Lies in the Deep

The Lakeville Project: Book Two

Lies in the Deep

By C.S. Robbie

Copyright ©2022 C.S. Robbie

Published in the United States By 7th Option Press

ISBN: 979-8-218-13135-7

DEDICATION

To Scott and Barb Shatzel
Larry and Fran Shatzel
Ruth Gollegly

This book is dedicated to my parents for all of their love and continuous support. And to my grandparents, who though they have passed, their influence, inspiration, and strength live on.

ACKNOWLEDGMENTS

Again, thank you, Alpha and Beta readers. Your input is everything.

Rockstar Reader Team: Nikki Gallup, Olivia Cardot, Autumn Maid, Carrie Cardot, Colleen Sadowski, Barb Shatzel, Jeanne Marquardt, Jamie Gallup

Consultation Squad: Sawyer Gallup, Jessica Cody, Joanne Malchoff, Michelle Peter, Nida Lelis

A big thank you goes to William Wadsworth for the amazing tour of the Wadsworth Estate and for sharing your vast knowledge of the area with me. If ever there is a must-see piece of history in the Finger Lakes Region, the Wadsworth Estate is the place.

Thank you to Keith Walters (The Gallery in the Valley, Geneseo, NY) for your visual inspiration. Your photographs continue to capture the beauty of the Finger Lakes like no one else.

And above all else, a big thank you to my husband and children. Bobby G, Camden, and Sawyer thank you for your words of encouragement, listening to me read the manuscript aloud, responding to my weird questions, and patiently allowing me to finish that one last paragraph. You are my world.

"Imma be what I set out to be
without a doubt
undoubtedly."

~Eminem

CHAPTER 1

~May~

Most people used the words picturesque, charming, and fairytale-like to describe Lakeville. Except there were no castles in my section of town, and I was anything but a princess. My house in this rundown, shanty town of a neighborhood was twelve doors down from even the slightest view of the so-called majestic Conesus Lake. And after eighteen years of living in this armpit, I couldn't wait to get the hell out.

I was already behind the wheel of my green Cavalier, wondering why my mother was passing by the kitchen window by the time I remembered I had left my keys on the counter.

"Why are you up already?" I mumbled.

The banshee, a.k.a. Tracy Finewood (also referred to as the woman who gave birth to me), was never up this early. As a matter of fact, she hadn't been up this early since the morning of my father's funeral, and that was ten years ago. Even then, my Aunt Stacy had to drag my mother out of bed and into the shower to get her to the service on time.

I waited a few seconds after she staggered by the window again, then snuck into the garage through the side door. Glancing at the time on my phone, I grimaced. I was running late.

"Please be back in your hole," I muttered.

I turned the knob to the kitchen door and quietly pushed it open. I should have known today was going to be wretched based on what I found: the banshee pacing the floor in her thin hot-pink robe with a fierce scowl and yesterday's makeup smeared under her bloodshot eyes. She was looking for a fight. But I didn't have time for that. Not today.

"Emma Rae! What the hell? If you weren't pounding around here all morning, making all that racket, I'd still be asleep right now. Stupid little mutt," she snapped without looking at me.

The banshee went to the cabinet and dug ferociously through the cough medicine, allergy medication, and expired antibiotics, undoubtedly looking for a painkiller cocktail to ease her chronic headache. Or was it knee pain today? Who could keep track?

"I forgot my keys," I uttered, ignoring her insult. It was easier that way.

I snatched the keys from the counter and darted to the door for a quick getaway.

"Stop right there. Where are my pills?" the banshee demanded. She slammed the cabinet door. "Did you take them? Give 'em back, ya goody-two-shoes."

One hand snapped to her hip while the other drummed impatient veiny fingers on the counter.

"I don't have them, Mom. Have some coffee; it should still be hot. But I have to go. I'm late for..."

"I don't want coffee, stupid. I want my pills. I'm in pain. If you were really that smart, you'd get that through your thick skull." She arched her back and squeezed her eyes shut. "Good God, Emma. My back... You're so selfish. Why do you do this to me?"

Today it was back pain.

"Honestly, Mom, I don't have them. They're probably on the table next to your bed."

My mother's eyes shot daggers at me. Then she stormed off down the hallway toward her dark, smoky room.

She waved her hand dismissively and grumbled, "Just get out so I can rest. Go to school, mutt."

I opened my mouth to remind her I had graduated last June. But then I didn't see the point.

She slammed the bedroom door. Beyond the paper-thin walls came the distinct rattle of pills tumbling out of a bottle and onto her side table. Yup— just another day in the Finewood household.

I felt a warm nudge on my ankle. "Novakitty, be smart, and stay out of the banshee's way today," I said, kneeling to scratch my calico's fuzzy chin.

Novakitty was *my* Novocain, my painkiller. She was the only thing that got me through the pain of living in this house with the woman who gave birth to me.

I took comfort in knowing I wouldn't have to face her again until maybe tomorrow afternoon when I expected the usual. After her chemical high kicked in, she would be gone before I got home and then maybe stumble in sometime late tomorrow, hopefully alone. I would have at least twenty-four hours of peace.

Shaking off the all-too-familiar exchange with the banshee, I escaped back to my car. I couldn't get out of the driveway fast enough. I clicked on the radio, looking for some music to distract me, and caught the tail end of a news report instead.

"...and he's been missing for two days. If anyone has any information, please contact..."

How long would I have to be missing before my mother noticed I was gone? I wondered.

I turned off the radio and drove through the village in silence, focusing on my destination. My goal had been to get into a college further than thirty miles away from Lakeville. But the Rochester Institute of Technology had one of the best engineering programs in the state, and they offered me the most financial assistance.

Today was my final interview with the RIT scholarship committee. I was one of three new entrants vying for four years of free room and board. And I was nervous. I grabbed my phone from the dash and dialed Frankie. Then I turned on the speaker and plopped it into the cup holder.

"Hey, sugar. I'm kind of busy. Call you back?" Frankie said.

"No. I'll call you after my interview."

"Oh, yeah. Sorry. I forgot... I have a second."

"I thought you were fishing today. Where are you?"

"I'm waiting for friends. So what's up? Freaking out?" he asked, diverting the topic.

3

My boyfriend (if we were calling each other that today) was the sweetest guy; the problem was his unfortunate habit of lying. I worried that maybe he was partaking in certain illegal activities that he swears he left behind a year ago.

"I'm a mess. And having a head-on collision with the banshee didn't help."

"You've already had the pleasure? It's kind of early," he said.

"Right? Anyway, I'm meeting with the whole committee this morning. All of them. Together."

"They're going to give you the cash, doll. Don't worry. And you know, you've inspired me. I guess I should tell you; I'm gonna start taking some classes next semester," Frankie said.

"That's awesome! Are you serious?"

"Would I lie to you?"

"You lie? Never," I joked. But I knew better. "Whatever you need, I can help. The financial aid stuff is the worst, although I'm a master now. Not that you need it, but I can help you with other stuff too."

For a moment, my day looked brighter. Maybe he did keep his promise and stop dealing cocaine with his family of criminals. Maybe we could have a future together after all. I had almost given up hope.

Suddenly, a loud noise echoed through the phone, much like a large overhead door slamming shut.

"Frankie? What was that?"

There was silence on the other end.

"Frankie? Are you there?" I checked the connection on the phone. "Frankie? Can you hear me?"

"I love you, Em. Don't ever forget that," Frankie said with a shaky voice.

"Hey, Franco! S'up?" yelled a man with a deep voice on Frankie's end of the phone.

"Hey, guys," Frankie said. Then quietly, he whispered, "Em, gotta go. I..."

As I wondered who he was talking to, the question on the tip of my tongue, I was struck by the ear-piercing clatter of what sounded like Frankie's phone hitting the ground.

"Frankie! Frankie!" I yelled. But he didn't respond.

4

Then— Pff! Pff, pff!

On the other end, Frankie let out an agonizing groan. Again, I heard another man's throaty voice.

"Bye-bye, Franco. If only you followed the rules, we coulda got along," he said.

"Wait. Stop," gurgled Frankie.

In my panic, I lost sight of my surroundings and drove thoughtlessly down the country road. I had no consideration for the left turn I missed or the stop sign I had blown through. Then a pothole seemed to come out of nowhere. My tire walloped in and out of the hole, jostling my car and everything in it. My phone bounced out of the cup holder.

With one hand on the wheel, I whipped off my seat belt and snagged the phone from the floor. I smacked it against my ear.

"Frankie? Can you hear me? What's happening?"

The last thing I remembered hearing was Frankie spluttering, "You're wrong. No one gets along with the devil."

Pff!

Had I been focused on the road, I would have at least had a chance to avoid the van crossing the center line and coming straight at me. But the fraction of a second I had been given wasn't enough time to stop my world from going dark.

There were no bright lights. No pearly gates. Nothing resplendent like angels in the wind. Not even so much as a feather.

I floated in a sterile hollow of nothingness. Seeing nothing. Thinking nothing. Feeling nothing other than the kind of cold that burrowed deep into the core of your bones.

But then came a hint of warmth. Next, a speck of light formed in the distance, and slowly, it began to grow. Then with increasing speed, the whisper of something from nothing hit me like a ton of bricks. Before I knew what was happening, floating turned into hurling through the dark abyss, and the pressure and terror of being shot forward forced my eyes shut.

And when my eyes opened, only one word slipped past my lips—

"James."

CHAPTER 2

My bare feet sank into the warm sand as I walked beside the ocean. I strolled closer to the water, bracing for the cold, except it was even more pleasant than the sand.

"Hello, Emma."

The tall, thin boy walking next to me had a friendly smile. He wore a light-blue button-up shirt and vintage jeans rolled at the ankle.

"Hi, James. This is a beautiful place," I said.

My short white dress billowed in the breeze. I caught it before more than a little leg was revealed. James smirked and took my hand. He led me away from the water toward a small cape cod with a large deck.

The deck was a tropical paradise covered with fragrant flowers and vibrant green plants. Extraordinary Boston ferns, towering palms, crawling grape vines, and chocolate-smelling purple akebia weaved their way through and across the structure, almost hiding it. We stepped onto a soft mossy floor under a canopy of wisteria and clematis.

James motioned toward an iron bistro set with a view of the ocean. On the table was a small pile of books, a bottle of wine, and a glass half empty.

"I was relaxing. Would you care for a glass?" James asked.

"Yes. I would love one," I gushed. Then it occurred to me, "No. I'm only eighteen. I don't know why I said that."

Out of nowhere, another glass appeared on the table, and James was pouring a white wine that I could instantly smell and almost taste.

"Good answer," James said. "Non-alcoholic Sauvignon Blanc for you." He handed me the glass. "Cheers, friend."

I sat at the table and admired the breathtaking view. The sun on the horizon wrapped around my shoulders like a cozy, comforting blanket.

"I have a silly question," I said, pushing the hair from my eyes.

He slid into the chair across from me and raised his brows.

"The sun— is it setting or rising? I can't seem to tell," I said, glancing at my glass. In my pause, he eyed my drink as I swirled it with my finger. I asked, "Are you sure this is non-alcoholic? My head is a little foggy."

"I would never do that. I would never deceive you."

James gazed at me like I was the only person in the world. Like nothing else mattered. I could easily have stayed lost in that moment. His soft golden-brown eyes, with prominent limbal rings, almost had me in a trance. Yet, the question wouldn't rest, and I had to know. "The sun?"

"Hmm. Good question," James said.

He slumped over, rested his chin in his hands, and gave me a quizzical stare.

"You don't know either?" I asked.

"Yes, I do know what I see. It's morning. I love to be up at the break of a new day when it's quiet. I get to enjoy uninterrupted reading time." James placed his hand on the small stack of books. "I guess you like to read too."

My face soured, and I shook my head. "Ooh, definitely not."

Upon closer inspection, I noticed one pile of books after another. They were on tables, shelves, under plants, peeking out from behind vines. "Wow. You have a lot of books."

"School must be tough when you don't like to read," James said with a longing sigh.

I shrugged, and changing the boring topic of books, I gestured to his glass and asked, "How old are you?"

"Just old enough to legally enjoy an occasional glass of wine." He grinned from ear to ear. "You will love school when you get to college. That new sense of freedom…"

"Freedom is exactly what I'm looking for. But to *love* school seems like a stretch."

James leaned in on his elbows. "I dream of being a college professor. English."

I laughed. "Professor? The lucky students," I uttered. "Anyway, here you sit with piles of books you read for fun, all while working up a good buzz first thing in the morning. Let's see what you have here."

I leaned to the side and removed a candle from a pile of books. Lifting *The Great Gatsby* from the top, I said, "A Fitzgerald classic." I picked up another book. "And here we have *Deliverance*, a creepy James Dickey book." Narrowing my eyes, I whispered, "Only saw the movie."

"The book is better," he whispered back.

"Then it must be creepier. Ooh, here's a good one. *The Satanic Verses*." I gasped, plunking it down on my lap. "Interesting choice for your collection. Salman Rushdie, right?"

James nodded.

"Such controversy with this one." I slid the book across the table.

He tapped the cover and said, "You could say that. But I'll read just about anything. It depends on how I feel that day."

I shuddered. "Glad I wasn't around when you were in the mood to read *this*."

His smile returned. It was mischievous this time.

"How could I stay away from one of the most controversial novels ever written? Take it. Read away. Because you want to, not because it's been assigned to you."

"I'll pass on that one."

He bent and snagged the following two books in the pile. "Then take *To the Light House* or *Native Son*. They're incredible."

"No, thanks."

He stood and scooped up another pile of books from under a plant stand and set them in front of me.

"Here's a great one, *All the Kings Men*."

"Nope." I shook my head, enjoying the playful banter.

He picked up another book and said, "This one. No, wait." He tossed it on the table and grabbed another. "This one is better," James chuckled. "You have to take one. Please. You'll insult me. How about *As I Lay*…" The smile dropped from his face.

"Dying," I finished for him. Then curious to look around, I got up and wandered toward a partially hidden door. "It's *As I Lay Dying*. And no thanks. Sounds depressing," I added.

I spied a stack of books on a short wooden bookshelf next to the door and removed the first of the Divergent Series from the top. James' eyes lit up, and the smile returned.

"Veronica Roth," I said, waving it at James. "I'll take these. I can't remember who, but someone told me these were good."

"Truthfully, I have never read one of her books. I didn't even know I had them," he said. "Something tells me they're meant for you."

"What? A book you've never read before? Professor, you'd best get to that. I'll leave them for you to read first."

"Oh, no, please. When you're done, I'll give them a shot." He paused, then said, "I have won, though. I have successfully created a reader. I just know it. And if you'd like, feel free to read them here." James gestured toward the bistro. "With me. Anytime."

James meandered in my direction, stopping to smell an akebia leaf. "I bet you're hungry," he said, stepping toward the house. He brushed aside the clematis, revealing a dark cherry wood door, then waved for me to follow.

The second James put his hand on the doorknob, I was struck with an odd sensation that I wasn't where I was supposed to be. Like I was lost. Or that something was missing. But the feeling left as quickly as it had appeared. James distracted me with a comforting hand on my shoulder as he gestured me into the house. The deep voice resonating from his dimple-framed mouth was calming.

"How hungry are you?" he asked.

I smiled, and swallowing that weird feeling, I followed James into the house and up several steps to the living area.

"Not very," I said.

"How about a snack then?"

"Sure," I responded.

The living room was a comfortable man cave decorated in warm neutral tones. An oversized leather sectional sat conveniently in front of the most enormous fireplace I had ever seen. I trailed James into the open kitchen. With the exception of the cherry wood floor and the solid wood top on the kitchen island, everything else was stark white. White cabinets, white overlay appliances, white marble countertops…

One entire wall was floor-to-ceiling accordion glass doors that opened to a balcony overlooking the ocean. The humid salt air blew in, pushing the bamboo ceiling fan blades to a slow glide.

James dug through the refrigerator and pantry as my eyes absorbed this completely unfamiliar place. The wondering began.

"You have a cat?" I asked, noticing the water bowl on the floor.

He stretched his head from the pantry and followed my gaze to the floor. "I guess so."

"You're not sure?" I asked.

How does one not know if they have a cat?

"Well, I haven't seen one. But there is a bowl." He reached into the pantry and emerged with a can of wet cat food. He plunked it on the island. "Yup, we have a cat."

We?

"James, not to sound stupid, but do you live here alone?"

The smile dropped from his face. And as he stared into my wondering eyes, my stomach began to turn.

He shook his head and said, "No?"

"That sounds like a question."

James closed the pantry door. And just like the books he had never seen before, a prescription bottle and a set of car keys suddenly appeared on the counter. I knew the keys were mine. I knew the cat bowl was mine. And I *knew* that even though the bottle of pills wasn't mine, it was meant for me.

Then from the corner of my eye, I caught the shadow of a woman walking away down a dark hallway.

"Mom?"

I caught a chill and shivered. My mother— that was the absence I felt. Where was my mother?

"I live with my mother," I mumbled. "Where is she?"

Leaving James at the island, I wandered toward the shadowy hallway to search for her.

"Mom?"

As I made my way down the hall and peeked in each room, my eyes scanned the modern furniture, the landscape paintings on the walls, and the overall clean, uncluttered decor. This was not the home I shared with my mother.

"Mom!" I called out.

Finding no one, I hurried back to the kitchen.

"James, I thought I saw my… James?" I said. But suddenly, he was gone.

CHAPTER 3

Confused, I traipsed into the living room and plopped down on the sectional. It was as if a chunk of my life was missing, and I didn't know where to find it or even when I'd lost it.

I heard footsteps behind me and turned to see James coming from the dark hallway.

"Where were you?" I asked.

"I was just giving you some space."

My head dropped into my hands. I rubbed my face vigorously and said, "Something is wrong. All of this... it's not right."

The next thing I knew, James' fingers were combing through the back of my hair.

Softly, almost as if talking to himself, James said, "Your hair is so dark. Such a contrast to your ice-blue eyes."

I turned my body so I could see him. He still held a few strands of my hair in his fingers.

"James?" I froze, my eyes locked on his.

He dropped my hair and crouched until we were eye to eye.

"I truly thought you were here just for me. I have to admit... " He stopped and looked away. Then he found my eyes again and said, "I am more than a little crushed that I was wrong. So very wrong."

He reached out and skimmed my cheek with his fingers.

He said, "I want you to stay."

I jolted up; the sectional was the only thing between us. Questions exploded all at once.

"Stop! What's going on? Who are you? Tell me! Where am I, and what is this freaky place?"

"Calm down. I didn't mean to scare you," James said, inching his way around the sectional.

"Stop right there," I barked.

Again, my instincts kicked in, and I yelled a name I had forgotten until that moment. I hollered for the one person I trusted and knew would come to my rescue.

"Frankie! Oh, God. Where is Frankie? Is he here too?"

James continued to close in.

I said, "Stop! Stay away from me."

I ran to the kitchen and grabbed a knife from the knife block on the island. James followed close behind, talking calmly, reassuring me that everything was going to be okay. A butcher knife shook in my hand.

"Answer me. Where am I, James? Answer that question. And stop. I don't want to hurt you. Please, back off."

James retreated with his hands in the air.

"The last thing I wanted to do was scare you. I was confused when I first got here too."

"Yes, I'm confused." Then it dawned on me. "My drink… You drugged me?"

I stepped forward, waving the knife at him. How stupid of me. No wonder I went along with everything. Nothing made sense, and now I understood why. But he denied it.

"Absolutely not. I could never do that here, Emma."

"Where is here?"

"I don't know. I could start with what I've figured out so far."

"I don't care where you start. Just start talking."

"What is the last thing you remember before we met on the beach?" James asked.

I searched my memory for a second, but nothing came to mind. The knife swayed in my hand.

"I don't know." My eyes slammed shut for a fraction of a second as I tried to focus. It was hard to think. "I don't know. Tell me what's going on."

"I am trying to help. Please, put the knife down. I won't hurt you. I promise."

I squeezed the knife and clenched my teeth. I wanted to believe James. Something in me trusted him, but still, I was afraid. It was

13

like I knew him, yet I could not for the life of me remember anything other than his name.

"Give me a reason to believe you, James."

"Your instincts told you I was a good person. You have good instincts. Trust them."

He stared into my eyes. Though I tried to appear calm, my shaky voice exposed my internal panic. I was about to lose it.

"I thought I trusted you, but you said you want to keep me here, wherever this is. And I want to go home— wherever that is." A frustrated snarl slipped from my mouth.

"It's going to be okay," James said.

"It's all so confusing. I remember Frankie; he's my boyfriend. And my mother— I thought she lived with me, but not here," I said, waving the knife erratically in the air, gesturing to my completely foreign surroundings. "That's it. That's all I remember."

"I only said I wanted you to stay. Not that I would keep you here against your will," James said.

I shook my head and grumbled, "Where are we?"

"I'm not sure. But you'll calm down soon. It takes some time to adjust."

"Oh, yeah? Exactly how much time will that take? An hour? Two? And how are we supposed to know since there are no godforsaken clocks in this entire place? It seems like at least a couple of hours have passed, yet the sun hasn't risen an inch," I said, raising the knife to the glass doors.

"I know. What would you like the sun to do? Should it be high noon?"

"Yes, it should be higher!"

Instantly, the sun shot up in the sky, momentarily searing my eyes and blinding me long enough to throw me off balance. Suddenly weak and tired from my emotional tirade, my knees buckled. Before I could protest, James was at my side, holding me up.

He laughed.

"What's funny?" I murmured.

"Ask, and you shall receive, my lady."

14

I let him take the knife from my hand and help me to a stool at the island. James went to the cupboard and came back with two mugs. By the time he placed them on the counter, they were full. My coffee tasted exactly how I liked it.

I felt James' stare from across the counter and met his eyes.

"What were you talking about earlier when you were touching my hair?"

"I didn't mean to scare you. I was mostly talking to myself. You showed up on my beach, in my world, so I thought you were something I created. Then after talking to you, you seemed so real. And when you made those Veronica Roth books appear, that strengthened my suspicions."

I found myself drawn to him. Trapped by the deep tone of his voice and the way his dimples framed his mouth. What was it about him? Or was it this place that kept distracting me from what I should really be thinking about? I had to force myself to focus. Then something he said hit a cord.

"Your world?" I asked.

"I thought this was my world. This," James gestured to our surroundings. "This is so familiar to me. But at the same time, it's wrong. I can't remember past this morning. And it seems like this morning has lasted days." His head dropped, and his elbows came to rest on the table. "I can tell you what I think. You just won't like it."

"Tell me."

He sighed. "Maybe we're in limbo. You might call it purgatory if that's something you believe in."

"I thought purgatory was where you suffered for your sins until God decided if he'd let you into heaven. This doesn't seem like suffering," I pointed out. Then, seconds later, it began to register. "Wait. Are you trying to tell me that I'm... that we're... dead?"

James shrugged, then his gaze drifted to the ceiling fan.

He said, "For me, this is heaven. I love the ocean, the sunrise on a warm summer morning, reading books, and of course, fine wine." James gestured to the wine fridge embedded in the island. "And that's exactly what I have. Earlier, I read a book about a couple in love, and then out of nowhere, a beautiful girl walks onto my beach. 'Is it a coincidence?' I asked myself."

"What else could it be?"

James didn't answer. We were quiet for a long moment. Finally, I stood and walked to the bay window in the living room. It looked out over the sandy side yard. To the right were the mossy steps of the deck. To the left was a solid green wall of arborvitaes and a golden arched trellis. Beyond the trellis, the air wavered like a steamy street on a hot day.

"I don't feel like I belong here. I don't know where I belong, though. This feeling— it's strange. Like I'm trapped," I said quietly.

I stepped away from the window toward the front door. Frankie's face flashed before my eyes. Anxiety burned inside my chest.

"I can't," I said. "I can't just sit around and wait."

I threw the door open and stepped onto the mossy deck.

"Emma, don't."

I ignored him. But I shouldn't have.

The arched trellis beaconed like a lighthouse to the ships at sea. "I'm here," it seemed to cry out. "This is the way…"

I glanced back at James and stepped off the deck. He was barely a step behind me.

"Wait. Stop," he urged.

"It must be a door," I said, gesturing to the wave of hot air billowing beyond the trellis. "This has to be the way out," I said.

Then I did the one thing I was always good at. I ran.

CHAPTER 4

I ran without looking back and like my life depended on it. Before I knew it, I had run straight to the opening of the trellis, where waves of heat rolled out so thick I could not see beyond it. One way or another, I had to get as far away from this freak storm as possible. So if this wall of smoldering air was the exit, I was taking it.

The closer I got to the trellis, the more I could see that it wasn't actually made of gold. Instead, dandelion-like flowers snaked their way up and around a wooden arch, giving it a bright golden hue. I didn't give much thought to the weed after that. I didn't care what my exit was made of as long as it brought me home.

Without pause, I ran straight through the opening. But one step into the heat waves and the smell of salt water and sand hit me hard. I gasped, then stumbled a bit and dropped to my knees. The urge to vomit was strong, but I managed to hold it back as long as I kept my eyes squeezed shut.

James rushed over and dropped to his knees beside me. "Give it a second. You get shaken up in there before it spits you back out."

A moment later, I was able to stand. I took a deep breath, again inhaling the fresh ocean air. The nausea was gone. I turned in circles, realizing how small my world was and feeling even more trapped than before.

"That smell never gets old," James said.

My pout landed on James. "What happened?"

"I've tried everything," he said. "And in case you're feeling persistent, you just end up back here no matter how many times you try."

"What about the beach? Where does it take you?"

"Back to the beach house," he said, gesturing to the mossy carpet of the deck.

"The water. I'm not the best swimmer, but…"

He shook his head, his mouth straight, his eyes soft.

"You tried?" I challenged.

"Everything."

"How do we get out of here? Tell me."

"I don't know."

There was nothing reasonable or rational about this place. Nothing made sense.

"This is it for us then?" I squawked, throwing my hands in the air. "How can that be?"

James looked away, staring past my head and out across the ocean. While I wondered what he was thinking, the truth was that I didn't want to know. I didn't want to hear *his* truth— that he had already given up. Because there was *no way* I was ready to give up yet.

"I'm scared," I admitted. "I want to go home. To my real home, wherever that is. I feel like I had big plans."

"I know the feeling."

"Do you remember anything?" I asked.

"I do. Except there's no memory that goes along with the face and the love I feel for her. Sometimes I think I am waiting for her. Maybe then I can move on."

"And when I showed up, you thought I was her?"

James chuckled. "No."

"Oh." My cheeks steamed up. What a dumb, presumptuous thing for me to say. "So you think someday she'll show up on the beach, and then your memories will come flooding back?"

"I hope so."

"At least then you'll be stuck here with someone you love. How lucky," I murmured.

James took my hand. His lips parted as if he was about to say something, instead, he sighed. Finally, he said, "I feel this fundamental connection to you. Like gravity… oxygen… the blood that flows through our veins… "

He stared into my eyes until I broke away. There were so many mixed signals.

"I wish I had all the answers," he said, clearing his throat. "Obviously, I don't. I could be wrong about everything. I never cared very much until now."

Hand in hand, we walked to the deck in silence. My mind seemed to run on an infinite loop. One minute, I was content and even happy to be here with James. The next— I was an anxious mess, desperate to return to a life I couldn't remember.

When we approached the lush, living deck, James motioned for me to take a seat at the bistro; instead, I followed him. When he pulled back the clematis vines revealing the door, he caught me hot on his trail. He stopped in the doorway and turned around.

James dropped the clematis. Slowly, he bent like he was going to kiss me. Instead, he slid his arms around my waist and held me as if he never wanted to let go. His breath was strong and steady in my ear. When my hands ran across his shoulders, I was surprised to find how solid his tall, thin frame was.

"Emma," James whispered. "I hate the thought that you might leave. I hate it."

I pulled back and cupped his face. "Why can't we go together? When one of us leaves, we will take the other. Wherever it is we go."

I brought his face to mine and kissed him. At first, it was slow and warm. Everything in me stirred. Then he pulled away. He shook his head and ran his hands over his scowling face.

"I can't, Emma."

"I'm sorry, James. I don't know what got into me. I forgot about your girl."

As I turned to go to the bistro, he grabbed my hand. "It's not about her. I just don't think we get to make any of the decisions." He stared down at the back of my hand and then raised it to his lips. He kissed it and said, "Come inside. I have a picture of her."

"You have pictures?" I asked, surprised.

"Three," he said, leading me inside. "She's the only one, besides me, who I recognize in the pictures."

I followed him inside and to the vast mouth of the fireplace. On the mantle were three picture frames. James took one down and studied it adoringly, and then he handed me the picture of an elderly woman with long curly white hair.

"That's my great grandma Gallagher. I call her G3."

I looked at him quizzically. "G3?"

"Yeah. G3. Great Grandma Gallagher. Get it?"

I nodded my head, and a smile seized my face.

Her big golden-brown eyes stared up at me. She had a perfectly placed dimple on each side of her brilliant smile. "She's so pretty. It's too bad you don't look anything like her."

He grinned; there were those same dimples.

"Like you remember living with your mom, I know I lived with her," he said, pointing to the picture. "I only know who she is and how much she means to me."

"And the other pictures? Are they of her too?"

James shook his head and returned the picture of G3 to the towering mantle. He took down another. It was a picture of a German Shepherd and a boy about the age of five.

"My dog, I think. I don't know his name. I'm the boy. See any resemblance?"

He presented me with the same toothy grin. And once again, the dimples gave him away.

"Without a doubt," I said.

"Wait here. I'll get us something to drink."

James walked into the kitchen and pulled a bottle from the wine fridge. When he returned, he handed me a glass of sparkling red grape juice. I ran my hand across the live-edged wooden mantel and down the cobblestone face.

"Have you ever had a fire in this monster?" I asked.

"Absolutely. This is my second favorite place to read."

He held up his drink. "To chance meetings," he said, then tapped my glass.

I grinned. "My favorite kind."

As I took a sip of the sweet juice, James reached for the third picture on the mantel. He scrunched up his nose at it.

He said, "I'm probably about thirteen or so, those dorky, awkward years. I don't know about the little girl." James turned the picture to face me.

I studied the familiar girl for just a moment— then I realized who she was.

"That girl…" I choked out.

The juice in my throat took a sudden detour into my lungs. My glass tipped in my hand, hit the hearth, and shattered into a thousand pieces. Purple juice spilled across the cream-colored rug.

"Whoa! Emma. Are you okay?"

I pointed to the picture.

"Do you know her?" James asked.

I nodded and coughed for another few seconds before I could speak.

"Yes," I said. "This girl was your neighbor until you were eleven. Then you moved away when your great-grandmother took custody of you."

I cleared the rest of the juice from my throat and lungs and said, "That little girl is me."

CHAPTER 5

James' mouth dropped open.

"That was my favorite plaid skirt," I recalled. "My mother called me a stupid goody-two-shoes when I wore it. But I didn't care because you told me it was cool." I faced him again with genuine amazement and said, "James Gallagher."

I continued to feed his memory as it came to me. "You had just given me that daisy. You picked it from mean old Mrs. Regina's garden. You loved making her mad; you weren't afraid of her like I was. I kept the flower pressed in a book. This picture was taken the day you moved."

"Go ahead. You can say it."

"Say what?" I asked.

"That I was right. Showing up on the beach wasn't a coincidence."

I giggled. "You were right, James. Maybe showing up on the beach wasn't a coincidence."

Earlier, I wondered how it was possible to have such strong feelings after such a small amount of time. Now I knew. The connection had already been there.

"How do you remember all that?" he asked.

"I don't know. When I saw the picture, it just came to me."

And that was the moment when *true hope* finally appeared.

"To the deck, my lady. I have all the time in the world to clean up this mess. We have a lot to talk about."

When we stepped out onto the deck, the sky had changed. The sun was slightly lower, with a hint of fuchsia at the horizon.

As we meandered toward the bistro, I spotted someone walking on the beach, along the water. "Who is that?" I asked, assuming he'd know.

James shrugged. I walked to the edge of the deck, squinting my eyes. Like so many things here, he seemed familiar. That was when it hit me.

"Frankie..."

Frankie strolled casually along the beach. His toes dragged through the warm sand, his face tilted toward the setting sun.

"Go to him," James said.

"Come with me. He'll want to see you too. The three of us were inseparable once. Do you remember?"

"I don't. Either way, he's not here for me."

I started toward the deck steps, then stopped abruptly. "Wait. Is he really here? I mean, because he's like us— dead?"

James shook his head and shrugged his shoulders. "I would hurry. We don't know how long he has."

My heart sank as I stared into James' sad eyes, searching for the answer. Was Frankie dead? Were we dead?

I turned to see Frankie's smiling face. He appeared happy, like he hadn't a care in the world.

I slowly descended the mossy steps and sunk into the warm sand. By the time Frankie spotted me and his eyes lit, I was running. I threw myself into his arms. Silently, we held each other. Then reality seeped in through the cracks in my heart. How could he have died so close to the time I had?

I placed a hand on Frankie's cheek and said, "I'm sorry you're here. I'm so sorry."

"Don't be sorry. This is hardly a place I thought I would ever see."

I shook my head. "What happened to you? I mean, do you remember anything?"

"You know, doll, it all makes sense now," he said, gazing out to sea. "I wasted so much time. I was never good at managing that— or anything for that matter."

Frankie appeared lost in thought as I gazed up at him. A smile spread across his face, and he seemed to glow with a peaceful aura. And though I wondered what he was thinking, I hated to ruin the moment with words.

Several seconds passed. Finally, Frankie took my hands, searched my eyes ardently, and said, "It's important that you know I was on the right track. I was headed to a better place. And it's because of you. Because you're the one I wanted to spend the rest of my life with." He reached out and twirled a lock of my hair around his finger. Then he chuckled, "But once again, I'm too late."

"For what? What about now?" I glanced at James, who was sitting at the bistro reading. I could tell he was pretending. He glanced up at me over the black hardcover book.

"Now I move on. Maybe you could name your first kid after me, doll." Frankie smirked and kissed my hand.

"Wait," I said, pulling away. "Did something happen to us? Together?"

"We weren't actually together," Frankie explained. "It was a strange twist of fate that we should be on the phone. Remember? You heard me talking to the man who shot and killed me."

In the blink of an eye, the memory of the accident snapped on. It was as if it had always been there, but I couldn't see it until now.

On the other end of the phone, I heard a steel overhead door slam shut. There was a sudden unexplainable poof noise. Frankie's voice gurgled. Then more poof noises. At the same time, I knew what my own fate had been at that very moment.

"I was hit head-on by a van. That's how I died," I mumbled.

"No, no, no, doll. That's not right."

"Yes. I remember now. She crossed the line, and I was too distracted, too upset..."

"Ems, look at me." He turned my face to face his. "*You* didn't die. That's why it's too late for us. That's why you have to go back. There's more for you."

I shook my head. "I thought there was hope. But if you're dead, and I'm here with you, I must be dead."

I peered back at James, who now hovered on the edge of the deck. He looked ready to jump off and run to me. "James?" I uttered.

Frankie said, "I lived my life, the good and the bad. I'm ready to move on. You are not dead." He pointed to James. "Neither is he. You will be fine. Have faith. Have faith in him too. You have something else to believe in now. Eventually, you'll see the whole picture."

Now I was angry. I said, "James lied to me. He made me think I was dead."

"He doesn't know any more than you do. You can't lie here. Trust me. I wish I could. Because then I would tell you everything will be alright when you wake up. I would tell you the people who killed me won't come after you and that it's okay to trust those close to you."

Frankie shook his head, glanced at the sky, and said, "Look, I know you're not the fairy tale type, but you feel something for James. If I could lie, I would tell you that you and James will live happily ever after. I would tell you all of that..." He took a deep breath, and as he let it out, he said, "...if only I could lie."

"I'm sorry," I said, lowering my head, ashamed.

I felt as if I'd been unfaithful. My head had been swimming with thoughts of only James when Frankie had been dying all along.

"Don't feel bad. Like the inability to lie here, you can't deny your feelings either. Here... they are what they are. What you feel is the truth. It's literally your deepest subconscious where all truth lives.

"Listen, none of us know everything; all we can do is have faith. Have faith, and open your eyes soon. Everyone will worry. Even the banshee," Frankie said with a mock punch to my shoulder. Then he pulled me in for one final hug.

"Frankie, don't leave me," I begged.

"I'm not leaving you. I told you, have faith. Ya never listen to me," he said.

"I can't do it," I said. "I'm scared."

"You always managed to amaze me. The only thing you could never do was get rid of me." Frankie ran his fingers across my cheek. "I was no stinkin' good for you, Ems. No good. But you loved me just the same. Thank you."

"Frankie," I said almost inaudibly.

"Remember something for me, Ems. Trust no one."

"Don't leave me, Frankie." A tear raced down my cheek.

"Iron backbone," he said, extending his hand, palm up.

I brushed the teary streak from my face, placed my hand on his, and said, "Iron-willed."

Iron backbone, iron-willed. Our nerdy childhood mantra.

Frankie, James, and I professed those words a hundred times a day when we were kids. None of us had it easy growing up. That's why our gang of three, with our tough-guy mantra, somehow made life more tolerable. Sometimes, it even made us braver than we should have been.

My eyes widened as I began to understand. His wish to be able to lie to me and our mantra— they were warnings.

Frankie clasped my hand and gave me one stern nod before his hand slipped through my fingers like sand. He slowly backed away, his eyes never leaving mine as he quickly faded into the wind.

There was nothing left to say. I loved him, and now he was dead. Gone. I stood there for what seemed like an eternity, lost in a mirage of memories I had shared with Frankie. Life rewound from that moment all the way back to the day we met at the age of four when he showed up in my backyard with a friend. James.

From behind me, James whispered, "I'm sorry. He was right. I don't know everything. And the longer you're here, the more I wonder if I ever knew anything."

I turned to face him. As always, a calmness ran through me when I looked at him. The urgency in my chest from Frankie's warning was tucked away somewhere safe. And through my eternal sadness, in the wasteland of my heart, there sprang a bud.

"Do you know what this means?" I asked.

"Yes. You can go back to your life. I'm sorry Frankie won't be there for you when you get back. I truly am."

"And my heart will never be the same." I swiped the tear from my cheek and kneaded my hands together until the teardrop disappeared. Then I took a sturdy huff and said, "Don't you get it? We aren't dead. We can go back. Together."

James didn't seem to share my excitement. "Everyone I have come across comes and goes. Except me. I'm still here, waiting to go elsewhere, to some final destination. The end."

"What is the final destination?" I asked.

James shrugged.

"Frankie said you're not dead. So we don't get to go to our final destination yet."

I would have expected him to be happy about that; but I found only sadness in his eyes.

I took his hand. "What is it?"

"I thought I was still here because I was choosing to wait for G3. But I was wrong. I'm not waiting; I'm stuck. Do I want to believe we can leave here together? Heck, yes. But it's not going to happen."

"You thought you were dead. Now you know you're not. Maybe all you have to do is believe you can go back, and it will happen."

James shook his head. He didn't believe it. How could I convince him?

"Listen, when one of us leaves, we will hold on to the other," I urged. "There has to be a reason I'm here with you, of all people. I haven't seen you in years; we were children when you moved."

James dove deep into my eyes and gently ran his fingers through my hair. "So what brings us together now?" he said softly.

James didn't wait for an answer. He kissed me slowly. Talk about heaven. A drifting cloud, a warm breeze, the buttery taste of pastries, a sweet flowery scent… At that moment, I didn't want to go anywhere without him. Then, before I knew what was happening, he shoved me behind his back to shield me from something or someone.

"No, wait! Stop! Just give us a little more time," he hollered into the air.

"James, what is it?" My eyes darted from one direction to the other, but I didn't see anything or anyone.

"Look at you," he said, lifting my fading hands. "Something is happening.

Then, it was faint, but I heard a man's voice. He said, "She's been out for about five minutes."

"Five minutes?" I repeated.

James stared at me with a questioning look on his face.

"Did you hear that?" I asked.

"No. What?"

I threw my arms around James' torso and held on for dear life. If I was going somewhere, he was coming with me.

I felt James' hands running through my hair and the heavy sigh that made him shrink when all his breath had been expelled.

"I will see you soon," he said. "I will find you. I promise, Emma."

James kissed me on the top of my head and took a small step back. I wasn't ready to leave, not that I had a choice. Despite my grip, his hand slipped away as I was slowly carried backward. It felt as though I was floating on a cloud along the edge of the water. I watched James fade away until all that was left was sand and water.

Eventually, the sand turned to dirt and the water into a mucky puddle in a field. The smell of fire, burning rubber, and gasoline were suffocating me. Then, all at once, I was dragged from the ground, and someone was running with me in their arms.

CHAPTER 6

"James?"

"Hang in there, little lady. Gotta git you away from this burnin' car."

A toothless man carefully set me down in the grass. As my eyes focused on his weathered face, he said, "Don't worry. I think you're fixin' to be okay. By the grace of God, though. Sheez! Your car is a pretzel. Lucky that girl was drivin' by and dragged ya away from that inferno."

"Are you okay?" asked a young girl about my age.

I couldn't find the words to speak through the fog in my brain.

"Hey, she's alive thanks to you," the man said to the girl.

At that moment, there was an explosion. It was loud. The man warned the girl not to go across the street.

"That there's a bomb," he told her.

"What?" I mumbled. "A bomb?"

My mouth felt swollen, and my eyes throbbed. My skull was a heavily shaken snow globe, and my brain the tiny pieces of glitter and confetti.

The girl explained, "You were in an accident. Help is coming."

In the distance, behind the girl's head, flames and smoke rose from a van across the street. The van that hit me. Then from the corner of my eye, I caught the sight of flames engulfing my car. The car I was just sitting in. I glanced up at the young girl caked in mud.

Frankie's smiling face flashed before my eyes just as I was losing consciousness. I had to tell someone about Frankie.

"He's dead," I whispered.

* * *

No one was around when I woke up in the hospital. My first thought was of my mother. Would she come here? When the door finally opened, it was an overly sweet nurse with a high-pitched voice who thought talking to me like I was five was a good idea.

"Hi there, darling. I'm Brenda, your nurse."

She patted my hand and leaned in close.

With a hushed, sing-song voice, she said, "Now listen, no need to panic. You are going to be just fine, baby girl. You have a few scrapes and bruises, a mild concussion, maybe a teensy-weensy fracture in your wrist. Otherwise, you are one blessed child."

"Stop it. I'm not a child," I grumbled.

Anything else out of my mouth would have sounded much kinder, I supposed. But I was highly irritated and uncomfortable. And sadly, I was alone.

The nurse's smile froze in place.

"Of course," she said. "I bet you're feeling those ouchies now. Aren't you? This should help."

She popped the cap off a syringe and slipped it into the IV line. Within an instant, I was feeling warm and fuzzy from head to toe.

"I'm sorry," I sighed. "I was rude."

"Yes, you were. And if I were just hit head-on and thrown from a car, I would be grumpy too." The nurse walked away, then stopped at the door. With a cold stare and a forced smile, she said, "Maybe not as rude as you, but a tad grumpy."

I was pretty sure I was not forgiven. Then, as if on cue, my mother breezed in.

"Emma, Emma. What on earth were you thinking?"

"I..."

"Emma, Frankie is dead. They found that no-good-loser down by the rock salt mine in a utility garage. Must have been some kind of drug deal or something. He was shot."

"Ma'am," said the doctor, coming in the door behind her. "She's very weak. You might want to have that conversation later."

"I'm her mother. She needs to know."

"I understand, but..."

"Stick to what you know, doctor. She's my daughter, and I know what's best for her."

"Mom."

"Listen, you're better off. It would never have worked out with you two. Enough now. He's history. Literally," she scoffed and waved a dismissive hand in the air. And it didn't end there. Talk about ripping off the Band-Aid. "You know you killed the lady driving the other car," she squawked, plopping down at the end of my bed.

I swallowed the pain from her brushing against my sore leg and searched my memory for what exactly happened to land me in the hospital. The medication had put me in a bit of a daze. Then I remembered the nurse saying something about a collision.

"That rotten woman. She hit you head-on. Bam!" My mother smacked her hands together as if I needed audio-visual effects.

"Ma'am!" the doctor growled.

The banshee turned to the doctor and said, "She killed someone, and her loser boyfriend died, all in the same day. And just look at her; she looks awful. She's going to need some heavy-duty medication for pain and the mental issues she's going to have."

I can't say I was utterly shocked by her obvious motives, but I was as embarrassed as one could get. My mother's intent was selfish, and her words were venomous. The doctor's eyes widened at the cold-hearted words that spewed from the banshee's mouth. She clutched her stethoscope, and her lips parted as if she was about to say something, but she didn't. Instead, she completely ignored the banshee.

The doctor marched to my bedside, and standing uncomfortably close to my mother, she put a hand on my left, un-splinted arm and said, "I'm Doctor Julie Gordon. How are you feeling?"

My mother made a face at the doctor's back, then hopped off the bed. She stepped to the head of my bed.

"Tired. And sore," I said. "The nurse just gave me pain medication. It's kicking in."

"What did she give you?" my mother chirped.

"I reviewed your x-rays. You have a broken right wrist; we'll cast that this afternoon. You suffered a mild concussion and several

31

lacerations on your shoulder, back, and legs. Nothing severe like we'd originally thought. We need to run a few more tests to check for internal injuries. The ones we ran earlier were inconclusive. In the meantime, you need to rest," doctor Gordon said.

I nodded. My mother asked again, "What did the nurse give her, doctor?"

"A mild painkiller," she answered without looking at her.

"Which one? She might need something stronger." My mother glared at me and asked, "Do you need something stronger? That may not be enough for you. You're going to be sore for a long time. Heck, you may even have some permanent damage you aren't aware of yet."

"It's fine, Mom. It's already taken most of the pain away." I wiggled the fingers on my right hand. "See, I can move them now."

Ignoring me, she said, "Look at you, such a mess. You'll have to send her home with something for her pain, doctor." She turned up her dismal performance with a melodramatic stroke of my hair, using her chronically shaky hand. "Oh, my poor baby."

Wow, she was laying it on thick. I wondered if it was a challenge or if it came easy when drugs were involved. She was like the naughty child who became the most polite and angelic creature when some-one held candy within her reach. Though, it never took long for the banshee to break out of her disguise.

Doctor Gordon turned to my mother and said, "I need to check the laceration on her back. If you would please step out for a mo-ment…"

"I'm not leaving her alone with you," the banshee remarked in an elevating tone. "I'm her *mother*, not some piece of trash you can boss around!"

Yep— there she was.

"I'm fine, Mom. Go get some coffee. I could use one too, please."

She glared at the doctor and me as if we were plotting something terrible against her. Her mouth puckered, her brows furrowed. Ever the doubter, and certain we were out to get her in some way, she turned abruptly and stormed out the door.

With a crooked smile, Doctor Gordon asked me to sit up. She examined the cut on my back.

Her eyebrows perked up, and she said, "Healing quickly. Leave the bandage on this one for a few days to protect the glue. It was a clean cut. But now I'm wondering about the wrist. Technically, you shouldn't be able to move that."

She unwrapped my wrist and gently ran her fingers along the bones.

"This doesn't hurt?"

"No. Not anymore."

"Hmm. I'm going to order another x-ray. I think there must have been an error with the first one." She re-wrapped my wrist and asked, "Do you live at home... with your mother?"

"Yes. For now."

"If you do need some pain management when you go home, keep them on you. If you go out, take them with you," she stated matter-of-factly.

"M-hmm," I hummed.

For a split second, our eyes met. I looked away, embarrassed. Of course, the banshee was an easy read for any intelligent person, especially a doctor. My face turned beet red.

"Things good at home? Would you like to talk to someone?"

I shook my head no. I wasn't ten. But how I wished someone would have asked me those questions back then. I changed the subject.

"I was on my way to RIT for an interview. I was up for a scholarship to get full room and board. So much for that."

"I'd be happy to make a few calls on your behalf. Give me a number so I can explain your situation. Don't give up."

"You'd do that?" I stammered.

"Sure."

"You don't have to."

A moment of silence went by as she listened to my heart and lungs.

"Get me your contact at RIT," she said with a smile.

33

"The number is in my purse," I responded. "I'm not sure where that is."

"I'll have Brenda come in and get your purse; your belongings are in the closet. I'll be back in about an hour to get that number."

"Thank you. I really need that scholarship."

Doctor Gordon nodded her head and patted my hand.

"See you in a bit. Get some rest. That's an order. After you say goodbye to your mother, no more visitors tonight." When she got to the door, she paused and quietly said, "I'm sorry about your friend."

Dr. Gordon returned an hour later. She took down the number of the chairman of the scholarship committee and promised to call him. Then she handed me a short note on script paper to share with whomever I needed and wished me luck.

The dated note read, "Emma Finewood was admitted to Strong Memorial Hospital after this courageous young woman was involved in a serious car accident causing her several physical injuries. I have enclosed my personal contact number for verification and references."

I have to say, I was floored by the doctor's kindness. A stranger had nicer things to say about me than my very own mother— who, by the way, never returned to my room.

Later that night, the floodgate opened. I shot up in bed from a deep, medicated sleep in a panic with a burning need to find James. It wasn't that I hadn't remembered him when I first regained consciousness; I had been distracted by other, more immediate things. I had also been medicated just enough not to worry about anything. Now, with the meds wearing off, I knew what I had to do.

But as quickly as those panicking thoughts raced through my head, I was laughing out loud. The nagging feeling in my gut was ridiculous. I mean, come on. It was just some kind of weird trauma-induced dream about James. None of that was real. Why on earth would I have to find him?

I imagined showing up, out of the blue, on his doorstep to make sure he was safe when I hadn't seen him in years. I laughed again. My face dropped into my hand.

"I'm such a schmuck."

A few seconds later, Frankie spiraled into my thoughts. The funeral. I needed to get a hold of the obituary, or maybe my sweet nurse would be kind enough to look it up online for me.

Frankie's poor family. He had three older brothers who were always in and out of jail for one stupid reason or another. Frankie, believe it or not, was the good boy. Mama's little boy. Her angel. And don't get me wrong, he had a big heart. He was simply… misguided, mainly by his brothers and the company they kept. I could only imagine the revenge they were plotting. Someone, for some reason, had killed their baby brother. And they'd soon be answering to the Ardemoni family.

THE IVORY DOME

When you walk with confidence and purpose, no one questions you. As I walked through the busy emergency room and past the nurse's station, I casually picked up a white coat and slipped it on. The name tag read "Niki Gallup, RN, BSN." A gender-neutral name. Perfect.

I headed to the elevator and up to the fifth floor. Subject Number 14 managed to get herself in quite a pickle today, and I needed to assess the damage with my own eyes.

I'm not sure what caused her accident, but she has an important road ahead of her. With one distraction out of the way, she was supposed to be free to move forward with the others. They were finally coming together— just as planned.

I got off on the fourth floor and took the stairs to the next floor in a hurry.

"Nurse, let's go," a doctor said as she cruised by me and ducked into a patient's room. A team of nurses hurried after her. I ignored them and kept walking.

At long last, I found the name I'd been looking for. Finewood, Emma. I peeked in and caught her flipping through the stations on the television. She shot me a cold glare with her ice-blue eyes and scowled.

SN14 is intact. The Lakeville Project is safe.

"Nurse. Now!" hollered another doctor, running by me. "She's coding," he said.

With a grin, I turned to the doctor and said, "Yes, doctor, I'm coming," and hurried into the room behind him.

I gazed down at the unconscious woman in the hospital bed. Nothing was more invigorating than holding a life in your hands... or five.

I suddenly found myself faced with a new question: to live or not to live... I scrutinized the slight creases around the woman's closed eyes and down-turned, lifeless mouth. She was too old and of no consequence to this world. What contribution could she possibly make to humankind? Another mouth to be fed, a human bottom feeder, a burden to society, an infected member of our species who could corrupt the strong if given a chance. To make matters worse, she was unsightly.

Sometimes, you had to do what was blatantly right, even when it seemed wrong. I was always good at making the most necessary and logical decisions, especially when the morally and ethically challenged could not.

I glanced down at a chart the nurse had tossed to the end of the bed.

Sweet dreams, Amanda Hudson.

CHAPTER 7

On day two, after several more vials of blood and another MRI, I was allowed to go home. As it turned out, my arm had no break or fracture as the doctors had first thought. All I needed was a few days with a bandage.

The morning of my release, true to form, my mother was nowhere to be found. I wasn't allowed to leave on my own, so the hospital social worker called a car service to take me home. Splenda the Good Nurse was unlucky enough to be my wheelchair chauffeur to the lobby, where I waited for the car. During the last few days, I had learned how to throw a little salt and vinegar into Brenda's annoying cheery attitude.

"Hey, Splenda, is that a pimple on your chin?" I asked of the minuscule blemish.

Her hand automatically went to her face. "Uh, yes. It is. I tried to cover it up."

"Didn't work."

"Seems not. Thanks for pointing that out."

"I would want someone to be honest with me. That's all. You might want to put more makeup on that hideous thing. And stop picking at it. You're making it worse."

"I didn't… oh, never mind," she hissed.

If she hadn't been so relentlessly condescending for the last several days, I might have felt bad for my rudeness. But who was I kidding? I had zero tolerance for her phony kindness.

After our verbal exchange, she stepped up the pace and had me at the curb faster than if I had run there. If she could have dumped me onto the sidewalk and walked away, I'm pretty sure she would have done so in a heartbeat. Instead, she stood duteously and silently waited with me.

When a black cab pulled up, Splenda loaded me in, plunked my plastic hospital bag on my lap, then marched away with her nose in the air. She may have despised me, but at least she didn't pity me.

"Thanks for the hospitality, Splenda!" I hollered after her. She never looked back.

"Laphi! Where to?" the driver asked.

Laphi? I didn't know what in the world that meant, and in all honesty, I could not have cared less. I was in no mood for conversation.

"6497 Beachwood."

"Ooh, Beachwood. Nice," he commented, throwing the car into drive.

He smiled and winked at me in the rearview mirror. It was creepy.

"South end," I muttered, squashing his glamorous ideas.

"Okay," he chirped, not losing a beat with another smile.

We drove in silence, which was the way I liked it. Then he had to ruin it.

"My name is Javier."

I nodded my head.

"Javier Ardaya," he said with a strong Hispanic accent.

I nodded again and faked a smile. *I don't care, so please shut up,* I thought.

"You were on the news..." he started.

"I'm not much in the mood for small talk, Javio. And no offense, but who drives a cab anymore when you can Uber?"

"It is Javier. And this is a Cadillac. We are a luxury car service, one of very few in the county. We have a contract with the hospital."

Ugh, stop talking, I thought. I bit the inside of my cheek and stared out the window. But wait...

"Did you say I was on the news?" I asked.

"Yes."

"Why? And how do you know it was me?"

"I am certain it was you. I never forget a face. Not to mention, I recognized your name when the hospital called for the car."

"What did the news say about me?" I asked.

39

Was I the bad guy because of the lady who died? Because guilt aside, the RIT interview committee wouldn't be handing over scholarship money to a murderer, let alone allow me to attend their college.

"They said you were in a car accident, that you managed to survive. They showed what was left of your car. Have you seen *that*?"

"No. I haven't seen anything. What did they say about the lady I killed?"

I glanced down at my lap, knowing his smile would surely vanish. Then strangely, he laughed.

"What's so funny about that?" I said just loud enough for him to hear.

"You did not *murder* someone. That loca was on drugs and had consumed enough aguardiente to kill a man. She almost killed you. A guardian angel was looking over you that day. That is for certain. Anyway, I hate to see anyone get killed, but as good karma would bless you that day, the innocent survived. Can you even imagine someone being so drunk first thing in the morning?"

Yes, I could.

For about half an hour, I had silence. I counted the lines on the road as they ticked by, trying to think of nothing else. But unfortunately, the driver could no longer hold his tongue.

"Things happen for a reason, you know," Javier said.

Here we go.

"I lost my parents when I was very young. That is why I came to America to live with my tia y tio. I was just a small boy."

"Mmm…" I uttered, finding the window again.

"It was an awful thing, but I adjusted. My uncle told me, 'Javier, if you let it eat away at you, you will become nothing. You will be the boy who should have been eaten by the mountain with your father.' Tough words, I know. But necessary."

"Harsh," I mumbled.

"Harsh, but true."

"Look, I'm fine. Thanks for trying to make me feel better… or whatever it is you're trying to do," I mumbled. "That's my house. The gray one with the missing shutter."

40

"I am not trying to make you feel better," he said, turning into the dirt driveway.

"Good. It wasn't working."

"I was trying to get you to see the whole picture. That is all."

"Yeah. Thanks."

His point was lost on me. And who gets eaten by a mountain anyway? Thankfully, the ride was over. He jumped out of the car and opened the door for me. He removed my bag from my lap, and without missing a beat, he continued his spiel as I slid out of the car.

"My uncle pushed me hard at first, then less as I came to grips with what life handed me. I realized what I could do. Perhaps things even worked out for the best. Maybe that was the plan all along." He threw his arms in the air. Proudly, he said, "And now look at me."

I nodded and took my bag from him. For the first time all day, I giggled.

"I don't know how this helps, but thanks. You made me laugh anyway. And again, no offense, but you're just a cab driver."

"No offense taken," he chuckled along with me. "Just remember, whatever we choose to do in our lives..." He stopped laughing and looked straight into my eyes. "...we are never *just* that."

My smile faded. I cleared my throat and said, "Thank you for the ride."

I started toward the house when I realized I had never paid him. When I turned around, he was standing at the driver's side door, looking at me. He waved and opened his door.

"Wait! How much do I owe you?"

"Here is my card," he said. "In case you need a ride before your car is fixed."

He handed me a fancy business card that read: Rich Silver Car Service, Javier Ardaya, and the company phone number.

"You saw my car. It was totaled."

"Even more reason why you will need this."

I took the card, dug through my purse, and asked, "How much do I owe you for today?"

"Another call."

"Please, how much was the ride?"

"I never charge people who need a ride to or from the hospital."
I held out a twenty. He winked again. It seemed less creepy that time.
"I will not take your money today."

"It's bad business to give free rides. Your boss should rethink that
policy."

I had no strength to argue anymore. This guy had me giggling
one minute and almost in tears the next.

All the random acts of kindness bestowed upon me over the past
several days were catching up; it was overwhelming. And while I
hated that he felt sorry for me, or was attempting to hit on me, or
was using me to drum up business… I would call him again.

"Thank you, Javier. I have a funeral to attend tomorrow."

"What time?"

"I should leave at ten. If I call by nine-thirty, is that enough time
for a pick-up?"

"I will see you at ten," he said, getting in the car.

"You? How do you know you'll be free?"

"I will let the office know I have a scheduled pick-up. We are com-
peting with Uber these days. We do what we have to. Jakisinkama."

"What does that mean?" I asked.

"What I said was 'until tomorrow.' I am from a region in the
Andes where we also speak Aymaran."

He smiled and backed out of the driveway.

I nodded. "Til tomorrow," I repeated.

Javier was the kind of person who gave others hope for humankind. One of the few who did good by you and restored your
faith in humanity at no cost. For several seconds, I thought about
Dr. Gordon and Javier and wondered if maybe I had become too
cynical for my own good. Too judgmental. Too mistrusting of the
intentions of others.

When I opened the door, Novakitty practically tackled me to the
ground. Clearly, she hadn't been fed in days. Then, as I closed the
door, I remembered her.

42

It all came flooding back. People only act on what's best for them. Humanity is innately selfish. It's indigenous to our mind, body, and soul. What other excuse could there be for my mother's cruelty?

CHAPTER 8

As soon as I walked in the door, I went straight to bed. By six the next morning, I was awake and chugging coffee like nobody's business. As I devoured a chocolate pop tart, the phone rang. It was Aunt Stacy. We talked for a few minutes. She wasn't aware of my accident; she called to see how my interview had gone. My mother must not have felt it very important to tell our only living relative, her sister, that I had been in a car accident.

At first, Aunt Stacy insisted on coming to stay with me for a while, but she didn't press the issue. Who could blame her for avoiding my mother? I didn't tell her about Frankie, though. If I told her, it would become real.

I was only capable of dealing with life's challenges in small steps. I never looked up the ladder to see what was there; I focused on one wrung at a time until I got to the top. And as of yet, I hadn't seen any proof that Frankie was dead. I planned to keep it that way as long as I could.

Until then, I had other things to deal with. I swallowed the lump in my throat and got online. I Googled my name, and there it was. Gladys Stark was driving a medical motor service van on her way to pick someone up when she crossed the center line and hit me.

Toxicology reports revealed that her blood alcohol level was three times the legal limit. On top of that, she had traces of multiple painkillers in her system. According to the article, it was amazing I had survived.

After that, just for the heck of it, I Googled another name. James Nicholas Gallagher. There was a lawyer, a hockey player, and a police officer. Nothing about my James. There was a Facebook account with no photos or information and an Instagram account with nine followers and no posts.

As I scoured the internet for anything that might lead me to James, my bubble of hope slowly deflated. In the back of my head, logic began to take over that hint of belief that James and I had somehow connected. What happened on the side of the road a few days ago was nothing more than an injured brain making up a good story to fill five minutes of my life while I regained consciousness.

I slammed my laptop shut and pounded the table with my uninjured fist. When did I become a hopelessly romantic dreamer? The answer was simple. I didn't.

For days, my goal had been to get out of the hospital, deal with Frankie's death, then find James. But that last part, the idea that lingered in the back of my head, that need to find James— it was ludicrous. Find James? And then what?

Novakitty jumped up on my lap. I kissed her and scratched her chin. I jokingly said to her, "Hey, James. Long time no see. Oh wait, I just saw you a few days ago in purgatory. No, purgatory is not the name of a bar. It's down the street, turn left, get hit head-on by a drunk driver, and there you have it. Lovely place. What, you don't remember?"

As dumb as I felt, if I was honest with myself, I had to admit I was disappointed. Certain parts of that memory, or to be more accurate— dream, were incredibly real.

"I'm losing it, Nova." She purred and meowed a few loud words at me. "I know, I know. It was a dream. I can't help that you weren't in it. It was a beautiful house. You would have loved it." After another loud meow, I promised, "Yes. One day we'll have a place of our own."

Before long, it was time to get ready for the funeral. I showered and dressed like I was going to a stranger's funeral— with little thought to whom or what I would find when I got there. One wrung at a time. Just one.

At 9:55 a.m., Javier pulled into the driveway.

"You're prompt," I hollered, locking the front door behind me.

"Part of the job," he said.

I moved slowly that morning. I didn't want to race to the inevitable. I knew that once I got into the car, there would be no

45

turning back. The truth waited at the end of this ride.

Javier opened the passenger side door and asked, "Where are we headed? What's the final destination today?"

Suddenly, I remembered James saying, "*I'm still here, waiting to go elsewhere, to some final destination.*"

"*What is the final destination?*" I had asked.

"I do not need the address. Just the name of the funeral parlor. I know where they all are," Javier said.

"Oh, sorry. It's at Morris and Gibbs."

I hovered at the back door of the car for a minute, my fingers on the handle. He stood, holding open the front passenger side door. Did I want to sit in the front with him? That could be awkward.

"I do not bite. But if you are more comfortable in the back…"

I shrugged my shoulders and slid into the front seat. He closed the door for me and hurried to the driver's seat.

"I just never sat in the front of a cab before."

"Then let me introduce you to the front seat of my girl, Potosi," he said, running his hand adoringly across the dash.

"Potosi? What kind of name is that?"

"It is a reminder of where I come from," he said.

Oh no, not another story.

"Is the funeral home far?" I asked, quickly changing the conversation.

"Fifteen minutes away. Seat belt, please."

I hesitated for a second, remembering how I wasn't wearing one days ago. So I obliged. With the click of my belt, he pulled out of the driveway.

"The meter isn't on," I reminded him.

He glanced at the meter and ignored me.

"Do you want me to get it?" I asked, reaching for the power button. No charity today.

"It is broken," he stated. "Have to get that fixed. In the meantime, I have a meter in my head. I shall not scam you. I promise."

"Maybe you should have taken a car that works," I said.

"This one pleases me," he responded with a chuckle.

46

"Does your boss know it's broken? He probably won't be happy you're driving one with a broken meter."

"He knows," Javier said. "Enough about the car. You look beautiful. I hope that is not rude, seeing as you are heading to a funeral."

"Your idea of beautiful is pretty basic," I said, glancing at my black pants and white silk shirt.

He grinned and said, "Your bandage is magnificent. Did you do that?"

I eyed my bandage. Between last night and this morning, I had doodled funky sphere designs, crosses, and willow trees all over it with a black Sharpie.

"Those would make fantastic tattoos," he continued.

"Thanks. I do my best thinking when I draw."

"You are talented."

"No. I'm not."

"I disagree," he chirped.

"I saw it in an art show a few months ago," I explained.

Maybe I could draw a little better than some people, but that didn't make me talented. Just ask my mother.

A few minutes of silence went by before Javier began to tap on the steering wheel. He asked me, "Is it a grandparent?"

"Excuse me?"

"The funeral. A relative? Friend?"

"Oh, uh, his name was Frankie."

Javier nodded.

"He was sort of a boyfriend. I guess. Maybe we were broken up..."

"I am so very sorry. I do not recall hearing anything about a man in the car with you."

"He wasn't."

"Right. Because you were broken up."

"It's complicated," I mumbled.

My relationship with Frankie had always been hard to explain. People had trouble understanding that we were so much more to each other that it was almost impossible to label.

Frankie and I started as childhood friends, then became best buddies, and eventually, we began dating. There was a cycle we ran through every few years: friends, best friends, friends with benefits, dating, then almost engaged. That's where it always stalled, and the cycle would run again. It seemed now the cycle was over.

I always believed he was my soul mate. Not that he was the one I would end up marrying, and not necessarily the love of my life, but the person whose soul was simply my other. My other half. My missing piece. My echo soul. No matter where in the world we ended up— he was my person.

I snapped out of my fog when Javier said, "All good things are complicated. That is the reason we work so hard to have them."

"You missed your calling, Javier."

"Do tell me what you mean."

"You could have been a motivational speaker, minister, a fortune teller." I laughed.

"A fortune teller? They are not real. Perhaps a professor? That could be interesting." He offered his hand to shake and said, "Good afternoon. Just call me Professor Ardaya."

And there it was again. A reminder of James, or somehow, a cry for help. James told me he loved school and that one day I would too.

"*When you get to college, I think you will love it. That new sense of freedom…*"

Yet now, freedom seemed so far away.

I stared blankly at Javier's hand until he shrugged and put it back on the wheel. He made a few more turns, stopped at a light, and before I knew it, we were at the funeral home. The ride was far too quick. The parking lot was packed. Javier pulled up front to let me out.

"I shall wait," he said.

"You don't have to. Someone will offer me a ride home."

"Or I could wait. Then you would not have to bother someone for a ride."

"It won't be a problem," I said, imagining how much it would be to use the car for several hours. I would walk home if I had to.

"Then why didn't you have someone bring you here?"

I was taken aback by the bluntness of his question and somewhat annoyed by it.

"I didn't want to put anyone out before the funeral. And honestly, I don't have a lot of close friends. But someone will offer me a ride." I paused. We stared at each other defiantly. "And I'll accept it," I growled.

We stared icily at one another for a few more seconds before we burst out laughing at our silly exchange. I dug a small wad of bills out of my pocket and handed a twenty to Javier.

"Will this cover it?"

He shook his head. "It is too much. Do you have a few ones?"

"It has to be more than a few dollars. I'm not a charity case. Don't make me feel like one." I waved the twenty at him.

"All joking aside, it was roughly a five-dollar ride."

I glanced at the front door of the funeral home. Frankie's brother, Anthony, stepped outside and lit up a cigarette. This was the last wrung of the ladder. The time had come, and I had things to deal with. So, even though I knew full well I owed Javier more money, I gave him five dollars and thanked him for the ride. Reluctantly, I opened the door and got out.

Javier rolled down the window and said, "You have my number? Just in case."

I patted my back pocket and smiled. "See you later. But not today," I said as he drove away with a wave.

Something about Javier always left me smiling.

CHAPTER 9

Other than Frankie's brief but powerful words in a dream I had while unconscious on the side of the road, and my mother's cruel words, I didn't know the full story behind Frankie's death.

I waited for Javier's car to be out of sight before approaching Anthony. I hadn't seen him in months. The puffy dark circles under his red eyes aged him by at least ten years. Despite that, he looked as impeccable as ever.

Anthony's dark brown hair was short around his ears and neck, while the top was long and perfectly gelled into place. The material of his charcoal gray designer suit hugged his muscular shoulders, then tapered around his waist. His shoes shined flawlessly, and his Rolex gleamed in the late morning sun. Until now, I never realized how handsome Anthony was.

Anthony tossed his cigarette to the ground and turned to walk back into the funeral parlor. He caught my eye. I smiled and waved as I walked toward him.

"Hey, fine lady," he said. "About time."

"I'm sorry I couldn't make it yesterday…" I began. But I couldn't finish. I had reached the top of a very unstable ladder.

He grabbed me and hugged me so hard I could barely breathe. I squeezed my eyes as tight as I could, holding back tears. They tried to fall, so I pushed my face into Anthony's suit coat. My body began to shake when I heard his quiet sob. I almost lost it.

After several seconds, I pulled away, smoothing out the wrinkled spot on his coat where my face had been planted.

"Don't worry about that," he said. "What happened to your arm, Finewood?"

"Nothing. Well, something, obviously. I just sprained it. It was dumb." I shook my head. I didn't want to get into my accident. Today was about Frankie.

Anthony's brows furrowed, and he asked, "Seriously? *She* do that to you?"

"No. My mother didn't do this. It was me. It was a dumb accident. Completely my fault."

"You would tell me?"

"Yes. Enough about my stupidity. Where's Mama?"

"With Frankie. Hasn't left his side this morning. She was upset that it couldn't be an open casket." He took a deep, angry breath and wrung his hands together. "Come on," he said. "She'll want to see you."

He took my good hand and led me into the funeral parlor. Time seemed to run in fast forward at that point. The world around me raced at ten times its speed as Anthony shuffled me past Frankie's friends and relatives. All familiar faces. We were on a straight path for Mama Ardemoni.

When she saw me, she stood up, looking frail, but embraced me with the same strength as Anthony. Over her shoulder, Frankie's smiling chocolate eyes stared at me from the picture atop his casket.

"Emma, Emma," she cried.

"I'm sorry, Mama," I whispered.

"Can you believe it? He's gone. My baby's gone!"

"I know. I know."

She pulled back and stroked my face. Then she stared into my eyes and slapped me with her pointed words.

"He loved you. He was going to marry you. Soon. He told me. We all knew it was only a matter of time. And now..." she sobbed harder.

I struggled to hold Mama up as she collapsed in despair. Anthony took her and helped her back into her chair. She reached over and placed a shaky hand on the casket.

"Frankie. Oh, Frankie!" she hollered. Then she looked at me and screamed, "Why! Tell me why!"

If only I knew. I felt like I should have an answer for her. Someone should. I glanced at the crowd of mourners assembled in intimate groups throughout the room. They shook their heads and wiped their crying eyes. Frankie's brothers, Dominic and Mario, came racing to their mother's side and relieved Anthony. Anthony took me by the hand and led me to the back of the room, where one poster board after another, decorated with pictures of Frankie, lined the wall. Flower arrangements scattered amongst the posters formed a garden most would envy.

"Ma's been like this for days," Anthony said. "She's way better than the day it happened. We thought it was gonna kill her."

"Maybe it will be easier when all this is over."

"The priest is held up in traffic across town. Services are supposed to start in ten minutes. Father Joe better get his ass here before I lose it."

That was Anthony. Straight to the point and rarely forgiving.

Without warning, a hand slapped down on my shoulder. I turned to find Dominic.

"Finewood. Lookin' fine," he said with a smile and warm embrace.

Dominic wasn't as tall as Anthony, though he had been taller than Frankie. He wore a designer suit like the rest of the men in the family, and his dark brown hair was long and wavy. He moved in close to Anthony and whispered, "There's talk about the Gallagher family."

"What?" asked Anthony.

"There's rumor that they done it," Dominic snapped.

"I knew it. Damn! Didn't I tell you?" Anthony said, a bit too loud.

His mother glanced at me, then stared at Anthony knowingly. I suspected Dominic had already told her. A second of silence passed.

"What the devil happened to you?" Dominic asked, grabbing my bandaged arm.

"Wow. You're so gentle," I sassed.

"She's a klutz," Anthony said.

"No, I'm not. It was a stupid accident."

Dominic's eyes could read people like a book. I could tell he didn't believe me. He knowingly pushed the hair off my forehead for

52

no other reason than to look for something more. And he found it. The purple and yellow bruise on my head was healing fast, just not fast enough to hide it from Dom.

Anthony took my arm and snapped, "You better tell me what happened, Finewood. Now."

Had I not known them all my life, I would have mistaken their aggressive tone for something other than extreme concern. I didn't want to get into it, but now I had no choice.

"I was in a car accident."

"Yeah?" Dominic said in his keep-talking tone.

"It was a few days ago. I just got out of the hospital yesterday. That's why I wasn't here for the calling hours."

They glared at me as if they weren't sure I was telling them the truth. Then Anthony asked, "How'd it happen?"

I explained how the drunk woman in the van crossed the yellow line and hit me head-on and how I had to stay in the hospital for days because of my injuries. I left out the pertinent fact that I was on the phone with Frankie when I was hit.

Anthony turned to Dominic, and through clenched teeth, he mumbled, "Why didn't we know about this?" Dominic shrugged.

"You've been a little preoccupied," I said. "It happened the same day…"

"I'm glad you're okay."

"I killed the lady," spewed from my mouth like hot coffee.

Anthony took a deep breath and said, "Drunk tramp deserved it. Better her than you."

Behind Anthony was a picture of Frankie running through a sprinkler with his brothers when they were small. They were all so innocent then. If you looked closely, you could see James and me sitting on the front porch, soaked and exhausted.

"Hey, Dom. Remember this?" I asked, pointing to the picture. Dom was the same age as James.

"Yeah," he snickered. "If only we had the in-ground then."

I pointed directly at James. "What happened to him?"

"I see him around. Why?"

"No reason. We were all friends back then."

"Except now, he's rolling in the family business," Dominic said.

"Just because his father joined a gang that doesn't mean he's in it too."

"Oh, yeah? How do you know? When's the last time you saw him?" he asked.

"I haven't seen him since he moved away." *Or had I?*

"Then I would know better. Right? And trust me, Finewood, Ty Gallagher went to the dark side with the rest of his family. And he probably took Jamie with him. So don't fool yourself. You don't have to have red hair and freckles to be an Irish punk. James may not look the part on the outside, but his blood is still green," Dominic spewed.

"Relax," Anthony said, resting a hand on Dom's shoulder.

Though I realized that it might not be the best time to talk about James, it could be the last time I had with the Ardemoni family. The only reason I was so close to the Ardemonis was because of Frankie. The family had moved off of Beechwood a few years ago. When Frankie's father died, they sold the old house, and Mama Ardemoni moved into Mario's mansion with his wife Carmella and their brood of children.

I swallowed hard. "When's the last time you saw James?" I asked casually.

Dominic tilted his head to the side and glanced at Anthony. His eyes slowly shifted back to me. "Saw him going into The Green as I was leaving. That was, oh, five days ago. I had dinner with Frankie and Mario. The boys stayed for a drink at the bar." He whacked Anthony on the arm. "So I'm walking out, and in come the riffraff. Good timing on my part." He cleared his throat and said to me, "It was the night before Frankie died. Now tell me, Finewood, why the sudden interest in old friends of the Irish descent?"

My heart skipped a beat. James had been at the same restaurant as Frankie the night before he died.

Just then, Father Joe rushed in full of apologies for being late. It looked like my questions would have to wait.

"Sorry, Dom," I said. "I didn't mean to upset you. Just making small talk, catching up. I haven't seen you guys in a while. That's all."

"I know, I know," he said, nodding his head and throwing his arm around me. "We're all a friggin' mess."

I eyeballed Mario, standing near the casket with his wife and five children. As the second oldest son with a less volatile temper, he might be more willing to talk than Dominic.

CHAPTER 10

Somehow I ended up wedged in between Anthony and Dominic in the front row with the Ardemoni family. I didn't belong there. My fingers fidgeted in my lap incessantly. Anthony gripped them at one point to stop me.

When my face was buried in Anthony's suit coat today, I almost cried. I had weakened since my father's funeral. This was supposed to be a time to mourn. A time to grieve. A time to remember the good times. But it was different for me. Funerals (and I'd been to my fair share) were a time of numbness. No tears of grief and no smiles and laughter at shared memories. For me, it was a time to watch sadness pass in front of me and retreat into my own world until it was over. Then life could go back to normal.

Today was different, though. I let memories in. All those damn pictures. Those damn people. I almost cried. I couldn't wait to escape. And at the same time, I couldn't leave. I needed answers.

I expected nothing less from the Ardemoni family than an elaborate funeral. I accompanied them from the funeral home to the cathedral, then to the cemetery in a shiny black Hummer limo. Mario owned Ardemoni Limo Incorporated, simply known as ALI. It seemed as though the whole fleet was there.

The morning soon turned into late afternoon. As the grand luncheon came to a close, I spotted Mario out in the hallway, pacing the floor with M.J., his eight-month-old son, his only son. Finally, he was alone.

M.J. was in a whiny semi-crying mood. He looked tired. But what did I know about babies? This was my chance to ask Mario if they had spoken to James the night before Frankie died. Somehow, I had to bring it up casually.

"Oh, look at him," I said, playing with M.J.'s tiny fingers. The infant stopped fussing and stared at me. "He's so cute."

"You should see him when he's happy."

Mario handed me the baby as if I had asked to hold him. I forced a smile and cringed at the slimy string of drool running down M.J.'s face and onto his drenched bib.

"So, uh, how are you handling everything?" I asked, swaying back and forth like I'd seen Carmella do.

"It hasn't sunk in yet. How about you?"

"Same here. I try to think about other things, so I don't think about Frankie. Of course, I'm bound to hit the wall eventually."

M.J. started to fuss again. I hoped Mario would see that as a sign to take the baby. When he didn't, I rocked a little quicker.

"Anthony said you took a cab to the funeral today. We could have picked you up."

"I know. You have a crowded car, and I didn't want to put anyone out."

"Crowded car? The limo seats a soccer team," he said.

"I know. I just..." My head bobbled as I searched for an excuse.

"You'll take one home. No arguments."

"Thank you."

"You're the baby whisperer, Emma," Mario said quietly.

I glanced at M.J. and found him fast asleep in my cradling arms. Drool poured from his mouth even in sleep— gross. At least he wasn't crying. Then I noticed something.

"Look at his chin. He has a cleft like Frankie," I said.

Mario had a cleft too. Although it was less noticeable, and you needed to be at the right angle to see it.

Mario nodded his head. "Frankie loved this little guy."

The opportunity presented itself.

"I heard you had dinner with him the night before he died. That's cool. You know, to be able to spend time with him before..." I hated to say the words.

"Yeah. We had a great dinner and relived some fun memories. It was nice."

"And you guys ran into an old friend?"

He nodded his head and smiled. "Jamie Gallagher showed up. I hadn't seen him in years. Frankie tell you about that?"

"No. He never mentioned it."

"I'm surprised. They hung out long after I left. You guys were all so close back in the day."

"Then he moved. And back then, traveling to the next town was like flying to another country." I rolled my eyes.

"I wonder if Jamie knows about Frankie. I didn't see him at the wake or the funeral. Did you see him at church today?"

"No. But he would want to know. Any idea how to get in touch with him?"

Please tell me you have his number, his address, something... I thought.

Mario shook his head and said, "Nah. I don't know. He said something about living with his grandmother while he finished getting his master's degree. Or doctorate? Some degree. Smart bastard."

"Hmm. James moved to Livonia, right?"

"Yeah. That's it. Now I remember. Jamie lives on Big Tree Road. Some old Victorian." Mario smiled and said, "Frankie gave him a hard time the other night because his house is purple with pink trim. A true Grandma's house. Do you know the one I'm talking about?"

I shook my head and said, "I never go that way." *But I will soon,* I thought.

Out of nowhere, Mario scowled and said, "Anyhow, don't ask Dom about Jamie. He thinks he had something to do with Frankie's death. It's stupid."

"What makes him think that?"

He shrugged his shoulders. "You know about the Gallaghers?"

Mario carefully took the baby from me and managed not to wake him up.

"A little," I said. "I don't know any of them personally. Unless you count James."

"The Gallaghers run drugs through the local colleges. A lot of them are college students trying to make a buck. Dom thinks Jamie is one of them now."

As each word dropped from Mario's mouth, I could only think of one thing. People who live in glass houses shouldn't throw stones.

"It's not like he's loaded with drug money. He lives with his great-grandmother."

"I know. I said it was stupid. I heard Jamie hasn't even seen or talked to his father in years. But for some reason, Dom is convinced he's involved."

"And Anthony?"

"He's open to the idea. So's Ma."

I took a deep breath and released it slowly.

"James would never hurt Frankie. Never," I reminded Mario.

Mario's mouth flattened, and his eyebrows raised. That look was doubt, and it could only mean trouble.

At that moment, even though I hadn't seen James in years, I knew I had to find him. Not because of my purgatory dream episode, but because Dom had convinced his family that James had done something atrocious, something unthinkable. And that put him in grave danger. Dom would never let James get away with what he thought he did. He would make James suffer for what happened to Frankie.

But I knew that already, didn't I?

"*Iron backbone*," Frankie had said.

"*Iron-willed*," I had replied.

It was a warning I could not ignore.

CHAPTER 11

When I woke up the next morning and my mother wasn't home, I began to worry. I hadn't seen nor heard from her since I woke up in the hospital. Three days was almost standard for her to be gone. After that, it meant trouble. Even though I despised her in many ways, she was the woman who gave birth to me. And we were going on day four.

I tried calling her cell phone only to hear it ringing in her bedroom. It was never wise to go in there and "poke around." To contact her, or "hunt her down," as she would call it, would infuriate her. But I had to look for clues as to where she might have gone. I would deal with the consequences later.

The banshee's room reeked of cigarette smoke; the ceiling was yellow above where she chain-smoked in bed. I didn't see her pills anywhere, which led me to believe she planned to be gone for a while. Next to her phone were several small pieces of paper, a few lame-looking business cards (the do-it-yourself kind), and a loaded ashtray with three different brands of cigarettes.

The entire room was dark, smelly, and disgusting. I snagged the random papers and business cards and left the room. I shuffled through them and found a few that sounded like names I'd overheard when she was on the phone. On a few drunken occasions, she had even mentioned some of these guys to me by name. Of course, at the time, they had fallen on I-could-give-a-crap ears.

I paced the floor in the kitchen for a bit, shuffling through the papers and the cards, then decided to give her another few days. While three days MIA was her standard, it was still far from her longest absence. She had skipped out once for two weeks. When I was eleven.

I tossed the phone numbers on the table and called for a ride. I needed to go to Livonia to find a big purple and pink Victorian on

Big Tree Road. When the car showed up, I expected to see Javier. To my surprise (and annoyance), I found myself disappointed when it wasn't him.

"Hi. Main Street, Livonia, please," I said, getting in the car.

"What number?"

"I don't know."

"Excuse me?" he said. The driver peered over his shoulder with an arrogant sneer.

I shrugged and said, "I'll know it when I see it."

We made it to Livonia in under five minutes. The driver glanced over his shoulder with an arrogant eye roll. His words dripped with sarcasm as he asked, "See anything familiar yet? Are we hot or cold?"

"Cold," I said, eyeing the houses we passed. "What's your name?"

"Jack," he replied. "What are we looking for here? This is ridiculous."

"Jack, if I were to call for another ride, can I request someone specific to pick me up?" I asked with a sweet smile.

His face lightened. His eyes perked up in the rearview mirror.

"Sure. If the person is free, they can. You want to request me for another day, baby?"

"Oh, no. Not you, *baby*. I had someone else in mind. I prefer the not-an-arrogant-prick type."

Just then, I spotted the house.

"There it is. The purple one."

"Yay," he mumbled.

I paid him and stepped out of the car.

"Need me to wait?' he asked.

"Hardly," I said, slamming the door.

He called me a bitch as he drove away. Not that I cared. You didn't grow up to be a sensitive person in my neighborhood and in my family. If you didn't have an iron backbone, you may as well have wilted with the weeds because you would never have come out unscathed. That's what Frankie and I always said. That's where our mantra came from.

I hesitated for a second before walking up the desolate driveway. It didn't look like anyone was home. Maybe I should have thought things out better. I sucked in a breath, then walked onto the front porch and peeked in the windows. The decor in the house screamed "old woman." This had to be the right house.

I knocked, then rang the bell. No one answered. I rang the bell once more, and still, no one came to the door, so I banged on the old wooden door with the rusty door knocker. After a few minutes, I pulled my phone from my pocket to call for a car.

"I should have had the jerk wait," I mumbled.

Just then, the door cracked open.

"Hello, there," said a frail elderly woman. Her white hair was pulled tightly into a perfect bun at the top of her head. She was the spitting image of the lady from the picture in my dream. "May I help you?" she asked.

"My name is Emma. I'm looking for James. We're old friends. Someone said he lives here?"

The door flew open. "James?" she gasped. The small woman reached out and grabbed my bandaged arm. "Have you seen him?" she implored.

"No. I haven't. That's why I'm here. I was hoping to talk to him about something."

Her eyes went cloudy as the glimmer of hope drained from her face. "I was hoping you knew something. James hasn't been home for days."

"How many days?"

"Six or seven now. I know he's a grown man, but he never stays away without telling me. It's so unlike him. The police are finally looking for him. I called them when he didn't come home the other night, and they said he was an adult. That sometimes, men do that. I know my James Nicholas; he always calls. He knows I worry."

I didn't know what to say. The last thing I expected was to learn James was missing.

"So..." I had so many questions that I didn't know where to begin. "So... the police consider him a missing person?"

62

"Yes. It's all over the news, and the police have no leads. You look familiar. Have we met?"

I nodded and said, "We were friends on Beachwood. What have the police told you?"

"They've told me nothing. I pester them every single day. I'm just a bothersome old lady to them. I don't know what else to do."

"Could he be with one of his parents?" I asked.

"No, honey. He doesn't talk to his daddy. And his mama passed years back."

"I didn't know. I'm sorry."

"They lived an unhealthy lifestyle. I've checked with all his friends. Maybe you know of some friends that I don't. Would you call them?"

Then it dawned on me. Friends she didn't know. Friends I knew. Dominic suspected James was involved with Frankie's death. It was only yesterday when Dominic informed Anthony and Mario about his suspicions. Could he have known something sooner? Could James' disappearance be linked to the Ardemonis?

G3 swayed like she was going to fall over. I took her by the arm and led her to the rocker on the porch.

"Sit down. Are you alright?" I asked.

"Yes. Yes. As well as can be expected. What was your name again?"

"Emma Finewood."

She put a shaky hand on my cheek and said, "I don't mean to burden you. I apologize."

"Don't be silly. I want to help." I wondered if James lived the same unhealthy lifestyle as his parents. And would she tell me? "G3, do you think maybe James left town? Maybe to get away from something?"

She smiled. "Oh, my. You called me G3. James calls me that."

Yes, I know. I thought. But I said, "He must have referred to you as G3 when we were kids."

She was shaking her head. "No. He started calling me that when he moved in here with me."

"Do you mind if I call you that?"

"Not at all. Oh, I miss him. I hope he's safe. He really would tell me if he wasn't coming home."

"When was the last time you saw him?"

I was trying to put together the timeline. James had been at The Green Sunday night. The night before my accident. The night before Frankie was killed. I asked G3, "Could it have been last Saturday or Sunday?"

She shook her head, and her eyes wandered like she was trying to think.

"Okay now, it was Saturday when I last saw him. I remember because that morning, he left for the library and never came home that night. I called the police; they weren't worried yet. I didn't know what else to do. So I started calling his friends."

"Do you know if anyone saw James after that?" *Besides the Ardemoni family*, I thought.

"Yes. The police said that James was seen at the restaurant in Geneseo."

"The Green." Good, other people saw them all together.

"Yes. That one. Then nothing. He disappeared."

I reran the timeline through my head. James leaves home Saturday morning. On Sunday, Frankie and James, two old buddies from the neighborhood, meet up at The Green. The next day, Frankie is dead, and James is missing. Did it take a genius to figure out the two were related? It did not.

After about half an hour on G3's porch, Javier's car pulled into the driveway. He sat patiently in the car. I gave G3 my number in case something else came up and promised to keep in touch.

I walked down the driveway toward the car.

"I didn't call for a ride," I declared as I walked by the car and down the sidewalk. I needed to think, not listen to stories, analogies, and proverbs.

Javier hopped out of the car and hurried after me.

"Emma, wait," he said. "You are not walking home."

"You're kind of like a crazy stalker now, Javier."

64

"Emma." He gripped my hand. "Please."

I stopped, and instead of taking my hand back, I let him hold it.

"Javier, you're a nice guy. My boyfriend was just murdered, and now my best friend is missing..." I stopped. His eyes went wide. "Please don't lecture me. I need some space. I don't know if you have a thing for me, or you feel sorry for me, or whatever. But I don't need advice or a pep talk."

He said, "You have friends?"

I took my hand back and smirked. "You're so awkward." I shoved his shoulder. "Go away, Javier."

"I cannot. I mean, I will not. You only seem to have one friend, and now she is missing. You need me."

"It's he. He's missing. And no, I don't need anyone."

I walked away, and he followed. After a few more steps, I stopped again. He was relentless.

"Seriously, man?"

"Let me take you home." He zipped his lips and said, "I hereby promise to keep my mouth shut."

"Impossible."

"Completely possible."

"Want to bet?"

"What are the stakes?" he asked.

"Ten bucks?" I said.

"No. Not money," he responded. He looked down at the sidewalk. "I want something more."

I considered what he could have meant by that. And I could only come to one obvious and disgusting conclusion.

"Wow. I have some seriously bad judgment," I said.

I shook my head and stormed off down the sidewalk. I couldn't believe it. He didn't seem like the type who would expect me to give up my body on a bet. It goes to show that you never really know someone. He had some nerve.

He raced after me.

"Go away," I said over my shoulder.

"Wait!" he hollered.

I stopped abruptly and said, "Beat it, Javi. My body is not on the bargaining table. But thanks for thinking I'm trash."

He waved his hands in the air. "Trash? No. If you think I am anything less than a gentleman, you are mistaken." He shook his head, and with pleading eyes, he said, "I think very highly of you. I wish only for your friendship. That is all."

I wasn't sure if I believed him. I tried to read his face, but the only way to describe it was pathetic.

"So you didn't mean…"

"No," he said. "Absolutely not."

Feeling foolish now, I tapped the sidewalk with my heel and studied my shoe.

"You must be desperate for friends," I said.

Javier said nothing. He waited for an answer.

"Whatever." I shrugged.

"It is a bet, then? I am silent for the entire drive to your home; then we are officially friends?"

I bit my lip and studied his eyes. Then after deciding to give him another chance, I responded, "Fine. But if you open your mouth even to yawn, that's it. You're strictly my occasional driver until I get a car. Deal?"

"Deal," he said, holding out his hand. I gave it a firm shake.

Javier didn't utter a single word for the entire ride. I tempted him to speak by asking random questions, but he didn't fall for it. Once we reached my driveway, he got out of the car and finally spoke.

"I do not take money from friends. Rides are free. Friends and family benefits."

"That's not right. You'll lose your job."

"No, I will not."

"Yes. Your boss will find out eventually, and then your dream job will be over. I don't want to be responsible for that."

"I shall worry about my job. Not you."

I shook my head. I glanced through the front window of my house and didn't see anyone. There was no unidentified vehicle in the driveway. And suddenly, I had an unexplainable need to tell Javier everything. That's what friends were for, right?

"Do you have time to come in for a minute? I could use someone to talk to."

"For you, I have all the time in the world."

CHAPTER 12

Javier and I sat down at the kitchen table. I opened my laptop, typed a few words, and hit enter. Then I slid the computer to Javier.

He stared at the screen for a minute, reading some of the article.

"Emma, this Frankie Ardemoni, he is the friend, sometimes boyfriend?"

"Yes."

"He was murdered?"

I nodded yes.

"Do you know what happened?"

"No. Not exactly. But I need to find out. I think my friend James is involved, and that's why he's missing."

"Let the police figure it out. They may know things they are not sharing."

"I think James is in real danger." I paused long enough for Javier to find my eyes. "I think I am in danger too."

"What? Why?"

"Frankie tried to warn me. Something he said made me think whoever did this might come for me."

"When did Frankie give you this warning?"

On the beach— after he died, I thought. But I said, "I was on the phone with him when he was shot. That's why I was distracted. I heard the shots; they were muffled. I didn't know at the time what was happening. I heard the shooter's voice, his words. And Frankie referred to him as the devil. Maybe that meant something."

"Perhaps. Why assume someone is to come after you, though? How would they know who he was on the phone with?"

"I checked my phone this morning. It has a cracked screen, but it still works. There was a call from Frankie's phone about ten minutes after my accident. Someone could have seen him on the phone and heard some of the conversation. They must have hit the call back on Frankie's phone and got my message."

Javier shook his head. "It could have been Frankie calling you back. He may not have died right away, Emma. I am sorry to say, but he may have been calling to talk to you one last time. Or calling you for help. Did you consider that?"

No, I hadn't considered that for one second. I knew it wasn't him calling. I knew I was in danger, and I knew from the bottom of my heart that James was in even greater danger. Every second counted.

For some reason, I assumed I could explain this to Javier without telling him what happened after my accident, about that place deep in my brain where I ventured for mere minutes. I supposed it didn't matter what I called it at this point. A dream, a trip to limbo, a figment of my imagination. Whatever it was, it was hard to deny that I believed in it. Whatever it was.

"Something else happened. Something I haven't told anyone. It's… strange."

"Tell me."

"It's weird."

"You do not drive strangers around without hearing strange things."

Javier didn't laugh or smile. His face was serious. So I told him.

"I'm pretty sure I almost died," I started. I took a deep breath and continued. "I think I went to some kind of purgatory or limbo. At first, I couldn't get out. Then, suddenly, I was picked up and thrown back here." Biting my thumbnail, I uttered, "Even God didn't want me."

Javier said nothing. He stared at me for a second, then dropped his face into his hands.

Ugh. Why did I tell him?

"Javier?"

He lifted his head and took my hands.

"Oh, Dios mio… Continue," he said.

I shifted around in my chair because my story sounded ridiculous. Plus, I was uncomfortable because Javier was holding my hands.

Uncomfortable because his eyes never left mine. Still, I sat there and explained it all. Then I got to the part where I saw Frankie.

"He said he was dead. He warned me that James and I were in danger. When I woke up, what happened seemed so real. And as I got better, I realized I probably just hit my head too hard. Or maybe it was a dream, or my mind was playing tricks on me. And now things are pointing to the fact that it was all true. That maybe, somehow, it was real."

Javier remained quiet.

I said, "That's it— kind of. Well, there was more. Anyway, that's the gist of it."

Again, not a word from Javier, the man who couldn't stop talking.

I rolled my eyes, got up, and marched to the fridge. I snagged the bottle of OJ and two glasses from the cupboard.

"Want some?" I asked Javier.

"Um, no thanks," he said.

He sat quietly with a strange look on his face. The silence was eating away at me. I was afraid that I had made a mistake in trusting him.

"Say something," I said.

He looked away.

"What?" I asked.

I poured what I thought was OJ into my glass. But it was transparent with a slight yellow hue. It was my mother's wine.

I jumped back from the table and exclaimed, "See. This is another sign telling me the ridiculous dream I had when I was unconscious was real."

"How do you mean?" he asked. "You simply took the wrong bottle."

Javier walked to the fridge and returned with the bottle of orange juice.

"It's my head, my subconscious. It's trying to tell me something. In purgatory, James offered me a glass of wine. But I said no, and he gave me non-alcoholic instead. I don't drink any of that stuff, not even non-alcoholic. But I did, and I loved it." I collapsed into the chair. "Or was it him that I loved?" I said quietly.

"Emma, let's talk this through. You see, I was raised catholic, so I believe in purgatory. When people enter into purgatory, it is to suffer for their mortal sins. It is where they try to find redemption for their tainted souls." Javier hesitated. "They do not get to come back."

"But I did." My voice was weak.

"Perhaps it was not purgatory, and maybe your energy is better spent elsewhere. You are smart; you know the tricks our brains can play on us."

In a deflated voice, I said, "You're right. I don't know what I was thinking."

"Now, all that said, tell me what these clues are. These warnings. It cannot hurt to check them out. Just in case."

I jumped out of my chair and tackled him with a hug.

"Thank you," I said.

"The world works in funny ways, Emma."

"You don't have to tell me."

"So, you have not seen nor heard from James in years?"

"At least seven years. Frankie never mentioned James or the meeting at The Green."

"And this Irish versus Italian conflict? Is that for real?" Javier asked. "I did not know such an old-fashioned battle existed anymore. It sounds like early 1900s New York City to me. At least, that is what the history books tell us."

I shrugged and responded, "Small town, lots of drama."

"Do you think Frankie was involved with drugs?"

"Anthony said the local colleges are riddled with drugs. Dom thinks James was involved, maybe even dealing. Maybe Frankie was dealing on James' campus, his territory. That would have made the conflict even worse. Why else would Frankie decide to enroll in college? He told me it was for me, but he lied. Don't you think?"

"I suppose. And if that is the case, you must share this information with the police. You must tell them what you heard on the phone," Javier urged.

"There are two problems with that plan. One, I just don't buy it. I don't think James had anything to do with dealing drugs on campus or anywhere else, for that matter. The last thing I want is the police thinking James is a criminal. And two, going to the police is what will put me in danger."

"Finding James is the most important thing right now. Once he is found, they will know he had nothing to do with Frankie's death or drugs on the campus. The Ardemonis believing something does not make it true," Javier said.

Javier had a point. I knew Frankie like no one else. He couldn't have been dealing again, which meant something else was going on. And on top of that, James had a new problem. The Ardemonis.

"Take me to the police station?"

Javier pulled his phone from his pocket and said, "Of course. I shall tell work I have a pick-up. Vamonos, mi amiga."

CHAPTER 13

After half an hour, Javier and I wandered out of the police station perplexed.

"I have never seen an officer so disinterested," Javier said.

In disbelief, I said, "When I told them I was on the phone when it happened and heard the shooter's voice, it was like I was telling him what my favorite color was."

"They did not even question you about Frankie."

I shrugged. "Maybe they've already talked to enough people, and what I had to say wasn't anything they didn't already know."

"Did you hear what he said when I asked about leads on James?" Javier asked.

"Yes. I couldn't believe it. I wanted to jump over the table and smack him."

"I am glad you did not."

"James is considered a missing person, and they have no leads? None? And it's not my concern?" I scoffed.

We stood in quiet disbelief for a moment. Then Javier asked, "Coffee?"

"Definitely," I responded.

I hopped into the passenger seat of the car, something I was more comfortable with now that we were friends. Javier took off down Main Street. Then he pulled into the parking lot of The Green.

"New plan," Javier announced. "I do not know about you, but I am starved. Perhaps a quick bite at The Green?"

"Yes! Great idea."

We were hopeful that the bartender was working the night Frankie and James were last seen here. We bellied up to the bar as soon as a spot opened. Javier ordered a coke, and I ordered a ginger ale.

"No drink?" I asked. "Don't let me stop you."

"Four more months is stopping me," he said with a smile. "I drink at home with my family. It is not so much a big deal with us. Wine with dinner. Homemade moonshine. It is the Bolivian way. But out and about with the car? Not worth the risk."

"Right. It's enough that you already give away free rides. You don't need more trouble than that."

He nudged my shoulder and said, "You worry for me?"

"I don't want to be the reason you lose your job. It seems to make you very happy."

"It does. Stop worrying."

The bartender came back with our drinks.

"There you go. You here on business or pleasure, Javi?" the bartender asked, eyeballing me.

The bartender had a look that you couldn't easily forget. Despite that, I couldn't put my finger on why he looked so familiar. He was well over six feet tall and built like a professional bodybuilder. There was a striking resemblance to Roman Reigns, one of Frankie's favorite WWE wrestlers, except this guy had shorter hair. That had to be why he looked so familiar.

"Just dinner," Javier responded. "Got a question for you, Adam."

"Shoot," he said.

"Who was here last Sunday night? You or Seth?"

Javier had obviously spent a fair amount of time at The Green to know the bartenders by their first names.

"That would have been me. Why? What's up? The Ardemoni kid?"

"As a matter of fact, yes. Emma here was his girlfriend."

"Aw... man. Sorry, Emma." Adam reached out and shook my hand. "I'm Adam," he said.

When our hands touched, what felt like several volts shot through my arm and continued through my body.

"Sorry," Adam blurted. "I didn't mean to shock you."

"It was probably me. I'm kind of a shuffler," I explained.

The shock took me several months back to the night I had gone to the Lakeville Sheer Art Gallery opening with Frankie, Mario, and Carmella. Carmella loved art and had been dying for a night out without kids, so Mario had asked Mama to babysit. Frankie and I tagged along.

Upon entering the gallery, we were welcomed by a glass wall emanating a soft, shimmering white glow. Water flowed through it, snaking around a dozen strategically placed black and white drawings. One caught my attention immediately; it was a girl with long hair, running through a field. Behind her, five large boulders rolled downhill directly toward the girl, her face full of angst as she tried to outrun them before they bowled her over.

I remembered how the anxiety had risen in my chest as I imagined her desperation. Her fear. Without thinking, I had placed my hand over the boulders, trying to shield her from them. And that's when I was shocked.

The zap had been hot and lightning-fast the second my hand touched the glass. Somehow I'd managed to stifle a yelp. Through the grimace on my face, I'd caught a girl on the other side of the glass who looked as though she'd also been shocked. Further down the wall, two guys were shaking and grasping their arms as if they'd met the same fate. Adam was one of those guys.

Adam said, "Frankie was a nice guy. The cops came in asking about him. I guess this was the last place he was seen. I heard his buddy is still missing."

"Look, Adam, I know you already talked to the police, but Emma has many questions about that night, and the police did not have much to tell her."

"What do you want to know?" Adam asked me.

I wasn't sure where to begin. So I said, "Did you know his friend? The one who's missing?"

"Yeah, sure. James Gallagher. We went to high school together. But he didn't have dinner with the Ardemonis. He showed up around ten and had a drink with Mario and Frankie. Mario only had one, but Frankie and James closed the place down."

"Any idea what they talked about?" I asked.

"I was busy cleaning the bar. But they were the only guys left in the place, so I caught a few things. You sure you want to go there?"

Javier and I exchanged looks.

"Yes," I said.

"Drug stuff, I think. Did you know Frankie used to deal?"

I cleared the sudden onset of phlegm from my throat and croaked, "Yes. Although I thought he left that behind years ago."

Adam replied, "I thought he did too. James seemed worried about something. Or someone, I should say."

"Who?" Javier asked.

"Keegan Flynn. Another guy James and I went to high school with. And I'm not positive, but I had always heard rumors that Keegan ran with the Gallaghers." Adam raised his eyebrows knowingly at Javier.

Javier asked, "Where can we find Keegan?"

"You can't. He's missing," Adam said.

He nodded to a couple who walked in and sat at the end of the bar.

"Hang on," Adam said and headed to pour a drink for the customers.

"Javier, do you see what I mean? This is a drug thing. Maybe Dom was right about James. And now this Keegan guy is missing too. Frankie told me Keegan was a bad seed. This can't be a coincidence."

"Do not give up on James yet. Trust your instincts, Emma."

"I have good instincts," I said, repeating James' words. "You're right. We're missing something. But what."

Javier shrugged and sipped his coke.

"How do you know the bartender?" I asked.

"Work."

"Work? Did you give him a ride or something?"

"Not him. When he has a drunk customer, he calls me. I pick them up and take them home."

"That's cool."

"We will talk to James' great-grandmother tomorrow."

76

"We also need to talk to Anthony and Dominic," I said.

"Did you not tell me Dominic was angry when you brought up James' name at the funeral? Perhaps reaching out to Dominic is a bad idea."

"This isn't all about James. It's also about who killed Frankie."

"Have you considered that Anthony and Dom have something to do with James' disappearance?"

"No way. They're two-bit troublemakers, not kidnappers and murderers. They deal drugs. Bookie stuff, minor burglaries. They got caught breaking into cars when they were younger and got into a bunch of fights. But kidnapping and murder?" I shook my head.

"Let me play the devil's advocate for a moment," Javier said. "James may be missing on purpose. Perhaps, he took off after something happened... like Frankie's murder. He may have had something to do with that or know something about it that has put him in hiding."

"I thought of that too," I said, interrupting. "But after I talked to G3, I was convinced he couldn't be a dealer. He has too much going for him."

"You told me yourself the college dealers fly under the radar. They are students, not gang members. He knows Keegan Flynn, a known dealer, according to Adam."

I shook my head vehemently. "Uh-uh, not James. I believe there is some kind of connection, but he is not jeopardizing his future to deal drugs on campus."

"Then let us consider something else. Most low-life criminals will eventually rise to the occasion. Do you understand?"

"I don't think I like you playing the devil's advocate." I crossed my arms.

"Gangs have initiations, expectations for new members or members rising in the ranks."

"You watch too much TV," I said, dismissing the idea.

"It would be wise to consider that Dom and Anthony could be more involved than you think. And James may be playing a greater role in all of this. Keep an open mind."

I couldn't completely deny the possibility that the Ardemoni family had something to do with James' disappearance. At the very least, they may know something about it. But my gut told me James was no criminal.

"Which brings me back to Dom and Anthony," I said. "I *have* to talk to them."

When Adam returned, he didn't have much more information to offer. Adam promised Javier he would keep his ears open and ask the other bartender to do the same.

We headed out the door around eleven. As I stepped around a bottle in the parking lot, a meaty hand captured my arm. Before I understood what was happening, I was getting dragged behind a parked van. As I began to yell, a hand slapped across my mouth. I caught the shocked look on Javier's face just before someone punched him right between the eyes and knocked him out cold. His body didn't have a chance to bend at the hips; he simply fell like a tree.

As I struggled to break away, my captor gave me a savage shove into the back doors of the van. My head bounced off the steel. My mouth was now free to scream, except I couldn't. I was sure my eyes deceived me.

"Mario?"

"Emma, stop with the questions. Stop now, or you're going to get hurt." he snarled, pinning me against the van.

"Let go of me. What are you doing?" I stretched my neck in search of Javier and called his name. "Javi!"

Mario pulled my shoulders toward him, then smashed me back against the van.

"Shut up. Shut. Up," he growled.

I had never seen this side of Mario. He was always the sweet loving one who stayed out of trouble since getting married. He was a family guy. But then again, this was a family issue.

"Take this warning with all the seriousness in the world. Keep out of this. We are handling everything. You're just getting in the way. You're stirring everything up and in the wrong direction."

"How did you…"

"You went to the cops. Campo called me after you left."

"Officer Campo? You know him? That explains his indifferent attitude."

Mario glared at me.

"You know then?" I asked.

Mario said nothing.

"Did he tell you, Mario? Did he?"

"You should have told us you were on the phone with Frankie. But it doesn't matter. There's no longer a record you were there tonight."

"Would you let go of me? I'm not going anywhere, and you're hurting me."

I was so angry with him that, in all honesty, I could feel no pain, only disgust.

As he lightened his grip, I shook his hands off me and pushed him back a few inches.

He said, "Go home, Fine. And do what I said, leave this alone."

I shook my head no. There wasn't a chance in hell that I was leaving this alone.

"Why are you hiding things from the police? You need to tell them so they can find Frankie's murderer and find James. He's missing, you know?"

Mario looked beyond the van. I followed his gaze to Dom, dragging the now conscious Javier around the corner with one arm sharply cranked up behind him. Javier winced and let out a groan.

"What's with the cabbie?" Dom asked me.

"He's my friend."

"Suddenly, you have friends?"

"Let go of him. You're hurting him."

"Aw, Finewood is worried about the cabbie," Dom whined sarcastically.

"You're a jerk, Dom. And you, Mario. It's like I don't even know you."

Without warning, Javier got loose from Dom's grip and elbowed him in the gut. Then turning on a dime, he slugged Dom straight in the nose. Dom stumbled back, clutching his face. Blood poured from both nostrils.

It took a second for Mario to register the scuffle and dive at Javier. But Javier was fast. He dodged out of the way and still managed to catch Mario with an upper right hook.

"Mario!" I yelled.

When I looked back at Dom, Adam had him pinned to the ground. It was like he appeared out of nowhere.

As Mario lunged at Javier, Adam hollered, "Ardemoni! Enough. I know a few cops who aren't in your pocket and will be here any minute."

Mario, already an object in motion, didn't look like he could have stopped even if he wanted to. All of a sudden, two parking lot lights exploded above us. We were all visibly startled, except for Mario. He barreled on.

As a shower of glass and fiery sparks dropped into the parking lot around us, Mario slammed head-first into Javier's waist, but it didn't take him down. Instead, it allowed Javier to scoop up Mario's torso, yank his lower body up into the air, and throw him onto the pavement.

The sudden audible expulsion of air and Mario's panicked chest grab made it clear he'd had the breath knocked out of him. Javier, the front of his shirt smoldering from the raining sparks, stood over him, ready to defend himself again. This time Mario stayed down.

Dom said, "Adam, let me go, man. I'm cool, I'm cool."

Adam slowly dragged Dom off the ground. Dom shoved Adam away and muttered some obscenities under his breath. Then he glowered at me and said, "Leave it alone. Do you hear me?"

I didn't respond. I went to Javier's side.

"Javi, you're hurt."

"I'm fine," he said, wiping a small trickle of blood from his forehead.

I would have expected more blood from his face-plant into the pavement and the glass that fell on him. He was lucky. He was also kind of cute.

80

"You're bleeding," I said.

"Not the first time."

In the distance, sirens began to blare.

Adam said, "They're coming here. I'd go if I were you."

"Let's go, Dom," Mario said, staggering to the far end of the parking lot where they had parked.

Dom and Mario jumped in Mario's matte-black BMW X6 and peeled out of the parking lot. A few seconds later, the police sirens stopped. I searched the street, ready for them to pull in.

"I don't know where they're going, but they're not coming here," Adam said. He pointed to a flexed bicep. "Do I look like I need cops?"

I said to Adam, "So you're the bouncer too?"

"Only when my friends are getting their asses beat."

"Thanks," Javier said, patting Adam on the back.

"I've got your back, man," said Adam, pulling something from his back pocket. "You forgot your credit card at the bar."

Javier laughed, took the card, and turned to me. "See? Everything happens for a reason."

We all looked up at the shattered light, then at Javier's smoldering shirt and the mess on the ground. Glass was scattered about the parking lot and sprinkled over nearby cars.

Javier and I turned our gaze toward Adam, who shrugged and said, "Uh, yeah. I'll have someone fix that."

CHAPTER 14

"You must be made of stone," I said, sliding into Javi's car. "Your face isn't bad for a knock-out punch and collision with the pavement."

"My modeling career could have been ruined," he said with a smile.

"Ha, ha," I said. All of a sudden, I saw him in a different light. "You're kind of a badass."

"You say that as if you are surprised."

"You're just so nice. I didn't take you for the type who would… you know…"

"Defend a lady or myself?"

"No. I don't know. Never mind."

Javier stared at me, then the crooked smile returned.

"I do not like getting punched. Sometimes I am forced to use my powerful ninja skills on people."

I poked my finger into a fresh burn hole on his shirt sleeve and laughed aloud. We both did. Then the laughter died down, and he turned his body toward me.

He said, "I know you come from a rough side of town, but so do I. Living here in America could never compare to where I spent the first ten years of my life."

"Where is that?" I asked, welcoming a story for a change.

"Potosi, Bolivia."

"Like the name of your car."

"Yes. Potosi sits at the foot of Cerro Rico, Rich Mountain."

"Rich Mountain?"

"Yes. That is what we called it. Its real name is Cerro de Potosi. The people of Potosi have worked the mine for its rich supply of silver for hundreds of years. Like my father, and his father, and his father's father."

"Not you?"

"I always thought I would end up in the mountain with my father. Too many times, we saw the mountain swallow our friends and family."

"You mean, the mine made them sick? Like coal miners?"

"Sick is not what I mean. Potosi has another name. They call it the mountain that eats men. Quite literally.

"My great grandfather was swallowed by a mine when he was only thirty-five years old; it collapsed and killed twenty-eight others. He left behind my great-grandmother with six children and nothing else. My grandfather was a little older when the mine took his life. That time there were fifty-two men."

Javier glanced down at his hands and continued.

"Then there was my father. He was not going to ever work in those cursed mines. Never. Until my mother got sick, and the bills were too much to handle on his baker's salary. He was forced to close the bakery and work in the mines.

"One morning, I returned from the mouth of the mine where, each day, I left a shiny stone as a gift to the Devil's Miner. The doctor was just leaving and explained there was nothing more he could do; my mother was dying. My mother said I would go to America to live with my aunt and uncle. I would go to college like her brother and never have to work the mines. But I refused to leave my father. I told her no."

"Who is the Devil's Miner?" I asked.

"What, not who. It is a statue that sits at the opening of the mine my father worked in. He is also called El Tio. The legend is that if you left a gift to the Devil's Miner, he would protect the mine and the men who worked inside. The shiny stones were all I had to offer. Sadly, my stones were not enough."

"Oh, no," I gasped.

"On my father's first day back in the mine after my mother had passed, I was at home and felt the rumble. The earth shook under my feet. There had not been a collapse in our town since I was a baby, but I knew what it was. I remember running to the opening and staring into the Devil's eyes. I picked up a large rock and threw it at him. I broke his nose off."

I put my hand on his arm. "I'm sorry, Javi."

He caught my eyes and said, "That is why I am here, though. I did not make it to college. Instead, I got a job at fifteen and started to save money. When I was eighteen, I bought my first car and became an Uber driver. By the end of that year, I had nine cars and eleven employees."

I gave his arm a playful shove. "This is your car company?"

"Yes. Rich Silver Car Service. Rich mountain full of silver; a place I will never have to work."

He lowered his head, then looked up at me through long dark lashes, and with that accent that I suddenly found sexy, he said, "Also, a place that will not be the death of me."

"I thought Rich Silver was a person. Your boss. Why all the mystery? Did you enjoy having me worry that I could be the reason you get fired at any moment?"

He smirked. "It never came up."

"And here I thought you were just some unmotivated cabbie. Instead, you are a smart, brave entrepreneur."

"I do not know about brave."

"Of course, you're brave. You left your country after both parents died and came here to start over. You took a risk on a business. Your parents would be proud. Your aunt and uncle must be."

"Yes, they are proud, but I had to convince them to believe in my dream. I dreamed of a high-end car service. Nicer than Uber and Lyft, yet affordable. Of course, my aunt and uncle wanted me to attend college as my mother wished. But they allowed me two years to make it work. If it failed, I would go to college. But I do not believe in failing."

"Me neither."

"We will not fail, Emma. We will find James."

"I know. I just hope we aren't too late."

CHAPTER 15

The following day, Javier and I went to see G3. She didn't have much more to tell us except that James gave her an important large green envelope the day he went missing. He needed her to mail it on Monday because it was a part of his final grade in English. Unfortunately, she didn't pay attention to the address.

After Javier dropped me off at home, I walked up to the cemetery. Mama Ardemoni visited her late husband at the mausoleum every day at noon. Rain or shine, she drove herself to have lunch with him. And now, with Frankie resting in the family crypt, she had even more reason to visit.

I found Mama sitting on the marble bench in front of the old stone family crypt. Ivy raced up the sides and filled in the cracks of the weathered stone. Mama was unpacking her lunch and chatting away in Italian to Anthony Senior and Frankie. She appeared happy for a change. Her face seemed a bit softer, and her voice was lighter as she laughed at something she had just said. I almost hated to interrupt.

"Mama?"

She looked over, surprised to see me.

"Emma. Hello. So good to see you."

She stood to greet me.

"I was visiting my father," I lied, hugging her. "I figured you might be here."

"Oh, your papa was such a good man. Always checked on me and the boys when Tony was away on business. How is your mother?" she asked, lowering her voice.

"The same. She's always been…troubled."

"She's young. She needs to find a good man to take care of her."

Oh, she's trying, I thought.

I sat down next to her on the bench.

"Grapes?" she offered.

"No, thank you. How are you doing, Mama?"

She patted my hand and said, "One day at a time, angelo. That's all we can do."

"One day at a time," I repeated. I took a breath and wondered if she already knew what I was about to tell her. "I saw the boys last night."

"Cheese?" she asked, holding out a bowl.

"No, thanks."

I was silent as I processed what to do next. The bottom line was that James might not have time for her to ignore this conversation. Once again, I laid it out there.

"I'm worried about what they're going to do."

"They can take care of themselves."

"I thought they were going to hurt me," I blathered to catch her off guard.

The look of disinterest on her face was heartbreaking.

"For Frankie, they are trying to help you, angelo mio," she responded with a bite to her words. Then she shrugged her shoulders and said, "You and your big ugly mouth."

Instantly, my pity for her disappeared. I stood up and took a step away from the bench. Was I treading on thin ice? Clearly, she was not in the dark, and if she told Mario, Dom, and Anthony I came here, I would end up in more trouble than I was already in.

"I'm not trying to start a fight, Mama."

"Aren't you? Hunting me down at Frankie's grave and accusing my boys of trying to harm you."

"I'm not accusing anyone of anything."

Mama Ardemoni stood, small and bulldoggish, and walked toward me with her crooked finger pointed in my face.

"Frankie's gone. Now go away, Emma. Seems you've already moved on anyway. Didn't take you long. Right? Right?" she snapped.

Mama sat back down on the bench and mumbled something in Italian. The only words I understood were "Frankie" and "Emma," and because I'd heard Anthony and Dom use the word, I understood *puttana*. I closed my gaping mouth, turned, and marched away without another word.

When I got home, I called Javier and explained my upsetting visit with Mama Ardemoni.

"She called me a slut."

"I knew that was a bad idea. They are playing a devious role in James' disappearance."

"I'm beginning to think you're right," I admitted. "I just can't figure out exactly what that role is."

"I am concerned for your safety. Is your mother home?"

"Why? Because she would protect me from them?" I laughed nervously. It was dawning on me that I might just need protection now.

"It would not hurt to have someone around. Is she there or not?" Javier asked.

"Not. And ninety-nine percent of the time, even when she is physically here, she's still not here. So what do we do now, Javi?"

"I am coming to get you."

"I don't need a babysitter."

"Let us have a late lunch."

"I don't have an appetite."

"Why not come to my place?" Javier said.

Too distracted by a nagging thought, I didn't answer.

"Hello?" he said. "Is that a yes?"

"Javi, I keep thinking about the envelope James had G3 put in the mail. Why the heck was it so important?"

"I agree. It is curious. Do you think perhaps it was not an assignment but something else entirely?"

"G3 insisted that he told her it was completely school related because of a project he was doing for his final. We need to find someone who can tell us about this project," I decided.

"Like Adam?" asked Javier.

Javier had a point. Adam may not have been in his class, but there was a chance he could lead us to some answers.

"Suddenly, I'm dying for chocolate mousse pie," I said. "Let's go back to The Green. What are the chances we'll run into an Ardemoni?"

"As good as anywhere else in this little town. See you in ten minutes."

CHAPTER 16

Javier greeted Adam while I checked the bar area, then peeked into the dining room.

"They aren't here," Adam noted.

"Good," I replied.

Javier and I pulled up stools to a bar table and sat down.

"When you have a chance, can we talk to you?" I asked Adam.

"Yup. Coke and a beer?"

"Two cokes," replied Javier.

When he returned, Adam gave us the names of two people possibly enrolled in the same accelerated senior thesis English class as James.

"I heard the class is brutal," Adam shared. "James bragged that this project would be epic. He said when the time came, it would basically guarantee him entrance into any doctoral program he wanted."

Javier asked, "Did he tell you anything about the project? Any details or maybe if he was working with anyone?"

"He said he couldn't give details because his project was 'unthinkable.' He even said it was dangerous once. But come on, it's an English class." Adam snickered. "How dangerous could that be?"

"Uh, he's missing," I reminded him.

"Yeah. But at the time, it seemed a little over the top." Adam leaned over the bar and said, "James never came out and told me he was working with anyone, but he was here with Keegan Flynn a few times."

"Seriously? Did they come in together?" I asked, dumbfounded.

"Yup. James, Frankie, and Keegan came in together last winter for drinks. It was back in February," Adam said.

"All three together," Javier said. "Is that typical?"

"No," Adam and I said together.

Everything Adam just told us bothered me. First of all, Keegan was known to work for Ty Gallagher. If anyone was a known troublemaker in town, it was him. He was in and out of jail for burglary, fights, and vandalism, just to name a few of his violent offenses.

Second, I would have sworn to anyone Frankie hadn't seen James in years. How could Frankie keep that from me?

Adam said, "Keegan and James never got along in high school. So I was surprised to see them all here together. Frankie and Keegan in one place usually meant trouble." He looked at me. "Sorry, Emma. You knew him better than I did. But Frankie had a bad rep. Cool guy, he just made bad decisions."

"Yeah, I know," I agreed. "Was Keegan enrolled at SUNY Geneseo?"

Adam tipped his head to the side and narrowed his eyes. "What do you think? In case you're wondering, I assure you it wasn't because of his scholarly ambitions."

"Strange coincidence that Frankie is dead, and James and Keegan are missing," said Javier.

"It's not a coincidence," I decided. "I need to find out what this project was. It must involve the three of them. Don't you think, Javi?"

He nodded his head. Adam agreed too.

"There is one person who must know what this project is about," I said.

"The English Professor. His name is Doctor Fahrer," Adam responded. "I had him one semester. He's cool."

*   *   *

When Monday rolled around, we went to see Dr. Fahrer. What he told us could be the key to what happened to James.

"He submitted an underwhelming proposal to investigate drugs in our small community," Dr. Fahrer said. "Honestly, I expected more from him, something deeper with elements of higher level thinking and research. Maybe something with a twist I never would

90

have seen coming. His proposal was stodgy at best; I figured he was playing it safe. Again, not like him."

Javier and I exchanged glances when Dr. Fahrer mentioned drugs in the community. Leave it to James to find that twist Dr. Fahrer was hoping for. My gut told me it was that twist we should be worried about.

"Do you think I could take a look at the report?" I asked.

He shook his head and said, "James never turned it in."

Javier responded, "He would have mailed it. You must have gotten it a few days ago. It would be in a large green envelope."

Dr. Fahrer said, "I think I would remember that. Let me check."

He went to his desk and rifled through a stack of papers. He dug through a small pile of mail, carefully reading the return addresses. There was no green envelope.

I turned to Javier and asked, "Where could he have sent it?"

*   *   *

Later that night, my mother stumbled in higher than a kite. Whatever she had taken made her extremely mellow. She mumbled that she was starving, then marched to her room without eating anything.

A few minutes later, I brought my mother an apple and a few crackers, only to find her out cold on the floor, curled up in the fetal position. Her closet door was wide open, and her head, half in the closet, rested peacefully on a balled-up sweater. Her purse strap was wrapped around her wrist and looked like it was cutting off circulation to her hand. So I unwound it from her arm and placed it on her nightstand.

I stuck my hand under her nose. Her breathing was a bit labored, but at least she was breathing. She twitched when I brushed my fingers over her clammy arm. She grunted when I said her name. She was her typical self, a hot mess. But still, I had been worried about her.

Startled by a sudden pounding at the front door, I quickly threw a blanket over my mother and hurried to the living room.

"Hey! Tracy! Open up. What the heck," hollered the man on the doorstep.

He continued to pound and yell.

I peeked out the window, and he saw me. He was a large, menacing-looking man. Heavy, but not muscular, and very tall. He had a shaved head, and tattooed sleeves covered both arms and made their way up his neck.

"Hey, girlie. Open the door. I'm with Tracy," he said. As if I'd ever open the door for him.

I walked away from the window, hoping he would go away. I checked on my mother, unconscious and oblivious to the racket. The man kept pounding. I was afraid he would break the door.

"Come on! The wench has my car keys," he yelled.

Geez, mom.

I went to the nightstand and rifled through the banshee's purse. I found cigarettes, gum, a few crumbled dollar bills and a handful of coins, a sticky shot glass, a lighter, a bottle of unmarked pills... But no keys. I went to her room and felt her pockets. Still— nothing.

I marched to the door and hollered to the fierce-tempered beast, "She doesn't have them."

"Yeah, the wench does. Let me in!"

"Go away," I said.

"I'd like to— if I could get my mother 'effin keys."

"She doesn't have them. I checked."

After that, he got quiet. He stopped banging on the door. I peeked out the window and didn't see him. His beat-up car was in the driveway, though. I paced the floor and figured he walked home or called someone for a ride or an extra set of keys.

Several minutes passed, and his dumb car was still in the driveway. Fine, I thought. Sit out there all night for all I care. I went to the kitchen for a cup of water. The banshee was down for the count, and I didn't look forward to the morning. My plan was to get up and out early before she saw the light of day.

As I walked down the hall to my room, the floor in the kitchen creaked.

"Come on, Nova," I said. "Come on, kitten."

"Never been called kitten before," said the beast, standing by the kitchen door.

"What are you doing in here? Get out."

"I'd love to."

"She doesn't have your keys," I stammered, taking a step back. "I checked."

Without hesitation, Jabba the Hutt barreled toward me, clamped onto my throat, and pinned me against the wall. My cup of water crashed to the floor and splashed all over my legs. The beast was crushing my throat; I couldn't breathe. I tried desperately to pry his hands off my neck, but he was too strong. I pounded on his head with my fists. Subsequently, it hurt me more than him. He wasn't phased in the least.

"Keys?" he demanded.

He loosened his grip long enough for me to choke out, "She doesn't have them." Then he throttled my neck again.

The next thing I knew, I was in my mother's room. She sat on her bed wearing a beautiful sundress and full makeup. Soft golden waves of hair brushed her shoulders.

I sat next to her. "Mom?"

"I know. I know. Billy wants the keys. I dropped them, honey."

"Where?" I asked.

Looking back at that moment, I should have been bewildered by her appearance. But strangely, I wasn't.

"Outside the door. By the front bushes," she said. "Tell him, and he will go away. Tell Billy to stop being such a bully."

"Thanks, Mom."

"Go on now. Hurry," she urged.

"The door," I grunted.

"What?" he asked. "Don't go passin' out on me. I need them keys, or I ain't gonna be able to leave. Does wenchiness run in your family, stupid?"

He let go of my neck, and my lungs burned with the sudden gasp of air.

"The door," I said again. "Look by the front door. Maybe she dropped them when she stumbled in."

My neck burned like it was on fire. The beast pounded his way to the door and stepped out. He bent over and pushed the dead leaves around. Soon, I heard the delightful sound of keys jingling.

"Got 'em, wenchie."

He snarled at me and stormed off toward his car.

"Billy!" I hollered after him.

He turned around and grunted, "What? I got the keys."

I guess I expected him to keep going— not to turn in response to the name.

"Your name is Billy?" I asked, short of breath.

"Uh-huh." He shook his head. "What? What do ya want, wenchie?" he said with a sinister grin. He started to walk back toward me, and I got scared.

"Nothing. Go!" I scurried to the door, slammed it in his face, and locked it.

I listened at the door until the keys jingled away from the house. What had just happened? I ran to my mother's room, where she still lay unconscious on the floor, covered by the blanket.

How had I known about the keys? I stared at my mother from the doorway. She hadn't moved an inch. Coincidence, I decided. Where else would the keys have fallen if she'd had them when she stumbled in the front door? But how did I know his name?

When I checked all the doors, I discovered that the lock on the door coming in from the garage didn't work. So I jammed a kitchen chair under the knob. Then, as long moments passed, I stood in the dark silence with my phone in my hand.

I was shaken by the beast. Terrified, if I was being honest. I thought for sure he was going to kill me. I wondered for a brief second, would my mother have taken responsibility for my death? Or would she expect everyone to feel sorry for her, like when she let my father die on our living room floor as she slept off her synthetic coma?

I shook my head dismissively and began to dial Javier's number. But then I stopped. With a deep breath, I shoved the phone into my back pocket. I didn't need him. I didn't need anyone.

"Iron backbone," I muttered.

CHAPTER 17

"It is too warm for a scarf," Javier said when I opened the door.

"Shh… my mother's sleeping. Let's go," I said, dragging him to the car.

Quietly, he said, "She has returned? That is good news."

I scowled.

"And bad," he said.

When we were safely in the car and leaving the driveway, I said, "She came home last night and went straight to bed. That doesn't mean she'll be there when I get home." I shrugged my shoulders.

"Again, that is good. And bad."

Javier drove in silence for a minute. I wasn't sure where we were going. I hadn't asked when he called that morning and said he was on his way to get me. All I could think about was getting the heck out of the house before the banshee woke up.

"It's supposed to be eighty today," Javier said, eyeballing my scarf.

"It's not for warmth; it's for fashion."

I fingered the lightweight blue scarf around my neck to be sure it still covered my bruises.

"Makes your eyes pop."

Stupid eyes. I hated that they made people look at me like they did. Changing the subject, I asked, "Don't you ever work?"

"I am working."

"I mean, real work."

"This is real work, Emma. We are going to the station."

"The police station," I said, getting excited. "Did they find something?"

"No. I meant the car station. I thought you might like to join me. You do not mind, do you? I have a few things to take care of. Then we can get to business."

I slumped back in the seat. "Anything is better than being at home."

"Why have you not moved out?"

"I have nowhere to go. I had to reschedule my scholarship interview for August. I need to get it." I shook my head. "If I don't, I'm stuck at home."

We pulled up to a large red brick building covered in vines. The sign on the top of the building was white with blue writing. Very plain. It read "Rich Silver Car Service." Except for the boring sign, the building was beautiful. The beautifully maintained landscape with fresh black mulch, an array of various colored flowers, and a freshly sculpted miniature willow tree reminded me of James.

The building itself was old. The antique garage doors resembled barn doors with flecks of old paint visible here and there. The moldings were carved with intricate details and adorned every corner of the building, doors, and windows.

"You need a fancier sign," I blurted out rudely. "It doesn't fit this amazing building."

"It fits me. I am simple."

When we stepped inside, there were four black metal desks in a large, soft-green room. The ceiling was vaulted and painted black, along with the ceiling fans, pipes, and ventilation that ran across it. The style was very industrial yet surprisingly warm. It seemed like a room where everything happened.

"Hi, Javier," said a young woman at the front desk.

She leaned back in her black leather chair, gave me the once over, and greeted me with a nod.

"Kate, this is Emma Finewood. Emma, Kate Salen. She runs the office."

She smiled, then sat forward, resting her elbows on the desk. Kate said, "They're calling in fifteen minutes. Cutting it a little close, Javi."

"I am fifteen minutes early," he replied.

"Sandy is in her office waiting to go over vehicle details before the negotiation."

Javier smiled at her, then turned to me. "If you will, please wait in my office while Sandy and I strike a deal."

We headed to the black sliding barn doors at the back of the room and stepped into office A. Javier's office. He turned on a small flat-screen television that hung on the wall and handed me the remote.

He gestured to the couch. "Please, make yourself comfortable. Relax, watch TV, read a magazine... I should not be long." ·

I plunked down on the dark brown leather couch. "I didn't sleep last night. I might shut my eyes for a few minutes."

"You are not well?" Javier asked. He sat next to me and casually put a hand on my knee.

"I'm fine," I responded, trying to play it cool.

I had to remind myself to keep breathing as the heat from his hand sank into my skin. Finally, he removed his hand to slide a piece of my hair behind my shoulder, but then he placed his hand back on my knee.

"Is there anything you would like to talk about, Emma?"

I shook my head no and fiddled with my scarf. I wondered if he had caught a glimpse of my neck.

"You can tell me anything, you know."

"Um, yeah." I bit my lower lip and fiddled with my scarf. I couldn't tell him about Billy.

"Javi!" cried a woman from next door.

"That must be Sandy?" I said. Damn her and her bad timing.

"The one and only." He stood up, walked to the door, and turned around. "We will talk more when I return."

When he left, I fluffed a fuzzy gray pillow and put my head back. I couldn't hear Javier and Sandy very well through the wall. But I was able to make out a few mumbled words. Sandy giggled and said something about his heavy accent. Then they were talking about me. First, I heard the words "not my girlfriend." Then Sandy said, "not your type."

"As if...," I mumbled. How could she say that? She didn't even know me.

I closed my weary eyes. I was only going to close them for a few seconds while I continued to eavesdrop. When my eyes opened, I was sitting at G3's kitchen table. She walked over and handed me a mug of tea.

"G3, do you know specifically what was in the green envelope?"

"Oh, my. I did tell you about that, didn't I." G3 shuffled the newspaper to a basket on the floor. "It was papers, a report of some kind for his English class."

I nodded; I sensed she knew more than she was willing to say.

"If it were a research paper, he would have a copy or draft, wouldn't he?"

"Most likely," she agreed, taking a sip of her tea.

"I feel like you're not telling me everything, G3."

"His laptop is in his room. That school paper was very important. I wouldn't be surprised if he has a copy on his computer. He's a smart boy."

"You're right about that." I ran my finger along the lip of the mug and asked, "You think he's alive, right?"

Her eyes shifted to the old phone on the wall. She became quiet; I hadn't meant to upset her. No doubt the poor woman wanted nothing more than for James to call her and tell her he was alive and well.

I started to apologize when she said, "I don't know that he will ever be okay."

"Stay positive," I said. "I believe we'll find him. And thank you."

"Thank you for what?" Javier asked.

My eyes popped open. I couldn't believe it; it had happened again. But this time, all I had done was close my eyes.

"Javi?"

"I walked in, and you were talking. I thought you were awake."

"How long was I sleeping?"

"I do not know. I was only next door for a few minutes." He sat behind his desk and wrote a few things in a notebook. He said, "The deal is done. I managed to acquire three gently used luxury vehicles and two SUVs."

99

I rubbed my hands over my eyes. They were blurry.

"Emma, what is the matter?"

Javier dropped his pen and stood up.

"I'm just tired," I said. "You know, I was thinking. James must have had a copy of his paper. And I think I know where to find it."

*   *   *

Moments later, we were at G3's front door. We knocked and rang the bell for several minutes before she answered. She looked tired.

"Emma, I was just thinking about you."

"You were?" I asked. Coincidences were piling up. "I'm sorry to bother you. Would you mind if I took a look around James' room?"

She glanced at Javier suspiciously.

"He's a friend."

I introduced them to one another. Javier had a way with people. So it wasn't surprising she took an instant liking to him.

We started with James' room. It was spotless and organized. I went directly to the bookshelf while Javier booted up James' laptop.

"I will start with his computer. It must be on here," he said.

I scanned his shelf for what I thought would be an obvious place to stash a hard copy of this mysterious report. I shuffled a few books around.

"It's not here," I said, perplexed. "I'm going downstairs to ask G3 if she knows where that book is."

"Why would he hide a hard copy in a book? I would bet it is in here," he said, tapping away at the keyboard.

"There has to be a copy here somewhere."

"And if there is no copy?" Javier asked.

"There has to be."

I went down to G3 and asked for the book I needed.

"I don't know, honey. If it's not in his room, I would have to say he doesn't have it."

"Maybe it's under his bed or something."

G3 nodded. "I wish I could be more help." Then as I jogged back upstairs, she called to me, "I'm not sure what that book has to do with anything."

As I passed G3's bedroom, I spotted a few books on her night-stand. There was an off chance James had put it in her room without telling her. I scanned the few books in G3's room and didn't find the book I was looking for. Disappointed and feeling that perhaps this was all a mistake, I turned to leave the room. That was when I spotted the shrine.

"Would you do that, James?" I whispered.

Kneeling in front of the shrine, I removed the statue of the Virgin Mary and carefully moved the crucifix and rosary beads aside. I peeked my head behind the small nightstand table and checked underneath. I didn't find anything.

I remembered James' deck in purgatory and how books filled tables and lined shelves. He had even piled some of the larger books to use as tables. Finally, I removed the white linen cloth covering G3's table. And there it was— *The Satanic Verses*.

CHAPTER 18

The book trembled in my hands. The dingy red edges of the partially torn cover, the dark battling figures too busy trying to kill each other to notice anyone was watching… I imagined James' ominous mood after writing a report that would put his life in danger.

For so many reasons, it made sense that he would hide it in this book. But there was a problem. The book was too light. I opened the cover, and just as I had suspected, it was fake. Inside was a dull green envelope.

"It never got mailed," I uttered.

I pulled the large envelope from the phony book. It had no label, but I could feel a stack of papers about an inch thick inside. I opened it and slid the contents out.

The cover page read: "STOP! Before you go any further, you must know that reading this paper could put you in grave danger. Should you decide to proceed, please do so with caution. You are accepting responsibility for the lives of many. Know that when I began my research, I never expected to stumble upon such disturbing information. You should also know that if you have found this…"

My eyes read the next phrase, but my brain refused it. I sucked in a deep breath, and with a lump in my throat, I began the sentence again.

"You should also know that if you have found this, I am most likely dead. Please take this paper into the city and hand it over to the FBI. Trust NO ONE."

Startling me from thought, Javier hollered from the other room, "Anything yet?"

Trust no one, it had said.

I shoved the report back in the envelope, slid it into my backpack, and stuck the phony book back in its place. After I repaired the shrine, I tiptoed into James' room, where Javier was still at work on the laptop.

"I cannot get in," he said. "It is password protected, and I cannot figure it out. Did you find the book you were looking for?"

I hesitated.

At that moment, I considered shoving the ugly green envelope back under the stupid shrine. I could pretend I never found the damn thing. Javier and I could spend the rest of the summer hanging out before school started in the fall. It would be easy to distract myself and forget everything that had happened in the last several days. Right?

All I had to do was just turn around and put the dumb envelope back where I found it, then I could walk away. *We* could walk away. The fact was, I didn't even know James anymore. I could forget about him. Couldn't I?

When I blinked, those ominous words flashed before my eyes. Trust no one.

Javier had been there for me from the start. He was literally the only person I trusted at the moment. But in the end, the answer to my questions was no. I couldn't forget the last several days, and I certainly could not forget James.

"You okay?" Javier asked, his eyebrows jacked up.

I realized I had been looking at him with a blank stare. I nodded my head and smiled.

"Yes. Fine," I replied. "No luck. I didn't find anything." Then I heard G3's mumbled voice. "Shh… She's on the phone," I said, pointing to the stairs.

He cocked his head to the side and listened. We heard G3 in the kitchen below us through the vent and the open windows.

"No. She's upstairs. She's looking for the research paper," G3 said.

I looked wide-eyed at Javier and leaned closer to the open window.

A second passed, then G3 said, "A young man. I forgot his name." After a pause, she asked, "How am I supposed to do that? You know, this nonsense needs to end." Another pause. Then she said, "He'd better not dare send them... What do you mean you're not with him? Where in the world are you, James?"

Javier and I gawked at each other. He mouthed, "James?"

Javier slid his fingers down my arm and took my hand. We crept through the hallway. He motioned to the front door, but I couldn't leave. I broke my hand free from his grip and tiptoed down the stairs. Javier reached for my arm. I waved him off and signaled for him to wait where he was.

I hurried because I didn't know how much longer they would be on the phone. I snuck up behind G3 and gently removed the phone from her frail hand. I looked into her wide worried eyes and smiled. I mouthed, "It's okay," and held the phone to my ear.

I heard, "I love you, G3. I'm trying to make things right."

"James?"

"Emma?"

"James, where are you?" I gasped.

He cleared his throat. "I was supposed to find you," he said sternly.

"Seems I found you first. Kind of."

"You can't find me, Emma. Wait for me to come to you. It's too dangerous right now."

"But not too dangerous for G3?" He was blowing me off.

"That's different. I can't explain it without putting you in any more danger. Please stop trying to find me and the research paper."

"Aren't you curious why I'm here after all these years?"

"No."

"I want to see you," I demanded.

"Later."

"When?"

"Trust me. Trust your instincts, Em."

Trust my instincts. Was James with me in another place and time just days ago? That couldn't have been possible. Except there he was on the phone with me, unfazed that I was at his house after all these years. And on top of that, he was repeating those familiar words:

trust your instincts. All I had was one question. A question I had to ask once again.

"Is this a coincidence, James? Is it? After ten years, I show up at your house looking for you, only to find you went missing days before Frankie was killed. Is it all a coincidence?"

"I don't believe in coincidences anymore. I'll see you soon," he said.

"When?" He didn't answer. "James? James?" He was gone.

"G3, how long have you known?" I asked, hanging up the phone.

"He called yesterday. I wasn't allowed to tell anyone. He needed me to call him should anyone show up and want to look around." G3 held up her palms and said, "Sorry, honey."

"And the report?"

She wrung her nervous hands and said, "I honestly don't know what he did with it. He gave it to me, and then he took it back before he left."

Because it would put you in danger, I thought.

Javier appeared at the kitchen entrance.

"Unexpected turn of events?" he asked, leaning against the door jam.

"Very unexpected," I said.

"I thought James' father was out of his life a long time ago," I said to G3. "When did he return?"

"I'm not supposed to talk about it. If I do, they might hurt James. Ty was once my grandson, but now," she shook her head and frowned, "he is a dangerous man. I don't know him anymore."

"Does he have James? Do you think he would hurt his own son?"

G3 lowered her head and said, "I think he killed his own mother, my daughter. So, if James gets in his way— yes— I believe he wouldn't hesitate."

"In the way of what?" Javier asked.

"I've said too much. You must go. James said they're sending someone. And trust me, you'll be sorry if you're still here."

"We can't leave you. Come with us," I said, taking G3's hand.

"Like I said, if Ty has it in him to kill me, he will. In the meantime, I will deal with his criminal friends." She slipped her hand from mine and said, "Now go before it's too late."

Bright headlights flashed in the window and across the room as a white Cadillac Escalade screeched into the driveway.

"Hurry," she said. "Go out the back."

"Come with us," I urged.

"Go. I'll be fine."

She threw open the kitchen door and hurried us onto the back of the wrap-around porch. Quietly, we descended the steps and walked around the house. When we stopped to peek in the windows, we saw two large guys in her doorway. One had a curly bush of strawberry-blonde hair and a Celtic tattooed sleeve. With a booming voice, he demanded the research paper from G3. When she explained that she didn't know where it was, he shoved her aside and commanded the other man to follow him into the house. G3's protest went unnoticed.

While the strawberry-blonde marched upstairs, a slim boy with jet-black hair began pulling books from a shelf. When the shelf was empty, and the books were in a heap on the floor, he moved to a cabinet housing old VCR tapes, CDs, and photo albums. G3 sat in her chair calmly and watched. The brave woman called the boy by his name.

"Liam."

The boy kept on his path of destruction. She said his name again. That time he stopped and glared at her with surprise.

"What?" he said. "Do you want to save yourself a mess and tell me where it is, old woman?"

"I go to church with your grandmother. Does she know?"

Liam leaned back from the cabinet with a stack of old newspapers in his hands. He glared at G3.

"There's nothing to know," he said. A threatening scowl grew across his face. He tossed the newspapers to the floor and stood. "Do you think you have something to tell her?"

Javier started toward the front door.

"Wait," I whispered.

"Liam, you were her smartest boy. I have to wonder who her smartest boy is now."

She was clever to engage him in conversation, making him feel like there was even the slightest connection between them. But her words were fighting words.

He walked directly to her chair and stood over her. Javier was ready to pounce should he raise one finger to her.

Liam said, "I'm still the smartest, old woman."

He stared at her for a long time. She never broke eye contact with him.

Eventually, he scoffed and went back to ransacking the house. Something crashed above, and then the other guy pounded down the stairs, again demanding the research paper. He threatened to "put her in the ground early" if she didn't talk. Clearly, he watched too many gangster movies.

Liam said, "Let's go. She's just a dumb old woman. It's not here."

Javier and I ran to the car and ducked inside. We waited for the SUV to leave, then Javier started the car. I let out a deep sigh of relief now that I knew G3 was safe.

"It doesn't make sense. If James' dad is holding him against his will, why would he let him talk to G3?" I wondered.

"Perhaps he is not with Ty," Javier said. Then after a second of silence, he said, "Perhaps he is not held against his will. There is a chance he is not who you believe him to be."

Javier followed the two guys who ransacked G3's house. He stayed several cars back.

I thought about the picture from James' mantel. Most of my memories were of Frankie, James, and me running around, getting into trouble, and being wild kids.

"I don't remember Ty ever living next door with James and his mom," I said. "I remember James telling me his father was mean. He said Ty didn't want him, and that's why James had to go live with G3 when his mom died."

"It sounds like Ty has not evolved much."

Javier slowed down when one of the cars between the Escalade and us turned north at an intersection. We continued to follow the Escalade.

"James said he would contact me," I said. "Although there's a chance these guys might lead us right to him."

Javier pointed out, "They looked dangerous. You have been told you are in danger. We must decide our next move. Are we going to the police with an address? Are we walking up to the door and asking to see James? What is the plan?"

"Maybe we can go to the FBI." Then I thought about the page I read in the report and sighed. "I need someone to tell me what to do."

"You want me to tell you?" Javier asked. "Thank you for finally asking. I think…"

"No. Not you. I need James to tell me. Look, it may seem like an odd time for a nap, but I want to try something."

I put my head back against the headrest and closed my eyes.

"You are going to sleep on it?"

"Sort of," I whispered.

"Seriously?"

"Shh," I said. "Just give me a second."

I rolled out the tension in my shoulders and thought for sure I would be face to face with James any second. A minute passed, then another. Finally, I growled, frustrated that I couldn't channel James like I had G3 and my mother.

"Emma," Javier said, gesturing to the Escalade. Its blinker was on, and it was turning into a parking lot. "What am I doing here?"

"Crap!" I scoffed.

"What exactly are you doing?"

"I don't know what to call it. Nothing, I guess."

Javier drove by an old white brick mansion. It was most likely gorgeous during the light of day. However, in the pitch darkness this time of night, it was purely creepy.

"Where are we?" I asked.

"Had you been paying attention, you would have seen us drive by the rock salt mine about a minute ago. We are in Mount Morris. The village is five minutes up the road."

Javier pulled into an empty restaurant parking lot, two buildings past where the truck stopped. He parked the car and killed the lights.

"Are you leaving the master plan to me?" he asked.

"I suppose. Mine isn't working."

"We know where they are. Let us stay on our mission to find the report. We should go back to G3's house."

Knowing what he didn't, I said, "Or we could go home. I can't begin to imagine where else to look."

Javier threw his hands in the air. "Or there is that."

"James said he would see me soon."

"How soon?"

"He said later. Maybe he's coming to me."

"If you believe he is held captive, then he is not coming to see you anytime soon."

I closed my eyes to concentrate. Things were so confusing that I couldn't keep up. I needed to take a step back.

"I can't think, Javi. I thought this would all fall into place. So far, that's not happening. Let's go back to my place to make a plan like you said. It needs to be done right so no one gets hurt."

And maybe when I'm more relaxed, I'll be able to connect with James again, I thought. I was so frustrated. It was like my ladder was crooked, and I couldn't get to the next wrung.

Thankfully, Javier agreed. He put the address into his phone, snapped several pictures of the brick mansion, and headed back to Lakeville.

"What if your mother is home?" Javier asked.

I smirked. "What, you don't want to meet my mother?"

Javier rolled his eyes and shook his head. "No. I really do not."

When we returned home, the driveway was empty, and the house was dark. Once inside, I hollered for my mother, and no one answered. Javier sighed in relief. He excused himself to the bathroom while I grabbed a notebook and a pen from the kitchen junk drawer.

I tossed them on the table, then turned on the coffee pot next to the sink. And just as I had almost convinced myself that everything was going to be okay, life took a nose-dive.

I heard a door open and assumed it was Javi coming out of the bathroom. At the same time, through the kitchen window, I spotted something.

With a lump in my throat, I said, "Javi, there's a motorcycle out back."

"That's mine," Billy said, exiting my mother's bedroom.

I whipped around to find the bathroom door still shut. Big-Billy-the-strangler stood in the middle of my kitchen. He wore a smug grin and a sleeveless t-shirt donning the body of a half-naked woman with a skull face.

"What— what are you doing here?" I stammered. "Is my mother here?"

"She'll be back in a few. Ran out for smokes."

"Oh. I just popped in to grab a few things," I said. "I'll be out of here in a sec."

"Don't be in such a hurry," he said, practically clotheslining me as I attempted to walk by. I stopped, and he said, "You and me got a few things to talk about."

CHAPTER 19

"Really? What riveting conversation would you like to have with me?" I asked Billy.

No lie, I was nervous. I was afraid of the beast who almost killed me last night. I almost called out for Javier. But in all honesty, this man could kill us both single-handedly. He was a starving grizzly bear, and I didn't want Javier to get hurt. I needed to get out of here with Javier unscathed.

Billy leaned against the refrigerator, a little too close for comfort.

He said, "Picture this. I'm having drinks with some associates last night, and they tell me about a little girlie making all sorts of trouble for them. Seems she's all up in their business. Funny how the description fit you right down to those piercing baby blues. Then they tell me where she lives."

He leaned in closer, squelching any possibility of fresh air existing in the room.

"Because they're watching you," he grumbled, grasping my shoulders.

I swallowed hard. Billy knew more than he was saying. Did he know where James was? Did he know about the report?

"They start asking me questions," he said, pulling me millimeters from his face, suffocating me with his wretched breath. "They says, 'What are you doin' with the trolls mother? Why did we see you leave Emma's house?'

"Imagine my luck?" Billy's laugh was almost jovial. "There's a price on your head bigger than the horsepower of my Harley."

"Is my mother here?" I asked again.

Billy smiled. "Nah. It's just me and you, baby. Now tell me— where's it at?"

"Where's what?"

He eyed my backpack.

"In there?" he grumbled.

He released my arms and snatched my backpack from the kitchen chair. He shook the empty bag and glared at me. Then he dug into it as if the report would magically appear.

I hugged my shoulders and said, "I don't know what you're looking for."

He whipped the backpack at the fridge and marched toward me. I took a step back, but before I knew what was happening, Billy had latched onto my wrist, swung me face-first into the wall, and locked his arm around the back of my neck. My head was facing the bathroom door. Despite the commotion, Javier still hadn't come out of the bathroom.

I thought, *I'm going to be the reason Javier dies today.*

My heart skipped a beat; maybe Billy had already taken care of Javier. I pushed off the wall as hard as I could and gained about an inch of space between the wall and me. That worked for a mere second before he slammed my head and body back into it. I yelped in pain.

"Where's the report, wench? I need it now."

"I don't know what you mean."

"I know you have it. You took it from Granny's house."

"I didn't take anything. But I have a Shakespeare essay lying around somewhere. Lots of betrayal, revenge, murder. It's right up your alley, and it's yours for the taking," I quipped.

He slammed my head into the wall again. And again, I yelped. The blood was warm as it dripped from my nose and slithered over my swelling lip and into my mouth. But I refused to let this beast break me— though he might kill me first.

"Come on. Green envelope. Give it up."

I said nothing.

Billy added, "You need some motivation?"

He flipped me around like a vertical blind and slammed my back to the wall. Billy got in my face and said, "First you, then mama wench... Maybe little old granny too. Why not?"

With a forced smirk, I said, "You have no idea what you're getting into."

"Think so? The way I see it, you're the one who ain't got no clue. I may not have all the details, but at least I'm gettin' paid. You're just gettin' dead." He stood to his full height and pulled back his right fist.

In an instant, just before his fist hit my nose, I kneed him in the groin as hard as I could. He buckled instantly, and I ran to the cupboard while he collapsed and writhed in pain. I ripped open the door above the coffee pot, snatched the green envelope from behind the dinner plates, and headed for the door. I was mid-jump over Billy's body when he caught my foot.

I went down hard, my elbows and knees taking most of the blow. The dingy brown carpeting burned my skin as I slid a few inches. I lost my grip on the envelope, and it went flying against the far wall in the hallway.

I wasn't delusional; I didn't stand a chance of getting to the envelope first, but I sure as hell was going to try. Billy and I scuffled across the floor for it. He made his way to his feet and kicked me in the ribs. I grabbed for his leg but caught air as he dashed toward the envelope.

Billy scooped up the envelope, but instead of just taking it and leaving, he plunked it on the kitchen table. From the floor, I watched as the angry bull rubbed his groin, turned, and charged at me. It was apparent that before killing me, he fully intended to torture me. Ultimately, that anger, that uncontrollable decision to pummel me, was the mistake that would cost him the game.

From the corner of my eye, I caught a figure burst through the front door and barrel directly into Billy. They collided inches in front of me. My first thought was that it was Javier. That somehow, he had climbed out the bathroom window and crashed through the door to save me just in the nick of time. Except it wasn't Javier. It was James.

James caught Billy around the waist and slammed him so hard into the wall that his backside made a monster dent. Billy swayed for a brief second and then managed to steady himself. After that, Billy's face became James' punching bag. Billy was down and out cold in seconds.

As soon as Billy tumbled, James rushed to my side. I managed to pull myself to my knees. Blood dripped from my nose and mouth.

"You're here," I gasped.

"Are you okay?" he asked.

"Yeah. Peachy," I retorted.

He tossed me the dishtowel from the sink. I wiped my bloody lip and nose, and for a second, I stared quietly in awe. I technically hadn't seen James in years. Only in some kind of unconscious brain injury dream. Yet, he looked exactly like he had in the dream, right down to the vintage jeans and the tattoo peeking out from under the sleeve of his light blue button-up shirt. Granted, the shirt was disheveled, dirt-stained, and had a small hole in the shoulder now.

That was when it hit me. With my face and ribs throbbing, and my head spinning like I'd just gotten off of a high-speed merry-go-round, a stockpile of emotions ambushed me all at once.

As the shock that James was alive and well and standing in my living room faded, a wave of relief and gratitude washed over me. He couldn't have shown up at a better time.

But the whirlwind of emotions didn't end there. I was scared as hell because I was almost beaten to death by a psychopath. And damn it, I was angry. James just showed up as if he'd been a free man this entire time. I opened my mouth to say— well, I don't know what. But he didn't give me a chance to speak.

He skimmed the green envelope from the table, folded it in half, and stuck it in the back of his pants.

"Where's the other guy, Emma?"

"What other guy? It was only him," I said, pointing to Billy's limp body.

"Javier. Where is he?"

"He's in the bathroom," I stammered. "I think Billy got to him first."

James kicked open the bathroom door. I expected to find Javier tied up, or worse, beaten up or maybe even half dead. Instead, I learned that Javier was gone.

"Can you walk?" James asked. I nodded. "Good. Take what you need," James snapped. "We have to get out of here."

Within minutes, we were racing toward Geneseo. Despite the queasy, Indie 500 drive, I still felt safer than I had five minutes earlier in my own house. And for the entire ride, James refused to answer any of my questions.

Before I knew it, we were pulling into The Green. James parked in a dark corner of the parking lot. Then he unlatched his seat belt, turned to face me, and grimaced as if I were green.

Rubbing my achy head, I grumbled, "Why are we here? It isn't safe."

"They aren't here now."

"How do you know?" I asked, looking around the parking lot.

James opened his door and said, "Come on."

I got out of the car cautiously, searching the darkness for danger.

"Wait," I said as James headed to the back door. "They might be in there. Or the Ardemonis. Or whoever is looking for me. Us. It would help to have answers. I mean, maybe you're the one I should be afraid of," I said, stopping in my tracks.

Suddenly, rock music blared through the door as it flew open.

"Let's go, Emma," boomed a voice in the doorway. "We'll tell you everything once you're safe."

Though I couldn't see his face, with the light shining from behind him, I knew it was Adam by his sheer size and deep voice.

Adam led us down a back staircase to the basement. We walked through a long shelf-lined hallway full of pans, tubs of mayo, bottles of ketchup, and cleaning supplies. At the end of the hall, we stopped and faced a stone wall.

Adam said to James, "You good with this?"

"Absolutely. I know he's right."

That was it. I'd had enough of being in the dark. I wanted answers.

"I'd love to know who *he* is, and what *he's* right about, and why we're here, and why you aren't surprised to see James, and..."

"Okay," Adam said. "You're frustrated. I get it."

Adam slid a shelf over about four feet to reveal a hole in the old stone basement wall.

"How dungeonesque," I said, following the guys through the hole and into a dimly lit, musty-smelling room.

"I'd like to think of it as more of a lair like the bat cave," said a young, cute guy sitting inside at a small, round wooden table. "Dungeon implies but is not exclusive to a prison or cell in a medieval castle. And while this structure was once a…"

"Stop," Adam said dryly. "It's embarrassing when you do that."

Adam then turned and introduced me to the boy at the table.

"Emma, this is Caleb Maxwell. Just call him Max."

CHAPTER 20

"Nice place, Max." He smiled and stood. I said, "Not gonna lie though, dungeon or not, it's creepy down here."

A strange and uncomfortable energy radiated through the room. I wondered if perhaps The Green was haunted. The rhythmic beat of the drums and bass from upstairs, and the occasional dust and dirt, which fell from the ceiling as people danced to the music, didn't help calm the anxious feeling building in my chest.

Max reached out and shook my hand. And bam! There it was again. It was not as powerful a shock as when Adam touched me, but it was strong enough to burn.

"Sorry," he said. He threw a side glance with a grin at James and Adam. "Welcome to our... lair."

We stared at each other with uncertainty for a few seconds until I became annoyed and snapped, "Well? Somebody start talking."

Max gestured toward Adam. "I think we should start by getting the lady some first aid."

"I'm fine," I said, wrapping my arms around a bruised rib. "Talk."

"Maybe it would be best coming from James," Adam suggested, handing me a napkin.

"Oh my God," I sighed heavily.

I crumbled the tiny one-ply napkin, whipped around, and headed for the hole where I entered the room. While I was elated that James was fine, and I did want to know more about what happened to him, these guys were acting too weird for comfort. Not to mention, I had this unexplainable urge to get as far away from this dark, smelly room as possible.

"Wait," James said, catching my elbow. The shock that accompanied his hand stung my funny bone. So not funny.

"Geez. What is wrong with this place? Get a humidifier."

"It's not the place, Emma," James said. "It's us. It's the four of us. And a couple more kids, we think."

I scowled at him and said, "Look, James, I thought you were missing and that I was in danger. But you seem fine here with your buddies. Now I'm thinking the only people I should be afraid of are you guys and whatever you're involved in with that unconscious meathead on my living room floor. So I'm removing myself from this entire equation. When you get things straightened out, call me. Until then I'm going to find Javier. Then I'm going to get my life back in order."

"You can't," James said, lowering his voice. "Your life is not what you think it is. But you know that. Don't you, Emma? Let's talk about the beach."

I glanced at Adam and Max. My jaw tensed, and I glowered at James with the sting of betrayal. Why would he bring that up in front of other people? Whatever had happened between us, it was nobody's business.

"We know what it was," James said, motioning toward Max and Adam. "We know what really happened between you and me."

My nails dug into my palms. My eyes flashed to Max, then Adam. When my gaze hit James, I shrugged and said, "Since the three of you have already figured everything out, I guess you don't need me."

"There are things you don't know, Emma," James said.

"Clearly. But guess what? I don't care. I'm out of here," I said. I spun around and stormed through the hole.

Behind me, Max said, "Stop her."

"Emma," James called.

I ignored him and marched on.

Once again, for some reason, I was fighting the urge to cry. And scream. And punch something. And tell someone off. I didn't have a clue what was going on, what had just happened at my house, or where Javier was. So obviously, I was having feelings. Crappy, confusing, maddening feelings. With a hard swallow, I pushed them from my head and walked faster. His footsteps closed in behind me.

"Em, please. You need to know the truth. This is important. It's not something you can run away from."

Darn him. Darn him for pointing out that I was running away. Again. Self-recognition sucked.

I stopped before ascending the stairs and said, "I'm not running away. I'm going to find Javier."

"Javier works for the Gallaghers. They threw him a boatload of money to get the report."

I turned and said, "He was helping me. He wouldn't take money from them."

"Maybe he started out helping you; I don't know. He needed the cash for his business. They knew exactly what to offer. And he took it. Then he hired Billy as a backup in case you found the report before he did. He wasn't in the bathroom, Em. Because he left Billy to do the dirty work."

Lies. "How do you know this?"

"I just do. Plus, Max looked into his personal and business finances."

"Is Max a cop?"

"Uh, no. He's just really freaking smart." James shifted his weight to the other foot and nervously rubbed his hands together. "Em. Please, come back in."

I weighed my options carefully. I didn't want to go back into that creepy room. Maybe it was the smell, or I had seen too many scary movies, or maybe it was possessed by some kind of demon. Either way, I didn't like the idea of returning to that maleficent cave. And even if I did go back in, what would I be hearing? Did I want to know anything other than what classes I would be taking in September? No, not really. But as always, it all came down to James' wickedly big brown eyes.

"Fine. I'll give you five minutes. Make the most of it," I said.

James held out his hand, and without thinking, I took it. Instantly, I yanked my hand back and growled. The zap was less intense that time. I followed him into their stupid lair, where Max and Adam were seated at a round wooden table. James sat down, and I stood behind an empty chair. Adam eye-balled me and pointed to it.

"Fine," I huffed and sat down. "Go."

"I'll start with what happened to me," James said. "I was with Frankie when he was shot. I was outside, and I was shot first."

James unbuttoned his dirt-stained shirt to reveal a bandage on his left shoulder.

"That's not dirt," I gasped.

"It's a blood stain," James said. "They didn't care if I lived or died because it was Frankie they wanted. They left me for dead. I hid out for as long as possible, but I was losing too much blood. That's when I came to Adam."

James and Frankie were together when Frankie died.

"You didn't try to save Frankie?"

James looked away, then said, "The casket was closed for a reason, Em. He was dead."

We were all silent for a second. Then to Adam, I asked, "You knew all along?"

Adam nodded.

"Why were they after Frankie?" I asked.

"Keegan stole the original report from the Gallagher family, and they found out," James explained. "They had seen him with Frankie and assumed he had it. They assumed Frankie got it for his brothers. But you see, Keegan stole the report for me, not the Ardemonis. Frankie was my source. He got me in touch with Keegan and convinced him to give it to me."

"What does the report have to do with what happened to us?"

"It has everything to do with what happened to us. Frankie was killed because of that report. And possibly Keegan too."

James tossed out the envelope. The antique chandelier above the table lit up the envelope like a spotlight.

"This is the report Frankie and Keegan got for you?" I asked, pointing to the envelope that had briefly been in my possession.

"Part of it is the original report. The rest is mine. It outlines an experiment in layman's terms and describes its significance." James sighed and sat up straight and tall. "It's about an experiment, and we, the four of us, are subjects in that experiment."

I sat back in my chair and thought about what he had said. I waited for them to smile, laugh it off, or make a joke about me being gullible. When they didn't, I reached for the envelope, and no one stopped me. I slid the thick stack of papers onto the table.

I turned to Adam and Max and asked, "Did you guys read this thing?"

They nodded their heads yes. Initially, when I found the report and read the first page warning of its danger, I was afraid to read further. I questioned if I would ever read it at all. But in light of what James had just told me, I now had no choice.

When I turned that first ominous page and learned it was written in a foreign language, I was pissed.

"What is this?"

"Latin," Max said.

"I can't read Latin," I said, shoving the pile of papers away from me.

"Lucky for you, I can," Max said. He stretched across the table and flipped through the report. Then he tapped a page and read the title, "English translation."

James said, "It was written in Latin on purpose. The average person can't read it. It has a summary in English on the last page. Of course, it barely touches on the real details of the experiment. Whoever wrote the summary was extremely vague."

I read the first paragraph of the summary.

"It's called the Lakeville Project. There are five subjects." I looked around the table. "We are the subjects? Where's the fifth subject?"

Max said, "There's actually two more."

"I'm confused. Even if math wasn't my strong point, I'd still be pretty confident that four plus two is six."

Adam jumped in, "Let me cut to the chase. Some whack job poisoned us with a toxic oil given to our parents about ten years ago. They thought it was organic. An all-natural essential oil. And maybe it was. Except for us, it was toxic.

"It was intended for us. Specifically. It could only work on someone who hadn't gone through puberty and hadn't finished growing.

That way, if our parents touched it, it did nothing to them. But, for us…it changed everything. It got in through our skin, got into our blood, and changed our DNA. Mutated it. And now, years later, here we are. And we can do weird crap."

Adam looked to Max for confirmation. Max nodded, and with half a grin, he said, "Way to sum it up."

"Whatever," Adam said. "Anyway, you and James shared a vial of the oil. It was meant for you, but he accidentally got infected too."

I scowled at James. "You're saying that… that thing… that happened between us was a part of that weird crap?"

"Yes," James confirmed.

"I had other episodes. With my mother. With G3."

"I have too," James responded. But he stopped there and didn't elaborate without a little pressure.

"Tell her," urged Adam. "Or I will."

"Javier. That's how I knew you were in trouble. When he texted that big guy to tell him you might have the report and to meet at your house, I saw it. It was odd because I think he was completely conscious. It was like I saw what was happening through his eyes."

Just then, I saw it too. It seemed to pop over to me from James' head. The letters ticked through my head one at a time as Javier texted the message that almost had me killed.

"I think she has it. You're up," he wrote.

My mouth hung open. It seemed unbelievable, but it was true. I just knew it. Deep in my bones, I felt different, and suddenly, the unexplainable power and energy that filled the room made sense. It wasn't the room that overwhelmed me. It was the people in the room.

Heat resonated from Adam, who sat to my left, and oddly, I felt smarter just sitting across from Max. After a second, I began to see it. Without telling me, I knew what their "weird crap" was. I knew what their power was.

I turned to Adam and said, "You're full of energy. Literally. I can almost see it being sucked from the room and funneling through you."

In sheer amazement, I studied the air around Max's head and said, "There's a glow around your head. It's a different kind of energy. I feel like I can even channel it.

"And you, James. It's a connection I can't put into words. When you told me you saw the text, I saw it too. On top of that, I haven't laid eyes on you in years, yet I knew exactly what you looked like, the clothes you were wearing, you have some kind of black tattoo on your arm, you love to read. How could I know that stuff, right?"

Relief washed across their faces. The tension in the room melted away like ice cream on a hot day.

"Show me where Javier went," I demanded.

"I can't. I don't know exactly how to control it yet. I think he has to be thinking about it. Like I was thinking of you when I saw the text. Javier was thinking about you at the same time. And I believe if he's unconscious or asleep, I can go in and ask him."

"Just try."

He closed his eyes for several seconds. When his eyes popped open, he shook his head.

"Nothing?" I asked.

"Zero point zero," he responded.

I paused, gathering my thoughts for my next round of questions.

James smiled. He was reading my mind.

"I'll start with the others," he said, answering my first question. "Max met a girl. We think she's like us. But we aren't sure what her power is because he hasn't been able to reach her."

"That makes four original subjects. And there's one more?"

"Yes. But we don't have a clue," Max said. "It's frustrating. I should be able to figure it out."

"What does all this mean," I asked. "Are we some kind of supernatural beings? Freaks of nature? What exactly are we?"

Max shrugged. James and Adam muttered under their breath that they had no clue.

I said to Max, "Look, smarty pants, you must have an answer. I mean, we're still human, right?"

"Technically, yes. I suppose you could say we are advanced humans. Evolved humans."

"Okay. So..." I began.

"We don't know exactly why we were created or by whom," said James. "The report is very technical, very scientific. Therefore, it's safe to say the project was created by someone with a very strong scientific background."

"How do we find him?" I asked.

"It started as a rumor. Frankie had heard it too. Then according to Keegan, all of a sudden, there was talk amongst the Gallaghers about an old experiment and lost money and the return on their investment."

This time, it was I who cut in. I knew what James was thinking.

"And your dad is right in the middle of it. You followed the buzz to find him. When you started looking into it, you found this," I said, placing my hand on the report sprawled out in front of us.

"I had no idea what I was getting into," James said, dropping his head.

We were all quiet for a moment.

Then Adam smacked his hands together, and we all jumped. He smirked at me and shook his head. "Yup. That's why you look familiar."

I pointed to myself with a wondering face.

"You're the girl from the head-on collision. Both cars caught fire. A girl pulled you from the car just in time." He jabbed a finger in my direction. "You're the girl who escaped death."

My mouth dropped open. "You were there?"

"Volunteer fireman," he said. Then, instantly dismissing his recollection, Adam demanded, "Let's wrap this up, folks. I have a restaurant to run."

"Are you for real?" I gasped. "Don't you think the fact that we're mutants is more important?"

"You'll get used to the idea. We've known for a while. The shock wears off quick." Adam grinned. "No pun intended."

"Should you be going back up there like nothing happened?"

"They aren't after me and Max, sister. You guys can stay down here. I'll be back in about an hour. Then we can talk about our next move."

"What is our next move?"

"Max, fill her in," Adam said. "I gotta jet. And someone get her a Band-Aid or something. She's a mess."

Adam ducked through the hole and was gone just like that. I was left with James and Max to explain what the next twenty-four hours of my life were about to look like.

CHAPTER 21

Max had an organized outline of our plan of action based on importance and safety. He was thorough. He was smart. Then again, that was his ability.

Before finding the scientist, we needed to find the other subjects. Since he already had a bite on one, he left James, Adam, and me in charge of finding the last one.

"Easy," I said. "Let's get out there and shake as many hands as possible."

"Except my father is trying to kill us," James pointed out.

"Right, there's that little snag. We can't hide forever, though."

"We should just give them what they want," Max said with a crooked grin.

"Us?" I asked.

"No. The report about the experiment. Except it will be spurious. Why didn't I think of that before?" Max said under his breath.

I glanced at James, and we shrugged.

"That means fake," Max explained. "The main description is in Latin, so I highly doubt they can read it. I'll change what it says. So, if by chance they know a priest or an altar boy who reads Latin, they won't have real details.

"The summary is the only part in English. In case someone already read this, I'll leave the part where it says this experiment will enhance human athletic performance on an evolutionary scale. But I'll change the time frame, so they think this experiment already failed."

"Keegan said this thing was locked away in Ty's safe for years," James said. "Who even knows if anyone read the synopsis at the end? You work on that, Max. I will reach out to my dad and tell him I want to make a deal: Emma and I get left alone, and in return, he can have the report."

"My thoughts exactly," Max said.

"Let's hope he's a man of his word," I sighed.

"That's doubtful, but it's worth a chance," James replied.

James got on the phone and stuck a finger in his ear so he could hear over the music pounding above, and Max got on his computer. I paced the floor.

All I could think about was Javier. I couldn't shake the sick feeling that he had betrayed me. I thought he was different. I thought he was good. How could I have been so easily swayed by his kindness, his good looks, his sexy confidence…? Swallowing my disappointment, I pushed Javier from my mind.

I glanced at James. He was here and safe, and that had to be my focus.

I rested my hand on James' shoulder and asked, "Well, does G3 have Ty's number?"

"Dude," Max hollered to James. "Don't try to call your dad. Wait until the man falls asleep and do your thing. Convince him it's his idea for the swap."

James hung up and said, "G3 doesn't know how to reach Ty. He comes around when he feels like it."

James was standing across the room. He wandered over to me. "How do I do this on purpose?" he asked. As if I knew.

I looked up into James' desperate eyes.

I said, "Focus on him. Isn't that what happened with Javier? Tell me about growing up with your father."

I plunked down on the brown, beat-up, flowery couch squished into the corner of the room.

"Sit," I commanded, patting the cushion next to me.

James sat down. He uttered, "I barely remember him being around. My mom and I lived next door to you, then one day, she didn't come home. The next day, G3 took custody of me. G3 said they looked for my dad and couldn't find him. When he finally came around, he didn't want me."

"Were your parents married?" I asked.

"No. They dated in high school. My mom got pregnant, and they moved to Beachwood. My dad left before I was a year old. The proud father."

James glanced at the floor, tapped his feet, and continued.

"Anyway, G3 said I was a fussy baby. Maybe if I'd been an easier kid, he would've stuck around. Instead, he left us. Every now and then, he would show up to G3's because he needed money."

I had been curious about something, so I asked, "Did you choose this topic for the paper to reconnect with your dad?"

"Hardly. I was taking a brutal English class and trying to get a decent grade. The outline for a final paper was laid out at the beginning of the semester. I racked my brain, trying to come up with something good to research. Something relevant, current, exciting… And I find I can't stop thinking about the rumor."

"How did you hear about it?"

"I ran into Frankie one night last winter."

With a tug to my heart, I said, "He never told me,"

"You were broken up at the time. After that, he didn't want you involved. So much for that." James paused for a second. Then knowing what I was thinking, he said, "There was no way he could have known about you. We had no idea who the subjects were when we started this.

"Anyway, Frankie brought it up to me; he learned about it from Keegan. So I asked Frankie to hook us up, and we met here." James pointed to the table.

"In the dungeon?"

He nodded. "We tried not to be seen in public. Certain people would get suspicious. The guys agreed that if I kept them anonymous, they would tell me what they knew.

"One night, Keegan shows up with the report. He said he found it collecting dust in Ty's safe. The only thing he could read was the outline in the back. None of us could read the actual report, but what I read from the outline was interesting. Eventually, Adam found out what we were up to and brought Max in on it. He read the full report. It doesn't name any of us. But we knew."

"Your dad obviously knows about the report."

James snickered. "Yes. If you think about the timing, my grandfather, Donnacka, had his stroke right after the project started. That was when my father took over the business. I'd bet Donnacka and my father never read the fine print. All they saw were dollar signs."

James stood up and threw his arms in the air to stretch. He pulled one of the rickety old chairs from the table, turned it backward, and plopped down in front of me. He rested his chin on his crossed arms as he leaned forward on the back of the chair.

"I've always known my dad was a loser. He went from loser to monster once I read this and realized he stands behind this project. A project I don't think he understands. He only cares about the money. If he brings this back to life in the Gallagher world, and they end up making a lot of money on this, he'll finish what his father started." James shifted in his chair. "The Gallaghers go from third-string player to quarterback just like that," James uttered, snapping his fingers. He scowled.

"I feel your pain," I said.

"This is depressing," James said. "Do we have to keep talking about this? We could kick back on the couch and sleep until about two. He's got to be asleep by then."

"True."

"Hey, check this out," Max said from across the room. "I changed the report. It says the blend will be absorbed into the host's system and fail to work if it hasn't done so within five years. Case closed. It failed years ago. No point in pursuing it."

"Not a bad idea except for one thing. The rumor is that the scientist is back in town. If that's true, why would he be here if it failed years ago? If he is here, he already knows something," I said.

"I have turned every page into a report with the same outcome. Failure. They'll think they got scammed, and if the scientist is here, the sucker who did this to us will have to pay whatever price the Gallaghers dish out," Max said.

James nodded his head. "That sounds good. Now one more question. What if this report was translated and copied? Just because Keegan brought this to me, that doesn't mean it's the only one. If I can reach out to my dad…"

"And survive," I reminded him.

James sighed. "Let's say I survive a meeting with my dad. If I can get info from him, and confirm this is the only report in existence, then we are good to go. Of course, we'll have to rethink this plan if there is a translation in circulation."

"Let's not worry about that yet," Max said. "A report indicating the experiment is doomed to fail is our best hope right now. What would anyone want with a bunch of failed subjects?"

James turned to me and said, "Then we need to focus on my dad. We need to get in his head and make him want to meet with us."

"You keep saying 'we.' Am I allowed to join you?" I asked.

For some reason, I was excited about the idea of willingly jumping into someone's head with James.

"You're the best bait I have, whether I like it or not."

"Gee, thanks…" I replied.

Then I blinked. Literally, I blinked, and everything changed.

CHAPTER 22

I was no longer in the dungeon of The Green with Max and James. The music that blasted from upstairs had morphed into a concert of crickets. I was sitting in the cold, damp grass, leaning against the wall surrounding the Wadsworth Homestead. The estate was located smack in the middle of Geneseo, a stone's throw from the college, a few blocks from The Green. It was dark, and all I could see were the trees swaying in the warm breeze, dimly lit by the half moon.

"I've been looking for you," a voice boomed from somewhere in front of me.

I scanned the tree line and didn't see anything. I hadn't a clue where James was.

"Stand up," a man commanded.

Slowly, I stood, wondering if the man was talking to me. That's when I saw two figures to my right in a clearing. I hadn't been able to see them when I was sitting on the ground. A broad-shouldered man in dark clothing stood over a boy about my age. The boy, with sandy brown hair and wearing a Notre Dame hoodie, was kneeling on the ground in front of him.

He said to the man, "I don't know what you want from me."

The man nudged the boy's head with the barrel of his gun.

"Stand up," he repeated slowly.

When the boy wobbled to his feet, the man said, "One last chance. Tell me who you gave it to and why."

"Okay, okay, okay," he whimpered. "It was Frankie Ardemoni. But I didn't give it to him. He must have broken in and stolen it from your safe."

The man nodded his head. His angry eyes never changed as the grin grew on his face.

"I didn't tell you it was in my safe."

Without hesitation, he shot the boy in the head— point blank. Blood and brain matter exploded from the back of the boy's head.

While struggling to comprehend what I was seeing, my mind turned the next ten seconds into slow motion as the boy crumbled into a mound of flesh. The man then pivoted, pointed the gun in my direction, and said, "Now it's your turn. The report, where is it?"

Startled by the sudden turn of events, and with what little breath I could muster, I stammered, "Wh- what? Who are you?"

"Ty!" someone called from the shadows.

Ty turned his head, keeping the gun aimed at me. James walked out from the shadows and said, "She doesn't have the report."

"We checked G3's house. Billy said if the girl doesn't have it, she knows where it is."

"I know where it is." James nodded toward the dead boy and snarled, "You killed Keegan?"

I gawked at James, then looked back toward the boy. But now he was gone. That's when it dawned on me— I had just witnessed Ty's memory of how he killed Keegan.

"I had to," Ty responded. "I *need* that report. And this piece of garbage stole it from me." Embedded in Ty's tough-guy tone was a hint of desperation. He begged James, "Just give it to me. The scientist has returned. It can't be in the wrong hands."

"You know it says the experiment failed, right?"

"The experiment didn't fail, James. It was a success. The scientist says in mere months, I'll be a billionaire. A billionaire. And all because of the Lakeville Project that Donnacka funded. This belongs to me."

Ty's face was plastered with that cruel grin again, yet he was sweating profusely, and his hands were shaking. I was worried he would accidentally shoot me.

"Put the gun down, and we can talk about this," James said.

"Why? She's special to you?" Ty stared at me for a second. "She *is* pretty. Are those freckles across her nose?" he asked. Then Ty said condescendingly to James, "Not your usual type." Ty cocked the gun. "I need the report. Now."

James walked over and stood next to me. He took my hand.

"Aw. Aren't you the cute couple? Kind of makes me want to vomit, though. Where is it, James? You should tell me now. Otherwise, I will shoot her and let her die a slow and painful death. After watching her suffer, you'll suffer the same fate."

James said to Ty, "Emma and I will be in Vitale Park at dawn."

I found that an odd choice of conversation, considering Ty was about to kill us. Everyone has heard it: If you die in your dreams, you die in real life. I didn't want to test that theory. I squeezed his hand.

James continued, "When the sun comes up, we'll be in the gazebo."

Ty tilted his head, "You won't be going anywhere at dawn, James. It's a shame you have to be as stubborn as Keegan."

James said to me, "Time to go."

The shot rang in my ears as my eyes focused on James. Suddenly, we were standing at the entrance to the dungeon, facing each other.

Max said, "Hello? Don't mind me. Just trying to get to the little boy's room."

Max clutched James' shoulders and moved him aside.

"Thank you," Max said and hurried out the hole and up the stairs to the bathroom.

"Whoa," I said breathlessly. "That was…"

James shrugged and finished my sentence with a big smirk, "…perfect."

CHAPTER 23

When James said "perfect," he may have been jumping the gun. We waited in Vitale Park every morning, hours before sunrise, for over a week with no sign of Ty. We tried to get back into his head, but after a few days, we wondered if the man ever slept; it just wouldn't work. Stuck in the basement of The Green for all but those few hours a day, we were going stir-crazy.

As we walked upstairs to the bathroom to brush our teeth one morning, hours before dawn, I mulled over the situation in my head. Here we were, getting ready to head out yet again, only to sit in Vitale Park for hours and wait for the man who, by now, we knew was most likely not going to show up. James insisted we were not safe anywhere but here, in the dungeon at The Green.

I hadn't been home for more than minutes at a time during the last two weeks, and that was only late at night for clean clothes, to feed Novakitty, and to leave my mother a note so she wouldn't worry about me. That was Max's idea; he actually had people who *would* worry about him.

"Your idea was stupid," I snapped at James on the way up to the bathroom.

"My idea? I'm pretty sure it was Max. And you agreed."

"Whatever." I stopped abruptly on the stairs. James crashed into me, and I got shocked. "Ah! What the heck?"

"You're the one who stopped."

"I'm not going to the park. And I'm not living in this basement anymore. I'm not doing any of this. We are living like vampires. We never go out unless it's dark; we hide in the shadows. I'm sick of it. There has to be another way." I stomped my foot as my hands snapped to my hips.

"It's not safe for us out there."

"Have you considered maybe what you said to Ty clicked with him?" I said. "Maybe he woke up thinking the experiment failed, and he's letting the whole stupid thing go."

James yanked me down to his step. I didn't have time to react other than to grab the railing so I didn't tumble down the stairs.

"All this might seem stupid to you," he said, struggling to control his voice. "But in case you forgot, the experiment didn't fail. Someone is coming for us, Emma. Do not let your guard down even for one second."

That's when I caught a hint of panic burning in his eyes.

"What aren't you telling me?"

I should have known days ago. I should have asked more questions instead of subserviently agreeing to live in this dark, creepy, haunted basement with no windows, heat, or running water, all because the guys said that would keep us safe.

"What is it?" I demanded.

James stormed past me and up the stairs. I followed.

"Talk to me," I said. "Did something happen?"

I was out of breath— but not from rushing up the stairs. It was the look on his face as he turned around and found my eyes. His eyes fixed on mine like they had when I first saw him on the beach, when we talked about books on his porch, and when he realized I was more than just something conjured by his imagination. He was hiding something from me, not to protect himself, but to protect me.

James rolled his eyes and said, "He's here, in town. The scientist came here to The Green."

"When?"

"Early this week, a man came in asking a lot of questions. Then he came in with Ty's guys."

"And you waited this long to tell me?"

"I didn't want to scare you."

"You didn't want to scare me?" I gawked at him. "What do you think I am, some fragile little flower?"

"No. I didn't want to worry you."

"Worry me? Seriously?" I huffed.

135

I shoved past him, stormed into the bathroom, and threw my plastic bag of toiletries against the mirror. I turned on the sink faucet. Angry blue eyes glared back at me in the mirror.

"Scared? Worried? Everyone thinks you're a coward," I growled at my reflection through gritted teeth.

I took a deep breath in and then let it out slowly. I had to focus on my breathing so I wouldn't break something. As much as I needed to hit something, I didn't want to get in trouble with Adam. Unable to stand still, I began to pace. If I went back out there, I would only lay into James.

"This isn't his fault," I mumbled. "Although he was the one who got this whole thing stirred up with that stupid report. He couldn't have left it alone? Maybe just kept it to himself?"

I braced my hands against the wall and leaned my head against the cold stone. My fingers tapped away as I tried to calm down. But I was too frustrated; I smacked my palms against the wall, causing my head to bounce. My forehead struck the cold stone wall, and it hurt— but it felt good. So I banged my head a little harder. This time, with too much force. But again, the pain was strangely satisfying. When my angry eyes forced me back to the mirror, I was shocked to find they were wet.

"Damn it," I snapped and scrubbed my eyes with my sleeves. "Stop it. Stop it. I should have asked more questions."

The door creaked open. James dragged himself in.

The water was still running, so I quickly splashed it on my face and then caught him staring at me.

"What?" I yapped. I dried my face with my sleeve, and growing further annoyed, I asked again, "What do you want? What do you want me to say?"

He shrugged. I prayed he couldn't see what I had just seen in the mirror.

Then he said, "*I'm* worried. *I'm* scared. I don't know what's going to happen or what exactly the experiment did to us. We all had dreams for our future. We were just learning what we wanted out of life. Now..." James shook his head and rolled his eyes to the ceiling,

"Now none of us have any idea what our future looks like. But we know it won't be normal. And *I'm* afraid of that."

James wrapped me in his arms and held me. The shock was momentary and seemed to get less severe each time we made contact. At first, I barely reciprocated the embrace. Still, he held me gently. He stroked my hair and didn't let go when I tried to push away.

"We can get through this together," he said.

He knew me so well. He was waiting for the moment I broke free and walked away from it all. Or ran away from it. And he wasn't about to let me make that mistake. So I gave in. I gave in to him and realized I didn't want him to let go of me.

Eventually, the water overflowed in the sink. We scrambled to turn the water off and grabbed paper towels.

Mopping up the mess and cutting through the awkwardness of the moment, I asked, "How do they know he's the one who did this to us?"

"It's part educated guess, part eavesdropping. I should start by saying he doesn't look like your typical scientist. He was muscular with a mop of slicked-back hair and a fancy three-piece suit. He was more middle-aged GQ than nerdy scientist.

"The guy came in with two of Gallagher's men and sat in the far corner of the dining room. When Adam went to greet them, GQ wouldn't even look him in the eyes," James said with a humph. "He barely said two words to him. One of the other guys asked Adam about you, though."

"Me?"

"He described you and asked if you'd been in lately. Adam said no. Gallagher's guys kept asking questions. Finally, Adam got ticked off and said right to GQ, 'Welcome back. Nice to see you again.' "

"What did the guy say?"

"He got flustered and said it was his first visit to town. The cool thing is that Adam felt a burst of nervous energy coming from him when he said that. Because he lied. He's convinced he is the scientist."

"Adam is a lie detector now?"

"He described it like when we get caught in a lie, and our adrenaline shoots up. Our face gets red, our blood pressure changes, or we get hot and sweaty. Adam could feel that energy."

"Remind me not to lie to him." I gathered the wet paper towels and threw them in the trash. As I loaded my toothbrush with blue gel, I asked, "Do we know what they were talking about?"

"Max bugged the place a few weeks ago. Gallaghers, Ardemonis, the cops, they are here all the time. He thought it was a good way to know what was going on in town. So yes, we know exactly what they were talking about. The conversation was about money, mostly. One of the Gallagher guys said Ty wanted to know exactly how they'd make money from the experiment..."

James stopped and looked at the floor. I sensed he was choosing his next words carefully. I removed the toothbrush and spat into the sink.

"And?" I said, urging him to continue. My stomach flopped. How much had they been keeping from me? "Don't sugarcoat it. Just tell me."

"The scientist is selling the subjects to the highest bidder."

I scoured my brain for exactly what that meant. Sell the subjects? The subjects would be James and me, Adam, Max, and two other people we didn't know. Sell us to the highest bidder? That's impossible.

"Do you get what I'm saying?" James asked.

"The scientist is going to sell the oil mixture, right? The stuff that made us this way. Then other people can get these same abilities."

"Not exactly."

I shoved everything back into my toiletry bag.

"What then?" I asked.

"He's going to sell *us*. These abilities are apparently unique to only us. We aren't the first experiment. There were other groups that failed. But not our group. To use the scientist's words, we all appeared to have developed 'uncanny, perfect, and strong abilities.' It comes from the oil reacting perfectly with our DNA, personalities, and personal strengths— making us super athletes."

"He called us super athletes?" I giggled. "I can throw a wicked curveball, but that's about it."

"That's the thing. The guy's lying. He's selling our abilities as performance-enhancing. I doubt the Gallaghers know we have more than simply enhanced ability. They don't know we have actual super-human power."

"Power," I repeated, nodding and trying to absorb the word. I shook my head and pressed on. "Does he know about you? That six of us were exposed to the oils?"

"No. No one seemed to know. And we plan to keep it that way. The less they know, the better."

"How does he plan to sell us?"

"He didn't go into specifics."

"Of course, he didn't. The scientist knows exactly what we are capable of and doesn't want anyone else to know. Especially not the criminals who funded the project," I said, leaning against the sink.

I threw my hands in the air. "He's going to kidnap us. That's what he plans to do."

"To kidnap us, he'd have to find us. They have to think we are worth it too. Why would they want us if we don't work?" James responded.

Then he said, "They talked about the girl Max is trying to reach. The scientist told Ty's guys that he's sure she has advanced performance abilities, but he hasn't seen it yet. In other words, he doesn't know what her ability is."

"What if she doesn't have an ability at all? Then we're off the hook. We all have to develop an ability for the experiment to work. Right? God, I have so many questions. I mean, how does he know we have abilities? How does he know what they are?"

"If he's here, he's watching us," James said. "And the girl Max met definitely has an ability. He felt it when he met her. She sparked hard. Adam remembered sparking with a girl at a party in the art gallery. If it's the same girl, we know she can do something. Max has been trying to reach her and find out exactly what it is. The problem is, she's next to impossible to get a hold of."

"I remember that day. I was there too. Maybe Adam was talking about me. I got one heck of a shock from an exhibit that night."

Just the mention of it sent pain up my arm.

"Adam said he remembers handing a girl keys and getting a heavy shock. Was that you?" he asked.

"No," I shook my head. "But there was a girl who got shocked the same time I did. We both touched a glass wall that had water running through it. I figured it was from the lighting. Electricity and water... bad combo."

I stopped to think for a minute, to gather my racing thoughts.

I said, "We need to get Max's girl on board before the scientist figures out her ability. If the scientist can't confirm she has one, or if we can somehow convince him she doesn't, he won't want us. Then we'll be in the clear."

"So optimistic," James said with a smile. "But I don't know."

James shifted nervously from one foot to the other. After seconds of silence, he said, "Look, it's Memorial Day weekend. This town is going to be packed for the fireworks. Everyone will be out. We should stay clear tonight. Ty still needs that report. And he thinks you and I have it. So Max and Adam are bringing the party to us."

"Nothing says welcome to junior high like a good basement party. Will there be balloons, spin the bottle, cupcakes?"

James rolled his eyes and shrugged. "I'll take any kind of party I can get right now."

CHAPTER 24

The pounding music from the live band blasted above our heads. With the crowd slamming around upstairs, I worried that the ceiling would come down any minute.

"It hasn't come down in over a hundred years," James said.

"Honestly, I don't even care right now. I'm starving. I thought Adam was bringing us food," I said.

On cue, Adam ducked through the doorway with a tray full of bar food. Cheeseburgers, chicken fingers, french fries, and a six-pack of beer.

"Nice. Seventh-grade mixer to frat party just like that," James said, snagging a beer as Adam walked by.

The one perk of living in the basement at The Green was being well-fed by Adam. He put the food on the table.

"Thank God," I whooped.

James and I sprinted to the food. Just then, something outside exploded.

"Holy crap!" I yelled. "What the heck is that?"

I ducked down next to the table for cover. Adam and James broke out in laughter.

"It's the fireworks, goof," explained Adam through tears of laughter.

"Oh my God," I gasped and slid into a chair.

They continued to laugh at me. James was pounding his hand on the table.

"Alright, alright. Stop bullying me, losers."

I grabbed a burger and wolfed down a big bite.

"The fireworks go off on the college soccer field right behind us," Adam explained. "I didn't think we'd hear them over the band...

but, of course, everyone went outside to see the fireworks. Even the band."

We listened and heard very few footsteps upstairs. The radio played softly.

We sat there for another second until James said, "Let's go."

James took my hand and followed Adam out the back door.

"Everyone will be too busy looking up to care about you guys," said Adam.

It was true— not a soul noticed as we emerged from the back door of the building. The explosions were spectacular. Breath-taking colors and patterns filled the onyx star-speckled sky above us.

Just as the finale was winding down, Max pushed through the crowd, out of breath.

"What's the matter?" I asked. "Who are you running from?"

"I'm not running *from* someone."

Max bent over, trying to catch his breath. Adam grabbed Max by the shirt and dragged him to his motorcycle, where no one was standing. James and I followed.

"What is it?" Adam demanded. "Max, talk to us."

Max bent at the hips, hands on his knees. His breathing was becoming less heavy. Slowly, he stood straight up, a smile plastered across his face from ear to ear. Adam whacked him in the chest.

"What the heck, man," Adam growled. "Seriously. Before I crush you."

"Okay, okay," Max said with his hands up. "I found her." Max chortled awkwardly. "Yeah, I found her. Sort of."

James scanned the crowd as everyone meandered back into the bar.

"Where is she?" James asked. "Did you bring her back here?"

"Uh, no. I tried, but she… she…" Max's gaze wandered up to the smoky sky. He shook his head, and the grin never left his mouth.

"Who?" I asked.

James said, "The girl he's been trying to reach. The other subject."

"Seriously? What is so amusing?" I snapped. "You found the girl you think is another subject, so why is that funny?"

Adam's eyes narrowed. "What's the matter with you?"

Failing to stifle the grin, he said, "It was weird. She just showed up out of the blue. I was trying to ditch Mikey so I could come here, and there she was, walking to her car. She acted like she remembered me from a few weeks ago, but I wasn't sure at first." He chuckled and continued. "All of a sudden, we were making out in an alley."

"Excuse me?" James said. "Are you joking?"

Max shook his head no.

"You're something else, man," James said with a smirk.

"I guess she's not shy," Max said.

Adam smacked a hand over his smirk and mumbled, "Go on."

Max threw his hands in the air. "Then she was gone. We were making out when the fireworks started, and the next thing I knew, she was in her car driving away. I was ready to kill Mikey. Talk about a bad wingman."

"Why didn't you follow her?" I asked.

"My wheels are here," Max said, pointing to the pickup truck next to Adam's motorcycle. "I'm going there now."

I asked an obvious question. "If you know where she lives, why haven't you gone to her house?"

"I have. She's never home," Max said. "I thought about leaving a note with my number, but somehow that didn't seem cool. What would I say? 'Hey, girl. I have super-enhanced abilities, and I think you do too. Call me when you're free.' I'm not feeling like that's a killer move."

"Point taken," I agreed.

"However, after what just happened, I think I have grounds for another visit."

"Good. Go," said Adam. "Try to get her to come back here. Or should we go with you?"

"That could scare her," I said. "All of us showing up? Let Max go alone."

"I'll be back soon," said Max. "Hopefully, with a new friend. A new *hot* friend." Again, he smirked.

Max hopped in his truck and left. Adam, James, and I went back inside. Adam went into the restaurant to check on customers and make sure everything was running smoothly at the bar. Then he met us downstairs. Adam met us with a nasty scowl and company. Beaten and bloody company.

"Javi!" I yelled, running to him. I shoved Adam away from Javier, and Javier fell to the ground. "Adam, did you do this?" I gaped at him as I waited for an answer, even though I was sure the answer was yes.

He responded, "I wish."

"It was the Gallaghers," Javier said. "They were less than pleased with me."

Javier had a swollen black eye with a cut above it. Blood dripped from his nose. He must have put up a good fight; his knuckles were bruised and bloody. Javier slumped over, his hand on his side.

"When you play with fire, you get burned," James said.

"Yes. Clearly, I misunderstood what they were all about."

"You spent their money already, didn't you?" I asked. "You bought new cars."

He nodded. "And I did not deliver what they wanted."

"Do you expect us to feel sorry for you?" Adam asked. "You betrayed her," he said, pointing an angry finger at me.

Adam reached down, hoisted Javier by the shirt, then slammed him down onto a chair. I got a bottle of water and a cloth and began to clean Javier's face.

James snatched the wet cloth from my hands and tossed it across the room. I scowled at him. Was he mad that I was being kind to a man who almost got me killed? Was he jealous? I wasn't sure what made me angrier. I refused to believe Javier should be written off so easily. He was naive and unaccustomed to people like the Ardemonis.

As if reading my mind, and maybe doing so, James said to Javier, "Do you expect us to believe you didn't know the Gallagher family was full of criminals? Poor, pathetic Javier, new to the United States and all of our filth. Oh, wait. You've been here since you were ten."

"Plenty of time to know the good from the bad in this town. Not to mention the conversations we've had. Especially lately," Adam chimed in.

"I know, I know," Javier stammered. "Emma, you have to believe me when I tell you I had no idea they would try to hurt you."

I thought about Billy, the beast he lured to my house to steal the report from me. I pictured Billy's meaty fists wrapped around my throat. And that whole time, I was worried about Javier.

Disappointment stabbed at my heart. "You know, Javi, I would love to believe that. But I don't. You're smooth, aren't you? A smooth-talking guy who gets pretty much whatever he wants. A friend, a report. Anything. Except you didn't get the report, and you paid the price. I can't say that bothers me. Why did you come here? Why did they let you go?" I asked, my concern for him dwindling.

I walked around his chair, and his gaze followed me.

"Tell me why, Javi?" I demanded, my voice cracking.

"They did not let me go. I got away."

"No one gets away unless they want him to," James said.

"You would certainly know," Javier said quietly to James with a crooked grin.

James stiffened his jaw and straightened his posture.

I snapped a glance at James. In my head, I repeated what James said. "No one gets away unless they want him to." Before I could question James, Javier continued.

"Ty knows about you and Adam," Javier said to me. "And he knows about the girl Max is looking for; her name is Chelsea Raleigh," Javier spit blood onto the floor and then continued. "I heard them talking. He does not know about one last subject. Ty did not seem to know much about what was in the report. That could be why he wants it so badly now. The scientist is back, and Ty wants more details about the project. He thought I had more information. What am I missing?" he asked.

No one answered him.

"You do not trust me?" Javier said. "Well, Ty does not trust the scientist either. He is keeping secrets from them." Then Javier threw a dagger. "Perhaps you should tell them all about it, James."

My heart plummeted to the floor.

"What is that supposed to mean?" I asked. I gawked at James. "What is he talking about?"

"Ty was on the phone with James this morning," Javier said.

Silence cut through the room. All eyes focused on James. At the same time, my disembodied heart was getting drop-kicked by Javier's words. Adam looked ready to kill James.

"Ty called me. I offered to get close to you guys, keep an eye on things until they were ready for you," James mumbled. "I wanted him to think I'm on their side."

A heavy sigh escaped my mouth. I placed myself between James and Adam.

Why did you do this to us? I thought to myself. But with my head held high, I asked, "Why does Ty need the report when he has the scientist who created the project? Did Ty explain that?"

"Ty doesn't trust him. He doesn't trust anybody."

"You think he trusts you?" I asked.

Adam's face had turned the tenth shade of red when I suddenly felt a strong pulling of energy in the room. The lights flickered, then dimmed completely. The music upstairs morphed into a strangled drone as if the electrical instruments had lost power. I could feel a swell of heat coming from Adam.

When I called out to Adam, he didn't respond. He was glaring at James as if trying to shoot fire from his eyes or something, so I yelled at him, "Adam! Adam, stop!"

Again, Adam didn't respond.

"James, move!" I said, pushing him toward the door. "Go!"

Javier was completely bewildered.

"What the heck is going on?" he asked. "What is wrong with Adam?"

"Adam!" I yelled again, this time gripping his arms.

Besides the anticipated shock, his arms were hot as fire. I could barely touch him. With my hands tucked into my sleeves, I slapped his chest with all my strength. He never budged. He didn't even seem to notice me.

I looked to Javier and James as they stood wide-eyed by the door. Something dangerous was happening to Adam, and not one of us had a clue what to do.

CHAPTER 25

"I got all the way down Main Street and realized I've never been to her house when it's dark out. Hey, move," said Max, pushing his way past James. He spotted Javier standing next to him and said, "Well, well, well. Look what the cat dragged in."

James' arm shot out to stop Max from going any further. He nodded toward Adam and me. Sparks shot out of the wall outlets.

"Stay back," I told Max. "Something is wrong with him."

"Crap!" Max growled and grimaced. "This is gonna suck."

Max took three long strides toward Adam and punched him square in the face. Adam went down like a toppling building; dust flew up from the floor. We all gasped.

"What the hell!" I hollered.

The lights popped back to maximum illumination, and the band picked up playing where they had left off. Max straightened his shirt and shook out his hand. His knuckles were flaming.

"Did you want mass destruction? End of the world? An earthquake? A downed plane in The Green's parking lot?" Max said.

"Is that what would have happened?" James gasped.

"Let's just say one of them almost did a few months ago when we were just figuring out we were a little different than everyone else." Max eyed us for a second and asked, "Who pissed him off?"

Javier and James simultaneously chimed, "I did."

"I see. Double trouble," Max responded. He pointed to Javier. "You, I can understand. But what did you do, James?"

"He's working for Ty. He's going to hand us over to the Gallaghers and the scientist. Isn't that peachy?" I said, disguising my heartbreak with disgust and sarcasm.

Max clasped his hands together and said, "Excellent. So good times are on the horizon, I see." He looked down at Adam, who was beginning to stir. "Yup, good times."

I knelt next to Adam and rested my hand on his cheek. He was not nearly as hot as he was a few minutes ago, though he did feel feverish. James stood over me.

"If you would have let me explain," James started to say.

"You all might want to back off and let Adam come to on his own," Max warned. "Especially you, James. We don't need an instant replay."

As we shuffled to the doorway, Max sat down at the table next to where Adam had landed on his side. Adam rolled onto his back and rubbed a hand over his face. He groaned as his hand passed over his nose.

"Morning, cupcake," Max chimed. "Come on. Rise and shine."

"Taunting a beast is asking for trouble," Javier warned Max.

James and I exchanged an agreeing nod.

Looking James in the eyes, I couldn't believe he betrayed us. I should have known. I should have figured it out because of our connection. But he was so believable, so sincere.

"Oh, he's no beast. He's all beauty," Max said, patting Adam on the belly.

"Shut up," Adam growled. He sat up slowly, blinking his blurry eyes, squinting at the light.

Though I didn't recall it to be true, Max said to Adam, "Just so you know, everything got worked out. There's no reason to be mad at anyone. It's just us buds down here hangin'. Except for maybe Javier. He's questionable."

James took my hand. "Emma, let me explain."

I swatted his hand away and looked from James to Javier. I sure knew how to pick friends. I went to the side of the only guy I trusted at the moment.

"Adam. Talk to me," I whispered, kneeling next to him.

For some reason, I got a warning glare from Max. But I knew Adam wasn't going to hurt me.

Adam focused on my face and smiled. Something he didn't often do.

"Just another day in the life of an electromagnetic monster," he said.

Max said, "Technically, you're far more than just a…"

149

"I know. I know," Adam responded, cutting him off from a lengthy scientific explanation that none of us would understand.

Adam turned back to me and said, "My nose hurts. He packs a good one."

Max and I helped Adam to his feet while James and Javier sulked in the corner. Max explained that he returned because he left his phone here and couldn't remember the girl's house number. Since it was dark, he didn't think he'd recognize her house without it. We filled Max in about James' secret plan to infiltrate the Gallaghers and how Javier stumbled in here after escaping from the Gallaghers.

"The girl you're looking for," I said. "Her name is Chelsea Raleigh."

Max smiled and nodded. He said, "I think I should hang here for a bit. Time for a group meeting."

After much discussion, we realized that while Javier had betrayed us, the bottom line was that he was a small-time weasel who got caught up with the Gallaghers. He was valuable to us because he had information that we needed, and he seemed to want to help.

"I overheard Ty talking to an older man, the scientist, maybe. The man said he had been living in California and only just returned a few months ago. Apparently, he would return several times a year to check on the status of some experiment."

Max, Adam, and James exchanged looks.

Javier continued. "The man told Ty that he did not need details. His job was strictly funding. Then they started to argue about money, interest, and advances that someone named Donnacka gave to him years ago… I do not know. I heard bits and pieces."

"I know they are talking about Donnacka Gallagher, Ty's dad. My grandfather," James said. "The man who was talking about the experiment is our scientist. It sounds like we were right that he got money from Donnacka to fund this experiment, and now Ty is getting the payback my grandfather would have gotten. What else?" asked James.

"That is all. For days they would come in, ask me a mountain of questions about Emma and Adam and their connection to the

Ardemonis in a not-so-pleasant manner," Javier said, gesturing to his face. "They insisted I knew more. They seem to think you have great athletic skills all of a sudden." He glanced at Adam and continued. "Finally, they put me in the car to take me to another location. When we stopped at the light on Main Street, I jumped out of the car and ran."

Adam grabbed Javier by the shirt. "What did you tell them?"

"Nothing. I know only that they are not done with me; I owe them money."

"Or information," Adam responded.

"All I did was agree to help with the report in exchange for money. I thought, what harm could be done by that? I will cancel the car orders and give them their money back."

"I don't care what you do or how they get payback from you as long as it has nothing to do with us," James huffed.

"Look, I want to help you," Javier explained. He turned to me. "I sincerely want to make up for the dishonesty, Emma. I am truly sorry."

When Javier reached out to me, James smacked his hand away.

"Don't touch her," James snapped.

"James, stop," I said.

"You know, Emma…" he started.

Adam tapped James' shoulder and said, "Shut up, man. Shut the heck up and listen!" We all drew our attention to Adam. "Do you hear that?" he asked quietly.

James shook his head no. Max whispered, "Such a quiescent vicissitude."

Adam mouthed, "What the…?" to Max and scowled at him.

"Silence," Max restated in standard English. He pointed to the ceiling and asked Adam, "Why is it so quiet?"

We followed several steps behind Adam as he dashed to the staircase. He ascended cautiously and quietly.

The silence in the bar was deafening. We heard no band, no talking, and not even a footstep. Where in the world had everyone gone when the place was packed just minutes ago?

CHAPTER 26

When Adam reached the door at the top of the stairs, he turned to us and put a finger to his lips. Then slowly, he turned the glass knob, and the door creaked open. Adam let it glide on its own until it hit the wall. When he stepped into the bar area, all we could see was his enraged face.

"What the hell is going on?" he yelled as he moved from our line of sight.

James and Max pushed past me and into the bar, following close behind Adam. Javier came up next to me, then slid me behind him. I stood on the top step, peeking around Javier to see what was happening.

At the bar, two menacing men in black leather jackets sat on stools, patiently waiting as the man behind the bar poured a round of drinks. He was not the bartender. The men didn't so much as acknowledge Adam as he barreled toward them. They casually slammed back a shot while the man behind the bar poured them another.

The imposter bartender had to be in his mid-fifties, and he was jacked. He was of average height with shoulder length, slicked-back, brown highlighted hair. The man wore a tan vest and pants from his three-piece suit; the coat hung on the hook next to the cash register. The GQ scientist had arrived.

Adam marched behind the bar and stood chest to nose with the scientist. The scientist didn't back down. Clearly (and oddly) not intimidated, he poured a shot of vodka and held it out to Adam.

"Shot?" he asked.

Adam suddenly got that look. The one that happened right before he sucked the energy from the room and everything in it. Max recognized it too. He raced to Adam's side and put a hand on his shoulder. Adam's gaze was locked on the scientist.

"Hey, man. Look at me. Seriously," Max said. "Hold it together." With that, Adam turned his beet-red face toward Max.

Max shoved Adam out from behind the bar. Of course, shoving Adam was like shoving a skyscraper, so it appeared difficult and cumbersome. At least Adam was able to step away and regain his composure.

Luckily, Adam didn't see the scientist's smirk as he walked away. That would've been gasoline on the fire.

"Ok. We got that out of the way," the scientist said. "Now, let me introduce myself."

He put the shot in Max's hand as he stepped around him and said, "You're going to need that."

Max put the shot on the bar and followed close behind him.

"Introductions are always a good start," Max said. "However, we already know who you are."

The scientist walked straight to the basement door and gestured to a nearby table.

"Please. Sit," he said to us.

Adam stood in the middle of the room, purposely watching the ceiling fan going around and around, most likely trying to ignore the scientist so he wouldn't get upset. But that crazy man waltzed directly to Adam and got in his face. Taunting the beast, poking the bear.

"Do you want to put on a show for my friends here before we talk, buddy? Or should I do introductions first?"

Adam's head tilted slightly. He studied the scientist's face as if searching the pockets of his memory. He said, "You remind me of someone."

Strangely, the scientist laughed and quickly broke away from Adam's glare. For the first time, he showed a crack in his armor.

"The truth is, kids, this isn't the first time you've met me. But we'll have plenty of time to rehash old memories later. And I suppose, if you don't want to sit, that's fine."

The scientist walked over to his two friends at the bar, slid casually onto the stool between them, and began.

"My name is Doctor Jake Jones. I used to live here until being forced to relocate several years ago. These are a couple of my local friends." Then there was a long silence.

After several seconds, when it seemed like that was all we were going to get from Dr. Jake Jones, Max rolled his eyes and said, "And…?"

"You don't need details just yet. Basics, you need the basics, my friends."

"We already know you're some kind of a witch doctor," James said. "We know you infected Emma, Max, and Adam when they were little. We know you're here now to do something about that. We also know you can take your fancy suit, smug attitude, and your weaselly friends and beat it." James walked to the bar, picked up the shot glass Max had pushed aside, and threw it back like water. "Bar closed," he said, leaning on the counter. "Bye."

Jones let out a boisterous belly laugh and smacked his hand down on the bar.

"You don't want me to go. You have too many questions. And I have all the answers."

"Then stop playing around. You must need something from us. So talk or get out," snapped Max.

Adam sat down and began tapping his foot. I could tell he was trying to stay focused and not get angry. Javier didn't say a word. He sat next to Adam at the table and listened. And me… I tried to make myself one with the cold stone wall. I closed my gaping mouth and avoided eye contact with Jones. Everything about that man made my skin crawl. And at the same time, boy, did I want to punch this guy.

"I am here to help," Jones began. "Some of you may have noticed a subtle change in yourselves."

"Understatement," mumbled Adam.

"James, Javier, your friend Adam has been experiencing an elevated level of… how should I put it… I suppose the word energy would sum it up. Then we have Max, the intellectual sponge. A human Google, Alexa, Siri. Knowledge is at his fingertips in seconds." He smiled, and to Max, he said, "Not bad for a guy who barely squeezed out a high school diploma. Wouldn't you say? You're welcome, by the way."

The scientist got up from the bar stool and put his hands on his hips. I almost laughed at his superman-like stance, but then I realized he was dead serious when he said, "I'm not going to be humble. I am responsible for your gifts. I gave them to you. I chose you specifically. You three and another. Chelsea. Then one other inadvertently received the gift."

I glanced at James. Did the scientist know what had happened between us? I got a pain in my gut. I scrambled to prepare a response.

Then Jones said, "It was her mother's fault. And trust me, she's paying for that. Her child wasn't supposed to receive the oil. Yet, she did. Her name was Areli. Sweet, innocent, towheaded Areli. Unfortunately, I can't seem to find her. Apparently, she 'left' her family," he said, making air quotes. "This is where I need your help. We need to find her if this is going to be successful. You will need her to complete what I like to call the ring of fire ceremony. You need to find her to survive."

"Survive?" I said, surprised to hear my own voice.

The scientist chirped, "Finally, she speaks."

He rushed to my side and reached for my hand. I jammed it into my back pocket and scowled.

The scientist leaned close and said, "You will be the one to find her. I just know it. You have the ability that will make finding her easy. I will tell you all I know about her, and with the help of Max, you can find her and save everyone."

"I don't know what you mean," I said, leaning away from his creepy smirk. "What ability?"

"You are not the first to have this ability." I shook my head and shrugged. "Don't be silly. You cannot lie to me. I am familiar with your uncanny telepathic thymesia, Emma. There was once another. She is no longer with us."

"What happened to her?"

"The ring of fire ceremony was unable to take place. Therefore, the final step to ensure survival was never taken, and her group was dismantled."

Javier asked Max, "What is this tela mesia?"

Max corrected, "Telepathic thymesia." He walked toward the scientist. "What makes you think that? How would you know?"

"You can thank Ty for sharing his dream about his son and the blue-eyed girl who enjoy the park just before sunrise. But don't worry, I assured him you were in excellent hands and so was his report."

Now we understood why Ty never showed up at the park.

Jones turned quickly and clapped his hands once. He said, "You also had that dream, James? Emma pulled your sleeping mind into her beautiful theater, where she tricked you into spilling your guts." Jones lowered his voice and said to James, "I hope you didn't reveal anything embarrassing. I hear one tends to be too honest in that state."

James shifted uncomfortably from one foot to the other.

"My dear boys, Emma's telepathic thymesia is just like her. Exceptional. Details from memories of her own life events are not nearly as strong, fast, and exact as her ability to find and decipher yours, for example." The scientist grinned.

"I've never heard of such a thing," Max pointed out.

"Of course, you have not! No studies have been done because no other living being can do it.

"You see, while I have given you the greatest gifts, worth a king's fortune and a man's soul, it comes with a price. It comes with rules and…" He rubbed his chin as if searching for the right words. Then he said, "It comes with certain procedures. What I have done to manipulate your DNA requires the merge of all parties involved in that particular blend. That is the purpose of the ring of fire ceremony. It's complicated to explain. But please understand that if we don't find Areli so that we may follow all of these procedures, it will not end well for any of you."

"Elaborate," Max demanded.

Jones smiled and nodded his head. "For you, I shall."

Jones rattled on for about ten minutes, using words and terminology I did not understand. By the looks I was getting from James and Adam, they didn't get it either. Jones and Max exchanged a few heated sentences at one point, and Adam laughed.

"Do either of you speak English?" Adam asked. He turned to Javier and smacked him on the arm, "Is this Spanish, man?"

Javier rubbed his bicep and responded, "I do not think it is even human."

After an intense few seconds where Max looked like he might explode, he erupted with, "Are you freaking kidding me?! What kind of a scientist are you? A mad scientist? You're a full-blown cross between Dippel and Crick. Are you trying to outdo the infamy of Jekyll and Hyde? And your N13?"

Max turned to us astonished and said, "Because that's what we are to him— numbers."

He turned back to Jones. "That Subject Number Thirteen whose special talent you can't seem to figure out... and that sweet tow-headed Areli you need us to find for you... I mean, seriously? Do you honestly think we're jumping on the crazy train with you after what you just explained? Leaving out the most important facts, I should point out."

Then Max did something which took me by surprise. He lunged at Jones and slammed him hard against the bar. Jones' head bounced off a napkin holder, sending bloody napkins everywhere.

Then, all at once, chaos erupted.

Jones' two buddies reached for Max. But James, Adam, and Javier were on top of them before anyone could blink. And while I might run away from the invisible battles, like feelings and family responsibility and all of that annoying stuff, I never ran away from a good old-fashioned fight.

All in at five foot seven and 125 pounds, I ran straight at Jones' smallest sidekick, whom James was prying from Max's back. When James whipped the little guy around to face me, I kneed him in the groin. An animal-like squeal escaped his mouth as he dropped to his knees like a hot potato. Somehow, through his pain, he was able to clamp onto my ankle and attempt to pull me down. So I kicked him in the face with my free foot. With one hand on his groin and the other on his eye, he dropped backward. He groaned in agony, but he didn't move much after that.

Adam grabbed the bigger guy by the back of his leather jacket and dragged him through several bar stools head first. Then he tossed the half-conscious jerk into the corner. But that didn't stop him. The big guy jumped to his feet, shook the stars from his head, and ran straight at Adam. It became an angry game of chicken.

Without hesitation, Adam stormed at the big guy and faked a move to the right. The big guy fell for it and lurched toward Adam's right. But suddenly, Adam shifted left, and as the guy sailed by, Adam stuck his arm out, catching him in the throat. The guy landed flat on his back so hard that I heard the hardwood floor crack. Adam gave the guy a swift and brutal kick to the ribs, then stood ready in case the idiot decided to get up again.

Max pulled Jones' limp body off the bar, and he and Javier dragged him to a table and slapped him into a chair. Jones hadn't even put up a fight.

"Stop. Please," Jones whined, his hands covering his face. He was breathing heavily. "I understand your anger."

Blood ran from his nose and mouth. His slicked-back hair now hung limp in his eyes, making the GQ facade a thing of the past.

Quicker than it started, the fight was over. But the depth of what had happened to us and what was yet to come— that was just beginning.

CHAPTER 27

As Adam walked toward Jones, a heavily tattooed man waltzed into The Green like he owned the place. He walked swiftly past Adam, who had just taken Jones by the collar. Adam caught sight of the guy and shoved Jones back into the chair with such force that Jones slid off and ended up on the floor. Adam marched after the tattooed man.

"Good evening," he said to Max and James. "My name is Ty Gallagher. And it seems like I need to make something clear. You *will* help us find the last girl and complete the transition."

He turned and glared at Adam, who had been trailing fast on his heels.

"Do you understand? This is neither a request nor an instruction. It is a clear, concise command."

Ty peeked around Adam to Jones, who had shuffled into a corner.

"Doctor Jones, I'm sure you agree that we have waited long enough. You're on my schedule now. You have exactly one month to wrap this up."

"Whoa," Adam chortled. "You're confused about who I take orders from... dick."

The last word hung in the air. Adam stood over Ty.

Ty grinned and inched closer to Adam defiantly. "I'm afraid you've got my name wrong."

They stood toe to toe. Adam's fists opened and closed repeatedly, and I thought for sure he was going to punch Ty.

The smug grin on Ty's mouth melted into a thin snarling line. He said to Adam, "I understand that you've been placed in a difficult position. And I respect the hell out of your strong stance on the matter. I do. But if you look around, you'll see there's no question about who's in charge here."

That's when I realized we were surrounded by Ty's people. The men from G3's house came and stood beside Ty. Twenty angry-looking men and two daunting women gathered around us— each one built like an MMA fighter. A thousand novels could have been written with all the ink in the room. And some had more piercings than skin on their face.

Ty pivoted and charged toward James, leaving Adam's tense body behind. James stiffened up, ready to defend himself. My stomach turned. The fear of uncertainty when a parent rush at you like that was too familiar. What was coming? A slap, a punch, a shove? Or words just as painful?

"You still with us?" Ty asked him.

"I never was," James responded, his fists balled at his sides.

I started toward James, but Max stopped me.

"I no longer need you to infiltrate this group," Ty said to James, waving a dismissive hand at us. "It's pointless. We'll finish this and get our money."

James shook his head. "I'm not going with you."

"You're making a mistake. You're on the wrong side, son," Ty said.

"Thanks for the fatherly concern, but I know exactly what side I'm on."

"Don't come running to me when this explodes in your face. Run home to Grannie, for all I care."

"Yeah, because you care so much," James mumbled.

Ty spun around on his heels, stopped to glare at Jones, and motioned for his guys to follow him. And just like a pack of dogs, they did.

On the way out, they tipped tables, kicked over chairs, and cracked sconces on the wall. Glass flew everywhere. One guy, who must have had a death wish, shouldered Adam as he passed him. Adam grabbed the guy by the arm and spun him around to face him. When the guy raised his fist, Adam slammed both hands into the guy's chest and sent him flying across the room. Adam's eyes followed the man as he slid across the floor, knocking down chairs like bowling pins.

All the lights flickered. From the corner he'd crawled into, Jones stared at Adam eagerly. It was as if he was anxiously waiting to see what else he would do— or could do. I feared it would be something awful.

Two of Ty's guys rushed to help the crumpled man up; Adam was already storming his way. When they dragged the half-conscious sack of flesh to his feet, we realized his hair stood on end as if he'd been electrocuted. Two small black holes smoldered on his shirt. Adam stopped dead in his tracks.

The shocked look on Ty's face made me think he didn't know what he'd gotten himself into. Jones tried desperately to stifle a creepy girlish giggle but failed. That man completely made my skin crawl. Jake Jones was inarguably a certifiable loser and a clear-cut mental case.

Ty bent over, poked a finger into the smoky shirt, and glared at Adam. He looked back at the shirt. One of the guys holding up the groggy french fry tapped his cheek to get a rise from him. But the guy's eyes barely fluttered open.

Ty ordered his men out and then left me with some parting words.

He looked directly at me, chuckled, and asked, "Do you think you've been hiding from me? Do you think I haven't known where you've been all this time? That's sad." Ty shook his head with a cocky smirk that I wanted so badly to smack from his face. Then he said, "I hope you've enjoyed your imprisonment. It may not be your last."

With nothing further, he left Jones behind and sauntered out the door.

All of a sudden, Jones seemed smaller and less intimidating. With Ty gone, the coward and his two men shuffled to their feet.

Jones wiped the dust from his pants and said to Adam, "Nice. Imagine what I could do to help you gain greater control. You and I both know how that could have ended." He looked at each one of us. "You all know what could have just happened, right? Don't fool yourselves. You need me on your team."

Jones gestured for his two men to head to the door as he slowly backed up to it himself.

"Emma," he said, startling me. "You'll find the girl."

With that, he and his men left. The door slammed behind them, and the lights flickered again.

"Adam?" I said, rushing to his side.

After a heavy gasp, he exhaled slowly and loudly. It was more like a growl than anything.

"Team? We are not on his stupid team. This isn't a game!"

A busted sconce popped and started on fire. Max snagged the fire extinguisher from behind the bar and put it out.

"Someone take him downstairs and distract him," Max commanded.

Javier and James escorted Adam to the dungeon. If Javier was good at anything, it was distracting someone with a long-winded story.

When they were out of earshot, and Max had the sconce completely doused, I said, "You're the one who understands all that scientific stuff. What's your take on all this?"

He dropped the extinguisher and plopped down in the chair next to me.

"I'm not sure. Part of me thinks we should do it. If what Jones says is true, when we complete the ring of fire, we'll be strong enough to defeat Jones and his thugs." Max paused, then said, "That's the catch, right? Why would he be willing to risk that— unless he's not telling us something."

I nodded. It was exactly what I'd been thinking.

"What if we find this girl and complete this ring of fire ceremony without Jones knowing? Whatever control he thinks he might have will be lost," I suggested.

"How do we know that?"

"We don't," I sighed.

"The truth is, we have no idea what will happen to us if we go through the ring of fire. But also, no idea what happens if we don't. And although Jones acts as if he knows, I'm not so sure. We're an experiment. By definition, that's a test, an act of discovering that which is unknown."

"This is all one big educated guess?"

"I think so," Max responded.

"Jones said we'll only survive if we go through with the ring of fire ceremony. I don't know about you, but I don't feel like I'm dying. Unless he means Ty will have us killed. The report did mention the termination of subjects. Then again, maybe the infectious oil came with an expiration date. What if that's what happened to his other subjects?"

"Jones could also mean that our lack of control will kill us. Take Adam, for example," Max said.

"And what about you? Will you get so smart that your brain will explode? That's ridiculous," I snickered.

Max pondered what I said. "I think the first thing we have to do is get everyone together. This is a decision we all need to agree with."

"So we find the blonde girl?" I asked. "I feel like we're opening Pandora's Box."

"Pandora's Box opened ten years ago." Max stood and paced the floor. Then he said, "We look for the girl. And as far as Chelsea goes, I'll just have to stalk her house and find a way to get her here without ending up in jail."

"Girls hate that smart, good-looking combo. Somehow you'll have to find a way to use that to your advantage." I rolled my eyes.

His face got red. He motioned to follow him downstairs and said, "Let's check in with Adam and James. We start in the morning."

CHAPTER 28

~June~

After a long argument about whether or not we should let Javier continue to help us, I convinced the guys to give him another chance. Forgiveness wasn't my greatest attribute, but I had to start somewhere. I considered myself a pretty good judge of character, and I believed he was sorry and had no idea what he was getting himself into. James, however, had a whole different take on Javier.

The grueling search for a needle in a haystack continued for about two weeks. We spent long days tapping the shoulder of every blonde who looked to be around our age in Lakeville, Livonia, Geneseo, Avon, Lima, and Mt. Morris. All we needed was a little zap.

Eventually, we got it through our thick skulls that we needed to go directly to the sources. Being careful and trying to act normal wasn't working. Because Max had the most tolerance for Javi, they went to Chelsea's together. James, Adam, and I started from scratch. We headed out to find the man of the hour, the monster in the closet, the scientist with the most to gain. And eminently— the most to lose.

I squeezed into the back seat of Adam's fancy Camaro.

"Sweet ride," said James, taking the front passenger seat.

"This isn't mine. My friend Taylor is working on my truck, so we swapped cars for a few days."

"A very trusting friend," James said. "Where to?"

"How do we find Jones?" I asked.

Adam glanced at me in the rearview mirror, smiled, and said, "We don't. We make him find us."

Adam drove straight to Vitale Park on the north end of Conesus Lake.

"Obviously, Mister Professor Doctor Jones is already watching us. Or someone he knows is. All we have to do is get out there and make a scene."

I glanced at James.

"James and I can't make much of a scene with our abilities. So that leaves you, the power sucker."

"I don't suck power," Adam said, opening the car door.

"Yes, you do," I said.

"No. I borrow existing power. I don't get to keep it."

"That still sounds like power-sucking to me. Borrow or steal."

"Brain invader," Adam said to me.

"Hey," James protested.

We headed across the lawn toward the gazebo at the edge of the lake.

"Do you have a plan, Adam?" James asked.

"Nope," he replied.

We stepped into the gazebo. As I sat on the bench and looked around, no one appeared to be watching us. A lady walked by with two crying children in a stroller. An old man walked by with his dog, carrying a metal detector. And while no boats were docked at the water's edge, a few cruised by. Some boats sat anchored offshore as kids played in the water and people fished.

James stood with his back to me as he scanned the water.

"James," I said. "You never finished telling us about the master plan you and your dad had for us."

His head snapped in my direction. "I was never working with him. I was trying to make him think that so I could get information. Didn't we already settle that?"

"No, not as far as I'm concerned."

"Drop it," Adam said, scanning the cars in the parking lot.

"Easy for you to say. You weren't confined to a basement for weeks with a liar."

James glared at me in disbelief, but he didn't say anything.

"Truth hurts. Huh?" I said to him.

"I wasn't lying to you about anything."

"Knock it off. You two arguing won't bring Jones to the surface," Adam said.

"This isn't about Jones. This is about betrayal."

"I didn't betray you, Emma," James said.

He stalked across the floor of the gazebo. I met him halfway.

"Yes, you did. You betrayed everyone. You were going to snitch us out to Ty to save your butt after all your alleged concern for my safety. But you threw my safety into the trash," I said, raising my voice.

James marched to the steps of the gazebo.

"Don't walk away from me," I snapped. "I bet you thought everyone forgot about what you did."

"Stop," Adam said through gritted teeth.

I turned to face Adam and said, "No. This whole thing is a joke. How about this: I'm going to leave, go home, finish getting my ass into college, and get as far away from you people as possible. You can all deal with Jones and your mutated selves on your own. I have a life to live, and it doesn't include being trapped in this crappy town with a bunch of freaks."

I stormed past James on the steps and stomped away from the gazebo. I could tell by his voice that I had made Adam mad. Because if there was one thing we had in common, it was a quick and vicious temper.

"Get back here," Adam yelled.

"Whatever. Let her cool off," James said.

Adam ignored James and kept after me.

He said, "You can't just leave. I didn't think you were so selfish."

"Said the pot to the kettle," I replied and continued my journey out of the park.

I marched down the park path along the lakeside and toward the parking lot without looking back at him.

"What did you just say?"

"You heard me, Sasquatch. You're more selfish than I am. You like your big bad power. You don't care what happens to the rest of us."

I heard him jogging toward me, but I didn't look back. I was pretty sure he wouldn't tackle me. Not positive, but somewhat confident and certainly hopeful. I threw a dismissive hand in the air as I quickened my step.

"Get back here, Emma."

"Just leave her alone," James hollered from the gazebo.

I glanced back. James jumped off the gazebo steps and jogged after Adam. Adam, mere steps behind me, was too close for comfort. So I ran.

"Where do you think you're going," Adam huffed.

"Adam, stop!" yelled James. "I'm serious."

Suddenly, Adam nabbed my elbow and dragged me to a halt.

"Let go, beast," I growled.

"What is the matter with you? Have you lost your mind?" he asked.

His face was red, and his hand was on fire.

"You're hurting me," I said.

In my peripheral view, I spotted two guys walking our way on the path. They were watching our exchange. One guy had a dog, and the other carried a football.

Louder, I cried, "Ow! Stop hurting me."

Adam let go, but as I turned to walk away, he put a burly hand on my shoulder.

James was almost upon us, and the guys who were watching stepped up the pace toward us. The dog began to bark. I looked back at Adam. If steam could actually blow from his ears...

"Go ahead, tough guy. Turn me into a french fry," I barked. I leaned in, and lowering my voice, I said, "I dare you."

Next, I kicked him in the shin. And there it was.

Finally, James caught up to us.

"Took you long enough," I said.

The lights along the water's edge and parking lot popped in unison. A shower of sparks rained down on cars as their alarms blared. Engines cut out on boats in the water.

Adam keeled over as if in pain. His beet-red face scrunched up. His white-knuckled fists balled at his chest. Suddenly, Adam hollered out an angry warrior-like cry.

James snapped at me, "You are literally playing with fire. What is wrong with you?"

He tried to shake Adam. He said, "Hey man, come on. She's punking you."

James gaped at me with panic in his eyes. "Now what do we do? This is bad."

Just then, the two guys on the path rushed over. The German Shepherd continued to bark as the man held it back on its leash.

The man with the football said, "Is everything okay? Do you need us to call for help?"

"No, he's fine," said James. "We're fine, thanks. He has, um, seizures."

"That doesn't look like a seizure," he said.

Adam dropped to his knees. The ground seemed to shake.

"The only person we need you to call is your boss," I said to the man with the football.

The two men exchanged a curious glance. Adam gave out another howl as a fire hydrant blew into the air. Water poured down around us.

"Now would be a good time to call Jake Jones," I told them.

As the man with the dog pulled his phone from his pocket, he walked away, out of the shower of hydrant water.

Seconds later, a black Tahoe sped into the parking lot and stopped. Jones stepped out and rushed toward us. He shrugged.

"If only he could learn to control it better." He knelt beside Adam and said, "Breathe in through the nose and out through the mouth. Let the anger go. She got what she wanted."

He looked up at me and said, "You are a dangerous little thing, aren't you?"

CHAPTER 29

When Adam returned to his usual grumpy self, we convened in the gazebo.

His eyes narrowed. "I could have hurt you," he said.

"You didn't. You have more control than you think," I mumbled, brushing off his concern.

Adam dropped his head into his hands.

"You okay?" I asked.

"Just a little headache... thanks. Seriously, thanks."

I apologized to him for the headache I had given him. He looked awful. He glared at me, so I gestured toward Jones.

"I know. I get it," he responded with a nod and a grin.

Jones said, "Well, you have my attention."

"This girl you want us to find," James started. "How do you expect us to find her when we know nothing about her? You know more than we do and can't find her."

Jones beamed at our sudden need for answers.

"I see you are already hard at work. Your first mission." He clapped his hands together. "Fabulous!"

"Where did she live ten years ago? We need somewhere to start," I said.

"A last name," said James.

"Yeah, man. We aren't detectives," Adam said, rubbing his forehead.

"Areli Weaver. She was born on the United with Devotion Farm. To the pastor's family. His congregation grew all of my herbs and spices. They harvested the essential oils for my project. That was until Gloria, Pastor Allen's wife, stole one of my blends and used it on her daughter. Eventually, I had to move the whole production to California."

Everyone knew about the United with Devotion Farm. It was some kind of cult on the outskirts of town which owned hundreds of acres. They had their own religion that revolved around the earth and God. Or that the earth was God or something to that effect. You were lucky if you caught a glimpse of one of them down by the lake or in a field on the edge of their property. And it was never a child. Only the adults were allowed to leave the farm occasionally.

"Why would her mother do that to her?" I asked.

"The Weavers had no idea what the oil could do. It was my mistake to use their barn for my lab. I needed discretion, though."

"Wouldn't her parents know where she is?"

"One would think, dear Emma. However, she was excommunicated from the congregation a couple of years ago. Now she could be anywhere."

"Have you talked to her family or friends lately?" James said.

Jones chuckled and nodded his head. "I have kept tabs on every one of you for years. But when she left, it was like she had vanished. Her parents act as though their daughter never existed."

"Seriously? How could they disown their own flesh and blood? I'd think God would be pissed about that," Adam said.

Jones turned his back to us and raised his head to the sky. "You know, buddy, sometimes parents have to think about the greater good."

Jones paused, exhaled like he'd been holding his breath, and turned back to face Adam.

He said, "You must understand that."

Adam stared at him. It was a cold hard stare. Not the kind where I was afraid he would start to suck the life out of everything, though. It was a painful, confused glare.

Jones turned to me and said, "Parents always start with the best intentions, don't they?"

The miserable woman who'd given birth to me came to mind. She'd confessed more than once that she had never wanted children. My reply was simple.

"No," I said. Then changing the topic, I asked, "You seriously haven't any clue where she could be?"

"I would bet that she hasn't left town. Not one of those simpletons will talk to me except for her parents. And they came right out and said, and I quote, their 'glorified ray of light went out the day she created the likeness of God, making it tangible and vulnerable to the weakness of dark souls.' There you have it." Jones shrugged. "The one and only clue as to her whereabouts. Or not. If I could find her, I would.

"Emma, Adam, you are the ones with the abilities. Please use them to find her. The fact is, she can't be far. You all have this incredible, unspoken link. It's one that prevents you from being too far from each other for very long. You have circled each other's lives for the last ten years, whether you knew it or not."

Adam threw a questioning glance my way. He probably had the same question I did. How could I find a missing person when the only thing I could do was mentally channel someone's memory? Especially when I had absolutely no control over it.

I had had enough. I got behind Adam and shoved him until he stood up. Then I marched over to James, whacked him on the shoulder, and said, "Let's go."

They glanced at Jones, whose parting words were, "Work fast. Time waits for no one."

We walked straight to Adam's car.

"Got an idea?" Adam asked.

"Give me the keys," I demanded. "I'm driving."

Adam tossed me the keys and grinned. James crawled in the back, and Adam got in beside me. I could see him looking at me with a smirk.

I could tell what he was thinking and played along. "What?" I asked.

He nodded his head and shrugged. "It's a stick."

"Crap," I whined. "I don't know how to drive one of those. What will I do?"

Adam nodded again. "Yeah, don't worry. I figured as much."

He had his hand on the door handle to get out so we could switch spots. That's when I started the car, threw it into first, and slammed the pedal to the floor. James snickered in the backseat as I peeled out of the parking lot.

When I made a sharp right onto Big Tree Drive, cutting off a long line of steady traffic, Adam yelled, "What the heck! You're going to kill us."

James laughed harder. He knew me too well. Yet, not at all. It was so weird.

The light ahead was yellow, so I stepped on the gas.

"Emma, stop. It's turning red."

"Looks yellow to me," I said.

"I'm just going to close my eyes for a few. Let me know when we're there, Emma," James said.

"Where?" Adam asked, one hand on the ceiling and the other on the dash. I blew through the yellow light just as it turned red. "Okay, okay. I get it. You can drive a stick. Now slow down." The panic in his voice made me smile. "Emma, watch that car. It's pulling out!"

I swerved around the extremely slow-moving silver Honda Civic driven by the oldest woman I'd ever seen and kept going.

"What the…" Adam's head snapped around to look at the Honda still puttering along. Easing off the gas, I turned right onto East Lake Road. "You're going to give us whiplash," Adam said. "James, make her stop."

"If you don't want to puke, I'd apologize," James said.

"For what?"

"For insulting her," James said.

"Emma, I didn't insult you. Most girls don't drive sticks. It's too complicated."

My mouth dropped open. Again, I stomped on the gas. I passed three cars while managing to avoid a collision with a garbage truck. As I hit the brakes to make a ninety-degree turn onto Cleary Road, Adam's body slammed against the door.

"I said most girls. I'm sorry. I didn't mean to insult you. Slow down. I'm sorry!"

I put my foot on the brake and turned off Cleary Road.

"Apology accepted," I said with a poker face. I winked at James in the rearview mirror. "And just in time. We're here."

Adam rested his head against the dash and said, "Holy crap. I think I'm going to be sick."

"United with Devotion," I read.

The blackened wood sign was tiny and stood on a two-by-four about six feet high. It blended in with the trees and the twelve-foot iron fence surrounding the property. The entrance was basic in every way except for the barbed wire at the top of the fence.

Naturally, just about every mischievous kid in Lakeville had tried to break into the compound. I mean, if you put a fence around a mysterious cult-church-farm, what else would you expect? Even James, Frankie, and I had made a go at this fence before James moved away.

It seemed like yesterday that we rode our bikes to this place. We had climbed to the top, found the barbed wire, and quickly decided we needed a new plan. We considered throwing blankets on the barbed wire, sneaking in on a delivery truck, digging a tunnel; all the standard nonsense kids see in the movies. But like I said, James moved, and that changed everything for Frankie and me.

I pulled up to the gate and rang the intercom buzzer.

"May I help you?" the voice boomed.

"We are here to see Pastor Allen Weaver," I said.

"Do you have an appointment?"

"No, sir."

Adam whacked my shoulder and mouthed, "Make something up."

"You will need to call for an appointment with the pastor, please. Have a blessed day."

"I really need to see him now."

"What is the nature of your visit?"

The nature of my visit? Oh, gosh. To find his daughter. The daughter he disowned and probably never wants to see or hear about again. Crap! I hadn't thought this out enough.

"The nature of my visit is… umm…" I glanced at the colorful flowers lining the driveway and the bright green and yellow vines that twisted up the gate. The earth and God were the main priorities around here, so I said, "Nature. It's about our God-given nature."

There was a deafening silence on the other end of the intercom. I sucked in a gallon of air and held it. Adam smacked himself on the head and grunted.

James whispered, "Nature?"

"The nature of your visit is… nature?" the voice asked.

"Yes, sir. It's very important."

An idea popped into my head, and without thinking, I slapped Adam's shoulder. He scowled at me.

I said into the intercom, "Uh, yes. Please let the pastor know that I am here about essential oil blends. Like I said, it's very important." And now for the hail Mary. I cleared my throat and turned on my most business-like voice. "I work closely with Doctor Jake Jones. We have a proposal to discuss, and it can't wait."

"No," muttered Adam as he threw his head back.

After another long silence, a buzzer sounded, and the gate opened. Through the intercom, the voice said, "Go straight back to the rectory. It's at the very end of the road. You will see a large cobblestone house. Pastor Allen will meet you on the porch."

I shrugged at Adam and started up the stone road. I turned to James and raised my eyebrows at him.

I said, "Only took us ten years to get into this place."

"We need a plan. We can't keep winging this," Adam said.

"Hey, I got us in, didn't I?"

Adam said, "Maybe the straightforward approach is the best move. They're religious. Maybe they'll respect that."

"We need a cover story for how we know Areli, though," I said.

"We have to be careful," James said. "We don't know how much the pastor knows about the oil or what it did to Areli."

"I wonder if he knows his daughter was infected by the oil his wife stole?" I asked. "Would that make a difference? Would they care? Maybe that's why they excommunicated Areli."

Just then, we spotted the house up ahead, next to three large red barns and a silo. As we drove by the silo, James asked, "Are you guys seeing this?"

"Yup," said James.

"Guards?" I wondered.

Friendly-looking men dressed in khakis and white button-down shirts stood peppered along the road. Each one held a pistol or shotgun of various sizes as if they were ready to use them. Yet, they waved and smiled at us as we drove by. Some tipped their hats toward us as a greeting.

"Why does a religious farm need guards and a gate lined with barbed wire?" I said, my voice rising.

"Stay calm," Adam said. "I'm sure they just like their privacy. And they're weirdos, so they probably take a lot of slack. You know, losers trying to break in and mess with them and stuff."

"Some people are curious," I said, eyeballing James. "That doesn't make us losers. Geez…"

"Whatever," Adam said. "Here's how it's going to go down. We stick with the honesty thing. Sort of. Emma, tell Pastor Allen you were infected by the oil as a kid, and now you have health issues. Tell him Jones told you about Areli, and now you want to see how it affected her."

James said, "You guys go in first. I'll stay in the car. Maybe I can channel him like I did with Javier. I'll see if I can get in his head."

"That sounds like the best plan we have," I said.

"Gotta start somewhere," Adam agreed.

CHAPTER 30

James stayed behind in the car as Adam and I made our way up the dilapidated walkway to the well-worn front porch. The windows stretched from floor to ceiling, the dull red paint had peeled from the shutters, and pieces of stone had crumbled onto the porch. Adam casually strolled back and forth, peeking inside.

"It doesn't look like anyone is here," he said.

I pointed up the hill toward a silo. "That house is huge," I said. "Looks newer than this timepiece. I bet that's where they live."

Seconds later, a rickety, black golf cart pulled out of a barn and headed toward us, with whom we assumed was the man of the hour, Pastor Allen. He waved at Adam and me. Then despite the direct path, which was a straight shot from the barn to the rectory, he drove down the driveway and stopped at the car.

"Fancy c-c-car," he stuttered, parking the golf cart in front of the Camaro. He walked to the passenger side and tipped his head toward the window. "Hot in there, my friend. C-c-care to join us?" he asked James.

James quickly responded with, "Sure thing. Just have to finish this call first."

The silhouette of James' cell phone shook inside the vehicle.

The pastor glanced at Adam and me on the porch, then gave James a thumbs up. He left the golf cart in front of the car and headed up the walkway.

He wore a yellow short-sleeved button-up shirt. It was so thin you could see his man boobs. No lie— it was gross. He had his shirt tucked into his navy blue polyester pants, which I was sure he called trousers. And, of course, he wore sensible shoes: plain, brown, nondescript loafers. And to top off the look, he'd parted his thinning salt and pepper hair right down the middle.

"Whoa, nerd alert," whispered Adam. I scowled and hushed him.

As if to prove Adam right, the pastor's foot caught the uneven edge of a slate slab, and he stumbled. I cringed at the complete awkwardness as his arms pinwheeled and his greasy hair flew into his face. A vision of the pastor face-planting on the sidewalk flashed before my eyes. But at the last second, he managed to catch himself. He pressed on as if nothing had happened.

"I must say, it's not often we have unexpected g-g-guests," Pastor Allen stuttered as he smoothed his hair neatly back into place on either side of his wide part. He jabbed a thumb at the car. "A little warm to sit in the c-c-car."

"He doesn't mind the heat," I responded with a smile. "Thanks for meeting with us."

Adam and I introduced ourselves and shook hands with the pastor. He stammered out a warm welcome, unlocked the rectory door, and shuffled us inside to his own personal time warp.

The walls looked as though they hadn't been painted in fifty years, the floors were scratched up and discolored, and the furniture... well, it was just old. It made G3's house look brand new. Yet, despite the ancient decor, it was spotless.

I plunked down on a green and gold plaid sofa, and Adam sat beside me. The pastor took a dinky chair facing the couch.

"It's stronger than it looks," he said.

We all laughed a little. That's about where the pleasantries ended.

"Tell me, what brings you to our private little c-c-community? Surely, it's not about saving your c-c-cursed souls."

"Wow. Blunt," Adam said.

"Yes. I have to be. I prefer to c-c-call it honesty. For example, I don't know why your friend decided not to c-c-come in. I believe it is dishonesty that drives his decision. That said, I'll have you know that some of our loyal c-c-community members are c-c-currently watching him. Should he steal anything or destroy property, he will be fully prosecuted."

"We just came to talk to you. Relax," I said.

The nerve this guy had. I hoped James was "napping" and already deep into this guy's brain.

"Then talk. I am a busy man, and my people need me."

Adam waved a hand at me to begin.

"We have had the recent misfortune of meeting Jake Jones."

I let the name hang in the air for a moment. Pastor Allen seemed unfazed.

"The scientist, Jake Jones," I repeated. "Your farm did some work for him a…"

"I know who he is and what my business was with him. You don't need to tell me," he said coldly. "What does this man have to do with you being here today?"

I continued, "The oil blends that he made ten years ago, they were sort of poisonous…"

"We provided Doctor Jones with all-natural essential oils derived from our organically g-g-grown plants. What he did with them was his business. We are not responsible for his sins, nor should we be subjected to dealing with your problems."

I began to steam. "What he did with them changed us forever. And it did the same to your daughter. Now maybe you don't care about that either, but it turned us into freaks of nature. And since you and your community are all about nature, you may want to be aware of what you helped Jones do to us and who knows how many others."

I caught Adam texting from the corner of my eye.

"Modern technology has made people rude," the pastor said to Adam. Then he turned to me. "We live in a qu-quiet c-c-community and have minimal c-c-contact with anything or anyone outside these g-g-gates. All I can offer you is some words of wisdom. G-g-god has a way of weeding out the bad in the world. Perhaps Doctor Jones was His soldier in this c-c-case. That's a c-c-conversation to have with him. Now, if you'll excuse me."

The pastor stood, an obvious indication that he was done with us. I started to stand, then stopped when I noticed Adam sit back on the couch and get more comfortable. Then Adam went for the jugular.

"We want to know where your daughter is," Adam said.

"I-I-I d-d-don't h-h-have a d-d-daughter."

While completely obnoxious, I smirked when Adam sighed long and loud. He followed it with, "That's weird. Because I happened to know you do. Blonde girl, your wife gave birth to her about nineteen years ago, then inadvertently infected her with the *oh-so-natural* oil blend that Doctor Jeckle threw together to mutate a few local kids. How's that for being blunt? Or should I say— honest?"

The pastor stepped back, his eyes widened, and his mouth dropped open.

Adam continued, "Is she here on the property?"

"No," said the pastor, shaking his head feverishly.

I jumped in. "Does Areli live in town? Who does she live with? Friends? Tell us anything you know. Our lives depend on it."

Just then, Adam's phone beeped, and he checked a text.

Pastor Allen glared at Adam, then blinked slowly and furrowed his brows.

"Our g-glorified ray of light went out the day that child c-c-created the likeness of G-god, making it tangible and vulnerable to the weakness of dark souls. She had the audacity to g-g-give Him the face of an old man with c-c-color in the cheeks and emotion on His face! I assure you, my wife and I have NO such child. You will leave now."

"How often do you practice that line? Our glorified ray of light went out the day that child… blah, blah, blah," I sassed.

He marched to the front door and swung it open. Adam checked his phone again and then stood.

"Let's go," he said to me. To Pastor Allen, he said, "Hey, thanks for the help today…"

The pastor ignored Adam's sarcasm.

With the door slamming behind us, we strolled to the car, our eyes absorbing everything. We spotted several barns on the property, three large greenhouses, and four silos of varying sizes and stages of decay. Next to the big house on the hill was your basic playground: a swing, a slide, and monkey bars. The corn and alfalfa fields surrounding the property appeared endless.

James sat up in the back seat when we reached the car. He was grinning from ear to ear. Adam got in the driver's side; my driving privileges had been revoked.

"Anything?" I asked, buckling my seatbelt.

"Didn't you get my text?" James asked.

I whacked Adam's arm and threw a questioning hand in the air.

"Jackpot," James said.

"Oh yeah!" Adam hooted.

To avoid hitting the golf cart, he threw the car in reverse. But why leave it unscathed? Adam peeled out, spinning a one-eighty. Dirt and stones flew everywhere, enveloping the golf cart and Pastor Allen, who was marching down the walkway.

We flew past all of the loyal community members, who looked more like soldiers to me now. This time, no one waved as we sped by. Instead, they threw their angry fists in the air and shouted for us to slow down. We laughed and hollered our goodbyes out the window. We were victorious after all. Mission accomplished. James found out where blondie was, and now we could get to her before Jones found out.

As we rounded the bend, we noticed the gate was closed. But Adam kept the pedal to the metal.

"Dude," said James. He tapped Adam on the shoulder. "Uh, dude. The gate."

Adam kept on it. "Open sesame!" he yelled.

Holy crap, he was going to crash through the gate. Someone somewhere needed to hurry up and push the open button before that happened. I braced myself for impact.

"Adam! Stop!" I hollered.

James continued to yell at him from the backseat as the big iron gate raced toward us. "You're going to wreck the car!"

"Screw the car. You're going to kill us," I said, my heart racing. I grounded my feet to the floor and braced for impact. "Adam, stop.

If you're trying to get back at me for the way I drove earlier, then I'm sorry. Honestly, I am."

He glanced at me and huffed, "I don't care about that. I think I can make it open."

His eyes grew wild; the smile never left his face. He was a devious child about to do something dangerous just to see if he could pull it off— no matter the consequences.

James and I had no time to respond to his impulsive idea. We were close to one hundred feet from smashing into the gate. Adam filled his lungs and let it out hard and fast like a fire-breathing dragon, except there was no fire. But there was energy. I could feel it.

A loud animal-like growl rolled off his tongue, and the gate smacked open with a bang. Barely setting foot on the brake, Adam fishtailed onto Cleary Road. James and I screamed in disbelief. But not Adam.

"How did you know that would work?" I asked, breathless.

"I didn't."

James' words dripped with sarcasm, "Gee, thanks for letting us be the guinea pigs in your fun little experiment. What an honor."

Adam tried to convince us that he was just about to put on the brakes so we wouldn't get hurt, but then the gates opened.

"Maybe the pastor opened the gates," he said. "But I swear, I did that. Did you see how they flew open? Did you see that?"

"Yeah. You totally did that," I said.

"HandClap" by Fitz and the Tantrums was quietly playing in the background. Adam blasted the radio, and the three of us began singing and clapping our hands along with the song. We were flying high from the adrenaline rush. After a few seconds, Adam clicked the radio off and caught James' eye in the rearview mirror.

"Yo, James. Where to?" Adam asked with excitement.

James sucked in a deep breath and said, "Oh, um, I'm not exactly sure."

"What do you mean?" I asked.

"I saw something."

"What exactly?" I asked again.

Adam slowed the car and snarled into the rearview mirror at James. He said, "Your text said you saw something."

"Um, I did. Sort of. I'm just not sure what it was."

Adam pounded the steering wheel. I sunk into the seat. The high-flying atmosphere in the car dropped like a cement block.

James said quickly, "I saw *something*. So yeah, it worked. I can't control what I see, you know."

I sighed. "Tell us everything."

CHAPTER 31

We couldn't blame James for not seeing clearly. None of us had true control over our abilities yet. Even Adam was still learning. While our celebration had been somewhat premature, there was hope that we could use what he saw and still find Areli.

After James recalled his brief description of the strange yellow, red, and gray blob on a piece of paper, we headed to The Green.

Settling at the table, I asked, "Was it gooey?"

"No, it was flat."

"Like marker on paper," I suggested.

"Gum on the street?" Adam asked.

"No. And no. It was mostly two-dimensional, with maybe a little texture. Except for the yellow. It looked like fur from a golden retriever." James thought for a second. "It's hard to explain. I couldn't interact with anything like before. It was a flash of something."

Suddenly, I had another idea.

"Come with me," I said, getting up from my chair. "Maybe we are stronger together, and whatever it was will be easier to see. Hopefully, our visit will still be fresh on Pastor Allen's mind."

James followed me. I took the old leather recliner in the corner, and he sat on the couch.

"Think about the pastor and the farm. And think about the little bottle of oil. That worked the last time," James said.

Adam stood in the middle of the room like he was guarding us. I sank back into the recliner and closed my eyes. I pictured the pastor's face and the intricate small yellow bottle that the oil came in when I was young. Within seconds, I was standing before a red blob surrounded by what looked like milk chocolate and melted marshmallows. Behind that was a gray, flat surface.

My eyes strained as if I was too close to something. I backed up to see it better. As I stepped back, an image appeared. Hoping James could hear me, I instructed him to do the same.

Soon, the gray turned into a wall, and the red blob turned into paint. The further back I stepped, the easier it was to see that this was a painting. A splotch of red oil paint represented a tear of blood dripping from a man's eye. The man resembled Jesus, but older with long white hair— the melted marshmallow. His skin was a medium brown— the milk chocolate— with pink lips and pink in his cheeks. His eyes were dark brown and sad.

Suddenly, a ribbon of blonde hair blew in front of the painting, and I realized I was standing to the left of someone. I turned to find a young girl, about eight or nine years old, with long flowing blonde hair and a tiny frame. Tears grew in her frightened eyes.

"Areli," James whispered. "This has to be her. Look around. See if we can tell where she is."

When I began to focus on the room, it became clear that we were in the rectory. But it looked different.

"They used to live in the rectory," I said. Then it dawned on me. "This is a memory, James. This was Areli when she got in trouble with her parents. That's what the pastor meant when he said she 'created the likeness of God' and gave Him 'color in the cheeks and emotion on His face.' She painted a picture of what she thought God looked like. And for this... this... amazing painting, she was excommunicated. They disowned her because of *this*."

My heart broke for this once young prodigy whose painting looked as though it could have hung at the Louvre. She'd painted a masterpiece, but the cost was losing her family. Granted, they were crazy. So maybe that wasn't such a bad thing in the long run. Still, the idea that someone could be that cruel to their child... Then I thought about my own mother and wondered who was worse.

The next thing I knew, I was staring at Adam.

"Anything?" he said.

"She's an artist. With her talent, I'd find it hard to believe she's not out there somewhere painting murals," I said.

After James and I explained what we saw, Adam said, "We should start at the art gallery. Max's cousin, Drew, is an artist. Been there a couple of times." Adam pulled the phone from his pocket and started thumbing away as he talked. "Not too long ago, they found someone dead in the basement. I'm not even sure if it's open anymore."

James nodded his head and cringed. "Yeah, I remember that story," he said.

"Paint and Party. That's what it was called. Max just texted me. He and Javi are meeting us at the gallery in fifteen minutes. Someone there might know where to find her. It's worth a shot. After that, we'll try the art program at the college."

"Wait," I said. Things were falling into place. "The gallery. Think about it. Jones said we've all been traveling in circles, just waiting to connect. And we did, right? At the gallery in February, when we were shocked by the glass wall. We were there," I said to Adam. "You and Max were there. And Chelsea was there. Areli must have been at the gallery too."

"Wouldn't Jones have seen her?" Adam asked.

"She left the farm years ago. She could have changed since he last saw her." I raised my brows at Adam and asked, "Have you changed in the last three years?"

"I grew four inches, gained fifty pounds, cut my hair…" He rubbed his fuzzy head. "Point taken," he said.

We headed back toward the park, where the art gallery was just up the road, overlooking the lake on the hill. Less than a mile down West Lake Road, we turned into the town recreation center that housed the art gallery.

When we got to the door, we were greeted with a sign that read, "Lakeville's Sheer Art Gallery: closed until August first."

"Great," I said. "Now what?"

Adam brushed past me and tugged the door handle. It opened.

"Can't let a little scribble on a piece of paper stop us," he said, holding the door open.

The smell of fresh white paint from opening night at the gallery was gone, but the oak beams which stretched across the ceiling still smelled like fresh-cut wood. Coat hooks lined the wall as we entered. There was a bench, two old wing-back chairs, and a small round coffee table just past the hooks.

The entryway opened to an empty larger event room where the first gallery opening had been. As we approached the double doors in the back of the room, we spotted a sign that read, "Welcome to Lakeville's Sheer Art Gallery." Slapped on top of that was a "closed" sign. One of the doors was cracked open, and we could hear shuffling around inside. My heart sped up.

"Please be the blonde," I mumbled, marching to the back of the room.

I gave a light tap on the door before we entered. A tall girl with short bouncy brown hair was removing a painting from the wall. She turned and greeted us.

Short jet-black bangs framed her face. She had a diamond nose ring and several black and silver bracelets running up her left arm. She wore capri jeans ripped at both knees with a black studded belt, a black flannel over a black t-shirt with a purple skull across the front, and a pair of platform military boots. This girl was a beautiful cross between goth and grunge.

"Sorry, we are closed," she hollered from across the room.

She turned her back to us like we would simply hear that and leave. Standing amidst several empty easels, she continued to remove pieces of art from the wall. Rows of natural wood shelving were empty. Scanty areas of pottery, ironwork, and small sculptures could be found here and there, but you had to search behind boxes. What was once a cool showroom of creativity was now a desolate ghost town of random artifacts.

"Can I help you?" the girl asked, realizing we hadn't left.

James and Adam began to wander, checking out the few remaining art pieces. I walked over to the lanky girl and said, "We're looking for Areli Weaver. We think she's an artist here."

"Never heard of her," the girl said. "I'm Megan, by the way. I'm one of the artists." She gestured to the empty easels, "We're shutting down for a few months. Someone passed away, so we all decided to take a little time to get ourselves together. We're storing a few things here until we reopen."

"I'm sorry to hear that. I'm Emma. This is Adam and James."

The guys came over and said hello to Megan. Adam recognized her.

"You're Reznor's girlfriend, right?" he asked.

"Hey, yeah." Her face lit up. "He's my guy."

"He's awesome," Adam said to us. "Reznor is the lead singer for Public Executioner. Have you guys heard of them?"

James shook his head no. But heck, yes, I had heard of them.

"Seriously? Wow. They are totally legit."

"They're pretty badass," Megan agreed. "Sorry I can't help you guys. I can ask around if you want."

"That would be great. Reznor has my number. Call me if you hear anything. We could really use her help," Adam explained. He pointed to me, "Kid has a school project. A friend told us Areli has experience with what she's looking for."

We thanked Megan for her willingness to help and started to leave when a painting caught my eye. I stopped.

"Hey," said James, gently tugging on my arm. "Come on."

The front door opened and closed, and then I heard the unmistakable voice of Javier talking to Max. Adam and James met them by the front door, but I was glued to the painting. I hadn't realized Megan was behind me.

"Ali Sheer did that. Most of the stuff still here is hers. She hasn't come to get it yet," Megan explained.

I tore my eyes from the painting.

"Ali Sheer? As in the Sheer Gallery? Is she the owner?" I asked.

"Sort of. Her family fronted the money to get it running. I haven't seen Ali since the accident here."

I sighed and said, "This painting is weird."

Megan shrugged like she could care less about the painting. I laughed with nervous breath.

I said, "I mean, it's weird *to me*. This looks like my living room."

The painting depicted a woman hunched over a man lying on the floor. His eyes wide, staring up lifelessly. Emptiness stuck on the woman's face.

"There is something creepy about this painting. Do you see it?" Megan asked.

"He's dead," I said matter-of-factly, pointing to the man.

She shrugged and said, "I don't know if he's dead. I meant the kid in the picture. You almost don't even see him. Can you find him?"

I immediately found the small child in a dark corner by a door. The child, dressed in tattered sweatpants, a dingy t-shirt, and an oversized vintage Boston Red Sox hat, stood watching the couple from the bedroom door. You couldn't see a face with the child's back to us.

I closed my eyes for a split second and felt the child's confusion, the stolen innocence, and the years of pain that would follow.

"There," I said, pointing to the bottom left corner of the painting.

"Wow. You're observant."

No, I thought. *That's where I was standing when I found them.*

CHAPTER 32

"It's a girl," I said softly.

Megan leaned in close to the painting and studied the child for a second. "Looks like a boy to me," she said.

I stared right into Megan's eyes. "That child is a girl."

"If you insist." She started to walk back to her art when she turned and asked, "Did you say you know Ali?"

"No. Why?"

"You seem to know this painting."

"It looks familiar. That's all," I replied.

I leaned in closer to study the painting that coincidentally, or not, spoke of my own life. Chills ran up my arms. The side of the child's dresser was visible in the doorway. On top sat a small intricate bottle. It was a fancy glass bottle you might have seen in the early 1900s when they took time to hand-craft beauty instead of mass-producing everything with machines.

That yellow bottle told me this painting was unquestionably *not* a coincidence. When I was little, I had a bottle exactly like it. It was *that* little yellow bottle of oil that infected James and me. I was sure of it.

"I don't remember this painting from the gallery opening back in February," I muttered under my breath.

"She hadn't painted it yet," Megan said. Then after a second, she said, "If you're interested in the painting, I can give you her number. Not sure if she's taking calls about her work, but it can't hurt to try."

"No, thanks." I stared at the painting, then shook my head. "Maybe I'll stop back in August."

She shrugged and walked away.

I found James in the other room, deep in a quiet conversation with Max. Javier and Adam had gone out to the parking lot.

"Hey," I said, tugging on his shirt sleeve. "Come here for a minute."

He nodded and told Max to hold his thought.

"Look at this painting," I said, pointing to the child in the corner.

James studied it for a second. "Hmmm. Look at that. Your team," he said, pointing to the Red Sox emblem on the back of the child's hat. He smiled, but he didn't get it.

"And?"

"And what?" he asked. "Go, Sox." He gestured toward Adam, Max, and Javier out the window, walking to their cars. "We should get going. This seems like a dead end for Areli. We're going to head to the art building in Geneseo. Max bombed on getting in touch with Chelsea. She lives right down the road, you know."

"James, I think this is me."

"What? In the painting?" He chuckled. "Do you know this person?" He bent to check out the signature. "Ali Sheer?" He stood straight and looked at me. "Sheer Gallery."

"Her family put up the money for the gallery. And no, I don't know her." We stood staring at the painting. "Could this have anything to do with that thing we do? I mean, do you see what I'm looking at here, James?"

His head cocked to the side, his eyes narrowed. Then, finally, he got it.

"These are your parents. Em, is this what you saw when your father died?"

"Exactly," I said. I pointed to the raggedy stuffed bunny on the floor. "I'm barely noticeable in the painting. Ironic because I was always barely noticeable to my parents. And there, that's BunBun. And look at that— the yellow bottle. Except I didn't get that bottle until after the funeral. As a matter of fact, it contained that smelly oil we spilled all over the place. Remember?"

"As in *the* oil?"

"It had to be. My aunt got it from the pharmacy. It was supposed to help with stress and depression. Remember, it spilled?"

"And I helped you clean it up before your aunt saw the mess. It got all over us."

I rushed over to Megan.

"Megan, I changed my mind about the painting. Can I have Ali's number, please?"

I put Ali's number in my phone. We needed to talk to Ali Sheer about her painting and how she came to steal my memory and paint it. James and I hurried to the parking lot to tell the others what we had discovered.

"We had to make her paint it. Somehow, we influenced her to do this. But why?" I wondered.

"And how?" Javier asked.

"When we subbed with Pastor Allen, we saw his memory. So maybe somehow you projected a memory onto Ali without knowing," James responded.

"Subbed?" Javier asked.

"That's what Max calls it. We are in our subconscious and the subconscious of others. So, yeah, subbing," I said.

"As if things need to get more complicated," Adam said.

"Not complicated," Max interjected. "Maybe she works with Jones or knows the pastor. She is connected to this. There could be more of us out there than even Jones knows. Call Ali, Emma. We need to meet her."

I immediately dialed Ali. She didn't answer, so I left a message about my interest in one of her paintings. I asked that she return my call as soon as possible. Megan hadn't sounded very confident that Ali would speak to me. Now all we could do was wait.

Feeling like we had hit a wall, we returned to The Green. We took our usual spots in the dungeon. I plopped down in the leather recliner in the corner, James on the adjacent couch. Max and Adam sat at the round wooden table in the middle of the room, and Javier leaned against the door jam.

Max rapped his knuckles on the table, stood up, and said, "Let's review what we have so far. We sat outside Chelsea's house for hours, and no one came or went. We think Areli is an artist in town, although we can't confirm that. Now we have Emma projecting her memories onto Ali Sheer, who, in a creepy move, turns around and paints them and could be a possible link to Areli." He clapped his hands together. "We have a whole lot of nothing. Perfect."

There was nothing but silence. We had been defeated. We were freaks, and we would never know why or what would happen next. Life as we knew it had changed forever. My curiosity and fear had become rage.

"We ran around all day like a bunch of gerbils on a wheel," I said, throwing my hands in the air.

"Look at the upside," began Javier.

"No, this sucks," said Adam. "You suck too, Javi. Nothing good came of today no matter how you spin it in your sunshine, whipped cream, unicorn, Jolly Rancher jelly bean, doe-eyed world."

Seconds of silence passed again as we pouted some more. Then Javier stuck his chin in the air and said, "Surely you meant to be cruel, Adam. However, that sounds absolutely delightful. And I love jelly beans."

We all snickered. Then my phone rang. It was Ali Sheer.

Her voice was angelic. It was melodic and soft but not too quiet. She spoke as if she hadn't a care in the world.

"This is Ali Sheer. You called about a painting?"

"Yes. Hi. I was at the gallery earlier and saw some of your work…"

"I should tell you, I'm not selling anything right now. I'm on a break from the gallery. I know a few of my things are still there, so I'm sorry if you misunderstood. The gallery is scheduled to reopen in August. If there's a piece you like, it will have to wait until then."

"Ali, wait!" I said before she could hang up. "My name is Emma Finewood. I want to ask you a few questions. That's all."

There was silence on the other end. Then she said, "Are you a reporter? I don't have anything to say to you."

"No, I'm not a reporter."

I bit my lip and glanced quizzically at the gang who hung on my every word.

"Then I'm not sure why you're calling."

"Like I said, I wanted to talk about one of your paintings at the gallery. The one with the man on the floor and the lady looking down at him."

Ali didn't speak, but I could hear her breathing.

"You know," I continued, "the one with the little girl watching her mother and dead father on the floor."

Ali remained silent.

"Hello? Are you there?" I asked, worried that she'd hung up.

"I know the one you're talking about," she said. "What is your question?"

My question? What *was* my question? How could I word it so she wouldn't hang up?

"Can we meet and look at it together," I asked. "I need to see it to ask the right questions."

"No. I can't go back to the gallery yet. I can't. Maybe in August..."

"Can we meet somewhere else?"

"I... I don't understand." Ali's voice rose and sharpened. "What is there to talk about? It's a painting I did a few months ago. It's called Life or Death. It's one hundred and twenty dollars, and you can buy it in August." With that, she hung up.

I sighed, "That was productive."

"What did she say?" James asked.

"Not much." I shrugged. "She called it Life or Death. Interesting name for the painting because, obviously, it should be called Death."

"Emma," Javier said, putting a comforting hand on my shoulder. "It could just be a strange coincidence."

"Thanks, Javi. But I stopped believing in coincidences."

I dialed Ali's number and let it ring until it went to voicemail. Then I called again. I called until, finally, she picked up.

"What?" she snapped.

"When I was nine, my father overdosed. My mother watched him die all night, too afraid to call for help because they were drunk out of their minds and high on all kinds of drugs. In the morning, I woke up, put on my favorite Red Socks hat, and grabbed BunBun. I walked out the door and into the hallway. That's where I found my father on the floor, staring blankly at the ceiling. My mother was hunched over him. I knew instantly that he was dead. BunBun fell to the floor, and I thought my life was over. So I will give you the answer to your painting's question. It's Death.

"Now I have a question for you, Ali. How is it that you happened to paint the worst day of my life, and you don't even know me?"

"I... I don't know. This is like The Angry Peach," she mumbled. "I can't believe this is happening again."

CHAPTER 33

I hit the speaker so everyone could hear along with me.

"What is The Angry Peach?" I asked.

"It's another painting I did. There was a girl who came to the gallery, and she saw my painting called The Angry Peach. It was very upsetting to her." Ali swallowed hard. "She said it depicted one of the most horrible days of her life. But I had no idea. It just came to me. The vision came to me so often that the only way to make it stop popping into my head was to paint it. As if putting it on canvas took it out of my head. That's what happened with Life or Death."

"You had a vision of this?"

"I did. For weeks. It wouldn't go away until I painted it."

Ali's sweet voice was now sad and confused.

"I don't mean to upset you. I'm just trying to understand how you did that."

"If you want it, you can have it. Just go get it. I'll tell Megan to wrap it up for you."

"No. I'm not saying I want it. And I'm not trying to scam you out of your painting. It's just so weird."

"I imagine it is. I'm not sure how this keeps happening." Ali sighed heavily. "Listen, when the gallery opens in August, please come to see me. I'd like to meet you."

Max and Adam were mouthing to me that I should try to meet her now. Max touched Adam and acted like he had gotten shocked. It wasn't a crazy idea. My oil had infected James, and Areli had been infected because of her mother. Ali could also be an innocent victim of Jones.

"Maybe we could meet sooner. I was going to head to Main Street Coffee. Can you meet me?"

Adam smacked my arm and pointed to the floor. He mouthed "here" and rolled his eyes.

"Or at The Green?" I said.

"Um… I don't know. I don't have a car."

"I can pick you up," I blurted out. Ugh— desperation was creepy. "I mean, Megan said you don't live too far from the gallery. I live close too."

"Then you've been to the gallery before now? Maybe we already met."

"I was there the night it opened back in February. But my friends and I were looking for a particular artist today. That's when we came across your painting."

"I understand why you'd be looking for Megan. Her drawings and sculptures are amazing."

"Yeah, her stuff is cool. But we weren't there for her. We were looking for someone else. Maybe you know her?"

"Maybe. We've had a lot of artists come through. It's been a great platform for them." She sounded sad again. "It's too bad we had to close for a while."

"How about it then? Can we meet today?"

"I have a lot going on at home right now." There was a pause. Then she said, "I suppose I can meet you next week. That would work better. The Green around noon Wednesday?"

"Wednesday? Is that the soonest you can meet?"

"I'm afraid so. I'm dealing with a lot right now."

"Okay. If that's the soonest. Do you need a ride?"

"No, thanks. I can get one. Or I'll take an Uber."

"Great. I look forward to meeting you. If anything comes up and you can meet sooner, please call me."

"Sure. And I'll grab the painting on the way."

"That would be great."

"I can look into that artist, too, if you'd like. What was her name?"

"That would be helpful. Her name is Areli Weaver."

"I'm sorry. Can you say that again?"

"Areli Weaver," I repeated.

"Areli Weaver?"

"Yes, do you know her?" The tone of Ali's voice gave it away. She did know Areli.

After a pause, she uttered, "Not anymore."

"We need to get in touch with her. If you can help us…"

"No. You can't get in touch with her." And just like that, she was gone again.

"Hello? Ali? Hello?"

My mouth dropped open. The conversation had been going so well. We were so close to making a positive connection with someone who might actually be able to help us. Darn that Areli Weaver.

"Maybe you lost the connection," Javier said. "Call her back."

I tried calling several times, but it went directly to her voicemail.

"I think she turned off her phone. What are the chances she still meets me at The Green on Wednesday?" I asked, slumping back into the chair.

I chucked my phone onto the couch next to James.

"Slim to none," said Adam. "I say we go back to the gallery first thing tomorrow and ask Megan where Ali lives. We'll pay her a visit."

"No," said Max. "Give her a chance. She seemed ready to meet with Emma and talk about the painting. Maybe she'll still show."

*   *   *

I had hoped Ali would call me before Wednesday and want to meet with me. However, the days came and went with no word from her. I tried calling her several times to no avail. Max found out where she lives and drove by slowly every time he went to Chelsea's.

By Tuesday night, I had had enough. All the waiting and hoping had become exhausting. We had all spent days at The Green brainstorming ideas on how we would get Chelsea and Areli to buy into what had happened with all of us. There was also the matter of how we would proceed with the Jake Jones situation once we were all together. But none of it mattered if we couldn't do two simple things: find Areli and get in touch with the elusive Chelsea.

197

Frustrated, I stood abruptly. "Since I am no longer in lockdown, I'm going home to sleep in my own bed tonight."

In unison, Javier and James said, "I'll drive you." They scowled at each other.

"Emma, I would feel better if someone stayed with you tonight," James said, gesturing toward himself.

"No problem. I am happy to stay with her," Javier said with a big smile.

"I wasn't talking about you. You betrayed Emma. Or did you forget? The last time she was in your care, you had Billy the Butcher beat the crap out of her," James said.

"In his care?" I repeated.

"That was unplanned. I had no idea he would try to harm Emma," Javier said, pointing at me.

My blood began to boil.

"I'm the one who had to save her from your unplanned beating, asshat," James said.

"All they wanted was that ridiculous report. A few sheets of paper. And let us not forget that you betray all of us. You agreed to tell Ty everything. And for all we know, you still plan to."

"I was trying to protect everyone. You, on the other hand, made money off of what he did to her!"

They were toe-to-toe now. I won't lie. Part of me wanted them to just throw down here and now. Get it over with. Spill the testosterone and blood and move on. Especially after implying that I was some kind of feeble child who needed to be cared for, protected, and saved. Adam and Max appeared to be thoroughly enjoying the show; no doubt, also hoping for a good fight.

As the macho showdown continued, I slipped out the door and made my way to the bar. I ordered a drink and dumped it into a plastic to-go cup. Halfway through the parking lot, Max caught up with me.

He put a hand on my shoulder and guided me toward his pickup truck.

"I'm heading your way."

Max reached for the cup in my hand. I took a quick swig of the Titos and water with lemon, then handed it to him. He drank a big gulp and dumped the rest. Then Max held the passenger door open for me.

Before closing the door, he said, "First, you don't need vodka. It's not you. Second, I'm going to check that your mom isn't home and that you have no other visitors in your house. Promise me you'll call one of us if you need something."

What I needed, no one could give me, I thought. Frankie and I might have had a relationship that seemed messed up to everyone else, but at least with him, I knew where we stood.

As it turned out, my mother wasn't home. It looked as though she hadn't been home in a few days. Max checked all the doors and once again headed to Chelsea's house. He was sure he'd run into her one of these times. According to him, it was statistically impossible not to.

I piled food into Novakitty's bowl. Then I cleaned the loaded sink full of dishes from the few times the banshee must have been here. Far be it for my mother to clean up after herself.

Evidence of her stellar cooking skills littered the counter. An empty macaroni and cheese box, half a can of SpaghettiO's, bread that had gone stale because she left it opened next to the package of moldy American Cheese. I swept up the Doritos and Fritos that crunched under my feet, then vacuumed Nova's hairballs that rolled across the floor like tumbleweeds in the breeze.

It was two in the morning before I went to bed. Even then, all I could do was think about Ali. Why did I have to bring up Areli Weaver?

The exchange between Adam and Max when I was on the phone with Ali popped into my head. They pretended to shock each other. Could Ali be like us? Could there be more kids like us than we originally thought? At that point, I supposed anything was possible.

At three in the morning, I got out of bed for a glass of water. I double-checked that the doors were locked and went back to bed, wondering if Max had gotten in touch with the elusive Chelsea. My mind didn't seem to want to stop. I thought I'd never fall asleep. Yet, at seven a.m., my alarm buzzed, pulling me from a few moments of rest. I hit the snooze button and tried to go back to sleep, but my phone kept vibrating.

I groaned. I had wanted another half an hour of sleep. But apparently, someone wasn't going to let that happen. I slapped my hand around my pillow until I found my phone.

"We need to talk now. Come to Long Point Park. Alone."

It was Dominic Ardemoni. Perfect. Just when I thought that wretched family was in my past, I found myself summoned.

CHAPTER 34

Even though I was curious about what Dom wanted, I responded that I was busy and probably couldn't get away. Dom wouldn't hear it. That created my dilemma: tell the guys and risk the consequences of meeting Dom with them by my side, or go alone and risk my life.

I texted Dom, "Just call me."

He responded, "I'm trying to help you! Meet me. ALONE."

I typed out that he was crazy if he thought I would meet him. Then I erased it.

I wrote "no way" and reminded him what he and Mario did to Javier and me at The Green. I erased that too.

I typed that he and his family were psychos and they needed to stay out of my life. Once again, I erased it.

"Fine," I typed. That one I sent.

I rolled out of bed. Despite my lack of sleep, it had been nice to snuggle into a clean set of sheets with my flat malleable pillow. Although the recliner and couch at The Green were fine in a pinch, I usually had to deal with a few hours of a sore neck the next day. I made my way to the kitchen. On my way past my mother's room, I peeked in. Her bed was untouched.

I downed a cup of coffee and tossed on a pair of worn jeans and my gray Dope Shirt hoodie. On my way out the door, I noticed the arm of my dad's old Genesee Brewery jacket sticking out from the closet. It seemed to call out to me. I tugged it from the broken hanger and threw it on. It was too big, but I didn't care. For some reason, it comforted me. Then I headed out the door toward Long Point–alone.

Javier would have given me a ride, but I had a couple of reasons for not calling him. First, Dominic would remember Javier from when they jumped us at The Green, and that would mean I broke his one command to come alone.

Second, I was still furious with Javier. I wanted to let it go, but it's not like we'd argued over pizza toppings or disagreed about politics. Because of Javier, I was almost beaten to death. Just thinking about it gave me an emotional blow to the stomach. Even though Javier was trying to help us and make up for what he did, it was hard to forgive and forget.

I walked through the village until the sidewalk ended at West Lake Road. The street was wet and muddy from the rain last night. Under a sky of gray, heavy clouds, I marched along with my hood up to shield my head from the spray of passing cars. The wind blew steadily, keeping me hedged in the damp, chilly air.

After thirty minutes of complete annoyance, I reached the park. Dom's yellow Corvette was the only car in the parking lot. As I checked my phone for the time and to see if any of the guys had texted me, the word "ALONE" jumped out from Dom's text message. My stomach pinged again, this time with dread.

I casually stuck my hands in my pocket. I fingered the Buck 110 hunting knife Frankie had given me for my birthday a few years back. This time, I came prepared for whatever popped into Dom's impulsive meat-headed brain.

I went directly to his car, but he wasn't there. I continued past the towering willow tree toward the park restroom and the pavilion and called out his name. Several blackbirds flew away from the water fountain, startling me. Again, I called his name, but he didn't answer.

As I headed toward the north end of the park, a cold mist started. A Livingston County Sheriff's Department trailer sat at the water's edge. I had hoped to see the Marine Patrol boat at their dock, but it wasn't there.

I was sure Dom wouldn't be waiting anywhere near the trailer, especially if he was up to no good. So I turned to head toward the beach area. That was when I thought I heard someone call my name. The voice was so quiet that I second-guessed myself. It could've been one of those annoying blackbirds. I scanned the park and didn't see a single person.

"Finewood," said a faint voice.

"Dom?"

"Over here," he said.

"Where are you?"

"Over here."

His voice was muffled and came from the direction of the restrooms. When I began to walk that way, I was surprised to see Dom in the window of the Sheriff's trailer. As I approached the front door, it swung open.

"Good girl. You came alone," he said.

"What can I say; I excel at following directions."

He ushered me in and pointed to an old wooden chair at a small metal desk. It was in the back corner of the room, which left me no means of a quick escape should I need one. I stopped halfway across the tiny trailer and leaned against a mini fridge. Dom shrugged and sat down in the rickety chair.

I threw my hands in the air, and breaking the uneasy silence, I said, "You call me here to show off your new place? I won't lie; you should hire a decorator."

He shook his head with half a grin. "You're such a smart ass, Finewood. I called you here with a proposal." His chair made a loud crack as he sat back. He quickly stood up. "What the heck? This place is a dump."

"Your choice. I would have been happy with a phone call."

I stiffened up as he stormed toward me, and through clenched teeth, he said, "I take it back. It's not a proposal. It's a gift. One that you need to take, or you and your idiot friends will suffer the consequences."

I could smell the hangover on his breath.

"And who is this gift from? You or Mama?"

"Consider it a gift from Frankie."

"Unfortunately, he's dead. Or I'd thank him for thinking of me."

Dom punched the wall inches from my head. On the outside, I didn't flinch. But on the inside, I was practically peeing my pants.

"Shut up, Finewood! Are you gonna listen to what I have to say or keep running your big mouth?"

"I'm listening," I said, slipping my hand into my pocket. I breathed in, soothed by the coolness of my weapon.

"Here's what you're gonna do. Go home, pack your bags, and go to Buffalo. Summer session at the University of Buffalo starts in a few weeks. You're a liberal arts major. You can change that later if you want. Don't matter to me. You pickin' up what I'm puttin' down?"

I shook my head no and asked, "Why would I do that? I have a scholarship to RIT in the fall."

"You'll get a full ride at UB. Carmella even arranged free room and board and spending money. Pretty generous gift. All you gotta do is show up."

"A few weeks ago, you and Mario tried to shut Javier and me up about Frankie's death. Now Mario's wife is pulling strings to get me a free ride to UB?"

"Good, you're hearing me."

"I hear you, Dom. But you are sadly mistaken if you think, for one minute, I'm accepting a *favor* from you and your family."

I slowly slid along the fridge to the wall, inching my way toward the door. He watched me, his eyes growing narrow and his mouth beginning to pout.

"I'll be going to RIT in the fall. Just like I planned. You know me better than that, Dom." When I finally reached the door, I said, "I don't take charity. I also don't respond well to threats."

When I opened the door and stepped out, Dom followed me. I was far from free yet. I had no means of getting away from him. I fingered the knife in my pocket as I skipped down the steps. Then keeping my eyes on Dom, I walked backward.

"We done now?" I nodded my head toward the road. "I have plans."

He shrugged, but the crap-eating grin on his face said we were far from done.

"Finewood, you know me better than that. There's a plan B if you choose to ignore this kind and generous gift."

My stomach flipped. Plan B was a term I hadn't heard in a long time. It was more than just the Ardemoni motto; it was their creed.

"Plan A would be Accepted because Plan B was Brutal and Bloody." I had heard it a thousand times growing up. It was cliche and sounded ridiculous when they said it, but that didn't mean it wasn't dangerous.

His father had said it about men who had wronged him. Dom, Anthony, Mario, and Mama had said it to people who crossed them. It was always true. Even Frankie had said it in high school. When Joey Carpenter didn't accept Frankie's suggestion to stop calling me, Plan B went into play. Joey Carpenter walks with a limp to this day. Bad things happened when Plan A wasn't accepted.

"Dom, I don't want to go to Buffalo."

"But you will."

"No. I won't. Plan B me if you have to. I'm not going."

I held my breath and prayed Plan B didn't go into action right then and there.

Dom shook his head. His eyes were sad for a brief moment. Then he smiled and pointed a stubby finger at me.

"All you had to do was walk away when I told you to. Anything that happens after today is on you, Finewood. I hope you can live with that."

"I loved Frankie. Why don't you think I would want justice for him too?" I snapped. "Just because I'm not blood?"

A smug grin grew across his face.

"Screw you, Dom! I loved him!"

Suddenly, a boat was approaching the cove and heading for the dock. Dom quickly began walking toward his car, leaving me frozen near the trailer. The Sheriff's boat pulled up and tied off. For a second, I considered telling the officer about Dom threatening me. Maybe I could have him arrested and get the family in trouble so they would leave me alone. Or, at the very least, if anything happened to me, the police would know it was the Ardemoni family.

"Go, Finewood," Dom said when he reached his car.

"Why can't you see we want the same thing?"

"Maybe we don't. That occur to you? Maybe Frankie didn't want the same thing as you, either. Hell, he didn't want the same thing as any of us. That was his freaking problem."

205

Dom got in the car and peeled out of his parking spot. The deputy stepped off the boat and asked, "Hey, was that Dom Ardemoni?" He smiled, shook his head, and said, "Gotta love that crazy guy."

"No," I said. "You don't."

Defeated, I walked away from the deputy.

About halfway home, my phone went berserk. It was almost ten; according to his text, Javier was planning to pick me up at ten thirty. Then the next text came in. James said he was coming to get me at ten thirty as well.

I shook my head and tilted it toward the cold mist. It now felt good as it hit my heated face.

"Boys are idiots," I whispered to the sky.

CHAPTER 35

Max pulled up next to me in his pickup truck.

"What are you doing out here?" he asked. Before I could answer, he popped the lock and ordered me into the truck. "Do you need to stop home for anything?" he asked.

"Definitely not," I responded.

I didn't tell him about Javier and James. They would have to deal with each other when they both showed up at my house. If I was lucky, my mother would be there to greet them. I giggled to myself at the thought.

"What's so funny?" Max asked.

"Nothing," I said with a grin.

He narrowed his eyes, then said, "I went to Chelsea's again this morning. No one is ever home. Seriously, never. It's weird."

"Does she have a job?" I asked. "Maybe we can go there and talk to someone."

"I haven't the foggiest idea. I met the girl once, instant spark, you know— literally. Not romantically."

"Uh-huh." My eyes rolled unintentionally.

"Then I ran into her in town Memorial Day weekend, and things…uh, things got romantic. Maybe. Sort of." Max cleared his throat, and his face turned red. "Now— nothing. It's like she vanished."

"What about Adam? He said he ran into her at the gas station once."

"Yes. But you know Adam. He doesn't always make a great first impression. So she refused to talk to him. He tried to follow her and lost her."

"How did you guys find Chelsea in the first place?"

"You know the gallery opening in February?" I nodded yes. "I don't remember seeing her, but Adam said he sparked with her when he handed her some keys. After that, I met her at the lake. She had fallen in, and I pulled her out of the water. That's when I sparked with her. Of course, I didn't know what that was."

Max's cheeks flushed. He glanced at me and smirked as he turned a corner.

He continued, "Then Adam saw her again at the scene of an accident, and they sparked again. By that time, we had been noticing our changes for months and figuring out that the shocks had to mean something. Then she came into The Green with some loser, and once more, they sparked. That's when Adam became convinced that she had to be like us. I didn't see her again until Memorial Day weekend. And you know how that went down."

"Maybe she's gone for the summer. That would suck."

"I asked Jones about her too. The idiot said I already know where to find her. Helpful guy."

"You should drop me off at The Green, then go back to Chelsea's house. Wait there. Someone has to show up. Knock on the neighbors' doors if you have to."

"I'll look like a stalker. You want me to end up in jail?"

"At this point, who cares if you look like a stalker? Think of a good story. Tell them she was supposed to meet you but never showed, and you're worried."

"You're right. I'm going to have to sit on that house today."

"It's not like we're going to see Ali anyway."

"If we're lucky, not only will she show, but she might bring Areli."

"That would be too easy," I said.

Just as we hit The Green, the sun came out. Steam eerily wafted from the hot wet pavement. The parking lot was already packed. We entered through the front doors, something we never did.

Adam was behind the bar, so I let Max talk to the hostess to see if Ali had come in, and I went to see Adam.

"She's not here," he said right off the bat.

"Why, I'm fine, thank you. How are you?"

"I'll be better if she shows up."

I glanced at my phone. "Still early," I said.

"So optimistic today. I thought Javier was picking you up."

"So did he," I said. "Max found me first. Maybe you guys should communicate a little better. I'll take a coke, please."

Adam poured me a coke and grinned.

"This is going to be another long day. I can already tell."

Max took a stool next to me and ordered Titos and water.

"It's not even noon yet," I said.

"My brain hurts. I need to dull the pain."

I sighed. "We're wasting time by sitting here and waiting for Ali to show up. She's not coming."

Max's phone buzzed. He checked the message and glared at me.

"Did you know they were both going to pick you up?"

I shrugged.

He started to text frantically. When he was done, he put his phone down on the bar. I could see that he had been texting James. I only caught the words "Ass beating," so I grabbed the phone.

"I was joking. He's not really going to do it," Max said, laughing. "You should see your face."

I punched his arm. "Not funny. He might do it."

Max took his phone from me and texted, "FYI: that was a joke. Do not beat Javi's ass— today."

James didn't respond.

A few explicit words toward Max fell out of my mouth like there was a hole in it.

"I see why those boys can't help themselves," Adam said, nudging my shoulder as he walked behind me. "You're so incredibly lovable."

"Very funny."

"Look," Adam said, "If you like one of them, you should just tell them. Then maybe they will stop fighting over you."

"Because I have time to think about any of that, right?"

"That answers that question," Adam said. "If you liked either one, you wouldn't have to think about it."

209

"Unless she likes them both," Max said. "And that would be normal. Only three to five percent of mammals form a monogamous bond. Of all the species…"

Adam held a hand up to put a halt to Max's spiel.

"Don't you have a girl to stalk?" I asked Max.

He slid off the stool and said, "As a matter of fact, I do. I will see you guys later. Hopefully, with Chelsea."

We wished him luck, then not ten minutes later, I got a mysterious text from Max ordering Adam and me to the basement immediately.

"For real?" Adam said. "Didn't we just see him walk out the front door?"

I rolled my eyes and sighed. When we got downstairs, Javier was sitting in my recliner, chewing on a fingernail.

"At least you don't look beat-up this time," I said.

"I found him in the parking lot. The guy is a wreck. He won't talk to me," Max said. He pointed a finger in my direction. "He wanted you."

When I asked what had happened, Javier simply shook his head. But I could feel it.

"Is it James?" I asked.

"Oh, Emma." Javier rushed over to me and took my hand.

"Did something happen to James? Talk to me."

My heart flopped around in my chest. Javier's mouth turned upside-down, and his eyes narrowed. His breath raced. All I could do was imagine the worst.

I dropped his hand. "Javi, what?" I demanded.

"James is gone, Emma. He and I were fighting, arguing in your driveway. A red van pulled up with a bunch of guys. They took him."

"Who were they," Adam asked. "Did you get a good look at them?"

"It could have been the Gallaghers, but I cannot be certain. I did not recognize anyone from the other day. It all happened so fast. I am very sorry, Emma. They hit him on the head. Hard." Javier hesitated, then he said, "With a baseball bat. There was a lot of blood."

My hand flew to my mouth. "Oh my God." I swung around to Adam. "What do we do? We have to help him."

Adam stood glaring at Javier. "Did you have anything to do with this?"

"Me? No. I swear," Javier said, placing one hand on his heart. "One minute, he and I were arguing, and the next, he was gone. I had nothing to do with it." Pressing his palms together, he begged, "Emma, believe me. I know I did wrong by you a few weeks ago. Please know that I learned my lesson. I would never do anything to hurt you or those you care for."

Javier stepped away from me and uttered, "I know how much you care for him. I do."

Deep down, I knew this boy would never purposely hurt a soul. I had been holding on to so much anger, and it was time I let it go.

That's when a terrifying thought popped into my head.

"This is plan B," I uttered. I turned to Max and Adam. "This is my fault."

"How is this your fault?" Adam asked, pacing the floor.

"I met with Dom in Long Point Park this morning." I looked at Max. "That's where I was coming from when you picked me up. He warned me." My voice wavered. "I should have listened. This is my fault."

"Dominic Ardemoni?" Max asked.

I nodded. I couldn't look them in the eyes.

Adam said, "Dom Ardemoni. That's..." Adam glanced at the ceiling.

"Bad," I said, finishing Adam's sentence. "That's very bad."

"Um, yeah. You dated his brother. Don't you have any pull?" Max said.

"Pull?" I scoffed at his silly question. So much for being a genius. "I turned down Dom's offer this morning. This is my punishment."

"Then take him up on the offer. You must call him," Javier chimed in.

I nodded my head. There was no question now. I had to take the offer to save James. I had to leave Lakeville and head to Buffalo immediately.

"Wait," Adam said. "What was the offer?"

With a heavy heart, I said, "That's the thing. It's not just me who will be affected by this. It's all of us."

"Whatever it takes," Javier said.

At that moment, I realized something about Javier. I always knew he was a sweet guy. Sincere and caring. Did he make dumb mistakes? Sure he did. We all make mistakes. But Javier, despite how he felt about me, wanted nothing more than for James to come home safe. Even if that meant I chose him over Javier. A lot of guys would have been happy to say sayonara to the competition. But Javier genuinely wanted to help James. His heart wasn't made of silver; it was made of gold.

I found myself drawn to his kind eyes. My hand touched his cheek. "You're so good, Javi," I said.

Max cleared his throat and broke the silence. "Are you going to tell us what we have to do to get James back?"

"Yes," I replied. "We have to stop looking for Areli. And I have to leave town."

Adam shook his head.

"Dom got me into the University of Buffalo. Full scholarship. I have to leave immediately. And all of you have to forget about what happened to Frankie."

"No way," Adam said.

"The Ardemonis have some kind of conflict with the Gallaghers and their connection to Jones. I don't know what it is, but somehow, we're screwing things up for them. So either they take us out one by one, or we drop this," I explained.

"Are we supposed to believe the Gallaghers will accept that?" Max scoffed. "They want the ring of fire ceremony over and done with immediately. A deadline of less than one month, to be exact. Don't forget that they're in this for a big and long overdue paycheck. Where does that leave us?"

"Dead either way," Adam pointed out.

"No. We have to walk away and let the Gallaghers and Ardemonis fight this battle," I replied. "That's the only way."

I headed out the door and started up the stairs. Wasting no time, I was off to pack.

"Wait!" Javier hollered to me. I should have kept going, but I paused as I stepped outside and into the parking lot. "There must be another way," Javier said.

I shook my head and walked toward his car. Javier's sneakers echoed in the stairwell as he hurried after me.

He closed in on me and said, "It is not like you to give up. There is a bigger issue at stake. Bigger than you and me."

Javier's accent was thick, his voice deep and sincere. His words pulled relentlessly at my heart.

"Bigger than James?" I asked without looking back.

"Bigger than all of us."

He took my hand and tugged me to a stop.

I looked him straight in the eyes and said, "You don't understand, Javi. My mother is my only family, which is a joke. I mean nothing to her. I'm a burden she can't wait to get rid of. I've spent my entire life with only two people who cared, two real friends. Just two. And I have always been okay with that."

A tear welled up in the corner of my eye. Javier took my other hand. He held them both and had that…that look in his eye. I cringed. For a second, it looked like pity. As if he felt sorry for me. Then his eyes softened.

I thought about how he lost his parents and left his country to start over and live with an aunt and uncle he barely knew when he was just a child. If anyone could understand the fear and pain I felt at that moment, it was Javier. Just as Max and Adam appeared in the doorway, the urge to push him away faded.

My gaze washed over each of them, and I said, "Now I have what I never dreamed of having. I have all of you. You're like a real family. I've already lost Frankie, and I can't lose James too. Or any of you, for that matter. You guys are all I have in this world. So is it like me to give up? No." I glanced at each precious face before me, then said, "But this isn't giving up. This is the only way to keep you all safe."

"We won't let you leave," Adam said. "A full scholarship sounds great. And if that's what you want to do with your life right now, then go. We'll support you. But we aren't going to let this drop, Emma. Leaving is no guarantee that James or any of us will be safe. And there's something else you need to consider. The payback. What will you owe them after you've taken the free ride to school?"

"I thought of that. But sending me to Buffalo is their way of getting rid of me. It's my punishment. I won't owe them anything for banishing me."

"That's not the way they're looking at this. They're criminals, Em. Don't play their games. You won't win," Adam urged.

"None of us should be pawns in this game, Adam." I walked over to him and placed my hand on his chest, paying no attention to the shock. "But we are. And right now, I can make a move that will save lives. I'll hate every minute of leaving. But if it means that today James comes home safe, then I'm already gone."

Suddenly, someone came pounding up the stairs behind Adam and Max. The hostess stuck her head out the door and said to Adam, "There's a girl here. She's looking for Emma."

Adam looked down at me, then leaned in, and with a sarcastic grin, he uttered, "It looks like you're not going anywhere just yet."

CHAPTER 36

I sat across from Ali Sheer at a dark table in the corner of the bar. Her long, tousled, mousey brown hair glistened with red and green tones from the tiffany drop light over the table. She was skinny, but not in a healthy, athletic way, more like in a starving child way. Her impeccable sense of fashion offset her dull physical appearance. She was such a bazaar contradiction.

I removed my father's old jacket, smoothed down the front of my hoodie, and pushed the hair from my eyes. Ugh. What must she think of me?

Then the waitress came and took our drink order.

"I almost didn't come," she said softly. She raised her eyebrows. "But I'm curious."

"I'm glad you came. I'm sorry if I offended you in some way. And we don't have to talk about anything you're uncomfortable with."

She flashed an ill-at-ease smile that made her look like she wanted to crawl out of her skin.

Adam was behind the bar where Javier and Max bellied up with menus. They casually glanced over at us. I looked away. For obvious reasons, I was drastically afraid she would leave before I had a chance to get answers. One wrong move, one stupid comment, one misinterpreted glance in the wrong direction... Who knew what would set her off?

When my coke and Ali's iced tea showed up, it was a relief from the silence. She ordered a caesar salad. Seriously worried that a cheeseburger would have offended her, I followed suit. I mean, she could be a vegetarian. That said, I let her lead the conversation.

"Are you an artist? Megan said that was why you came to the gallery?"

"No. I like to draw sometimes. That's it. Your painting, though— that's amazing."

I tried to make her comfortable talking about the painting.

"I think I was initially drawn to it because it was so sad. You brought out a lot of emotion in that painting." I channeled the one art class I took in high school. I waved my hands in the air as if I were actually painting. "The way you were able to tell such a, um, story. You know, with the vibrant colors and the, uh, with your choice of texture."

Then feeling stupid, I paused, hoping for her to jump into this with me. *Geez, help a girl out, Ali.* But she just sipped her tea and waited for me to finish.

"Did I mention the emotions? The people in the painting, they just…" I grabbed my shirt at my chest, "They tugged at my heart."

She studied my face as she put down her glass. "You don't know anything about art, do you?"

"Nope. Not a thing. I never seemed to make it to that class."

"As you can see, I didn't bring the painting. We should talk about it first. I'm curious about your connection to Life or Death."

Curious, huh? How do I respond to that? The exact words that ran through my head were, "*Well, weird little girl, who I have never met in my entire life… Let's start with the obvious fact that you painted my dead father on the floor with my murderous mother hovering over his body. Or the fact that you managed to capture the single most pivotal moment in my life that changed the world as I knew it forever in one creepy painting.*" But, of course, that's not what I said.

"Umm, I'm curious myself," I sputtered.

"You mentioned a specific personal connection on the phone."

I nodded.

"You said it has to do with an event in your life?"

"Yup."

"A while back at a Paint and Party Gala, another girl said the same thing about one of my other paintings. She said I had painted a significant piece of her past, right down to the finest detail. I told her she could have the painting, except she didn't want it. I tried to give it to Megan, and she wouldn't take it either. I don't know why these things seem to happen. I never meant to hurt anyone."

"Megan from the gallery?"

"Yes, Megan Raleigh."

I gestured to my hair, "The girl with the cute bobbed hair. The emo, alt-rock girl?" Ali nodded. "Why would you give it to her?"

"Sorry. I assumed you knew her."

"Her last name is Raleigh?" I said, consciously closing the gap in my thoughts.

"Yes. Her sister, Chelsea, seemed tortured by my Angry Peach painting."

"Chelsea Raleigh is Megan's sister?" I gasped.

Ding, ding, ding. Of course, she is!

Ali went on to explain that Chelsea is Megan's younger sister, and she only met her that one time. Chelsea lost it when she saw the painting. She claimed it was a painting of her specifically. As she spoke, I was processing the fact that Ali has a significant connection to this whole thing. I had to figure out what it was. I had to know how she knew Areli Weaver.

When Ali finished her spiel about Chelsea, Megan, and The Angry Peach, I excused myself to use the bathroom. I snagged Max's shirt as I went by to signal for him to follow me. A few seconds later, he was outside the restroom door.

"Megan from the art gallery is Chelsea's sister."

"For real? Ali told you that?"

"Yes. Ali painted a picture of an event in Chelsea's past, and it totally freaked her out. This is too weird."

"Can I come and talk to her?"

I whacked him on the chest. "No. Are you crazy? We have a good conversation going over there. I need to know more. She *must* know where Areli is. But look at her."

One glance at Ali and Max couldn't deny it. As she gnawed on her lower lip, her foot and fingers tapped in unison. Max winced.

I said, "She's a nervous wreck. I'm afraid if I say one wrong thing, she might leave."

"Make it the last thing you talk about. I'm going to find Chelsea. If she's not there, I'm going to the gallery to look for Megan."

"Got it. Go."

We broke off and went our separate ways. When I returned, Ali was sitting politely in front of her salad, waiting for me before starting her meal.

I stabbed at my salad. "Back to Megan. She has a super funky sense of style. In a good way, I mean. I wish I could pull it off." I poked at a crouton. "I didn't know Megan had a sister," I said, stuffing the lettuce and crouton into my mouth.

She stopped chewing, wiped her mouth, and said, "Yes, Chelsea is not quite as unique with her style as Megan. And she's nice, even though she was upset by the painting."

I nodded my head and hoped she would just keep talking. Interrogation wasn't really my thing. She explained that Megan had her teaching degree. When the gallery opened, she decided to give freelancing a go before pursuing, as Megan had put it, "a dead-end teaching career."

Ali said Megan had seen the painting hours before Chelsea. All Megan had said was that it looked like her grandparent's farm and that she thought it was cool. She had even considered buying it for her father for his birthday. Then Chelsea saw it and freaked out. According to Ali, Chelsea seemed almost afraid of it.

"A friend of mine knows a girl named Chelsea. She lives on the lake. Probably not the same one, though. There must be a ton of Chelsea's in Lakeville." I waved off the idea. My acting skills were definitely improving.

"She's the only Chelsea I know. And she lives on the lake with her parents. Up the road a bit from me, not too far from the gallery. So it could be the same girl. It's a small world, you know."

"Yes, probably smaller than we think."

Ali put her fork down and sat back. I glanced up from my salad and smiled at her. She seemed to be studying my face.

"How's your salad?" I asked.

She crossed her arms and cocked her head to the side. "You seem nice. But I sense there's more to this than just your interest in my painting and your connection to it."

"Oh?"

"Mm-hmm."

Since she brought it up (with a hint of attitude), I said, "Alright then. I *am* wondering how it is that you paint the memories of others." I threw my hands in the air. "And I'm not trying to upset you. Any ideas? I mean, have you talked with anyone I might know? Someone who could have given you certain details. Like my mother, Tracy Finewood, maybe?"

She shook her head and said, "No. It just popped into my head. I can't explain it. To be honest, the real reason I came today was not out of sheer curiosity. It doesn't even have anything to do with that painting either."

Tell me about Areli, I thought. That had to be why she showed up.

"I was hoping you could help me with a vision I keep having. I wondered if it had anything to do with you. Then I walked in and saw that guy." Ali pointed to Adam behind the bar. "Now I know it must have something to do with you.

"It started after you called the other day, and I can't get it out of my head. It's… it's pretty awful. I'm almost afraid to paint it. But I think I'll have to because it won't stop. Every time I close my eyes, every time I blink, it's there." She closed her eyes and shuttered. Her eyes popped open. "It won't stop."

Crud. This wasn't the conversation I wanted to be having. With the breath I'd been holding, I asked, "And?"

"You may find this hard to believe, but that guy at the bar," she pointed to Adam again, "did something terrible." She sat up straight and leaned in. Hesitantly, she whispered, "He killed someone."

"Adam? No, he wouldn't do that." I glanced over at him, drying a glass and shooting me half a grin. "He can be an arrogant jerk at times, but a murderer? Definitely not."

"There's another guy too. But I don't see him here." Ali squinted in Adam's direction. "I keep seeing the same thing. It's always the same. It's him."

Again, she pointed to Adam.

Then Ali's eyes shifted to the table, and staring at her knife, she said, "Two guys are standing at the end of a dock looking down into the water. There's a man in the lake at the base of the dock. He is under the water, staring up. Lifeless eyes. Gaping mouth. Blood floats all around him. Adam's friend just watches. The old man is dead, and they don't care."

Suddenly, Ali seemed to snap out of her trance-like vision. Her overcast eyes glowered at me, and she muttered, "He is a murderer, Emma. Something is wrong with him."

"If the guy in your vision is already dead, how do you know Adam did it?"

"His hand is red with the old man's blood. It's hard to explain. He has this smug look on his face. And the look on his friend's face isn't shock, it's satisfaction. They're happy the man is dead. It feels all wrong."

I glanced at Adam, innocently serving a man and woman lunch at the bar. He smiled at them. I read his lips as he told the couple to enjoy their food. Is it true? Was this big, burly, adorable bear of a man a murderer? He was the volunteer fireman who helped when I crashed my car. Adam was the "come-to-the-rescue hero" who saved Javier and me when we were jumped in the parking lot. Adam— the smart-ass, quick-witted, completely loyal, and fearless friend. There was no way he had killed someone.

Maybe I was mad that Ali was accusing Adam of murder. Maybe I had simply had enough for today. Whatever the cause for my sudden directness with Ali, I could no longer hold back.

"Since we're being so open, I have a question for you. I need you to answer it. Not run away. Not give me a bunch of cryptic bull crap that you expect me to figure out myself. And certainly not a freaking lie. I need an honest, straight-out, truthful, clear-cut answer. Can you manage that?"

"First, let me say, about Adam…"

"Just stop. Will you answer one question for me or not?"

Ali was silent for a second. Part of me was preparing to chase her down should she decide to run. The fact was that when it came time to leave The Green, I'd have only two choices. Two places to go. I was either going home to pack, leave my mother a note, and head to Buffalo. Or I was never going home again. Because chances were, I would be back in hiding, and I wouldn't be alone. I was done beating around the bush and following her lead. I was going to get answers before I made my choice, and that was going to be by the end of lunch with Ali Sheer.

"Fine. If I can answer it, I will."

"This is a simple question. One that I am confident you can answer."

Ali picked up her tea and sucked the last of it from the ice in the bottom of the glass. She shook the ice as if hoping to find a little more tea. When she put it down, I asked her.

"Where is Areli Weaver?"

She leaned forward with her elbows on the table. "Why do you want to find her?"

"Don't answer me with a question. Where is she?" I demanded. "I need to talk to her. Today."

Ali shrugged. "I'm sorry to disappoint you. Areli Weaver died a long time ago."

"She's not dead. Someone told me to find her. She must be alive. Tell me where she is."

"She lived on the farm, United with Devotion. And that's where she died."

She was convincing. I wanted to believe her, but she had to be lying. Jones wouldn't send us looking for her if she was dead. Unless he didn't know.

"How did she die?"

"I don't know the graphic details. Rumor is that she was sent into a cornfield and got lost. By the time they found her, she was gone."

"How do you know this?"

"Why are you asking about her?"

"How do you know Areli?" I demanded.

"I knew her a long time ago."

"Did you live on the farm too?"

"I think you've asked enough questions. And I answered yours. She's dead."

I slumped back in the booth, having once again hit a wall. On the upside, if Areli truly was dead, that could solve our problem. According to Jones, he needed all of us to complete the ring of fire. If one of us were dead, his sick plan was history. *That* might get the Ardemoni family off my back and set James free. However, Jones must have a reason to believe Areli was alive, or he wouldn't be wasting his time. She had to be lying.

"I need her," I said. I leaned forward and jabbed my finger in her direction. "And I promise you, I won't stop until I find her. Either you can tell me where she is, or I will stalk you, day in and day out until you tell me. This isn't about me *wanting* to talk to her. I literally *need* her. So you decide; stalker or no stalker?"

She shifted uncomfortably in her seat. I seemed to have hit a nerve. She stole a glimpse of Adam nervously. Then she scowled at me and said, "She's dead. Do you not understand what that word means? Stalk away, but unless you can raise the dead, you're out of luck."

Ali nabbed her sweater, threw a twenty on the table, and stormed out of the restaurant.

Adam came rushing over. "What the heck? I thought things were going good."

"They were. Then she lied."

CHAPTER 37

I went home to pack. For now, it was for show, in case the Ardemonis were watching me. They had to think I was leaving so they wouldn't hurt James or anyone else, for that matter.

Adam agreed to meet me with Javier tonight at my house. The plan was clear now. If Ali used to live at the farm with Areli, what better head to jump into than Pastor Allen? If lucky, I would catch him off guard. And if that didn't work, the next step was to go directly into Ali's mind. That could prove to be challenging, though. She knows something, and she's clearly guarded about the whole situation. But I had to try. And since I didn't have much experience doing this alone, it wouldn't be easy.

Max checked in from operation Chelsea throughout the day. Apparently, she was pretty much MIA. He went to the neighbor's house and spoke to an elderly couple who found him highly suspicious. They asked if he was her mysterious boyfriend, which threw Max into a nasty mood. Eventually, he gave up and came to my house.

I was nervous doing this without James. But desperate times meant desperate measures. Max and Adam argued about where I should start. Max said we should start with Ali instead of the pastor, but Adam was afraid that would spook her.

I didn't tell anyone what Ali told me. No one else needed to think Adam was a murderer. It was a ridiculous notion to believe he killed someone. It wasn't fair to put doubt in anyone's head.

There we were, sitting around my living room at eleven fifteen. Novakitty had curled up on Javier's lap and fallen sound asleep. Max was on his phone researching essential oils, DNA, and stories related to people who claim to have had special abilities throughout modern and ancient times. All while Adam dug through the cupboards in search of food and vodka. The start time was set at eleven thirty p.m.

"I don't think I can do this," I said, standing up and pacing the floor. "I have never successfully done this on purpose without James. I think I need him to be able to control this."

"Won't know unless you try," Adam said, his head in the fridge. "Got any lemon?"

"Bottom drawer," I responded. "What if I make matters worse?"

Max stopped scrolling through his phone and pointed to the suitcases next to the door.

"It can't really get worse."

"Emma, you must believe this will work. Even Doctor Jones said you were the key to finding Areli Weaver," Javier said as he scratched Nova's chin.

"Maybe this is a test," I said. "What if Areli is dead, and he knows that? Maybe he is trying to string the Gallaghers along. Then again, what if he truly thinks she is alive, and she's actually dead? We should tell him."

"No. Bad idea. Max, want a Complete Vodka with lemon?"

"Complete Vodka?" Max said.

"No Titos," Adam explained.

"I want one," Javier said surprisingly.

"If that's all she's got," Max responded. Then, he turned to me and snarled, "Complete Vodka?"

"What can I say? My mother's not picky about what she washes her pills down with."

The clock on the end table read 11:26 p.m.

"Maybe we should wait until midnight," I mumbled. "Just to be sure the pastor is asleep."

"Emma, chill. You got this," Adam said. He held his glass out to me. "Sip? Maybe it will help you relax." I shook my head no. Adam shrugged and said to Javier, "You and your buddy get off the couch. Emma needs room."

Javier picked up Nova and pulled a chair in from the kitchen. He sat down, placing Nova back on his lap. "You need to think positive," he said.

I sat back on the couch and propped my head up with a pillow. I closed my eyes. Peeking at everyone through one eye, I said, "I feel so dumb." I giggled and closed my eye.

"Be serious," Javier said.

"I know. I'm sorry." I said, straightening my nervous grin. "But I can feel you all staring at me. So stop."

I peeked an eye open again, and everyone was looking at the ceiling or the wall. I closed my eye and sighed. I tried to focus on the pastor. But no matter what I did, my only thought was of James.

"I knew you'd look for me," I heard.

When I opened my eyes this time, I was back on the beach. The warm water lapped against the shoreline, and the sun sat just at the horizon, neither going up nor down.

"I tried to think of the pastor," I said, looking into James' golden brown eyes. "You kept popping into my head."

"I was thinking of you. It will be great when we figure out how this craziness works." James touched my cheek. "Remember when we met here before we understood what was happening? Just two people meeting for the first time."

A warm breeze brushed by me. "Although it felt like I'd known you forever."

"You didn't know who I was. There was no past getting between us. There was no Javier. There were only our true feelings." James looked down at his feet.

Being here made it easy to remember the strong feelings I'd had for him. They were innocent and pure. And it had felt new, even though it had always been there. We hadn't a problem in the world. I was sure he longed for that feeling again, just as I did. But we had a dark cloud looming over us. And it had to be dealt with before we could move forward.

"Do you think we can find the pastor here?" I asked.

"I believe we can. Be open-minded. We have to use our re-sources."

"Got it. What are we waiting for?" I grabbed his hand and began to drag him to the yellow dandelion trellis. "I know this didn't work the last time. But this is the way. I can feel it."

"Wait," he said, stopping abruptly. "I have to tell you something first."

"Time is different here; we need to hurry."

"This is important." James pulled me close. "For this to work, where we all come out alive, you have to trust me."

"I do trust you."

"No matter what you think, are told, or are led to believe, always remember there was a reason. And for me, it's that reason that matters most."

The finality of his words worried me. "What's happening, James? I am assuming you've been taken by the Ardemonis. Am I wrong?"

He ran his hand down my cheek.

"One day, I will be able to explain it to you. For now, please don't ever forget how much you mean to me. You are the only thing keeping me strong enough to get through this. Just don't lose faith in me."

"You're scaring me."

Just then, the ground shook, and James' sunny sky went black. Without warning, he wrapped me in his arms and kissed me. It was five seconds of heaven.

Before I had time to think about the blackout or the kiss that came with it, James had whisked me under the trellis. And instead of ending up back on the beach, we were on the farm, standing in thick fog in front of Pastor Allen's hilltop home.

We ascended the steps to the wrap-around porch and noticed someone on the swing.

"I don't know why anyone would want to find her," the pastor said, scooting from the swing. He tapped it to stop it from moving, then turned back toward us. A creepy shadow from the porch light formed on one side of his face. "You c-c-came here for her, and she is long g-gone. She is no one to us."

James responded, "She is someone to us. We need to find her. I don't care about your differences. I don't care what happened between the two of you. Just tell me where she is, and you will never have to hear her name again."

"You're not the only one looking for her. I know what people think. They think we should have stood by her, been more lenient. But she was our g-g-greatest test. And we passed. We did what we were supposed to do to protect the g-g-greater g-g-good."

"Who else is looking for her?" I asked.

"Why Doctor Jones of c-c-course. He c-came here first. I told him she was g-g-gone. But he refused to believe me. We did the right thing, you know. We are all better off without her. That includes you."

"Is she dead?" I asked, point blank.

"Yes. Very much dead to us."

"No, I mean truly dead. Not alive. Buried. Cremated. Dead dead."

The pastor looked at us sorrowfully and said, "She was shameful, sinful, a demon in disguise."

"Why can't anyone just answer the freaking question?" I muttered, rolling my eyes.

"When someone leaves this farm, which rarely happens, they are c-c-c-considered dead. So that is the answer you will g-get every time."

On a hunch, I threw an implication out there, hoping for him to catch it. "Still, you must feel bad for sending your daughter away, out into the world all alone."

From the corner of my eye, I caught James' head snap in my direction. It was a risky move, and I could blow this whole thing by being so blunt, but he was also in a dream state. That meant his reactions could be very different than expected. The pastor didn't even think twice.

"No. I don't feel bad. She was Lilith, Jezebel, the devil himself sent here to test me. I am only ashamed that it took me so long to rid the c-c-community of her ung-g-godliness."

"She was a child."

"An evil child. Not all children are innocent, you know. And she wasn't a child when she left. G-God punished her with the death of her bastard child. In the end, He will always reign. He will always make right what the sinners try to destroy."

The pastor went on and on as if we weren't even there. He paced in front of the swing and continued talking, mostly to himself. It was like he was trying to justify what had happened.

"When all was said and done, we had learned from her nefarious ways. We are a stronger c-community. Our children will hear the tales of Areli the Harlot for years to c-c-come and take it as a fair warning and an example of His great tests. And now she c-c-can be the test for others. All the unsuspecting lost individuals, whose souls are up for g-g-grabs, will be taken by her."

The pastor sucked in a breath like his lungs had been empty. "God help them all," slowly drifted out of his mouth into the cool night air. He collapsed onto the swing. It swung back and sideways as he sat limp and exhausted.

"Have you warned anyone on the outside?" I asked.

"That is not my responsibility."

"Isn't it? You're a man of God. You do his work for him. Would He not want you to save others from the suffering she will cause them?"

The pastor's face went white, and he shot to the edge of the swing.

"Did He send you here?" he asked incredulously.

Bingo!

I glanced at James and said confidently to the pastor, "Have you asked yourself that question?"

It was impossible to lie here, so I said nothing. The pastor stared into my eyes as if searching for some kind of truth. I sensed he believed that I had a connection to the God he served. So despite his uncomfortable soul-diving glare, I didn't look away for even a second. Eventually, his head dropped in shame.

"No. No, I have not," he uttered.

"Then how will you proceed?"

"As I should."

"Has it occurred to you that He sent us here not to fix what you have done but to help you and guide you to fix it yourself?"

He stood again, the swing rocking behind him. He pleaded, "Please, I pray every day that He will not punish me for the sins of mine own daughters. I hope He forgives me. I knew not what I had done. As I look into your heavenly eyes, I know now that I should have made this right long ago."

"Daughters?" I asked. The pastor did not respond. This was the first we'd heard that the pastor had more than one child.

The pastor's boney and leathery hands latched onto my shoulders, and he shook me. When James stepped forward to stop him, I threw my hand up before he got too close. We were on the verge of something important.

"Tell me," the pastor snapped. "Tell me what He wants me to do."

Slightly flustered, I said, "We will go to her." The words tumbled out of my mouth. "We will stop her from causing pain to others at the expense of your negligence."

With barely a whisper, he said, "Yes."

"I assume you know where to find her; those around her will need your help."

"I do," he said. "West Lake Road. The Sheer Family needs us."

The next thing I knew, my eyes popped open, and I shot upright. I was back home without even a chance to say a word to James. And what seemed to be at least an hour was mere minutes, maybe seconds.

"Oh my! Are you alright?" Javier asked, looking as shocked as I was at my sudden return.

"You are never going to believe what I just found out. Ali Sheer is hiding Areli. Ali has a sister."

CHAPTER 38

"What?" Adam choked on his vodka. "Areli is Ali's sister?"

"The pastor said it himself. He has daughters, as in plural. That has to be the answer. Ali is hiding Areli. Why else would she lie?"

Javier asked, "What is she hiding Areli from? The farm? Doctor Jones?"

"Only one way to answer those questions," I said.

"Field trip," Max chimed, rubbing his hands together. "In the morning, we'll hit Ali's house first, then head to Chelsea's."

We camped out at my house that night, only to be awoken at five a.m. by none other than the banshee herself. She slapped my feet from the arm of the chair I was curled up in and yelled, "What the hell is going on here, Emma?"

"Mom," I slurred. "You're home."

Max and Javier shook off throw blankets and jumped up from the floor, and Adam sat up on the couch.

"Who the hell are these people?" Her red, tired eyes darted from one face to the other until landing back on me. With complete disgust, she quipped, "Look at goody-two-shoes, shacking up with all the boys. Is that what you have been doing these past few weeks? Emma, you slut."

"Wait. No, Mom. Come on. It's not like that."

I shot off the chair and started folding blankets. We had been so tired, and I never dreamed my mother would actually show up after all this time, especially at the crack of dawn. Just my luck that she chose the one time I had boys sleeping in our house to crawl in early.

"Always so judgy, judgy, judgy when it comes to your mother, and here you are," she said, gesturing to the guys. "I'm gone for a couple of days, and you think you can take over the house with your, your… " she waved her hands around searching for just the right insult, "…your studs." She eyed Max up and down. "Are you prostitutes?"

Adam snickered.

"No, ma'am," Javier said.

Max said nothing as he marched to the door with his hands stuffed in his pockets. His head was down, and the brim of his baseball hat shadowed his face.

My mother sauntered to the couch. "Someone needs to explain what's going on. Now."

Adam stood, towering over my mother, looking down at her. He smiled, turning on the rare bit of charm he often hid, and said, "Obviously, you have this all wrong. You have a good daughter, ma'am. You should be proud of her."

My mom tisked. "Please," she said to Adam. "I doubt you know the real Emma." She pointed at me. "Emma is good at first impressions. But it's all manipulation. Do yourselves a favor and cut loose while you can. Now get out before I have you all arrested."

"They're my guests. You can't have them arrested."

"Shut up, Emma. You and I will have words when your little boy toys leave."

"Stop, Mom. They're my friends."

"Ha! Friends?" She got in my face and said, "You don't have any friends. The only poor soul who cared anything about you is dead. And he was almost as big of a disappointment as you are. And you can bet your ass that you are in huge trouble, so if I were you, I'd keep my mouth shut."

"Are you threatening her?" Adam asked.

"This is none of your business," my mother snapped. She pulled her phone from her bra and snapped again, "You have three seconds to leave before I call the cops."

"Don't worry, we are definitely leaving," Adam said.

He stepped past my mother toward the door. At that moment, I was torn with emotions. I was utterly humiliated by my mother's behavior and, at the same time, heartbroken that they were leaving

231

me here to deal with this woman when all I wanted to do was go find Ali and Chelsea with them.

"I'll catch up with you guys later," I said. "I'm sorry."

I went to the door and opened it. Javier and Max hesitated, waiting on Adam.

"You don't have to catch up with us later," Adam said.

Of course not, I thought. They didn't need me and my baggage.

I glared at my mother, who said, "She won't be going anywhere for a long time."

She grinned at me smugly and crossed her arms. My heart dropped like a boulder from an airplane.

Then Adam took my hand, glared directly at my mother, and said, "She doesn't have to catch up with us because we aren't leaving here without her."

My breath caught in my throat.

In a sullen voice, unlike anything that has ever come out of Adam's mouth, he said to my mother, "I know people like you. I would say you should be ashamed of yourself, but you never will be. You think you're justified in treating her this way simply because you gave birth to her. Except it doesn't work that way. You don't own her. She's old enough to make her own decisions, and because I *do* know her, I can confidently tell you that the last thing she wants to deal with are your meaningless lectures and verbal abuse."

She stepped toward Adam. "How dare you!"

"How dare you," he threw back at her without missing a beat. This time his voice was on the verge of booming. "You have a beautiful, intelligent, and kind daughter. The sad thing is, you can't even see that, let alone appreciate it."

"Whoa, she has someone wrapped around her little finger. Give it time; you'll see the real Emma soon enough."

"Mom."

"Didn't take you long to replace Frankie. That's nice, real nice. You leave with them now, and you can forget calling me mom, little miss."

Adam handed my hand to Javier and said, "Take her to the truck."

232

The banshee threw one hand on her hip and pointed her finger at me with the other. She said, "You are not leaving this house, Emma. Get in here right now or else."

I stopped and let go of Javier's hand. I was grateful they were so protective, but I couldn't leave without sharing my final thoughts. I honestly didn't know when I'd ever see her again after this.

"Or else what?" I asked. She just stared at me blankly. "Mom? Or else what? You'll hit me again? Tell me what a useless human being I am for the hundredth time? Call me stupid, a goody-two-shoes, a loser? Lock me in my room without dinner? Leave for days or weeks without coming home or checking on me? What, Mom? What exactly will you do?"

"I am the only family you have, Emma. Just remember that before you burn all your bridges," she spewed.

Adam put a consoling hand on my shoulder.

"Biologically, you're my mother. But *you* are not my family."

I turned and walked outside to Max's truck. I jumped in the backseat with Javier. Max and Adam got in, and we drove off. It was possibly the last time I'd have to experience her flared nostrils and gritted teeth, the constant look of disapproval and disappointment, and worst of all, the gut-wrenching look of hatred that escaped her eyes because I looked just like my father. The man she let die.

I glanced out the back window to catch one final glimpse of my mother's enraged face. It was a look that sent a clear message. If looks could kill— I would be dead.

CHAPTER 39

Dummies. That's what we were. While Javier headed into his office, Max, Adam, and I had an early breakfast at the Lakeville Diner. We had concluded that one of two things was possible. Ali had painted our memories based on what her sister, Areli, must have told her, or Ali had been infected by Areli just as I had infected James.

Minutes later, we were headed full blast toward her front door at eight in the morning. We had no plan of attack, gave no warning phone call, and showed no consideration for the fact that she didn't live alone.

I rang the bell.

"Good morning. May I help you?" asked a cheerful, older man with a smile. Clearly, a morning person.

"Good morning. Sorry to bother you so early. We're looking for Ali," I said. "Is she here?"

"Perhaps," he said, craning his neck to check the driveway. "David's car is here. They live in the carriage house."

"That's right. I forgot."

"No bother. They're early risers. If no one answers, check out back. Ali likes to paint on the dock in the morning."

"Thanks," I said.

"Sure. Ali should have had you come earlier to paint the sunrise. It was a beauty."

Of course, Ali is an art teacher.

"Uh, yes. That would've been amazing. She must have something else in mind for us."

The guys were already headed to the carriage house. I waved goodbye to the man who answered the door and hurried to the guys just as they rang Ali's doorbell.

"Good cover, Em," Max said.

"What are we going to tell her?" I asked.

Adam cleared his throat. "We're just going to wing it," he said, rocking on his heels.

After the third ring, the door swung open.

"Are you for real?" Ali said. "You shouldn't be here."

Ali's big brown eyes jittered through the yard behind us and glistened in the morning sun. She peeked out the door at the main house.

"We met your landlord. Nice guy. He thinks we're here for a painting lesson. Should we go out back on the dock?" I asked.

She sighed. "No, come in. That was my father-in-law." She held the door wide. "You have five minutes to speak, and then you must leave before my husband gets back from his run."

"Husband? You're pretty young to be married."

"Did you come here to talk about my marriage?"

"No," I said, shocked that she was married at such a young age. "We need to see your sister."

"My sister?" Ali shook her head. "Why would you want to see my sister?"

"We need to talk to Areli. Call it a hunch, but I believe she lives here with you."

Ali folded her arms and glared at us. She bit her lip and said, "You think Areli is my sister?"

"Oops. You said *is*, not *was*. That could only mean Areli isn't dead. Now tell us where she is," Max said.

"I do have a sister. Her name is Elizabeth. And I have never met her. She's two years old."

Adam's eyebrows slammed together. "Nope, try again."

"Did someone actually tell you that my sister is Areli and that she lives here? This is ridiculous. This is harassment."

"We have it on good authority that Areli lives here with the Sheer family," Max said, looking around the room, no doubt searching for evidence to prove it.

"Who told you such a thing?"

"You know that thing you do with painting people's memories?" I said. "Let's just say I have a similar ability, and it led me here. Is she living in the main house?"

"You've been misled."

"Come on. She's super blonde. Sad religious, cult-like background. She was excommunicated, got pregnant, and lost the baby. Her parents are the Weavers from the farm. Ringing a bell yet? You did say you knew her on the farm," I reminded her.

Ali stared at me blankly.

"We put two and two together," I said. "None of it adds up to Areli being two years old."

Finally, Ali said, "Math must not be your strong point." A deep sigh escaped her mouth. "Your time is up. You need to leave before my husband gets home. He will not take kindly to you all being here."

Adam turned toward the door. "Too late. Is that your husband?" he asked, pointing to the man walking up the driveway.

Ali's face went sour, and before we knew it, we were being shuffled out a door and down the stairs to the dock. Ali ran back toward the house and disappeared into a small shed. Seconds later, she returned with canvases, paint, and paintbrushes.

"Quick, open the blue paint and put a blob on your palette." We all did as she said.

Behind us, the squeaky screen door slid open.

Ali said, "Today is all about capturing the color. Start by looking out into the water. See the different shades of blue and gray? That's what we want to capture; that color. Start by dipping the tip of the brush in the blue paint, and use long soft strokes to paint horizontal lines across the canvas."

Ali came to my canvas and demonstrated the strokes.

From the corner of my eye, I watched Ali's husband casually stroll over to her. She waved at him as he approached and continued her instruction.

"Now mix a little black with the white on your palette, and with the same stroke, I want you to play with the color until it matches the lake. And don't forget, there are many varying shades, depending on where you look. Focus on one area."

"You never mentioned a class here this morning," he said to Ali under his breath.

"I'm sorry, David. I forgot until they showed up. I had the wrong date on my calendar."

He pinched her by the elbow. She winced. Through gritted teeth, he asked, "How long is this class?"

"Half an hour. It's just a color class."

"It's just a color class," he said, mocking her in a high-pitched voice. He released her arm and turned to us. "She's the expert."

My next thought was that he would know who was living in his house.

"Excuse me." I waved at him as he walked by. "Hi. I'm Emma. Thanks for letting us come here this morning."

I held my hand out to him. He begrudgingly shook it and glanced at Ali, annoyed.

He turned to me and said, "Nice of you to let my talented wife teach you about art. It's the only thing she's actually good at."

I swallowed my desire to slap the smug grin off his face and said, "She is good at teaching. That's for sure. She reminds me of my sister. She was always trying to teach me stuff. Hey, Ali, you have siblings, right?"

A nervous laugh slipped from Ali's lips, and she said, "Let's focus, everyone. Wouldn't want to waste your money with idle chit-chat."

David happily walked away and back into the house, where he proceeded to slam cupboard doors.

Ali came to my side. "Please don't," she begged. "Do not say anything to him. He is not a nice person."

"I can see that. Talk, or I'll have no choice but to start asking the other people in this house about Areli Weaver. Do everyone a favor, including yourself, and tell us where we can find your sister."

"Shh. Not so loud."

"Tell us," I demanded

"Areli is not my sister. *I* am Areli."

Max's brush went flying past my head. "Sorry," he said. "You're her?"

"I *was* her," she said quietly. She raised her voice and said, "Nice work, Emma. I'd call that shade a steel blue."

She walked past me to Adam. Lowering her voice again, she said, "When I left the farm and got married, I became Ali Sheer. I left my past behind. For good reasons. If you bring all this up now in front of David, I will suffer the consequences."

"Sounds like you went from one crappy family situation to another. I'm sorry," Adam said, sounding sincere for a change.

Ali shrugged. "It is what it is. I'd actually rather be here than on the farm, believe it or not. David doesn't talk about my past. It conjures up bad feelings."

"That explains your uncanny ability to recreate our memories on canvas," Max said.

Ali shook her head, dismissing the term "ability."

"It's weird. It's only happened a few times."

With that, she glanced at Adam and furrowed her brows.

"Is there somewhere we can go and talk?" Max asked her. "There are things you need to know."

Ali walked closer to Max. She glanced up into the windows. "I can't leave with you guys. He's a jealous man, and he would find it odd since I don't really know you."

"Then meet us somewhere."

"I can't today. But the Sheers are having a family brunch here tomorrow. Blood relatives only, so David will be in the main house most of the afternoon. I should be able to sneak away." Ali raised her voice, "Add a dab of black for greater depth."

"Meet us at the gallery at noon," Max muttered.

"No, I don't want to go there," she snapped under her breath.

I wasn't ready to blindly believe that Ali was Areli Weaver. I couldn't help but wonder if this was her way to throw us off track. "Can you look at my painting?" I asked. "I'm not sure if this is right."

Ali came and stood behind me. At the same time, she and I caught David in the window tapping his watch. She sighed heavily and tried to act like she didn't care.

"That's perfect," Ali said, picking up my brush. "Maybe add a touch of white to lighten the waves a little."

"Areli is blonde," I said, barely moving my mouth.

"Color needs to look real, guys. Not like a bad dye job," she said to me. "And I'm afraid we are out of time."

I looked closer at her hair as she threw it up in a ponytail and noticed the patch of blonde hair she missed in the back of her head.

"Thanks for the lesson," I said. "The gallery at noon," I mouthed.

"I can't go there," she insisted softly.

"That's where your paintings are," I reminded her, confused by her reluctance to meet at the gallery.

Ali glanced at David standing in the window, staring at her. "Fine," she uttered.

As we started around the house to leave, I looked back at her. She smiled at me with childlike innocence. She had no idea how we were about to shake up her already crazy life tomorrow. I almost felt bad, like maybe we should give the girl a pass and forget we even found her. As we shuffled out to the truck and slid in, we were silent for several minutes.

Finally, I shared my suspicion that maybe she wasn't Areli. But Adam and Max were certain it all made perfect sense. A disgrace to her congregation, Areli left the farm pregnant, married David, then lost the baby. She had left everything behind— including her identity. In Ali's mind, Areli Weaver died on the farm.

"Her husband seems like a real jerk," Adam said.

"Controlling," Max added. "He could be a problem. We need Ali to understand what's happening to her and what Jones wants from us." He put his finger in the air and said, "Under no circumstances are you to let Jones know that we found her. Emma, if you sub with James at some point, you cannot even leak it to him. Not even Javi can know. It stays right here. Got it?"

We all agreed.

"Good. We'll meet at the gallery tomorrow at noon."

I pointed out that Jones was most likely watching us and knew we went to Ali Sheer's house. Meeting with her again tomorrow could make him more suspicious. Someone had to distract Jones tomorrow. We got Javier on the phone right away.

Javier said, "This is probably a good time to tell you that while Doctor Jones is most certainly watching you, I am watching him. I thought that would be helpful."

Adam laughed. "Are you serious?"

Javier stifled a snicker and said, "I've had three drivers on him throughout the day since James went missing. My people are everywhere; therefore, they will not appear suspicious."

We all laughed and rallied with Javier. We didn't tell him about Ali. Instead, we said we planned to meet with Chelsea tomorrow and needed Jones to be kept busy.

"Luck may be on your side," Javier responded. "Jones has requested a car for tomorrow. And I know just how to keep him busy."

CHAPTER 40

Adam let me in the back door of The Green at nine the next morning.

"Do you have everything you need?" he asked me as I dragged my backpack full of bare necessities through the door and down the stairs.

"Yeah. My mom wasn't home. So it was easy."

I walked into the dungeon and threw my pillow on the couch. Both Adam and Javier had offered to let me stay with them until I started school in the fall, but for whatever reason, I had grown to like the basement.

I officially moved out, taking everything that mattered, including Novakitty. I left my mother a note explaining that I'd be staying with friends until school started, and if she needed me, which I doubted would ever be the case, she could reach me on my cell phone.

Adam came down the stairs with the cat carrier, closed the door, and let my little meowing calico out. As she explored the dank corners of the room, we discussed the plan and waited for Javier to call.

Max was stopping at Chelsea's again and then meeting us at the gallery, hopefully with her. Once we filled Ali in on all things supernatural and what we knew about Jake Jones, we were going to make sure Jones went MIA for a while. It sounded like kidnapping to me, but Javier assured us it was merely a bit of confusion resulting in Jones getting lost with one of his drivers. All day and maybe longer.

I was nervous. There was a chance Ali could completely reject us. She'd already been through so much. Finding out that she'd been cursed with an ability that none of us understood could throw her over the edge. If she turned her back on us and this so-called project, I wasn't exactly sure where that left the rest of us. But like Max always said, we needed to deal with one problem at a time. That was something I found easy; because that was me— one wrung at a time. Our first problem to tackle was getting Ali and Chelsea on board without tipping off Jones.

Adam and I got to the gallery fifteen minutes early to scope out a quiet and secure place for our meeting with Ali. As we expected, Megan was in the back. Adam and Megan talked for a few minutes about their mutual friend Reznor and his band, then Megan left.

Adam explained that we were meeting Ali about the painting I was interested in. It made Megan happy that Ali was getting out of the house. She said it was a good sign that the gallery might open earlier than expected. Little did she know, it could mean the opposite.

Adam checked his watch. With an edge to his voice, he said, "Max said he'd be here ten minutes early. It's already noon, and Ali will be here any second."

He got up and peeked out the window.

"Maybe that's a good sign." I was feeling optimistic like Javier all of a sudden. "Maybe he's finally talking to Chelsea. It would figure today would be the day."

"I texted him five minutes ago, and he hasn't answered. He should have waited for us."

I shrugged. "You know him. Any word from Javier and our lost friend?"

"Javier felt guilty sending a driver to do his dirty work. So he sort of went undercover."

"Seriously?"

Adam nodded his head. I marched to the window and stood beside him.

"That could be dangerous."

He nodded again and said, "Exactly why he didn't want someone else to do it."

"Hmmm, that's brave. Sometimes I don't give him enough credit."

Adam looked at me squarely. "Javi had a monstrous screw-up when he got involved with the Gallaghers. But at the end of the day, he's a nice guy. And I guess, good looking, and maybe he's brave. But if I were you, I'd wait until we figure out all this project, ring of fire crap, before you drag anyone into your life. He doesn't know too much, and he's not a freakish subject. That puts him in a good position to call this quits and not suffer any consequences. Right now, he can walk away easily and never look back."

I didn't look at Adam as he dumped his lecture on me.

I said, "Yup. I'm sure the Gallaghers see it that way. Like Javi is in a good position to walk away."

Adam crossed his arms. From the corner of my eye, I saw him glaring at me.

"For the record, I'm not the player you make me out to be," I said. "So if someone is interested in me, or if someone *thinks* that's the case, that's not my doing."

I turned and walked along the blinds, closing them one by one until I got to the end of the wall. Then I planted myself at a table in the back corner.

"She's here," Adam said. He sighed, strolled over to the table, and plunked down. "I'm not trying to be a jerk."

"So it just comes naturally?"

"Funny." He intertwined his fingers, put them behind his head, and leaned back in the chair. "We all need to stay focused. That's all."

To squash the desire to kick the chair out from under Adam, I got up and greeted Ali as she walked into the room. She was always put together in her perfectly preppy way. Despite her lack of height, her tanned legs looked long in her Old Navy khaki shorts and simple pale yellow button-up shirt rolled at the sleeves. She sported cream-colored Roxy slip-ons, perfect little boating shoes. I imagined her with her natural blonde hair color. Even with her mousey brown hair, she was still adorable.

Adam got up and gave her the once-over from head to toe. The grumpy giant smiled. I wondered how good he was at taking his own advice.

Ali asked where everyone else was. We explained that Max was on his way, and if we were lucky, he'd be bringing Chelsea, the fifth subject in the project. Adam wasted no time giving Ali the same blunt and brief description of what happened to us that he had given to me. I was hoping Max would hurry up because he was gentler in his explanation.

Ali sat silent for a long time. At one point, Adam was worried she might lose it. Her face contorted with a nervous smirk when Adam told her about Jake Jones and the Gallagher connection. He pulled his chair closer to hers, and she quickly stood and backed away.

"You don't have to be afraid of us, Ali. We're all in this together."

But it wasn't that she was afraid of *us*. She was afraid of *him* because she thought he was a murderer. I couldn't keep quiet about it anymore.

"Ali, I don't know what you saw, but Adam wouldn't kill anyone."

Adam chuckled. Then when no one laughed, he scowled at me.

"She had a vision," I told him.

"I painted it," she blurted out. "It wouldn't stop."

"I don't know what you're talking about, but I can assure you, I've never killed anybody," Adam chuckled again.

"I saw it. It wouldn't go away until I painted it. It had to be a memory."

"Are you sure the man is dead? I mean, in the Life or Death painting, you didn't know that my father was actually dead," I pointed out.

"In the painting with Adam, there is no doubt the man is dead. Blood is everywhere, and the man he killed is underwater."

This was the last thing we needed to deal with.

Adam started pacing the floor.

"Wait. Are you being serious?" he boomed. "I would know if I killed someone. Do you have other paintings that are memories?"

"Maybe. But I don't know until someone tells me. Unless it's my memory, of course. Lately, I'm seeing a trend. When I can't get a vision out of my head, but then I paint it, it goes away. Those are the ones that seem to be someone else's memory. In your case, you're actually in the painting. And the vision started before I ever laid eyes on you."

Adam checked his watch, then dialed Max.

"He's taking forever," he said, shaking his head. He let it ring for a while, but Max didn't answer. "We don't have time for this conversation now. I need to know where you stand with this whole ability thing, Ali."

"Are you in or out?" I asked, happy that Adam had changed the subject for now.

She shrugged. "It doesn't sound like I have a choice."

"We all have a choice," Adam responded dryly.

Just then, we heard sirens in the distance. We didn't pay much attention at first, but then they got louder, and an ambulance flew by the gallery, horn honking, sirens blaring. Next came fire trucks and police cars.

The three of us looked at each other.

"Do you feel that?" I asked.

Adam and Ali shook their heads no. But I felt a nagging physical discomfort. Anxiety was rising in my chest, and the first name to come to my mind was Max.

"Something's wrong," I uttered.

Adam ran toward the door and hollered for us to follow. We ran after him and out into the parking lot. Adam craned his neck to see down the road. All he could see were cars coming to a stop on the road and then redirected up Gray Road by a police officer.

"It's Max. No, wait. I think it's Chelsea," I said. "I feel it. Something is very wrong with her."

As we were getting into Adam's truck, his phone rang. Finally, it was Max. Through the phone connection in the car, Adam answered.

"We are on our way."

"No," said Max.

We heard a screeching siren through the phone at Max's end. A Mercy Flight helicopter flew overhead.

"What happened to Chelsea?" I asked.

"Mercy Flight is coming. They're airlifting her to Strong Memorial Hospital."

"Oh my God. Is she going to be okay?" Ali asked.

"I don't know. She's pretty bad. I tried to stop him, but the door was locked, and I couldn't get in fast enough. I'm going to meet her at the hospital. I'll call you guys in a little while."

Adam said, "We'll meet you there."

CHAPTER 41

While Adam and I headed to the hospital, Ali decided to go home before her husband realized she was gone. I found myself both sad and angry that she felt that way. But who was I to judge?

On our drive to the hospital, Adam called Javier to check on the status with Jones. Javier explained he was in the driveway of the old white brick mansion in Mt. Morris, waiting for Jones to come out. His plan was to head in the opposite direction of what Jones requested. He said he would keep us posted.

Out of nowhere, Adam pounded the steering wheel, his brows slammed together, and he said, "I bet it was that loser boyfriend she was with at The Green that time." He was talking about Chelsea. "I knew he was trouble. I should have beaten the crap out of him when I had a chance."

"Don't say stuff like that."

"I didn't say I wanted to kill him. And for the record, that's a bunch of bull. I would know if I murdered someone."

When we got to the hospital, we went directly to the ER and found Max talking to an elderly couple in the waiting room. We held back until he noticed us. A few seconds later, he took the chair next to me.

"She's unconscious," he said, taking a deep breath. "She has multiple broken bones, and they are apparently about to operate on her brain."

I sighed. "That sounds pretty serious."

Adam asked, "What happened?"

"Her ex-boyfriend did it. He's been stalking her." Max pointed to the elderly couple he'd been talking to. "According to her neighbors, they haven't seen much of her lately. She's either been out or shut in when she is home. It explains why I haven't been able to get in touch with her."

Adam got up and started a slow pace in front of us.

"When I got to Chelsea's house," Max shook his head, "there was so much blood. She couldn't even talk. She was barely conscious at first, then she just closed her eyes. I thought she was dead."

Max dropped his face into his hands. I rested my hand on his back. He glanced at me and asked, "How could someone do that to her?"

Suddenly, the lights flickered in the waiting room. "Adam," I cried, jumping up from my chair.

I placed my hands on his cheeks and forced him to look me in the eyes. His face was hot.

"Adam, calm down. This is a hospital, and they need their electricity to save people. Including Chelsea. You have to get control. *Right now.*"

Adam let out the breath he'd been holding and focused on my eyes for a brief second.

"I'm going to get a bottle of water," he said and disappeared around a corner.

Suddenly, the lights snapped back to normal.

"You look like you were in a boxing match, by the way," I said to Max.

"I was."

"I take it you won?"

"She'd be dead if I didn't."

"Thank God you were there in time. See, your stalking paid off. Good stalker beats up bad stalker." I snickered.

"Stop," he said with half a grin.

"What's your plan now?"

"I need to stay and make sure she comes out of this okay. We don't really know her, but I can't leave. She's very close with her neighbors over there." He pointed to the elderly couple he'd been talking to when we came in. They sat eagerly by the ER doors, worry written across their faces. "I want to talk to them and see if I can get any idea what her ability is."

"Where are her parents?"

248

"They went to Europe. Her sister should be here any minute."

He mindlessly flipped through a magazine and kept glancing at the ER doors. I wondered about the connection he had with her.

"You guys can go," Max said. "I'll be fine. I'll meet you at The Green when I leave."

"Good luck."

I got up to find Adam and leave when Max said, "Wait. How did Ali take the news?"

"Surprisingly well. She could feel it, just like I did. I have her cell number, so we can text her and keep her in play."

Adam strolled back around the corner with three bottles of water. He tossed one to Max and handed another to me.

"Text me before you leave," I said to Max. I pulled at Adam's shirt. "Let's go, hot head."

Adam threw his arm around me. "So you think I'm hot now? Sweet."

I jabbed him in the ribs, and we turned toward the stairs which led to the parking garage. We barely got a few feet before the commotion broke out behind us.

A gurney, accompanied by several EMTs, came crashing through the waiting room door. The EMTs hollered orders and stats about the patient on the gurney. He had bandages and IVs, and he was covered in blood. It rolled right by Max. When Max and the patient reached for each other, the EMTs ordered him to back off.

Adam and I bolted to Max. Just as the doors closed, another gurney rushed into the ER with a patient in an almost identical state. It was Jake Jones.

I swung Max around to face me and said, "The first guy was Javier?" He nodded, his hands digging through his hair.

We hurried to the front desk to find out what had happened and discovered the horrifying news that there was a ten-car pileup on the 390/590 north interchange. To make matters worse, this was just the first wave of injured people.

The waiting room quickly filled with people waiting to hear news about their loved ones. Soon, it was a madhouse. Frantic nurses and doctors shuffled about, hollering orders and checking on patients who lined hallways and overflowed into the waiting area. Orderlies, EMTs, and police officers ambled the waiting area and hallways, keeping order and helping people get information.

We moved to the far corner to stay out of the way. Chelsea's neighbors had gone to the cafeteria to wait while Chelsea underwent surgery. And that was when karma threw everything she had in our faces.

An orderly pushed a battered and bruised girl into the waiting room in a wheelchair. Her sneakers caught my attention. Cream-colored Roxy slip-ons speckled with blood.

I stood up, focused on the girl, and was lost.

I panicked for a second as I found myself in the middle of a high-way, burning cars compacted in a mangled line next to me. Emergency vehicles were strewn throughout the anarchic scene. My gaze followed the ghost-town-like disaster to the end, where a semi-truck concluded the accordion-style mash of jagged metal and burning oil and gasoline.

"Emma?" Ali said from behind me.

I whipped around and saw her standing next to a black Acura SUV with its front and back end smashed in and flames coming out of the engine. Blood dripped from her forehead and nose. A mass of chaos surrounded her.

"What happened?" she asked, assessing the mayhem. "Where is everyone?"

She wiped the dripping blood from her nose with the back of her hand.

"You were in an accident. You're actually at the hospital right now." The confused and lost look on her face tugged at my heart. I embraced her in a hug. "We're with you, Ali. It's going to be okay."

"Where are all the other people?"

"At the hospital. This is that thing I do. I'm physically with you at the hospital, and right now, I'm also in your head. This is what you're thinking about right now." I gestured to the accident, keeping my arm around her.

Her hand flew to her mouth. "Oh, God. I don't even know what happened. Shortly after I got home, David left to go golfing with his cousin for the rest of the day. So I snuck out to check on Chelsea and meet up with you guys."

My eyes scanned the line of cars, and I said, "This is a ten-car pileup. I only see eight, and none of these are Javier's."

I let go of Ali and started toward the front of the smoldering line of cars. Then all of a sudden, I was standing in the hospital waiting room again. I rushed to the girl in the wheelchair.

"Ali," I said, tapping her arm. I took her hand. "Ali, open your eyes. I'm here. Ali."

Adam and Max raced to my side. Adam knelt beside me and said Ali's name.

Frantically, he asked, "Why is she here? She's supposed to be home." He scanned the room and the other patients who were waiting for assistance. "Was she alone?"

"Yes. She was coming to us."

"How do you... Did you talk to her?" Adam asked.

"Yes. She's scared. But she'll be fine." I patted her hand. "Ali?"

Max rushed to the front desk and pointed to Ali. "That girl is unconscious. Do you know that?"

"Sir, we will get to her. We have to take high priority patients first."

"She is completely unresponsive. To me, that's a priority."

The lady behind the desk got a nurse who rushed to see Ali.

"She was conscious when she came in," the nurse said.

"Well, she isn't now," Adam responded.

The nurse wheeled Ali to the door, and we followed, only to get stopped again.

"There's no room back there. Are you family?" she asked.

We nodded yes, so she said she would keep us posted. Then she flew through the doors, called to a doctor, and disappeared.

Adam rubbed both hands over his face. "I don't understand what's happening."

Max threw his hands in the air. "I can tell you one thing," he said. "The five of us are now in one place. At the same time. And so is Jones. The exact opposite of what we want to happen."

"We can't leave," I said. "I won't leave until I know everyone is okay."

"I know. I know," Max said, shaking his head.

* * *

The hours dragged by until, finally, we learned that Chelsea didn't end up in surgery after all. And although her injuries seemed severe when she came in, they turned out to be less threatening than doctors initially thought. Still, she would need to spend a few days in recovery. Chelsea's neighbor, Ruthie, pulled Max aside. She requested that he stay distant from Chelsea while she recovered from the trauma. The doctors didn't want her to be stressed as she regained her memory, and Max's presence threatened to bring back memories of the attack.

Before the incident, Ruthie had been concerned for Chelsea's mental health, and she thought Chelsea would need as little distraction and confusion as possible as she recovered. Of course, who could blame Chelsea for looking like she had mental health problems? We figured she was coming into her ability and, like the rest of us, thought she was losing her mind. She had been going through her discovery alone.

Max agreed to keep his distance from Chelsea, but he was determined to stay close enough to keep an eye on her. Jones was here, in the hospital, and there was no way Max would let him get near Chelsea.

Right after we learned the news about Chelsea, a nurse came out and told us Javier was being admitted to a room.

"And the man who was with him in the car?" Max inquired.

The nurse shook his head and squinted his eyes. "What man?"

"There was another man in the car with Javier. His name is Jake Jones."

"The girls at the front desk can give you Mister Ardaya's room number." The nurse took a folder from under his arm and skimmed

252

over a piece of paper. Then he said, "You can also ask at the front desk about other patients. But everything I have here says Mister Ardaya was alone."

CHAPTER 42

"Can you give us the room number for Javier Ardaya?" I asked the lady at the front desk. "And we also need the room for Jake Jones? He was brought in today too."

The woman went into her computer, and after several seconds, she said, "I don't see anyone by the name of Jake Jones."

Thinking perhaps he was under another name, we about Javier's passenger.

"I don't have that kind of information. Javier Ardaya is in room 5377. Take the red elevators," she said, pointing to the left.

She handed me a small piece of paper with the room number and Javier's name. We weaved through the crowded hallway and headed directly to Javier's room.

While in the elevator, I got a text from Javier demanding that I call him as soon as possible. It appeared that Javier was awake and alert. The second we walked in the door, Javier began his rant.

"Doctor Jones wanted to go to Nunda. There is nothing but farms in Nunda, by the way. So, of course, I went in the opposite direction and headed north toward Rochester. He was on the phone and did not notice. I thought all was going smoothly. Then it happened.

"There was a car. It came speeding up alongside me and did one of those PIT maneuvers the police do to stop criminals on the run. But it was not the police. The next thing I know, I am waking up as I am rolling into the emergency room, and I see you," he said to Max.

"Just before the accident, Doctor Jones told someone on the phone that he absolutely was not changing the terms of the original agreement, and in no way was he willing to compromise the outcome of the project. I think that is why we got hit."

"Javi, Javi," Adam said. "Take a breath, man."

"Yeah. First of all, how are you?" I asked, taking a seat at the end of his bed.

"A broken leg is all that came from what sounds like an absolute disaster." He dropped back against his pillow, looking weak and sad. "I hurt many people."

"Look, man," said Max. "It wasn't your fault. Everyone is looking for the car that started the pile-up. Problem is that no one saw the license plate, if there was a plate at all. They're hoping a dash cam or security camera caught it somewhere."

"It almost sounds like a calculated hit," I said, thinking about big old Billy with the meaty fists. "Javi, they're saying you were alone in the car. But we saw Jones come into the hospital on a gurney. He was in bad shape. There is no record of anyone named Jake Jones being admitted. It's like he disappeared."

Max said, "Did you guys see him? He couldn't have walked out of here." He turned to Adam. "Speaking of that, why don't we take a stroll."

"Yep. Let's find you an unoccupied computer to poke around on."

"And we'll see if we can find out anything about Ali," Max said.

They left me to keep Javier company. He revealed more about his short car ride with Jones.

"Doctor Jones was clueless. He had no idea we were headed north. He was quite nervous. Not Mister Cool like the last few times we have seen him. Nunda, south of Lakeville, could not be more country and in the middle of nowhere. And even when he sees the city buildings, he is not phased one bit. I assumed he did not know where Nunda was located. Not to mention, he was preoccupied with phone calls…"

"I wonder why he wanted to go to Nunda. Do you think he has a new farm there?"

"My thoughts exactly."

"What was the address?"

Javier cringed. "It is in the car's GPS… which is most likely totaled."

"Maybe someone in your office has it."

"I am afraid not," he uttered.

A special news report suddenly popped on TV. The police were currently searching for the car suspected to have caused the accident today. I reached for the TV remote and turned up the volume. It had been on mute since we entered the room. They still had no leads.

Then as if a lightbulb had just gone on, Javier asked, "Wait. Did they say they were checking on Ali? What happened to her?"

"She was in the accident. She was in one of the cars behind you."

"You must be kidding me. What kind of terrible luck is that?"

"Strange luck."

I couldn't tell him exactly how strange it was because he had no idea Ali was actually Areli Weaver.

"Max is right. Jones has to be here, maybe under a different name. They need to find him before he finds us," I said.

An hour later, Adam and Max returned.

"This man is a genius," Adam said, patting Max on the back. "Jones was admitted under the name Kelly O'Riley. A name that, upon question, you would initially assume was a girl's name."

"A nice Irish name," I said. "Is he still here?"

"He was admitted, treated, and then released thirty minutes ago against doctor's orders. On a positive note, Ali is doing great. She's conscious and waiting for an MRI," Max said.

"We snuck into the ER and talked to her," Adam said with a big smile. "Doesn't look like she has any broken bones."

"Has anyone called her family yet?" I asked.

Adam responded, "She called and left her husband a message. She said she had car trouble."

"Little bit of an understatement," I said, raising my eyebrows.

"She's hoping to get released before anyone has to come up here." He shook his head and said, "It's ridiculous how she walks on eggshells with that family."

"I'm sure the car she was driving is totaled. That's going to be pretty tough to explain."

I turned back to Javier and patted his good leg. I said to Max and Adam, "Sounds like Javi might be here for a few days."

"You guys, go," said Javier. "I will be fine. No reason to stay here. I think I am going to need a little rest anyway." Javier yawned. It seemed as though the events of today were catching up with him.

"If you're sure," I agreed reluctantly. "Get some sleep. I'll be back first thing in the morning."

The guys said goodbye to Javier, and we headed to the elevator. Once inside, the bombs dropped. Max said he was staying to keep an eye on Chelsea. Then unexpectedly, Adam said he, too, was staying.

"Someone should keep Ali company. She's all alone, and we dumped a lot on her shoulders today." Adam shoved his hands in his pocket and gave me an apologetic look. "Take the car, Em. I'll hitch a ride with Max when he leaves."

"Yeah, sure."

Adam handed me the keys. We went our separate ways, agreeing to keep in touch throughout the night. But I'm not going to lie. We had spent so much time together during the last few weeks that I felt like I was getting dumped. It was weird to be alone.

Once I found the truck in the parking garage, I hopped in and fiddled with the radio stations until I found one I liked. I reached for the seatbelt when suddenly, a sickening feeling washed over me. I turned the car off.

At first, the feeling was an all-over body discomfort, like a thousand pointy balls were rolling around under my skin. Next came nausea. I opened the door in case I threw up; Adam would kill me if I puked in his truck. After a second, my emotions overtook my physical inclination to throw up. A strange rush of anxiety and fear flooded my chest to the point of feeling as if a heavy weight was literally on top of me, crushing me, suffocating me. I could barely inhale. Finally, I couldn't breathe at all.

I jumped out of the truck and tried to take a deep breath, but it was a struggle. It hurt. My heart raced. I slammed the car door and poppled my way back into the hospital, clutching my chest. Sadly, my first thought was that they wouldn't be able to get in touch with

257

my mother if something happened to me. But truth be told, my real family was already here.

The closer I got to the hospital doors, the better I felt. The heaviness slowly left my chest; my heart began to beat slower. The second the doors slid open, and I stepped inside, I could breathe, stand up straight, and think clearer. My only thought, as urgent and persistent as a siren, was of Javier.

I raced to the red elevators and hit the up button, even though it was already lit. A man stood casually by the doors and glared at me as I hit the button several more times. Soon, I heard the elevator descending. But when the flashing green number above the doors indicated a stop on the third floor, I knew I couldn't wait. I ran to the stairwell and didn't stop until I reached the fifth floor.

My pounding chest from the dash up the stairs didn't slow me down as I bobbed and weaved my way around people until I reached Javier's room. The door was closed. Normally, I would have knocked, yet something told me I didn't have time for that. I barged into the room, and though the curtain around his bed was partially closed, I could see Javier. His eyes were closed peacefully. The TV was still on.

Instant relief washed over me, and I laughed at how silly I was to think something was wrong. Strange, that unexplainable wave of feelings I had just had. I watched Javier for a few more seconds to be sure all was good and to catch my breath. As I turned to leave, I noticed the TV remote had fallen and gotten jammed between the mattress and the side rails of the bed. He'd be looking for it later. I pushed back the curtain and stepped closer to the bed. Catching a figure in the corner of my eye, I froze.

"I recognized him when he picked me up," Jones said.

He had been standing suspiciously behind the medical equipment in the corner. He came around and settled into the chair next to Javier's bed.

"That boy wore a hat and glasses," he chuckled. "Does he think he's Clark Kent?"

He slapped his knee awkwardly, enjoying his own dumb joke, but wincing as his hand made contact with his leg. Jones had a black eye and a puffy bottom lip. He had three stitches on the hairline of his forehead. Jones' eyes were bloodshot.

My mind reeled. What was my next move? I can't leave Javier here with this madman.

"How is the mission going, Emma? Find Areli yet?"

"No. You know more about her than we do. I'm not sure why you think she'll be easy for us to find if you can't even find her."

"Your special talents should help you. You aren't focusing enough. You're not practicing."

"I can't focus on someone I don't know," I barked.

He put a splinted finger to his lips to silence me. It was arrogant, and I wanted to slap his pudgy little, beat-up finger from his mouth and tell him where to stick it. Instead, I smiled and shrugged.

"Let's not make a scene," he said quietly.

Jones slid to the edge of the recliner, wincing again as he did so.

He said, "I'm going to share a little secret with you. I'm not supposed to be here right now. However, I felt this was the best place to get your attention." He stood and stepped toward me. "So much is going on 'behind the scenes,'" he said with air quotes. "You don't need to know everything, but you should be aware that while certain people wish for this project to fail, there are others who are highly invested in this project. Should it fail, heads will roll. Mine. Yours." Jones pointed to Javier and said, "His. I'd hate for that to happen. So you see, it's much more to our benefit to make this project successful."

Jones moved toward Javier's IV. With one hand, he fondled the bag. He slipped his other hand into his left pocket and retrieved a needle fully loaded with a mysterious cloudy liquid. My heart stopped. "This bag is helping him sleep right now. If you don't want him to sleep forever… you'll hurry up and do what I asked."

"What's in the syringe?" I said, trying to appear calm. Of course, inside, I was panicking.

"Merely a special concoction I whipped up."

"Javier isn't like us. Leave him out of this."

"You see, I need the *five* of you. Javier, not so much. Not at all, truthfully. He is expendable. But he means something to you and your friends." He slid the needle back into his pocket. "Don't play games with me. Find Areli. Get Chelsea, Max, and Adam, and meet me so we can finalize the project."

Dramatically, he studied his Apple watch. He said, "You have a new deadline. You will meet me at Vitale Park on the night of July third. Eleven o'clock. Go to your favorite gazebo; I have already reserved it."

"July third? The park will be packed."

Jones grinned, "You get it, right? I can see it in your eyes."

Yes, I understood the irony, his sick little joke. I glared at him. July third was Conesus Lake's Ring of Fire. At ten o'clock that night, every resident on the lake would light their flares at the lake's edge in celebration of the Fourth of July. That day was inevitably the busiest day of the year in Lakeville. Vitale Park would be jam-packed all day and into the night.

"We will complete the ring of fire ceremony," he said decisively.

He brushed past me, shoving my shoulder with his. I stepped to Javier's side and turned to face Jones before he walked out the door.

With pity written all over his smug face, he shook his head and said, "I suspect it's a burden to be you. Knowing things you don't want to know. People expecting things from you, forcing you to make decisions that affect so many others."

His pitch raised, and mocking me, he threw his hands wildly in the air and said, "How do I save James from the Ardemoni's evil clutches and at the same time keep the Gallaghers and Doctor Jones from killing Javier? All I really want to do is get away from my vicious mother and join a sorority. I'm so torn."

"I hate you," I spewed.

"Ah, hate. The fragile rock your depression cowers beneath. The weak armor which shields your heart against years of trauma. Your hiding place for fear and sadness. When you complete the ring of fire, it will be gone, you know. You'll no longer need to be the heretic you think you are. The suffering, embarrassment, anger... it all goes away. And on top of that, you will share what the others have, and you will have connections with powerful people for the rest of your life.

"Don't mess this up, Emma. Find the girl, gather the others." He nodded toward Javier and whispered, "Or people will die."

I glanced at Javier, and when I looked back at the door, Jones was gone.

CHAPTER 43

Back at The Green, my temporary home, I anxiously paced the floor. I had stayed with Javier for about an hour before leaving. I considered going to find Adam and Max, but ultimately, everything sat in my lap.

I could go to Buffalo and hope they release James or stay and convince everyone to finish the project so Javier and the rest of us survived. To choose one, crucified the other. How could I make everyone happy and get away with no one dying?

I would start with getting answers. First question: where did the Ardemoni's sudden interest in this project come from, and why do they want it to fail?

I sat down on the couch and put my head back.

"Get out," James snapped. "You're putting yourself in danger."

James stood in front of me in the middle of Vitale Park. Waves gently rolled up against the break wall. The moon was full and so bright that it lit the park.

"I have to figure this out. That's the only way I can get you back safely."

"No. Do not try to get me back. I'm trying to fix this so that no one gets hurt."

"What do you mean? How?"

"Don't worry about that. Stay low for a few weeks."

"No. I'm not hiding again. Where are you? I'll come for you."

He sighed hard and heavy. "Emma, listen to me. Do not look for me. There's something I have to do. Then this will be over."

"What are you going to do?" I grabbed James' arm. "You can't sabotage the project. Jones will kill Javier and God knows who else. If we find and save you and complete the ring of fire, we will be

stronger. We will be able to defend ourselves against the Ardemonis."
I let go of James. "Yes, that's the answer."

"We can't do that until you find Areli, and who knows if Chelsea even has any abilities. Jones said he couldn't figure it out." James was pacing now.

"Max said Chelsea does have a gift. He can feel it. She sparked every time they touched. He's going to talk to her in the morning. We should know something soon."

"Still, without Areli, this plan doesn't work." He stopped pacing and peered into my eyes. "Well?"

"Well, what?" I asked.

I remembered Max warning me against telling anyone about Ali, even James.

James asked again, "Do you know where she is? If you do, you have to tell me."

I hesitated long enough for it to be a red flag. "Do you?" he asked.

Unable to lie, I turned the tables, "I can feel her sometimes. Can you?"

"What does that mean?" He appeared too anxious for comfort. He stared intently at my face like he was trying to read it.

"We feel like we're close."

"Close to finding her?"

"And close to completing the ring of fire."

James nodded and smiled. "So that's the plan; you will go through with the ring of fire. *Do not* come for me until you've done that. Focus on Chelsea getting out of the hospital and finding Areli. Everything is going to happen fast. Just be careful."

Suddenly, I was awakened by Adam closing the door at The Green. My eyes opened, and I gasped.

"I didn't mean to wake you," Adam said.

Tears welled up in my eyes. My heart ached.

"What's the matter? Bad dream?"

He plunked down in the chair across from me. Bags hung under his bloodshot eyes.

"I just saw James."

"What's wrong?"

"He wanted to know if we found Areli."

"You didn't tell him, did you?"

"I didn't." I shook my head and sighed. "He knew about Chelsea. He knew she was in the hospital, and I didn't tell him that. So how did he know?"

Adam frowned. "Maybe he got in your head, and you didn't notice."

"I would know if he was in my head. It doesn't add up. He wanted to know if we found Areli. I have a bad feeling, Adam. I don't think the Ardemonis have him. What if he's with Jones and the Gallaghers." I stared at the ceiling, willing my tears to slide back into the ducts they had just slid from, and said, "He's with his father. I just know it. I can feel it."

Adam put a hand on my shoulder.

"I think we lost him," I said.

I didn't want to go to sleep after that. The last thing I needed was for James to hijack my brain. But somewhere along the way, after Adam had gone home, I fell asleep only to be awakened to more of the same chaos that had been chasing us like a rabid dog for weeks.

The noise jarred me awake. Glass was breaking, furniture was being overturned, and voices shouted words that didn't register. Suddenly, my head whipped back, causing shooting pain down my spine as I was yanked from the couch. Finally came the stabbing pain of a needle in my thigh.

That was when all went black.

When the light returned, I was alone on a beat-up, filthy cot in an otherwise empty and cold room. The room was barely big enough for the cot. Feeling claustrophobic in the rancid damp closet of a room, I immediately closed my eyes, trying to escape from wherever subbing had taken me.

When I opened them, I was still on the nasty cot in the dank room. The old wooden door reminded me of the one in the basement at The Green. The small, dim light bulb hanging from the low, spiderwebbed ceiling provided the only light in the room. I got up and tried to push it open; as expected, it was locked.

I plunked down on the cot, closed my eyes, and tried to imagine I was outside. I breathed in the musty air and let it out slowly. Truth be told, I needed to open my eyes and realize that I was subbing because I wasn't sure I could keep my sanity trapped in this tiny windowless hole.

I went back to the door and pushed harder this time. It didn't budge. It didn't make sense that someone would kidnap me. What would be the point? Jones needed me to find Areli so we could complete the ring of fire. Ty needed me to help Jones so he would finally see his payday. Then there were the Ardemonis— and I was pretty sure they didn't need me at all.

Deprived of any stimulation in this gray hole, my mind had nothing else to do but drill through the facts. I kept going back to the unknown in the scenario. The Ardemonis didn't want this project to succeed. But why? Would it interfere in one of their ongoing shady schemes? Dom blamed the Gallaghers for Frankie's death, and the Gallaghers stood to lose a lot of money if the project failed. So was it revenge?

Because of this project, Keegan was killed. Frankie had been killed. Javier's life was in danger. And maybe James' too. James. The man whose report threatened to expose everyone, who has powers Jones and the Gallaghers don't know about. James, who knows everything about us. The man who plans to sabotage the ring of fire by keeping Jones from getting control. James suspects we found Areli, and he knows Chelsea has a gift.

My head dropped into my hands. Why does it all seem to lead back to James?

Pounding on the door startled me. "You awake in there?" the voice boomed.

I didn't answer. There was more pounding. "Hey! Wake up."

I didn't recognize the voice. Keys fiddled at the lock, then the door flew open. In the hallway, a dirty block window high up on the wall let in just enough light to singe my eyes. A hand reached into the ancient chamber and yanked me out.

He growled, "Let's go."

I stumbled out of the room shoeless. The guard moved quickly, dragging me across the dirty stone floor by the elbow. Eventually, I was able to get my bearings and keep up.

In the narrow hallway, a single flickering bulb hung from the ceiling. The corridor was lined with multiple small arched doors similar to something you might see in Lord of the Rings. Old. Wooden. Rickety. Some had tiny windows with bars. I once thought the basement of The Green was creepy and dungeon-like, but it was nothing compared to this place.

"Emma!" I heard as I was shuffled past the last room before the stairs.

I looked back, and a hand reached out from the bars. I recognized that voice.

"Javier?"

I snapped my arm free from the lug who dragged me through the cold corridor and ran back to the door that trapped Javier. I grasped the metal bars and was nose-to-nose with him.

"Javi! You should be in the hospital!"

"Emma, what is happening?" he said. "What is going on? Where are we?"

"Hey! Get over here!" yelled the guard, barreling at me.

Instinctually, my knee came up as he approached and got him where it hurts. That move never seemed to fail me. As he went down, I whacked him square in the nose with my elbow. The guard fell like a ton of bricks right in front of Javier's door.

"Run, Emma! Go!"

I hesitated for a second, wondering how to move the big lug out of the way so I could get Javier out.

"Emma, go! Hurry! Get help."

"I'll be back for you, Javi! I promise!" I hollered over my shoulder.

I ran to the end of the Cimmerian corridor and up the uneven stone steps. The guard shuffled and groaned down below. Javier hollered for me to hurry.

As I approached the door at the top of the stairs, I prayed for it to be unlocked and that no one was on the other side. I stopped at the top and put my ear to the door. All was quiet, so I slowly turned the glass knob and pushed the door open. The hinges creaked; I cringed.

I stepped into a large foyer and became temporarily blinded by a massive collection of stained glass windows blazing down from the second story. The entry was breathtaking. The hardwood floors gleamed against the blue flowery wallpaper. An ornate white wooden staircase spiraled up at least three flights, elegantly framing the stained glass picture along the way.

Together the six colored glass windows created a large body of water under a partly cloudy sky. Four more stained glass windows on each side created pictorial green columns. The glass embodiment of a distant ocean glowed to life from the sun and shot shimmering rainbows throughout the entryway.

The floor was cold on my bare feet as I dashed to the front door. Escape was mere feet in front of me. Behind me, footsteps pounded up the stairs. Through the lead glass on the side of the large wooden door, I saw no movement. I ripped the door open and ran like I had never run before.

I flew down the porch steps two at a time and ran down the brick-paved walkway to the freshly sealed driveway. I didn't look back. After several yards, the driveway took a stiff bend, then turned into stones and dirt. Finally, I spotted the road up ahead and, just beyond that, the bronze bear. I knew exactly where I was.

In the middle of Main Street in Geneseo stood a bronze statue of a bear placed upon the Emmeline Austin Wadsworth fountain in 1888. The mansion, now behind me, was the old Wadsworth Homestead. While there were many legends about the bear and the fountain, one thing was a given. It was a symbol of home to all who lived here and went to school at the college. It was a beacon of strength, hospitality, and hope.

But as the wrought iron gates slowly closed up ahead and the black Jeep Rubicon pulled around and stopped abruptly in front of me, all hope *I'd had*— vanished.

The guard and his buddies jumped from the jeep and tackled me to the ground. Like a small calf, I was hogtied in seconds, lifted into the jeep, and hauled back to the mansion to meet my fate.

I was placed back in the same tiny cell after a brief interrogation as to the whereabouts of Areli Weaver, what I knew about the Ardemonis and the Gallaghers, and what I knew about the Lakeville Project. I basically told them to piss off. They warned me that my continued lack of cooperation would only lead to more severe consequences.

"*Remember something for me, Ems. Trust no one,*" Frankie had said. My gut kept telling me James wasn't being honest with me, and I feared the worst— that he was behind all of this.

Back in my dank chamber, I was able to talk to Javier. He explained that, like me, he woke up in the cell with no memory of how he got there. I told him about my conversation with Jones in his hospital room and regretted it the minute I did so. Javi sounded afraid.

"For the record, I'm sorry I ever doubted you, Javi. I'm sorry you're in the middle of this because of me. When we get out of here, you're done. Understand? Walk away. Go about life without this mess. You deserve the life you've worked so hard for."

"I appreciate what you are saying, Emma. But I would like to think I am a friend. Everyone's friend. I cannot just walk away. You must understand that."

While I got the whole loyalty thing and respected the heck out of him for it, I couldn't bear the thought of losing him. He had grown on me like moss. Moss: the soft, pretty, pollutant-absorbing plant often mistaken for a fungus. That was my Javi.

As much as I hated to admit it, my heart swelled when I thought of Javi. I loved being around him, talking to him, hanging out, and doing absolutely nothing with him… The fact was, I needed him.

* * *

Several days went by in the cell. The big old guard was replaced with a much bigger and meaner one. Javier and I got food and water twice a day.

"A shower would be nice," I said to the new guy as he scoffed away. But soon, he was back.

I learned the hard way that telling them to piss off every day wasn't an option. The first day of torture included open-handed slaps to the face because I refused to answer questions. While it hurt like hell, the truth was, I was already accustomed to this kind of cruelty. They would have to do better than that to get me to talk.

After a couple of days, they stepped up their game by tasering me. Still, I refused to tell them anything about Areli, the Ardemonis, or the Gallaghers. And I swore I had no idea what the Lakeville Project was because *that* was what they really wanted to know about.

I began to wonder if I would ever get out alive. Every time I closed my eyes, I tried to reach Adam and Max. A few times, I practiced with Javier, and I was able to connect with him. The problem was that no matter how hard I tried, I could not connect with Adam and Max... the very people I needed to reach.

Javier tried to keep me focused, but he was far down the hall and difficult to hear.

"Emma," he hollered. "Close your eyes and think of me again. I am going to meditate, and you will think only of me. Count to one hundred and then go."

"Hang on, Javi. I am too tired to concentrate."

"You can do this, Emma. Once you have perfected this with me, we can try again with Adam and Max. They must be crazy not knowing where you are."

I sat on the musty cot and closed my eyes. Instantly, I was with Javier in his cell. He seemed unaware that I was in his head every time. That made me realize that even when he was conscious, I could see where he was and what he was doing. I could see everything, including him.

I studied the details of his cell. Javier was lying on his cot with his leg in a cast. He wore a tan t-shirt with his sleeve folded up enough to see a tattoo on the inside of his bicep. It was some kind of green gremlin. Then I remembered Javi's story about the Devil's Miner. I got a sinking feeling. It might look like an evil goat, but the reality was that it represented a devil.

Javier's face was serious, as though he was concentrating. "Focus on your gift," Javier said. The word 'gift' didn't fit how I truly felt about this burden.

My eyes opened. I jumped up and went to the door. Unlike Javier, I had no opening, so I yelled through the door, "Javi, I saw my name scratched on the wall."

"Yes! I did that this morning. I could not see or feel you, though. Even meditation did not seem to work."

"I could see you on the cot."

"Yet, you could not talk to me. You did not get into my head. You should try to do that while I am still conscious."

"First, try to think of something else completely. Not me. I want to see if I can get in when you aren't thinking of me at all."

"I will try. However, it is going to be difficult. You are all I have at the moment." Javier stifled an uneasy chuckle. But I got it. It was hard not to think about the only other person held captive with you when her main goal at the moment was to jump into your head.

"Think of your family. Your parents."

"Right."

"Don't meditate, just chill and think of them." I slid to the ground along the wooden door and sat on the cold stone. All of my focus was on Javier.

As if seeing through Javier's eyes, I saw my name scratched on the wall.

My eyes snapped open, and I said, "Javi, stop staring at the wall. You're still looking at my name."

"Sorry. I did not realize."

My eyes closed, and again, I saw my name. I was about to yell at him when suddenly, everything changed. Javier was texting Billy; it was the memory James had shared with me weeks ago. The next thing I knew, I was in my driveway, and Javier and James were arguing outside my house.

James was red-in-the-face angry, yelling at Javier, and Javier…Javier was laughing. It was hard to understand James. His voice sounded muffled, almost like background noise. The smug grin never left Javier's face as an SUV pulled into the driveway. Two men got out and dragged James into the truck. *That* made Javier angry. His fists balled at his sides, and he screamed obscenities. I had never heard Javier swear. Never.

My eyes were open now. I sat silently on the floor, trying to process what I had seen. So much didn't make sense. I don't think Javier meant for me to see that. But somehow, I did. Somehow, I tapped into a memory, or maybe that was what he was thinking about at that moment.

Questions ran through my head. Why was Javier so smug? Why was it hard to hear James when I could hear Javier swear without sounding muffled? And Javier had said James was hit with a bat. Yet, that's not what I saw. The men who grabbed James didn't struggle to get him in the truck. It was almost like James wanted to go with them. What really happened? Why was Javier lying?

"Emma, you still there?"

"Uh, no. I went out for ice cream."

"If only. Did it work?"

"No. All I kept seeing was my name on the wall." I almost asked Javier about what I did see. Then I realized that could be a mistake. I needed to get out of here. With or without Javier. "I'm beat. This is taking a mental toll. I'm going to rest for a bit."

"Yes. Of course. We will try again later. I mean, what else is there to do after all?"

Exactly, I thought. *What else was there to do here*?

CHAPTER 44

Somewhere along the way, I became a conspiracy theorist. I began to doubt everyone I'd grown to care about and their intentions. I fell back into believing the world was out to get me.

Jones' words rang in my ears. "*I suspect it's a burden to be you. Knowing things you don't want to know. People expecting things from you, forcing you to make decisions that affect so many others.*"

His mocking voice sang, "*How do I save James from the Ardemoni's evil clutches and at the same time keep the Gallaghers and Doctor Jones from killing Javier? All I really want to do is get away from my vicious mother and join a sorority. I'm so torn.*"

That jerk. Did I want to join a sorority? Heck no. But I did want to go to college, get a good job, and get the hell out of Lakeville. And what did the world give me? Karma's trash can overflowing with crushed dreams, a loser for a mother, a dead best friend, and Jake Jones. Thanks, world. Thanks a lot.

Time seemed to crawl by. At one point, after having liquid soap rubbed into my eyes, I had almost fallen asleep. Or maybe I had been on the brink of passing out. Either way, Javier called out to me, "Emma, are you ready to try again?"

No. I'm not done dying inside, I thought. I didn't answer him.

"Emma, we should try before they bring us dinner."

"What's the point? I can't reach anyone on the outside."

I dabbed my burning eyes with a tissue. A moan slipped out.

"Where do they take you, Emma? What are they doing to you?" he demanded.

I couldn't tell him. So far, they had spared him. I didn't need him worrying about me when I could take care of myself. So I said, "They keep asking me questions. But I don't have anything to tell them."

"Okay, then you must practice. It will help. Maybe then you can get to Max or Adam. They must be thinking of you. Perhaps they are trying to allow you to reach them, and they are trying to sleep. They must be trying to find you."

"Us."

"Right. They are trying to find us. Please. I do not want to die in here," he said.

"If they wanted to kill us, we'd be dead by now, Javi. I don't know what they want from us. But it's not to kill us."

"Maybe they are waiting for the right moment. Who is to say?"

"We don't even know who they are," I snapped.

It was maddening to think we were trapped here and had no idea why. Why would they take Javier from the hospital? I mean, Jones had to be involved. He threatened Javier after all. What better reminder for me than to stick Javier down here with me?

Then I had a thought. Actually, it was more like another theory.

"One more try."

"Good. I am ready, Emma. What do you need me to do?"

"No, not you, Javi. Like Max always says, I'm going right to the source this time."

"What do you mean?"

"Jake Jones."

"Wait! That could be dangerous. Is it not most important to reach Max and Adam?"

"Nope. I'll let you know how it goes."

"Emma, wait."

And so, I did. I sat quietly and waited for a few seconds. I listened to Javier mumble under his breath, clearly annoyed with what he thought I was doing. I hoped trying something dangerous would throw him off and maybe keep him quiet for a few minutes. There was a trick I wanted to try without Javier's incessant coaching. And he was right after all; it wasn't Jones I wanted to reach. I needed Max and Adam.

After a few more minutes, I closed my eyes and thought long and hard about Max and Adam at the same time. I focused on their consciousness instead of their unconscious. I imagined them puttering around at The Green. Adam behind the bar, Max scouring the internet…

This time it worked. I was in the basement of The Green. Max was on the computer, jabbing away at the keyboard. He was pulling up maps and blueprints for the Gallagher's white brick mansion in Mt. Morris. Adam was on his phone researching Jones and getting frustrated that the scientist didn't seem to exist.

Max said, "Did you seriously think Jake Jones was his real name?" He laughed. "Come on, dude. One thing at a time. Let's focus on Emma and Javier. There is no way Javi checked out of the hospital and went back to Bolivia. He has too much going on here."

Finally, I managed to get into their subconscious without anyone being asleep. Now I needed to send a message. I tried to pick up a pen, turn on a light, push a chair… Nothing would move. Max was smart, and I knew he would pick up on a clue if I could leave one. But how? There had to be another way.

In the past, I could feel their gifts. I could feel it now. That was when it dawned on me. Max was a complete genius, thanks to his gift. And Adam could manipulate energy. That was the key.

I stood behind Adam, then put my hands on his shoulders and concentrated all of my thoughts on Adam and his phone. I focused on Adam getting angry and the phone getting hot. Then, suddenly, the phone popped, and sparks flew out of it. Adam growled, jumped up, and tossed it across the room. It hit the stone wall and broke into pieces.

Max rolled his eyes at Adam.

"Come on, man," he said. "Chill. Breaking stuff isn't going to help. We'll find them." He shook his head and looked back down at the computer. "I thought you had better control than that."

"Dude, that wasn't me." Adam was catching on. He shook out his hand and grinned. "Did you hear me? I wasn't mad. I wasn't trying to throw energy or anything. That just popped and sparked on its own."

Max glanced at the black spot where the phone hit the wall. Then down at the broken pieces of the phone on the floor. "Faulty phone?" he asked, popping up from his chair.

"No. It was working just fine."

They stared at each other, and I could see the wheels spinning. Max found a flashlight on a shelf. "Here," he said. "Don't do anything. Just hold it."

Yes, Max. You got it! I stood next to Adam and placed my hand on his arm. Again, I concentrated on the light and thought about Adam when he was angry. I pictured him when I had kicked him in the shin in Vitale Park. The next thing I knew, Adam dropped the flashlight as it caught fire.

Max's eyes grew wide. "Did you do that?"

"No. I was just holding it. But right before that happened, I felt a singe on my arm." He gestured to the spot where my hand had been. "Almost like when we spark."

Max rummaged through the shelves and found an old calculator. He plugged into the wall. "Here," he said, handing it to Adam. "Let's think about this. We still aren't totally sure what Chelsea can do. We know Ali paints memories. We know James and Emma can go into the subconscious of others when they are pliable."

"Pliable?"

"Yeah. When they're vulnerable. Usually, when they are unconscious or asleep. But James said he saw Javier texting the scumbag that beat up Emma, and both Javier and James were wide awake."

"That's completely different from them magically being here; last I knew, they couldn't become invisible."

Max stood, thinking for another second. I waited for the right moment. Then Max said, "James, if you're trying to get us a message, give us a sign with the calculator."

James? They had no faith in me. I waited.

Seconds crawled by before Max said, "Emma?"

I put my hand on Adam's shoulder, and he flinched knowingly and grinned. The calculator got hot, but Adam didn't drop it. When I removed my hand, the calculator cooled off quickly.

"It's Emma," Adam said. "Right, Emma? Do it again."

Once more, I placed my hand on his shoulder and focused through him. The calculator heated up and started to smoke. They laughed incredulously.

"Holy cow. I can't believe it," Adam said. "Is she here? How is she doing that?"

"She's not literally here. She found a way to tap into you and use your ability to send us a message. My guess is she can only channel your power. But I still don't understand why she hasn't subbed with us in our dreams. She'd be able to talk directly to us."

Little did they know how hard I tried to do precisely that. Every night, I went to bed thinking about them, confident I would be face to face with one if not both of them. But every morning, I woke up and didn't so much as remember having any dreams at all.

Max said, "Emma, let me think of a way for us to communicate. I don't know exactly what you're capable of, so we'll try a few things. If you're hearing me, show us a sign."

I heated the calculator through Adam again. This time, it was too much for the little old gadget; it popped, and the plug began to smoke. Adam dropped it on the floor and ripped the cord from the wall.

"Sorry," I said as if they could hear me.

"Damn," Max said as he ransacked the room for more electronic devices. I quickly put my hand back on Adam's shoulder and concentrated on his ability. I didn't have to channel his anger this time.

Adam said. "We don't need anything. I can feel her touching my shoulder."

"Wait a minute. Emma, take your hand off."

I did as Max said.

"She did it. I don't feel her anymore," Adam said. "Get ready, Emma. Do it again."

I complied.

"Yeah, I can feel a light shock when she touches me. How about a back rub, Em? It's been a tough day."

I grabbed both shoulders and focused. Adam's shoulders went up, and he lurched forward away from my grasp. "Ouch. Okay, never mind. I was kidding," he said. "That's definitely Emma," he said to Max with a grin.

"Hey, remember that game we played as kids where you wrote on your friend's back with your finger, and they had to guess what you wrote?" Max got excited and started talking faster. "Emma, tell us where to find you. Write it on Adam's back with your finger."

The guy was truly a genius. Slowly, I wrote the letter W. Max got a pen and a piece of paper, and Adam began to tell him the letters.

"W-A-P."

"No, not P. It's a D, "I said.

"No, wait. I think she erased it. I feel a wash of energy on my whole back." I started to write again. "Yes, she did a W again. A-D-C."

"No!" What was the matter with this guy? How do you mistake an S for a C? Again, I erased it. My annoyance came through in the strength of his ability.

"Ah! Sorry. That stung, by the way."

"What's happening?" Max asked.

"I screwed up again. She's starting over."

"Come on, man," Max said. He shoved Adam away and stood where he had been. "Emma, try to put one hand on Adam, and write the letters on my back with the other."

Adam scoffed at the idea. "Whatever, brainiac. Go ahead. Take over."

The minute I started to write on Max's back, he yelped and scurried away. "Never mind. Man, that hurts. Use Adam, please."

Adam laughed at him. "Yes, Emma. I'm much stronger and braver than him. I can take it like a man."

I rolled my eyes and started again.

"W-A-D-S-W-O-R…"

"The Wadsworth Mansion?" Max blurted out.

I grabbed both of Adam's shoulders. He jumped.

"Yes! Yes. I think she's saying yes." I grabbed his shoulder again. "Alright. Alright." He ran off to the corner, making a face and rubbing his shoulder. "She's at the mansion." He smacked his hands together. "Let's go."

Max said, "We can't just go busting in. We need to know if she's alone, if there are guards, how many…"

Like snapping out of a deep sleep, I was brought back to Javier calling my name.

"Emma! Answer me."

Darn him! I was back in my cell, and the guys were gone.

"What, Javier?"

I tried not to sound annoyed, but it was a challenge since he had just ripped me away from our only hope of escape.

"What happened? Did you fall asleep?"

"Uh. No, I was just thinking. It's kind of hard to hear back here."

"Oh. I was worried. Do you want to practice again?"

"Maybe in a little while."

"We should practice before dinner comes."

I shook my head and sighed, still annoyed. "Why? We go through this every day."

I didn't tell him that hopefully, help was already on the way. After seeing into Javier's head, I decided I wasn't going to share anything with anyone who I didn't completely, one hundred percent trust, no matter how much I cared about them.

"You seem to get sleepy after dinner. You are stressing yourself too much."

"That's because you're pushing me too hard."

"I am only trying to help."

The desperation was back in his voice. If Javier would stop talking, I might be able to concentrate and get back to Adam and Max. Then I could find out their plan. But Javier kept going.

"Emma, I can help you. Then you can help to get us out of here."

"Javier, I'm beat. I just can't do this anymore."

"Do not give up. You must believe you can do it."

"Javier, stop pushing me. Let me get some rest."

Javier went silent. Then he said, "You got to them, didn't you?"

I didn't answer.

"Emma. Talk to me. I feel as though you are shutting me out."

"Stop. I'm not shutting you out."

I crossed my arms and started to pace the tiny room. Three steps in one direction, three steps in the other. I almost told Javier that the guys were coming so he'd stop bugging me. But for whatever reason, call it a gut feeling, I didn't.

"What happened? Were you able to tell someone where we are? Is help coming? Emma? What is the plan?"

"I tried. It didn't work."

Again, he was quiet for a second. Then he said, "You were able to reach Adam or Max? That is good news. You know them; they will get us out. And on top of that, you have succeeded. You have mastered your ability."

"I'd hardly call it mastering."

"You need to believe you can do it. You carry such doubt."

Yeah, yeah. Be more positive was the message. I got it. "They don't know where we are, Javi. I couldn't communicate with them."

"Are you going to try again?"

I plunked down on the cot. *No, Javi. I'm not.* "Yes. I guess I should."

"Great. Maybe there is hope for us. Remember, you must believe. It has not been long, so I am sure whoever was asleep is still napping. Hurry."

"Shhh," I said.

I continued to have my doubts about Javier. I sat quietly and pretended to sub. After about three minutes, I heard Javier. His voice was shallow, almost a whisper.

"Emma?" I didn't say anything. Then again, he said, "Emma?"

When I didn't answer, he was silent for a few minutes. I quietly moved closer to the door and pressed my cheek against the crack in the door by the hinges. The unmistakable creak of the door at the top of the stairs meant someone was coming down.

I heard a man's voice and wondered if it was Max or Adam. Excited, I pressed my ear against the door harder. There was whispering, but I couldn't make out the words. I waited a few seconds more before I closed my eyes and concentrated on Javier.

Suddenly, I was in his cell, looking at my name scrawled across the wall. I turned around toward Javier. He wasn't alone.

CHAPTER 45

James and I were face to face. Startled to see him, I hopped back a step. I waved at James to see if he was physically in the room, but he didn't acknowledge me. I wondered if James could sense my presence.

"What are you doing here?" Javier whispered.

"Surprised to see me?" James responded.

"Yes. Hurry, get us out of here before those men return." Javier hobbled toward the door, and James blocked him.

"I'm not here to set you free," James said, slamming his hand into Javier's chest.

"What? Emma is here. Down the hall. We have to help her."

James nodded his head. Then he pushed Javier onto the cot. He fell back clumsily. Javier struggled to his feet again, bearing weight on his good leg. He threw his hands out protectively in front of him.

"Wait. Stop. Please, do not hurt me," Javier said.

After that, everything was a tragic flash...

James pulled a gun from the back of his jeans. Then he reached into his pocket and came out with a thin piece of metal that he screwed onto the barrel. I had only seen these in movies; it was a silencer.

"Wait, that belongs to... where did you get that?" Javier stammered in perfectly clear, unbroken English. Any hint of a Spanish accent was gone. "For real, sir. You don't have to do this."

James shot him a sinister grin I had never seen cross his face before.

"Stop! No!" I yelled.

James glanced in my direction. Javier followed his gaze to my name on the wall.

"Emma. Help!" Javier yelled. He pleaded with James, "You don't have to do this. I'm on your side. Please," Javier begged in an unfamiliar voice. How did one's accent simply disappear?

"Don't take it personally. It's just that you are no longer relevant, buddy." James turned in my direction and said, "This will be a memory you won't want to live with. Now… Go!" he screamed at me.

In a blink, I was back in my cell. I heard the muffled "poof" and the sound of a body slumping to the ground.

"No!" I screamed, getting up and pounding on the door. "No! James! Open the door. Let me out. What have you done? James!"

I pounded until my fists were red. Javier's cell door slammed shut, and I listened as heavy footsteps lumbered up the stairs.

"James! James!" I yelled. Tears streamed down my cheeks and into my nose and mouth. I leaned back against the door and slid to the floor, broken into a thousand pieces. Almost out of breath, I yelled, "Javi!"

Shortly after James left, a door opened upstairs. I was partly aware of muted voices, doors opening and closing, and someone calling Javier's name in despair. I heard a mad shuffle down the hall and the rattle of doors being pulled and pounded.

"Emma!"

Someone pounded on the outside of my door. And again, a distant voice called my name. But I couldn't move; I couldn't open my swollen and sore eyes. I didn't want to. If I were lucky, I would wake up, and this would have been nothing but a bad dream.

As the door was ripped open, my limp body slumped to the cold floor.

"She's okay!" Adam yelled. He scooped me up. My head rested against his shoulder.

I found his face and said, "Javi?"

Adam cradled my cheek and gently pushed my head down onto his shoulder. He kept his hand on my head, shielding me from seeing into Javier's cell as we walked by. I sobbed quietly.

He stroked my hair. "I'm sorry, Em. I'm so sorry."

Back in the safety zone of The Green, I rested on the couch with a cold cloth on my eyes. I was in a fog for hours as I tried to process what had happened. Eventually, after spending hours at the computer and on the phone, Max sat down and filled me in.

Without hesitation, Max and Adam had headed straight for the Wadsworth Homestead. They had been stopped at the gate by, as Adam described him, "a dumb little troll." Adam pummeled the troll, and they entered the property. They came into the house with no further confrontation. No one else was there.

Once they checked the first three floors of the mansion, they headed to the basement and found Javier. The cell had been unlocked. Next, they found me and unlocked the door with keys they found on a stool next to Javier's bed.

I explained what I'd seen James do.

Max said, "Javi had a gun, a bunch of cash, two burner phones, a bottle of bourbon, and a bag of M & M's in a box under his cot."

"Tell her everything," Adam said, patting my shoulder. "She can handle it."

Hesitantly, Max continued.

"Since we got back, I have been researching the Wadsworth Homestead. I made a few calls and got some interesting information. It turns out that the Wadsworth Homestead can be rented for special occasions like weddings, big corporate fundraisers, and charity events. According to town documents, the Wadsworth Homestead is currently being retained by a man named Doctor Jacob Jonesmith." Max grinned. "I know, obvious, right? Anyway, he's rented it for the entire month of June to do an agricultural and geological study of the property for historical purposes."

"And now for the kicker," Adam said with an introductory gesture.

Max's jaw stiffened, and he said, "The paperwork states that his lead assistant is Javier Ardaya. And that Mister Ardaya would be in charge of managing the study and be responsible for the property while the study is in progress."

They acted as though I should understand what the kicker was. Except when you were in complete denial like I was, it could take a while.

"Are you saying Javier was involved in my kidnapping?"

Max nodded yes.

I chuckled. "No. You're wrong. He was a prisoner."

Max sighed.

I said, "He didn't know I was being tortured. I could tell. He wouldn't..."

I remembered my vision of an enraged James and a smug Javier outside my house. Then there was the lie about James getting hit by a bat and dragged away. I thought about his accent disappearing and shook my head. "Wait. When did he..."

"The timing of when Javier came into your life and Jones showing up is a little suspicious," Adam said.

I slumped over, and my head banged on the table.

"It felt real." I lifted my head. "I fell for all of it. The accent, the stories, the fake kindness. That phony gave me hope. He made me think people could truly be good. God, how could I have fallen for that? I am so stupid."

I kicked the chair back and stood up. Adam reached for me, but I raised my hands to warn him away.

"Why didn't I trust my gut? I knew something wasn't right, and I ignored it. Why?" I slammed my hand on the table. "I'll tell you why. Because he was cute and nice and seemed to be such a sincere human being. Because I wanted to believe. He told me to believe in the goodness of people. What a liar."

"Emma. We were all fooled by him," Adam said.

"We thought he was legit too. But none of us really knew him," Max agreed.

"That might be true, but were you falling for him? Were you torn between two psychos? No!" I pointed a shaky hand at myself and uttered, "But I was."

I was losing it. I was more than book-smart; I was street-smart. How could I have fallen for this kind of unthinkable nonsense? How would I recover from the depths of the despair and agony that ravaged my heart and the embarrassment at how absolutely naive I had been?

Adam approached me cautiously. "Now I don't want to tell you to calm down. I know that wouldn't go over well. So tell us what we can do to help you." He glanced at Max.

"James is a murderer. He killed Javier." I walked toward the wall and kicked it. "My God. What's worse? Javier lying to me for months, kidnapping me and torturing me, or the fact that James went nuts and killed him. Why didn't he kill me?"

Max said, "I think James is working with the Ardemonis. Not the Gallaghers."

"Then he should have killed me too. That would have destroyed the entire project."

"I think they're trying to gain control of the project, not kill it. I believe Jones is playing everyone."

"We're not his toys," I snapped.

"I'm afraid there's more, Em," Max said. "They found some heavy-duty sleeping pills in the kitchen at the mansion. We think that's why you couldn't connect with us when you slept."

"Makes sense," I said. "Javi always wanted me to practice before dinner. It must have been in the food. So what? He didn't want me to connect with you while I slept, but it was fine if I did in the middle of the day?"

"Javi probably wanted to keep you focused on growing your power to find Areli. At the same time, he didn't want you to get to us too soon," Adam said. "If you connected to someone when you slept, Javi would have no control. And if it makes you feel any better. There is a chance Javi didn't know about the torture. Maybe that's why they took you upstairs. In the end, he is just another one of Jones' pawns."

"What does it matter now?" I sighed. "He was a traitor and a snitch."

"Damn, he was diabolical." Adam glanced over at me. "Max is right. None of us really knew him."

CHAPTER 46

Max anonymously called in Javier's death, and soon it was all over the news. Not only did word of his death spread like wildfire, but I learned exactly who Javier Ardaya was.

"Javier Ardaya Cruz, twenty-five-year-old owner of Rich Silver Car Service: found dead in Wadsworth Mansion," read the headlines on the local news site. The article went on to say that Javier's grandparents came to the United States from Bolivia in the 1940s when his grandfather took an engineering job at Kodak.

Javier was born and raised in Rochester, New York. He had received a bachelor's degree in business from SUNY Geneseo, where he fell in love with the town and decided to settle and start a business.

What they didn't include in any article or newscast was a fact that Max had uncovered. Javier had been working for the Gallaghers for years, using his car service as a cover. Drugs would come into Rochester from New York City, and Javier would use his cars to transport them across the southwestern counties. Occasionally, his cars would take the shipment all the way to Niagara Falls.

Javier was using me from the moment I met him until the moment he was murdered. Everything from his last name to his accent was nothing but a fat lie. He was working for Jones by keeping me locked away and afraid. His goal had been to force me to get better control over my gift and, at the same time, push me harder to find Areli Weaver.

Max even discovered that when the accident happened in Rochester, Jones and Javier had been driving to Williamson, up by Lake Ontario. Jones had his sight set on a new farm to make his oils.

As the days flew by, we grew closer to Ali and waited patiently for Chelsea to fully recover so we could tell her our secret. Our deep, dark, secret curse.

Sitting on Max's boat in the middle of the lake, Adam, Ali, Max, and I watched the sun sink slowly behind the hills. The air was heavy and still. We were desperate to think of a plan that wouldn't get anyone else killed. It was June thirtieth, and we had only days left before Jones expected us to meet him in Vitale Park for the ring of fire.

Breaking the silence, Max said, "I swear, Chelsea is heavily guarded. People are around her twenty-four-seven. How am I supposed to get her alone? How are we going to tell her? Time is running out."

"I don't understand why we have to go through with this ring of fire ceremony," Ali said. "He was threatening to kill Javier unless we did what he said. Isn't that a moot point now?"

Adam stood, got a beer from the cooler, and cracked it open. He said, "Javi may have worked for Jones, but he was expendable. He was a tool." Adam took a swig of his beer and turned to Max. "You're going to have to step it up. Get Chelsea alone and tell her. We have to be prepared. All of us."

"What about James?" I asked. "We're all assuming he's not on our side anymore. What if he is? What if he actually needs our help?"

Adam shrugged and scowled.

"He killed Javier," Ali said— as if I needed a reminder.

"But he didn't kill me. What if he somehow knew Javier had me kidnapped, locked in a cell, and was responsible for someone torturing me? James could have been trying to save me."

They shook their heads and rolled their eyes.

I said, "I know, I know, stop being so gullible, Emma. But the last time I subbed with James, he begged me to never stop believing in him. I can't ignore that."

"He isn't here," Adam said. "We need to worry about the five of us first."

Max and Ali nodded in agreement. Max said, "Look, Emma. Whoever he is working with, and whatever side he's on, he has his own agenda. We have to move forward. We have to get Chelsea in the know before July third."

I knew they were right. James hadn't contacted me since I saw him in Javier's cell, and though I tried, I couldn't reach him either.

Max peered through his binoculars and said, "Her mother is stuck to her like glue."

I took the binoculars from him and watched Chelsea sitting at the end of her dock next to her mother. Despite her chronic frown, she was beautiful. Her hair glistened in the light from the setting sun.

"She looks sad. Like she's going to cry," I said.

"She looks like that all the time," Max said. "Her neighbor, Ruthie, thinks it's a part of the trauma. Chelsea's idiot boyfriend, Brent, really did a number on her."

"It's hard to trust people after someone you love betrays you in such a tragic way. A part of you will always be broken," Ali said. I glanced at her, staring up the hill toward the United with Devotion Farm.

We had all shared that feeling in one way or another. Each one of us knew what she was feeling at that moment. I gave the binoculars to Adam and sat next to Ali.

"You have us now," I told her. I nudged my shoulder against hers, smiled, and said, "Whether you like it or not."

She returned the smile and threw her arm around my shoulder.

I looked out to the dark water, where the lake was at its deepest. While the maximum depth of Conesus Lake at sixty-six feet was nothing compared to some of the other Finger Lakes, it was still deeper than I would be willing to go.

"There are lies in the deep," I uttered, mostly to myself.

Ali grinned and scrunched her eyebrows. She followed my gaze to the lake and squeezed my shoulder. She asked, "Lies in the deep?"

"After my father died, Frankie and his brothers would take me fishing. Anthony would say, 'Emma, cast your lies in the deep.' He said if you tossed your secrets and lies into the deep, dark water, no one would ever find them."

My gaze shifted from the water to my friends, who seemed to be hanging on my every word.

"I was ten, so it seemed legit." I shrugged and continued. "The bait went on the hook, then you whispered all those deep, dark, terrible feelings and lies to it and cast it into the lake. It made you feel better for a little while."

I paused, letting it sink in. But to make sure they understood what I was saying, I spelled it. "Don't you see? Even when you throw your lies and secrets into the deep, they don't cease to exist. And while you may not *want* to search for the truth, that doesn't mean it's not there." I caught Adam's eye and said, "It's just harder to see."

After a few seconds of silence, Adam tossed his empty can into a bag. He gave a deep growl. "Okay, fine," he said, glaring at me. "Step one: Max, you *have* to talk to Chelsea. Emma, you could be right about reaching out to James. We need a better understanding of who he's working with. Ali, we need to look at your paintings. Maybe they'll give us clues about what this ceremony is all about or an idea of what Chelsea's ability is."

"About that," Max started. He tossed Adam another beer and grabbed a water bottle for himself. "I think I know." He smiled. "And if her ability is what I think it is, it's pretty awesome."

We waited for him to tell us as he settled into the captain's chair and continued to grin. Then he chugged his water. We stared at him anxiously, and he asked, "Oh, anyone need water?"

"Don't make me invade your brain," I threatened.

Max grinned and said, "I think she can heal herself."

Adam nodded his head. "Of course. That makes total sense."

"We all heal," I said.

"Not like her," Max explained. "When she was beaten up and almost killed by Brent, most of her wounds healed before she left the hospital. I saw her broken fingers right after it happened, and by the time she left the hospital, they were barely even black and blue."

Adam added, "Remember they were going to operate on her brain when a scan showed they didn't have to?"

"That's true. I've gotten close with her neighbors, Ruthie and Will. They said Chelsea was diagnosed with a brain tumor not too long ago, and within a week or so, it was gone. Disappeared. They chalked it up to a bad scan, but think about it. If she can heal herself, then it wasn't about the scan. She cured herself."

"So when she gets sick or hurt, she heals herself? No cast, no stitches? Cool," I said.

"All you have to do is look at her. When she went into the ER, she had broken ribs and fingers. She had a gash on her head, black eyes… She was a mess. Look at her now. Nothing is broken. She's flawless. She looked flawless when she got home from the hospital. Ruthie said her mom was all ticked off that they kept her admitted for so long and wrongly diagnosed everything. My question is— did they?"

"No," Adam said. "She healed just like that." He snapped his fingers.

"That's a handy ability," Ali said.

"Does she know?" I asked.

"I don't think she has a clue," Max said. "And that could be why Jones doesn't know. Her transformation seems to have started with the tumor. It was all in her head. Ruthie said she thought she was going crazy at one point."

"Well, she's about to think we are all crazy when we tell her what's really going on," I said.

"That's just my theory. I could be wrong," Max said.

Adam turned to me. "Obviously, if you reach James, you can't tell him this."

"Duh," I said and snarled at him. "Why do you think I'd do that?"

Adam shrugged and rolled his eyes.

"Jerk," I muttered.

We ended our sunset cruise and headed back to The Green. From there, Max went to talk to Chelsea, and Ali went home to get more of her paintings and move them to the gallery. That way, we could look at them without worrying about her husband. I urged Ali to let him know we were all friends, but she was sure he would disapprove. She thought he might even forbid her from hanging out with us. Why she stayed with him was beyond me.

"Is he that controlling?" I asked Adam when Ali left.

"Sounds like it. David reminds me of Brent. Arrogant. Snobby. Narcissistic."

"She's afraid of him."

"I know."

"Do you think he…"

"If I find out he lays a hand on her, her painting of me will become a reality," Adam said.

An hour passed, and we headed to the gallery. We hadn't heard from Ali yet, but we assumed she'd be there with the paintings. On the drive over, I got a call from Max. He said Ruthie saw him at Chelsea's door and stopped him from knocking. She forbade him from speaking to Chelsea because it could jeopardize her recovery.

"Ruthie said Chelsea doesn't know I stopped Brent," Max said. "She doesn't have her complete memory back, and the doctors want her to get it back on her own."

"She must have it back. If your theory is right, she's fine," I said.

"The woman is an ex-cop. She has a gun," Max said.

"I don't care if she has a machete. Go talk to her. Better yet, bring her to the gallery."

"I can't do that."

"You can. Now go," I said and hung up. "He's such a dweeb," I said to Adam.

"He likes her. He doesn't want to hurt her."

"If he doesn't tell her soon, we will all be hurt, along with everyone we care about," I reminded him.

Ali wasn't at the gallery when we arrived. The door was locked, and the place was dark. Adam and I sat in the car for another twenty minutes before I texted Ali to see what was keeping her. After several minutes, she texted back that she couldn't make it. David was home and expecting her to stay in for the night. Frustrated, I texted her back that we'd meet her at the gallery in the morning and that she had better find a way to get out of the house because tomorrow was July first. Time was dangerously scarce.

Adam called Max to check his status, only to find that Chelsea wasn't even home. Max was in the process of helping her father and sister's boyfriend repair the damage done when Brent attacked Chelsea.

"He's doing what?" I asked, throwing my hands in the air. "He's fixing a door?"

"He's a handy guy. And getting in good with her family is smart. They could override Ruthie. If he's lucky, Chelsea will come home when Max is there."

"We're in trouble; this isn't going to work. Nothing is working."

"Don't panic. We still have a couple of days. I'll take you back. Get some rest, and we will come back in the morning."

We headed back to The Green. It was late, and the restaurant was closed. Adam dropped me at the back door and waited until I got in before he left. I walked down the creaking back stairs and found Novakitty sound asleep on my pillow. I sat down and moved her to my feet. Unfazed, she closed her eyes and snuggled in.

It didn't take long for me to fall fast asleep, but I woke up around three in the morning to use the bathroom. Nova was still at my feet. On my way back down the stairs, I heard a noise. It sounded like someone was shuffling their feet across the floor.

"Adam, is that you?"

No one answered. These old steps always cracked and creaked, and the radiators banged and squealed constantly. When the place was empty, it was extra creepy. I made my way back to the couch in the dark. Nova had stolen my pillow again, so I moved her back to my feet and snuggled under the blanket. My kitty jumped off the couch, full of spunk, and took off.

I had almost drifted back into dreamland when Nova hissed. I shot up and stared into the dark. As my eyes adjusted to the blackness, I made out a figure sitting at the table.

"I didn't mean to wake you. I was trying to pet your cat," Jones said.

"How long have you been here?"

"I'll ask the questions," he said. He got up and made his way to the couch. "Where do we stand with Areli Weaver? You all seem to have forgotten about finding her."

291

"We haven't forgotten. We're looking. We have others trying to help us find her too."

"Such as Ali Sheer? She seems busier than all of you. Does she know Areli?"

"She said she used to know her. She's helping us."

He looked into the air in thought, then said, "Of course. That makes sense. Does Ali talk about her lover?"

"Uh. What? Do you mean her husband?"

"Her lover. At one point, I had good reason to believe he knew Areli. That turned out to be a dead end. Very dead."

I shook my head. Was this man insane? Dumb question— of course, he was. Why would he think Ali had a boyfriend? Her husband had her under his thumb.

"We haven't stopped looking. We still have a few days to find her."

"You do. I just worry that you may need some motivation."

"Well, we don't."

"James thinks you do."

I was silent. I didn't believe him.

"He said Chelsea has an ability, yet he doesn't know what it is. Why don't you tell me?"

I remained silent.

"People get hurt when you don't cooperate, Emma. Or did you forget about Javier?"

"I know he was working for you. So why was he killed?"

"You mean, why did James kill him? That's what you really mean. You see, I know you have many questions. And when the five of you complete the ring of fire, I can tell you everything. Until then, the days are flying by. The third is upon us, and you need to be prepared."

Jones sat at the edge of the couch. I swept my feet under me, ready to run if I had to.

"What is Chelsea's ability?" he asked again. His tone was less patient.

"I don't know if she has one for sure."

He nodded his head. "If I have to go to her myself, I will. If I have to coerce her into telling me, I will. I will do whatever it takes to complete this project. No matter the cost. I have waited years. I have worked toward one single end. Emma, that end is upon us. Do you understand?"

Annoyed by his threats, I forcibly pushed out the breath I'd been holding. Argh! He ticked me off.

"To be honest with you, Jake, I *don't* understand. Maybe it would serve you to explain a few things. Perhaps that's the kind of motivation that would make more of an impact. Because for all I know, that ring of fire ceremony you want us to participate in could kill us."

"Emma, so mouthy. So disrespectful. What will kill you will be your disobedience. Not the ring of fire." He shook his head and tisked. Then he stood abruptly. "Go ahead, keep your secrets for now. The Ivory Dome doesn't care. On July third, at eleven sharp, you, Adam, Max, Chelsea, and Areli had better show up. Otherwise, heads will roll. Yours, your family, your friends."

Jones marched out of the room and pounded up the stairs. I heard him walk through the restaurant and slam the front door behind him. With shaky legs, I ran upstairs and locked the door. Then I slipped a chair under the handle and called Adam.

"Jones was just here."

"Are you okay?"

"Kind of want to puke. But yeah, I'm okay."

"I'm on my way," Adam responded. "Get ready, Em. If the deep is where we'll find the truth, then it's time for a swim."

CHAPTER 47

~July~

Adam got to The Green in minutes. I had already changed into my jeans and a black hoodie. There was no going back to sleep after that.

I told Adam all about my brief but disturbing conversation with Jones.

"We have no choice. We'll meet him at the park like he wants. All of us," Adam said. "In the meantime, we don't have to go into this blindly. I'm going to find Jones. It's time to turn the table and find out what we can."

"I'm in," I said. "We have four hours until we meet everyone at the gallery. Let's get started."

Adam went for the jugular and drove straight to the Gallagher's brick mansion in Mt. Morris.

"Are you sure this is a good idea?" I asked.

He pulled into the driveway. "They can't hurt us. They need us."

"True," I said, getting out of the car and heading to the front door. "I just feel like we're making several assumptions here."

Adam marched ahead of me, up the winding red brick walkway, past the "private property" and "beware of dog" signs. Then he said, "Assume this: we knock on the door, find Jones, and grill him with questions for a change. And maybe get a few answers. And assume this: we find James in there chilling with daddy."

Adam and I stopped at the door. He glanced at me from the corner of his eyes and rang the doorbell.

"I'm not sure if I want you to be right or wrong. Where's Max when we need him?"

"Sound asleep, like most sane people." Adam tapped his pointer finger on his temple. "I got this."

"Right." I held my breath, waiting for someone to answer the door. Or shoot us.

Adam rang the bell again, and we heard shuffling inside. Lights began popping on all over the house. Then a man with messy hair pushed the curtain aside and peeked out the window next to the door. He shot us a menacing scowl, but what else would you expect? Adam rang the bell yet again.

"Stop. They saw us."

He hit the bell once more. "How long does it take to answer a door?"

He went to hit the bell again, and I grabbed his hand. "Stop."

"Bossy," he whined.

The door swung open. Jones wore a long maroon silk robe and tan UGG slippers. He said, "Welcome, friends," and stepped aside so we could enter. He hollered into the house, "Ty, get out the fine china and Waterford. Our guests are days early."

We stepped into an entryway with a vaulted ceiling. By the look of the outside, I shouldn't have been surprised by the grandeur of the entryway. A marble floor with inlaid gold tile led to an elegant split staircase. Fox heads adorned the newel posts. The wrought iron balusters and cherry wood handrails offset the bright white paneled walls. A sphere-shaped black iron chandelier hung above us.

Ty sauntered down the stairs in a pair of black Nike sweats and a tight white t-shirt. Tattoos scrolled down his muscular arms and up his neck. He stopped at the landing to scowl at us before continuing. I watched the stairs, wondering if James would trail behind.

"What are you doing here?" Ty asked. "Do you have any idea what time it is?"

Adam looked around the foyer, smiled, and glanced at his watch. He said, "It's come to Jesus time."

"You've got balls showing up here, kid," Ty said. He rolled his eyes and left the room, mumbling something about coffee under his breath.

"He doesn't like unexpected visitors," Jones said. "Come, have a seat in the den."

He threw open french doors to reveal a cozy room with a fireplace. In the middle of the room sat two caramel-colored leather couches, a black leather wingback chair, and a round black walnut coffee table. The walls were made of fully stocked bookcases. I peeked a glance at the stairs again. But no one else came down.

Jones took the wingback chair, and Adam and I sat on one of the couches. Ty returned, assured us that a pot of coffee was brewing, and sat across from Adam and me. He sat on the edge of his seat, looking ready to leap if needed.

I wiped my sweaty palms on my jeans. Adam appeared as calm as if floating on a lazy river raft. I wondered how he could be so cool and collected when we were literally sitting ducks who had walked straight into the fox's den.

"To what does the Ivory Dome owe the pleasure?" Jones asked.

Adam's eyebrows slammed together, and he stared at Jones for several seconds. Then he responded, "Just feeling chatty."

Jones nodded. Ty glanced at Jones, forehead scrunched, and said, "Seriously? You come here at the crack of dawn because you're bored?"

Two men with guns holstered under their arms passed by the door and peeked in. They nodded at Ty and kept going.

Ty hollered to them, "Check on the coffee! Bring it out if it's ready." One of the men grunted an acknowledgment.

"Was he in his robe when he swung by The Green tonight?" Adam suddenly asked me.

"Uh, no. Jake was fully clothed," I said.

"Good. But here's the thing," Adam started, "I think we can agree that unexpected pre-dawn visits suck." He glared at Jones, then Ty. "In this day and age, there are these highly effective communication devices called cell phones. Try using one the next time you need to send a message. Also, we don't need threats. We don't need intimidation. We only need you to be straight with us."

Jones shrugged with a look of protest on his face. Adam held up his hand before Jones could speak.

"Listen, Jones. Without us, there is no project. Now, it is what it is at this point. I'm not saying we're happy about being turned into freaky mutated humans, but it's a little late to hash all that over. Right?" He looked pointedly at Jones.

"Is that truly your first question, Adam? Are you asking me if this can be reversed? Because I'm afraid the answer is no. Your DNA has been altered. Completely transformed. You have all become a brand new and improved version of Homo sapiens as we know them. You're welcome."

Adam nodded his head and pressed on. "The ring of fire ceremony..."

Jones practically jumped from his seat. "Yes, yes, I know. You want details about how it all works. The only hesitation I have is that the whole group isn't here. I plan to fill you in on everything prior to the ceremony."

Out of the blue, Adam lunged across the coffee table and gripped Jones by his robe collar. He jacked him up, almost off his feet, and snapped, "I'm modifying your plan, Jones. Answer the questions, or when we leave here, the five of us will disappear."

Ty sat back on the couch with a grin and watched. I think he wanted Adam to kick Jones' butt. I sure didn't sense any sort of friendship between the two of them. Then one of the armed men came reeling around the corner with his gun aimed at Adam.

"Wait, no!" I hollered and jumped up off the couch. "Stop!"

Adam didn't let go of Jones. Yet, Jones calmly put his hand out and said, "Hold up there, my friend. No guns needed here." Unable to fully turn his head, he glared at the man with a sideways glance. "Come on now, let's all calm down."

"Adam," I pleaded, "let go."

Adam sent me a quick look that had troublemaker written all over it. The shifty half grin, one raised eyebrow. And that's when I realized that despite his anger, not even the smallest light flickered. I looked closer at Adam; he was *full* of energy. No one seemed to notice the bright yellow glow that grew around his body, which meant that only I could see it. He winked at me. He was completely in control of his power.

"I'll finish my sentence now," Adam said, letting go of Jones.

Jones dropped from Adam's grasp and fell back into the chair. Adam glanced at me again. He wanted something from me. But what?

"About the ring of fire ceremony, what will happen during this, and what will be the outcome? For us. And be honest," Adam demanded.

He glanced at me and raised his eyebrows again. That was it. Adam wanted me to get into Jones' head. He doesn't believe Jones will answer the question with the truth, but he will be thinking about it.

I didn't think twice; I just did it. I stared at Jones as he talked. I focused on his eyes.

Jones said, "It's simple, really."

But that was *not* what he was thinking.

One minute, I was in the den. The next, Jones and I were in the gazebo at Vitale Park. The sun was coming up over the hills, and he was saying, "If I tell them the whole truth, they won't do it. I must be careful."

Suddenly, I was in the den again. I glanced to the side when Adam said, "Explain now."

"Fine, fine. If you insist," Jones said. "We shall all gather at the park on the night of July third, eleven o'clock. At that time, the five of you will ingest one final oil blend that will, in essence, connect all of your powers. For example, Emma will be able to take and use some of your energy. Just not to the full extent that you can."

I thought about how I had already done that with Adam. Without taking his final oil. There had to be something more.

"And if we all use that power together?" I asked.

I bounced back to the park with Jones, who said, "I need to know they will be under my control before I tell them how powerful they are becoming. That gorgeous little capsule full of binding oil will ensure that. It will take away their free will and make them mine. Then they will have no choice but to do what I say."

"What?!" I gasped.

"Emma?" Adam said. Back in the den, I realized they were all looking at me.

"What?" I uttered in a more controlled voice.

"I'm sorry if that disappoints you, my dear. You won't be any stronger in that way. You'll just be able to share a bit of everyone's ability. And I am sorry to tell you that unless you ingest the final oil together, you'll physically weaken. Without the final oil, you will get very sick, and it will only continue to worsen. The good news is, I am certain the binding oil will protect you and make you stronger."

I dove into his lying eyes.

Jones sat down in the gazebo with a satisfied grin and said, "If they don't take the final oil and complete the ring of fire, I will have to get rid of them. Just as I did with some of the others. They can't be running around on their own with powers they don't understand or deserve. I don't want to start over again. Although I will if I have to."

"What else do you need from the Ivory Dome, Adam?" Jones asked.

"Why do you keep saying that? What does that mean?" Adam snapped.

"The house," Ty said. "He's talking about this house."

Jones snickered. "Not exactly, my fine colleague. But you've hit a bit of irony on the head." He snickered again and shook his head. Next, he said to Adam, "It seems to bother you for some reason."

There was an odd moment of tension between Jones and Adam that I couldn't explain. The lights flickered for a quick second.

Adam's head rattled like he was literally shaking off whatever was going through his mind. Then his brusque words cut through the room, "You're telling me if we don't do this, we could die? You basically gave us a death sentence when you infected us with this oil of yours?"

"Only if you don't get the final oil. Your DNA will begin to fall apart. The original oil still runs through your blood, and it will act as a poison. Think of the final blend as a neutralizer. It prevents the current oil from breaking down your DNA and solidifies your powers. You see, you need to meet me, and we need to finish this.

You must get Chelsea and Areli and bring them to the park with you, Max, and Emma. You have to. You have to take it at the same time, and you have to be connected."

"Connected by what?" Adam asked.

"Holding hands will do. There needs to be physical contact. You have felt the power with every touch. And when you take the final dose and combine energies, you will all be whole."

I remembered Jones mentioning "the others" and asked, "How do you know we will get sick? Have you done this before?"

Jones' head teetered for a brief moment, perhaps debating whether or not to tell us. Then he said, "Yes. And it had a tragic end."

I knew he was telling the truth. I also knew the tragic end he referred to was not from the oil. He had killed them.

Adam released a grueling breath and said, "I can't force anyone to come to the park."

"You will have to use your skills of persuasion."

"What if someone refuses?"

"Again, you already know the answer to that. But if you're concerned about anyone in particular, I would suggest finding a way to convince them. Otherwise... " Jones shook his head and looked at the floor. Then he glanced at me and said, "Emma, you'll have to help him. Make the others see that there is no other way."

"Fine. We'll be there," Adam agreed. He grabbed my hand, and we stormed out of the house. Adam marched ahead of me to the car and got in.

I opened the door and stammered, "I can't believe you just did that."

I slid in, and Adam started the truck. He was silent as he backed out of the parking spot and pulled out onto the street. We were headed in the direction of The Green.

"What will you tell everyone? That you took away their choice? That you've decided we are all giving up and that you've promised their lives to a crazy man?"

"What was he thinking, Em?"

"He lied. Just like you thought."

"About what?"

"Pretty much everything."

He looked at me and demanded, "Details. Tell me what you saw... or heard... or whatever it is you do. Tell me exactly."

I told him Jones lied about the strength of our powers and that the oil won't just connect us. It will connect us to him, making us his puppets.

"And that other group of kids he was referring to, their tragic end wasn't because they never took the final blend. He killed them for some reason. Maybe because they didn't all agree to the ring of fire."

As the words came out of my mouth, I realized we were doomed. Adam knew this; I could tell by the serious look on his face. Gone was the smug giant.

When we drove past Main Street, I knew we weren't going back to The Green. We were headed to Lakeville.

"We still have over two hours before we meet everyone," I reminded him.

"Text Max and Ali. Tell them to meet us at the diner now."

Adam and I arrived at the Lakeville Diner first. We talked out a thousand scenarios and came up with a million plans. Yet, they all seemed to end with us dead. Then I came up with an idea that just might work.

Max crawled in, demanding coffee before he spoke. Ali texted and said she couldn't get here until after David left for work. That meant eight a.m.

"I see there's no Chelsea in your presence," I said to Max.

He shook his bed-headed-mop no and closed his eyes. The waitress delivered his coffee. His eyes opened to a slit as he dumped three sugars and one cream into his drink. After a generous gulp, Max said, "I know, I know. I waved to her a few times, but her neighbor Ruthie won't let me get near her."

"Why are you letting an old lady get in the way? I'll go to her house and tell her myself if you don't," I snapped.

I couldn't understand why he thought he could wait this long. Why did he treat her like she was going to break?

301

As if reading my mind, and maybe he was at this point, he said, "I'm not trying to wait until the last minute. I'm just afraid because *it is* so last minute. This could freak her out. We don't know her ability for sure, so this could backfire. Then what? She seems super cool, but that doesn't mean she'll jump on board with this. I don't even think Ali is totally on board."

"She is," Adam barked.

"Okay. Chill," Max said, shifting his eyes from Adam to me.

Adam went on to tell Max what we discovered about the ring of fire ceremony. "Basically, if we go through with this and take the final oil, it would somehow give him control over us. We'd become his servants or soldiers. The alternative is not taking the final oil and keeping the powers he claims will soon kill us."

"But that's a lie," I said.

"That doesn't mean something bad won't happen. Don't forget the report said that we could be terminated. There were other people like us. Strangely, I haven't run into any of them. Have you?" Adam asked.

"Sure, he could try to kill us. But we have powers. We could use them to stop him from hurting us," I said.

"What, are you going to get into his head and tell him to knock it off? Think that will work? Short of terminating the creator— we're screwed." Adam said.

Instantly, I thought of Ali saying that Adam had murdered someone.

"You know we can hear you, right?" Adam asked.

Shocked, I said, "What do you mean? I didn't say anything."

"You must be projecting your thoughts or something," Max said. "I heard you earlier. The minute I walked in without Chelsea, you were chastising me and my ignorance." He sipped his coffee and smirked.

"Oh my God. How do I turn that off? That's so unfair."

"Just another thing to work on. And I am not a murderer. I have no intention of killing Jones. He deserves it because he's an ass. But again, not a murderer," Adam said, pointing to himself.

Just as the waitress brought our food, Ali came rushing in. She kept her sunglasses and navy baseball hat on as she slid in next to Adam.

"Nice disguise," I said.

She pulled off the sunglasses and said, "I don't want anyone to tell David I was here."

"Then maybe you should try to look less cute," I said with a wink.

A smile cracked on her face.

"Why don't you just tell David you have friends?" I asked.

"I told you; he won't understand."

She looked at the guys and then back at me, "He gets jealous. Anyway, what did I miss?"

Adam said, "We're meeting at Vitale Park on July third like Jones wants." He winked at me and said, "Em has a plan."

CHAPTER 48

Before we knew it, it was July third. The entire town was overrun by vacationers, the locals and their families, vendors, food trucks… you name it. The lake was a bustling madhouse.

Adam and I were in Vitale Park at the crack of dawn, scoping out the gazebo, the walking path, and the bathrooms. We wanted to be familiar with every inch of the park so we'd know any place where someone could hide. *We* had no intention of hiding, but when we made our getaway, we had to be sure it was secure.

After spending a few hours in the park, hashing over the plan, we split off. I dropped Adam off at the gallery so he could look at the painting of him allegedly murdering someone.

It bothered Adam that someone would think he had done such a thing. I didn't believe for one second that he was a murderer. I mean, maybe, somehow, someone had died because of something he did— or didn't do. But wasn't that true for everybody?

I went back to The Green to wait. I wandered around the basement like some kind of neurotic troll locked in a cellar. I was antsy to get this over with. I almost headed to the gallery to see the painting but was afraid I'd end up feeling like a third wheel.

I texted Max, "Hope you're a success today. It's only our lives that depend on it;)"

No pressure, I thought. But damn, he better get this right. His only mission today was to get Chelsea to the park by eleven p.m. and have her fully informed. Her family has a party every year for the Lakeville Ring of Fire, and Max was planning to crash that party, whether Ruthie liked it or not.

He texted back, "Thx for the wrds of encouragement :o"

I sent him a poop and an alien emoji just for the heck of it. He didn't respond.

The day pressed on until, finally, I couldn't wait anymore. At four o'clock, I got in Adam's truck and drove to Vitale Park in Lakeville. I stopped at Vincenzo's for a slice of pepperoni pizza and a mountain dew. I would need the caffeine.

I left the truck and walked across what was typically a quiet street. Today it was inundated with cars, bumper to bumper, moving at a snail's pace. I kept my eyes peeled for Jones. He had to be here somewhere, or Ty's guys were, at the very least.

Adam sent me a text. "Where r u?"

I responded, "Ground 0."

"C u in 5," he wrote.

When I reached the park, I found a large white Cadillac Escalade with its engine running in the parking lot. The two men in the car were the same guys Javier and I had seen at G3's house a while back. They turned away when I caught their eye. Dummies. They couldn't be more obvious.

Adam pulled into the parking lot in his friend's fancy Camaro and made his own parking spot in the grass.

"Could you be flashier? We're supposed to be on the down low."

He said, "Sure. Right. As you stand smack dab in the middle of the parking lot shoveling pizza into your face, wearing a neon-pink half-shirt and short shorts. I didn't notice you at all."

I gave him a saucy smirk. "Does it matter? They know we're here." I pointed to the Cadillac and waved my crust at the guys.

We walked around the park again. We reviewed our plan. Then we reviewed our alternative plan.

"What do I do until eleven?" I asked. "I can't sit around anymore."

"I'm going to make sure Max does his job at about eight forty-five. You're welcome to come."

I had a bad feeling Chelsea's party could get ugly tonight, and I did not want to be there. I tossed my napkin in the garbage and elbowed Adam in the stomach.

"No way," I said. "I'll get my blanket and hang in the gazebo until everyone gets here. I'll keep an eye out for Jones and his guys. Maybe I can catch them coming in and hunkering down."

Somewhere around eight, I must have dozed off because suddenly, I was face to face with James.

"You can't go to the park, Em. It's a trap."

"I'm supposed to trust you?"

"Yes. You have to," he urged.

I shook my head. "Where have you been? I have been trying to reach you. You have to tell me what's going on with you?"

I looked around, and here we were again, standing on the beach mere feet from his outdoor oasis. The water broke against the white sand and washed over my bare feet.

"There's something you don't know about Jones. I've been trying to dig up some dirt on him."

"Don't bother," I said. "Max has found nothing. And he's a freaking genius. It's like Jones doesn't exist. Not on paper anyway."

"No, I mean internally. Not the internet, Em. Inside sources."

"What did you find out?"

"I don't have a lot of time. So listen carefully," he urged, taking me by the shoulders. "Jones has been pitting the Ardemonis and Gallaghers against each other since he came back. At first, it was a bidding war. The Ardemonis want to pay off the Gallaghers and take the profit from the sale of you and the others once the ring of fire ceremony is over. The problem is that the Gallagher family already put up hundreds of thousands of dollars ten years ago and have no interest in changing the deal."

"How do you know all of this?"

"Ty plans to keep control of the project. Even if it means killing all of you and taking the oils to start from scratch."

"I know what the final oil will do. I know the truth. We have a plan."

"You don't have a plan for this. Trust me. Things are not going to go as you think tonight." He squeezed my fingers and peered straight into my eyes. He said, "Please. I beg you to listen. Do not go to Vitale Park tonight."

"James, I'm already here."

"Leave."

I glanced around, now annoyed by the once comforting surroundings. The warm water, the white sand. James.

Then maybe too loud and with a little too much attitude, I said, "No, I'm not leaving. This is all going to end tonight. We don't need your help. So leave me alone."

"The Gallaghers aren't going to let this happen. Jones is not going to come here." He kicked the sand as he started to pace, then let out a frustrated growl. Finally, he said, "If you won't listen, I'll just do what I have to do."

"I don't like the person you've become."

"I'm doing this for you. All of this. Infiltrating the Ardemonis, pretending to help them secure the project…"

"Killing Javier?" I asked. Why beat around the bush?

James scowled. "Jones did it."

"I saw you."

"That's what he wanted you to see."

"Stop playing games. I don't need your so-called help. I haven't needed you for ten years. Ever since you came back into my life, it has been a bigger mess than it already was. So stay away from me."

I slammed my eyes shut and willed myself to wake up.

When I opened my eyes, the sky was alive with fireworks. And I had done it. I had successfully and willingly left James in his own head.

However, staying out of someone's head wouldn't last more than a few seconds. While everyone was looking up at the fireworks, I searched the park for familiar faces. And I found one, but I was no longer in the park.

For a brief second, I was on the deck of a house on the west side of the lake. Adam was there with the girl, Chelsea. The fireworks were exploding, people were cheering, music was playing— and they were arguing. Then like a madman, Adam pulled out a small pocket knife and sliced open Chelsea's palm. I gasped.

Adam yelled to me, "Help me. Convince her she can fix this!"

It was clear what I had to do. But before I could answer him, everyone was gone— except for Chelsea and me.

We were standing in the field where I had crashed my car months ago. A thick fog rolled across our feet. The smell of burning rubber and smoke hung heavy in the air.

She asked me, "Are you her? Are you the same girl I pulled from the burning car?"

"It seems so," I said with a smile.

I wanted her to be calm. Yet, time was of the essence. I took her by the shoulders and said, "We aren't going to hurt you. We're trying to help you realize the truth. You can heal the wound. Believe you can do it. *Want* to do it. You're the healer, Chelsea. Do you understand what I'm telling you?"

And then she was gone.

I was standing on my blanket in the gazebo, staring blankly at the lake. I plopped down, sitting on my feet and feeling exhausted. Good God, I hoped that helped our imminent cause. I sat for a minute, shocked by what Adam had done. Chelsea being able to heal herself was a theory. Obviously, it was one Adam believed in completely. I was thankful I hadn't gone to the party. What a mess that had to be. I smacked my forehead. It was hard to imagine that after what had just happened, Chelsea would be willing to ride off with crazy Adam just because he asked her to. Ugh. What the heck had he just done?

That was when I realized what I had to do next. I needed to channel the front runners in the ceremony. So I started with the one I wanted to see the least of all. Dr. Jake Jones. And what I witnessed changed everything.

CHAPTER 49

~*10:46 p.m. Vitale Park, July 3rd*~

The park was bustling with celebration. All around me, people ate, drank, sang, and danced. They blew off fireworks and broke into laughter. But the reserved gazebo was empty. Except for me. I stood alone. Splashes of color from the fireworks lit up the floorboards behind me. The full moon beamed down on the gazebo like a spotlight from heaven.

Despite the hundreds of people in the park, I felt incredibly alone and empty. It was as if I were standing next to myself, watching life go by in slow motion. It was that feeling of being outside of yourself.

Not one person in the park paid any attention to the gazebo or me, the lone eighteen-year-old girl standing on the steps, scanning the park for the ones she waited for and the ones she was terrified she would see.

No one noticed the three seconds of relief on her face when her long dark hair blew in the breeze, shielding her from the real world. Hiding her for those three seconds. They didn't know her hands were hidden deep in her pockets because they trembled uncontrollably and that her eyes darted from one dark corner of the park to the other as she wondered, "Is it true that Jones isn't coming?"

Yet there he was at 10:49 p.m., standing on the path at the water's edge. Snapping back from my despondency, I took one step down from the gazebo.

"They tried to stop me," he said. "Once again, they fail to understand the significance of this project. This is my life. I will not rest until it is complete."

As Jones walked toward me, I stepped back into the gazebo. He threw his hands in the air. "My dear Emma. Where is everyone? The clock is ticking."

"James said you weren't coming," I said. "He said you were double-crossing the Gallaghers."

"I went to Chelsea's party, and they weren't there. So again, my dear, I ask you. Where is everyone?"

"Did James kill Javier?"

"Stop with the questions, and answer me."

"Did he? He said he didn't do it."

A gush of wind from behind pushed me forward. I turned to see what it was, and at the same time, Jones demanded, "Tell me where they are, Emma."

From out of nowhere appeared a guy with short brown hair. His left arm was in a cast from his hand to just below his elbow. He had yellowing under one eye and across his chin.

"I see you brought a friend," I said to Jones. "Hmm. Strange that he's a former subject, and yet, he's not dead. Brent looks alive and well to me."

"Someone has been doing her homework," Jones said with a big smile.

Brent looked at Jones, then back at me.

"How does she know me?" he asked.

"She's become quite the little spy," Jones responded. "You learn fast when you have to."

"I'm sure Chelsea will be thrilled to see you," I said to Brent. Then I turned to Jones and said, "Amateur move. Chelsea's not going to have anything to do with him. He tried to kill her, one of *your* subjects. That would have destroyed your stupid project."

"He was doing his job."

"Excuse me?" Brent snapped. "I'm not your puppet."

"You will be," I said.

Jones threw his hands in the air dismissively and said, "What I meant was I may have used his toxic relationship with Chelsea to my advantage. While I agree that killing Chelsea would have destroyed the project, that did not happen. Plus, he is quite useful. Important, I should say. He is of the utmost importance to this project."

310

He was backtracking with Brent. When I spied on their conversation earlier as I tapped into Jones' brain, I learned that Brent could transport himself from one place to another. Jones called it teleporting. I was assuming he planned to use this against us somehow.

I had also learned that Brent was now on the run. He had teleported out of jail after his father, a lawyer, refused to represent him in Chelsea's case. It seemed Brent had become an embarrassment, and the risk was too significant that he would ruin the law firm's reputation. Now Jones was all he had. Brent was a monster, so they deserved each other.

I said, "They're here. All of them. Even Areli Weaver."

Jones clapped his hands together and sat on the gazebo bench.

"Fantastic! Did you hear that, Brent? The gang is all here."

"Does Chelsea know what Brent can do?"

"Ahh, speaking of her," Jones said. "What *is* her special talent?"

"You can ask her yourself."

I had stalled long enough for everyone to finally arrive. Now they were walking down the path. I had already warned them about Brent when I called to tell them my new plan.

"Look, Max, it's the jackass," Adam said as they all stepped into the gazebo.

Chelsea nodded at me. Max reached for Chelsea's hand when they noticed Brent. She wouldn't even look at him.

Max's whole demeanor changed in an instant. "Why is he here?" he demanded from Jones.

Brent stuck his chin out and said, "The Ivory Dome thought I should come for a visit. Don't worry; I'm not staying long. Just here to make a point."

"Ivory Dome?" Adam asked.

Brent pointed to Jones. Jones popped up from the bench, lowered Brent's hand, and said, "All in good time. Let's not get ahead of ourselves."

"No. I want to know what that's supposed to mean. Who are you talking about?" Adam insisted. Jones had a way of firing Adam's temper.

Max said, "A dome is not typically a person. Its most common interpretation is that of an architectural nature. The term Ivory Dome according to the urban dictionary, however, tends to refer to an individual lacking intellect. Yet, that definition is almost the exact opposite of many other interpretations, which refer to an "Ivory Dome" as a person with great knowledge and skill in their area of expertise. It's a complicated term."

Adam scowled at Max and offered another definition. "Or it means bald idiot."

"Um, sure. That works too," Max agreed. "How is this relevant?"

"I used to call someone the Ivory Dome. I haven't seen him in years, though." Max eyed Jones up and down and demanded, "How do you know him?"

Jones shook his head. "I don't know what nonsense you're talking about. I am a master in my field. The field that has brought us all together. The one that is about to change the world forever."

With Jones' excitement, he let out a creepy little girl laugh and clapped his hands together.

Jones released a gasp of air when he noticed Ali and said, "Aren't you the clever one Ali Sheer? You even dyed your beautiful locks to hide from me."

"I didn't even know you existed," she responded dryly. Then squinting her eyes at him, she said, "But you *do* look familiar. Have we met?"

Jones cut her off with the wave of his hand and said, "Nonetheless. Areli, Chelsea, so happy to see you."

Jones made a beeline across the gazebo, arms outstretched as if he was moving in to hug them. Max put his hand out and stopped Jones dead in his tracks.

"Step off, man," he said.

"So sorry. I am just absolutely delighted. You have no idea how long I have waited for this moment. Come now, gather around."

"Whoa, man," Adam said. "Let's get a few things out of the way first. Number one," he pointed to Brent, who leaned casually against the railing, "this scumbag. Not sure why he's here, but he's got to go."

Jones ushered himself to Brent's side.

"Ooh, yes. As you may have figured out, sadly, he is a subject from an unsuccessful project. However, while the ring of fire ceremony was not anywhere close to happening for him, he still has a special talent. One that cannot go to waste."

I pointed out the obvious when I said, "You said if we didn't go through with the ring of fire, we'd all die from the oil blend you used. Why isn't he dead?"

"You didn't say anything about this killing me," Brent said sharply to Jones.

"Calm down, Brent. That's a part of the reason you're here tonight. While you can't participate in the ring of fire, I can give you the final blend. That will protect you."

"It sounds like you're forgetting your own rules," I pointed out. "Weird how Brent is from another group, doesn't need to be connected to us, and he seems to be feeling just fine. How long ago did you infect him?"

"You're getting caught up in the fine print, dear. Let's just move forward and get this going. Once it's finished, we can sit down, and I will explain everything from the beginning."

He pulled a prescription bottle from his pocket and held it up.

"I have condensed the oil and put it in these capsules. All you need to do is get into a circle, pop one of these beauties into your mouth, hold hands, and swallow. It is a rapidly dissolving capsule, so it should take effect within seconds."

Chelsea had been standing quietly behind Max until, finally, she spoke.

"You are insane. I was worried that *I* had mental issues, but you, you take it to a whole new level. If you think I am going to blindly swallow some mystery pill and even stand in the same space with Brent any longer, you have another thing coming."

Max pulled her close and whispered in her ear. She clenched her teeth, but she stayed. We slowly gathered, making a circle in the middle of the gazebo. Jones handed us each a pale-yellow capsule. I held mine in the palm of my hand and let it roll around as I studied it.

313

It was sticky, and it smelled like rosemary and lavender. It looked exactly like the Vitamin E pills I purchased at the pharmacy across the street after I had witnessed Jones show it to Brent on his front porch. I then hid the bottle under a rock next to the Vitale Park sign for the others to find.

I swapped my pill out with a large vitamin E capsule and casually slid Jones' mysterious oil capsule into my pocket.

Adam, to my left, tied a shoelace and switched out the oil pill with a vitamin in his sock. On my right, Max tucked his into his white button-up shirt pocket and plucked out the vitamin E. I didn't see where Ali and Chelsea hid theirs, but everyone looked ready.

When Jones finished handing out the pills, Brent held out a hand and cleared his throat. He marched into the circle and said, "Umm, hello. Forgetting someone?"

"Oh, right. Of course."

Jones handed a pill to Brent. Without hesitation, he popped it in his mouth, swallowed it, and marched back to the gazebo railing.

Jones then turned his attention back to us and said, "In a moment, you will simultaneously put the capsule in your mouth and take hands. Then you will swallow it. Do not break contact for at least thirty seconds. Do you all understand?"

I glanced at Brent. So far, he seemed fine. Brent leaned against the railing and watched. He didn't appear to react to the oil, which meant we could easily fake taking the pill.

Jones scanned the park and the dock closest to the gazebo. Vitale Park was much quieter now. The fireworks slowed, and families were packing up and leaving the park. Looking satisfied that no one was paying attention to us, Jones gave the "get ready" command.

I placed the Vitamin E in my mouth. The others did the same. I took Adam's hand, then Max's. As Chelsea and Ali joined the connection, the sting gained strength. Adam squeezed my hand and shook it. I looked down to find a soft orange glow surrounding our clasped hands. Everyone's eyes widened as they began to notice our hands were glowing.

Then Jones gave one final glance around the circle and said, "Now."

We swallowed the pill. The darn thing slowly slid down my throat. It was like going down a waterslide with no water.

As I counted to thirty in my head, Jones timed us on his watch. At long last, he let out a deep breath as if he'd been holding it for hours. On what would have been the count of thirty-one, Jones clapped his hands together and smiled from ear to ear.

Pop! Pop!

Two shots rang out from afar. At first, I thought it was firecrackers. Then Jones clutched his chest and went down hard on the wooden floor of the gazebo. We scattered, and within seconds, more shots rang out, and we all went down— one by one.

CHAPTER 50

Adam hit the gazebo floor like a toppling building. Mid-run, Chelsea collapsed next to Max's downed body. Ali fell on the gazebo steps. And the last thing I remember was a boat pulling up to the break wall. Then the strangest thing happened.

I couldn't see, but I heard people coming up the gazebo steps. I felt a poke in my side when someone walked past me. Next came a flash, like I had peeked my eyes open, and I saw a figure with a gun walking across the gazebo.

Then, in another flash of a second, I was looking at James. I was standing next to him on the boat that had pulled up to the park. James got off the boat and followed three men to the gazebo. I trailed close behind. First, I found Ali with her feet in the gazebo and her head face-down on the first step. Her arms cascaded down the stairs elegantly as if she'd been dancing.

After that— I saw myself.

I was lying on my side next to Ali's feet, where I had fallen. I could not see where I'd been shot. Since I could see no blood on my front side, I assumed I'd been hit in the back.

I continued to follow James and the other three men further into the gazebo. I stayed close to James as the others spread out. Suddenly, I caught Chelsea's eyes flash open. For that brief second, I was seeing through her eyes. I saw James from the front. And as soon as Chelsea's eyes closed, I was back behind him.

Chelsea was not unconscious like the rest of us. I couldn't understand how I was seeing through her eyes, when I was clearly subbing with James.

The three men James had been walking with turned to face him. Dom, Anthony, and Mario. As I scanned the park outside the gazebo, I recognized the other men as their cousins and several of their close

316

friends; people I knew were involved in their shady business deals. I hadn't seen them get off the boat, so they must have been in the park all along,

Dom yelled orders at the men.

"I want Finewood and Jones. Leave the rest. James, remember our deal."

James turned around and seemed to look right at me. For a second, I thought everyone could see me, and I gasped. And then, again, my point of view reverted to seeing James from Chelsea's angle. That's when it became clear that not only was I in Chelsea's head, but somehow, I was in James' head at the same time.

"Our deal doesn't include taking Emma," James said.

"My insurance policy," Dom responded with a grin. He walked by James and said, "Hold up your end of the deal, Gallagher." Dom poked James hard on the shoulder. "When you think about running, picture granny in a body bag."

Dom marched over to my body, crouched down, and shoved my shoulder.

He said, "Your scholarship to UB has just been revoked."

"I hate you and your whole miserable family," I mumbled.

James' head snapped in my direction.

Dom walked past Ali, gave her the once-over, and said, "They don't look any different." He turned back to James. "Remember, if any of you even think about leaving, your families and friends will suffer the consequences."

Dom, Anthony, and Mario boarded the boat. Their guys grabbed Jones' body and mine and loaded us onto what looked like the Ardemoni's Scout 420 LXF. Then while one guy started up the engine, the other guys disappeared into the park. My stomach churned as I watched the obnoxiously fast craft speed off down the lake until, eventually, they were out of sight.

James turned to me. "Em."

"What's happening right now?"

"We're subbing."

"I know *that*. I mean, you just let the Ardemonis take my body away. Now what? I get sold to the highest bidder? Maybe donated to science?" I scowled at him and marched toward Chelsea. "Thanks. Great way to redeem yourself," I quipped over my shoulder.

"That's not how it's going to work, Emma."

"How exactly will it work?" I asked, not turning around. I couldn't bear to look at him.

"No one knows the whole truth except for Jones and us."

"Well, now he's dead. And how long before everyone bleeds out, James?"

"The Ardemonis used tranquilizers. They need everyone alive. They're fighting for control over the secret ingredient. I gave Ty's guys a tip on where to find it. That's why they aren't here," James said through a smirk.

"Secret ingredient?" I asked. It was the first I had heard of a secret ingredient. Then I realized. "There is no secret ingredient. You made that up to throw them off."

"You gave me no choice. I had to buy us some time. Ty's guys will figure that out soon, and Dom won't be able to hold onto Jones for long."

"How do you know? Those guys are no joke."

"I'm pretty sure he has his own escape plan. Just like his buddy did."

Brent. I had almost forgotten about him. At some point, he teleported out of here with no one noticing.

I looked down at Chelsea and threw my hands in the air. "She's awake," I told James. "Give me a second."

I squatted beside her and whispered, "He won't hurt you."

Chelsea opened her eyes cautiously and scoured the gazebo. She shot up and said, "Emma?"

"Are you okay?" I asked.

She stared at James and said, "Did you hear that? She sounded like she was right here." She pointed to the floor in front of her. "But they took her. I saw them. Why did you let them take her?"

"Great question," I said to James.

"Emma? I swear, I just heard her," she said to James.

James and I glanced at each other.

"Chelsea, can you hear me?" I said.

Chelsea swung her body around to look behind her.

"Yes," she answered into the air.

Then she spotted Max on the floor and rushed to his side.

"Max! Max!" she hollered, patting his cheek. "Oh my God. Get help," Chelsea called to James.

"He'll be okay," James explained. "He was hit with a tranquilizer."

"Chelsea, Max will be fine. I need you to focus on my voice," I said calmly.

As I spoke, she rose from Max's side. Her head followed the sound of my voice. Then, suddenly, she looked directly at me. Her eyes widened.

"Where did you come from? How did you get away from them?" she demanded.

"We can both see you now. Our abilities must be getting stronger. Maybe because of the pill," James said.

I almost told him we never took the real pill from Jones. But I still didn't know if I could trust him.

He turned to Chelsea and said, "How were you not knocked out? Didn't you get hit?"

"No. I saw everyone going down, and then something grazed my arm, so I went down too."

She glanced at me, then back at James, and shrugged. Chelsea had a skeptical look in her eye; she was lying. She didn't want James to know that not only was she hit, but she almost instantly woke up. He didn't know she was a healer.

James reached out to touch my arm, and his hand went right through me. Chelsea jumped back.

"Holy geez. What the heck is going on?" she gasped. She marched over to me and did the same. Her hand disappeared in my arm.

With a look of awe, James said, "You must be projecting to both of us. You're in both our heads at the same time and while we're both awake."

"That's what you do?" Chelsea asked me.

I nodded. "Sort of. I think it's some kind of telepathy. But we can do more than just read minds. We can also interact on a subconscious level."

"We?"

"It's a long story, but James and I share an ability."

Chelsea's eye shifted from mine to James and back again.

"Speaking of which," James said. "I guess I should explain what happened."

"Oh, please do," I quipped. "And make it fast. We have things to do," I said, gesturing to our friends on the gazebo floor.

James explained that he was taken from my driveway by the Ardemonis because the family wanted his firsthand account of what happened to Frankie. James told them about the research paper and Frankie's involvement. He also gave them the same story he gave to the Gallaghers. He said there is a secret ingredient that "enhances athletic performance to an astrological level." He compared it to sports-enhancing drugs, but it was cutting-edge and stronger.

James promised Dom to keep the Gallaghers away from the park so they could get more answers from Jones about Frankie's murder and get control of the project that was bound to make billions of dollars.

"I went into Jones' head, Em. I know what happened to Frankie. Jones ordered Ty to have him taken out because he could ruin everything with one of his subjects. He had to mean you. He said Frankie could jeopardize the project. And you should know, it wasn't Ty who killed Frankie."

I shook my head. "Then who?"

James' eyes flickered from my face to his feet. He said, "Javier did it. I'm sorry, Em."

I stood motionless, trying to process what James had told me.

"No. He was a con artist and a liar, but Javi wasn't a murderer."

"Who is Javier?" Chelsea asked.

"He was a friend," I said. "But there's no way..."

Then I remembered Javier's devil tattoo, and it all fell into place.

320

I said to James, "Frankie had said that no one gets along with the devil. He was talking about Javi's tattoo. He was trying to warn me. He even said not to trust those close to me."

I held James' eyes.

"I'm not a killer," he said. "I didn't kill Javier. You think it was me, Emma." James shook his head. "That was not me."

"Javier said your name."

"I told you. There's something you don't know about Jones. Something no one knows. I saw it. It's the reason you can't dig up a single thing on him."

"Tell me," I demanded, my patience for him growing short.

"I was in his head, trying to figure out the truth about Frankie. He walked by a mirror, and his image was not what we see. I commented on his transformation, and he said he was so glad he didn't have to look like some skinny, ugly loser anymore. He had figured out a way to utilize his power when he discovered the final blend. He perfected it out west, where he's been hiding for the last several years while we developed our abilities."

"What is his ability?" I snapped.

"He can change his appearance."

Chelsea and I exchanged a wondering glance.

James said, "Don't you get it? He could be anyone, anywhere. I can't let anything happen to you guys. The Ardemoni family will take each of you out one by one and your families."

I let out a short growl. While I wasn't sure how much I believed him about Jones having an ability or whether or not he killed Javier, one thing was true. The Ardemonis didn't make empty threats. We had to stay.

I said, "Look, tomorrow is going to come, and it won't be pretty. We are all very different than we were months ago, days ago, yesterday even. And our future— it's no longer what we thought it would be. But there are a few things we can count on.

"First, the Ardemonis will be watching us, so we need to be very careful with what they see. Second, Jones thinks we completed the ring of fire and that we are now his loyal servants. And last, and

321

in my opinion, most importantly, we're family now. We need to be there for each other. Because no matter how bad things have been in our lives, something worse is coming."

"You know the drill," James said, throwing his hand toward me. "Iron backbone."

I paused, then I realized that in all my years, I didn't just *speak* the motto— I lived it. And if ever there was a time to remember that, it was now. It didn't matter at that moment if I trusted James or not. I needed to be brave, and I needed to be strong if we were going to survive. So I threw my hand on top of James's and motioned for Chelsea to do the same.

"Iron-willed," I said.

After that, James went to check Adam's pulse. Then he tapped his cheek and gave him a solid shoulder shake. Adam didn't so much as move a finger.

I stared at my new family scattered about the gazebo floor. They needed to wake up. We had no time to waste.

The reflection of the full moon danced across the lake as it retreated further up into the sky. I glanced out at the water, still bustling with boats. Fireworks were dying down, but the steady red glow of flares at the lake's edge held strong. The actual Ring of Fire.

Then Chelsea asked one last question.

"Tell me. How are we supposed to get you back?"

Suddenly, it occurred to me how simple the answer was.

Barely audible, I uttered, "Wake me up." I stepped closer to her so James wouldn't hear. "You saved my life once. You'll just have to do it again."

She shook her head. She didn't know.

"Think about it," I said. "EMTs thought I was a goner when they first got to my accident. You were the one who pulled me away from the car. Your touch healed me."

She shook her head again and muttered, "I can't heal other people. Just myself."

"How else could I have survived a head-on collision with a van at fifty-five miles per hour? The minute you touched me, I began to heal. I was a mess when they first brought me into the ER. By the time I left, only a few days later, I had nothing but a few bruises."

James had wandered over to Max and was giving him the same checkup he'd given Adam. I pointed to James and held a finger to my lips. Then I gestured to our friends scattered across the gazebo floor, and quietly I said, "James won't know it was you. You can wake them."

Chelsea's mouth scrunched up. She reached out and took hold of my wrists.

"Wait. I can't do it. I can't," she stammered.

Then at the same time, we felt the slight zap of her hands clutching my wrists, and she said, "Holy geez, I can feel you."

I looked her in the eyes and said, "We're getting stronger. Now wake me up." My eyes flashed to her hands, still latched onto me, and I whispered, "Then wake them all up."

Suddenly, she was gone. Everything went dark.

And when my eyes opened—I was on the floor of a boat racing across Conesus Lake.

ABOUT THE AUTHOR

C. S. Robbie is the author of the young adult series called The Lakeville Project. *Lies in the Deep* is the second book in this series. The adventures take place in and around the small town of Lakeville, New York. Just down the road from Lakeville is SUNY Geneseo, where C. S. went to college and earned a degree in Speech Pathology. Her passion for language and communication has finally brought her back to her love of writing. Inspired by the Finger Lakes region, where she continues to spend her free time, C. S. Robbie brings to life a dark and mysterious alternative to the quaint town of Lakeville.